WERECATS RESURGENT

BOOK 3 OF THE FOREST EXILES SAGA

MARK J. ENGELS

FAZED ANGLE MEDIA

Contents

CHAPTER ONE

MAWRO REACHED OVER THE gallery rail and fumbled at the dogs holding the porthole's storm cover in place with his oversized forepaws. He managed to swing the thing clear and peer through the porthole window in time to spot Hana stepping off the gangplank. She hiked her duffel's strap up onto her shoulder and shuffled off across the pier toward the waiting taxicab. But she stopped short of where the driver stood beside the taxi's open trunk, his arm outstretched so as to take her bag and stow it. Mawro followed Hana's gaze toward a black sedan with tinted windows, racing up the pier until it screeched to a halt in front of the gangplank.

Hana turned back toward their ship and brushed her long black bangs away from the sides of her pale face. She met eyes with Mawro an instant later, then stole a glance over at Oh and Min Soo exiting the car. With a curt nod, she acknowledged the general and his hacker lackey as they stomped aboard. They made quite the pair—Oh with his slicked back hair, designer sunglasses, perfectly tailored suit; Min Soo dressed in shorts and a T-shirt and a surveyor's vest, looking as if had just rolled out of bed before Oh summoned him. Which, to be fair, he might well have.

Hana turned back toward Mawro, one eyebrow cocked. Mawro shook his head then wagged his fur-covered chin toward the snowy peak of Mount Chilbo, rising in the distance beyond what passed for a skyline in Chŏngjin. *There. That's where you need to be.*

Her chin drooped to her chest as she handed the taxi driver her duffel. A moment later, the car sped off with Hana in the back seat. The taxi slowed to make its turn then darted between a pair of flagpoles. The North Korean standard flapped smartly atop each one from the stiff breeze blowing ashore. He glimpsed her sullen face staring back at him before the car disappeared behind the Chong Pol cargo ship berthed opposite the pier from their own.

Mawro sighed and stared down at the shaggy gray fur covering his enormous legs and feet. He appreciated Hana's reticence to leave him in what amounted to solitary confinement while their ship was cleaned and provisioned. Not like he could go ashore and take in the local color sporting, as he was, a gray spotted pelt and tufted ears and fangs grown out past his chin.

Regardless, Mawro had insisted Hana use their brief port-of-call in this rusted-out factory town to return to her birthplace near the Tumen River, in the remotest portion of Ryanggang Province. There she planned to observe a mountaintop vigil to honor her mother's memory on another lonely anniversary of her death. Mawro knew firsthand how badly it hurt being denied the opportunity to grieve the loss of one's family—that most of his loved ones were still very much alive notwithstanding. Because, as far as they knew, the man they knew and loved had died years before.

The clanking of deck plates above him announced Oh and Min Soo stepping aboard the ship. Mawro was in no mood for houseguests, but he knew the best way to get Oh to go away was to give him whatever he wanted. Right, then. Time to get this over with.

A sudden *whoosh* of air through the porthole from outside launched stray strands of shed fur on the floor billowing upward into the compartment all around him. The bulkhead door across the hold slammed shut, indicating his visitors had arrived. "Through the door at the end of the corridor," he said in a raised voice.

Oh grunted by way of reply and began weaving his way through the crammed cargo hold toward Mawro's compartment. Mawro couldn't help but chuckle, imagining his guest pinching his nose as he passed pens lining either side of the narrow corridor hosting goats and sheep, turkeys and chickens, rats and rabbits. A pounding at his compartment door came a moment later. "Open up. It's me."

Mawro daintily took the handle between his thumb and forefinger to open the door. He glanced down as it swung open to find Oh there, alone, stowing his designer shades into a case covered in what looked like alligator skin. Mawro stepped back so his hulking form wouldn't take up the entire doorway. "Sorry if my accommodations strike you as...less than suitable," he said with a wry grin.

"My father was a Party official in South Hwanghae Province, the heart of farm country." Oh snapped his sunglass case shut and returned it to one of his suit coat's inside pockets. Then, from his other, he produced a small box made from lacquered ebony and pulled out a cigarette. "The smell doesn't bother me much. Though what *reeks* is how you let the MGS slip through your fingers. When your ship came within hailing distance, the Party apparat called me, insisting I return immediately. Didn't matter I was in Panama, deep into negotiations with our drug cartel partners at the time." The cigarette dangled between his lips as he reached for his lighter. "They'll be grilling me straightaway as to our plans. So, this scheme of yours had better be good."

"It ought to suffice. So long as you don't go near it with a lit cigarette."

Oh frowned and plucked the cigarette from his mouth. "This way," Mawro said, stepping over to a rollup door in the bulkhead wall. It opened as he approached. He glanced over his shoulder in time to see Oh wince and wrinkle his nose. Surely from the strong odor the stewards had complained about to the ship's master whenever he sent them below to muck out the livestock pens.

Mawro knew the stuff had a powerful smell, but he wouldn't have described it like a cross between pig manure and drain cleaner as the stewards had. Pungent, perhaps, but not what he would consider putrid. Oh, however, made a face as if to suggest his nose found it decidedly objectionable regardless. "We're going in *there*?"

Mawro said nothing and stepped through the open doorway. Oh snarled and jammed the lighter and unlit cigarette into his pants pocket before pulling off his suit coat. He hung it on a hook fixed to the compartment wall beside the door frame and followed.

"I would have thought you would have been used to this stuff by now," Mawro said as Oh strode up beside him. A moment later they approached a steaming vat of foul-smelling dark goo. "Most of its base compounds are also now being fielded to our mobile psychotropic drug production facilities onshore."

Oh drew up beside the vat. He peered down at its contents, bubbling like tar in a roofer's kettle. "But what is this stuff to us?" he asked, drawing back after a bubble popped a little too near to his face.

"To you, nothing." Mawro strode over to the bulkhead and plunked down heavily into a makeshift chair made from two rolled-up lengths of canvas suspended from the compartment's overhead by steel cable. "Please," Mawro said, motioning to a normal-sized desk chair pushed in beneath an oversized display console.

"In answer to your question," Mawro said after Oh had taken a seat, "I guarantee this stuff will be irresistible to Katczynski and his family."

Oh crossed his arms across his chest. "What makes you so sure of that?"

Mawro waved toward the vat with one arm. "These are catalyzation proteins. The foundation material required to perform morphogenetic synthesis."

"What the MGS needs to run, you're saying?"

Mawro nodded. "Yes. Though on our voyage back from Gdańsk, I experimented with how to increase the morphogenetic yield of the material. This stuff here is a thousand times more potent than anything I've known the Opoworos to come up with."

Oh cocked an eyebrow at him. "Sounds to me you mean to bait them." He glanced over at the vat, wincing as more foul-smelling gas belched forth from the dark goo. "What would they possibly want with this...stuff?"

"To develop a tissue-replacement regimen with which to exorcise their family members of their bloodlust. Along with the entire Forest Clan."

Oh's eyes went wide. "They are in league? But how? Blaznikov shared at length the deep enmity between the Forest Clan and seafaring werecats like your family."

Mawro rubbed his chin. "And toward any other werecats for that matter, as Hana would be quick to point out. But they are a wily bunch," he went on, raking his claws through the thick ruff of white fur covering his neck. "If they weren't working together, the Forest Clan would've distracted the Katczynskis by goading Hana into fighting them. But they ran her off themselves instead."

"So, you think that they'll be interested in these...proteins of yours, is that it?"

"I do. This stuff ought to help Opoworo and his son keep their loved ones' bodies from breaking down further. Which is also why I need the Party leadership to authorize Office 35 to leak intel that this stuff is aboard my ship."

"And just what makes you think they'd be so inclined?" Oh replied with a sneer. "Without having delivered the MGS to them, you hardly are in a position of influence. Besides, they wouldn't dare risk compromising their supply lines for their onshore drug production facilities."

"They might if I promise them the werecat army they've been seeking."

Oh narrowed his eyes at him. "Quite a claim. The last time you made it, you put out to retrieve the MGS. Then came back empty-handed."

"Not entirely. I did suss out the youngling, as you'll recall."

"You plan to bring her to us?" Oh asked as he rubbed at his chin.

"No. Werecat clans are jealously protective of their own. The Katczynskis and Opoworos have come under the protection of the Forest Clan. Pyongyang has no idea the whirlwind they would reap from us trying to kidnap her."

Mawro walked over to a table full of aquarium tanks nearby. He knelt down beside them and peered into each one in turn, studying the features of the organs growing in the clear, bubbling liquid—here a lung, there a kidney, another a pancreas. "I do plan to detain the girl for a short while, though, to harvest samples from her. Given she is still growing, we will be able to morph her samples into ailuranthropic starter tissues."

"With which we can finally complete our human augmentation program," Oh replied, a lilt in his voice.

Mawro nodded but kept his gaze fixed on the organ tanks. "Yes, that was the alternative scenario I came up with during Hana's unfortunate rage episode. Which is why I allowed Katczynski and the Americans to make off with the MGS rather than risk Hana being captured." *Or shot.*

He turned away from the tanks and locked eyes with Oh. "Katczynski and his family get what they want, the Party leaders in Pyongyang get what they want. So, the latter need not ever engage the former again. Are we agreed?"

Oh stood and stepped quickly through the bulkhead door. "I shall have that cigarette now, thank you very much," he muttered as he pulled the door closed behind him.

PARTY HEADQUARTERS, PYONGYANG. LATER THAT DAY.

OH CLOSED HIS EYES and leaned back in his chair as the lights in the conference room came up. He listened for a moment while the ten highest-ranking members of Office 35 chatted amongst themselves. They marveled one to another about the images which had flashed across the conference room's screen moments before—footage of Mawro's aborted Gdańsk harbor operation, featuring a young weretigress fending off their operative Hana's savage attack. The girl's collapse had elicited a collective gasp from the Party apparat. The American lyncean woman drawing Hana away and out of the camera frame resulted in a relieved sigh from all of them.

He breathed a relieved sigh too. No one was calling for Oh to be fitted for a blindfold anytime soon—requisite equipment for either a one-way van ride to Kaechon prison camp or before being stood up in front of a firing squad. Far from condemning him, in fact, the general tenor in the room was one of jubilance. Oh made out snippets of conversation like "miracle girl" and "promised child." News of the youngling's existence would surely spread across Pyongyang like wildfire through a dry forest. Years before, the birth of Lim's stillborn child had caught them all unawares. DPRK's top doctors, after debriefing the field medics that had tended Lim following Mawro's flight from the Chinese, had assured Party officials the young woman's self-inflicted uterine damage would preclude her from ever again bearing children. As far as Office 35 was concerned, Lim's birth name—and Pyongyang's hopes of creating an army of ailuranthropes at the beck and call of their Great Leader—had died with her baby. She had been known to them simply as "Hana" in the years since.

After a moment, Chairman Ryuk stood and waved his hands so as to restore order. "Director Yin," he said, nodding toward a bald man leaning up against the wall in the opposite corner. "Is this the sort of 'fresh stock' you were talking about?"

"Yes. Yes, exactly," the man replied, nodding toward Oh. "And I'm eager for the General to brief us how he and Captain Mawro figure how we might secure the youngling's genetic material for ourselves."

The youngling. Oh couldn't help but crack a sly smile; Yin was barking like a trained seal. Referring to the girl as if she were a thing—an *it*—rather than a human being. Which befitted her life station being the granddaughter of that traitor Rhim Seon-Yeong. The same woman who had permitted herself decades before to succumb to the charms of a dashing young Polish doctor, Nikodemos Opoworo. Not only marrying him, but then running off with him to America.

Ryuk waved toward Oh and took his seat. "So, General, is it the captain's assertion that drawing samples of this the girl's DNA obviates the need for that morpho-...morphogen-...oh, what was it now?"

"We have come to know it simply as the 'MGS,' honorable chairman."

"Yes, this MGS thing," Ryuk replied, nodding. "The one he was on about before he left."

"The same, honorable Chairman. Captain Mawro and I discussed that very subject well into the evening aboard his ship in port at Chŏngjin. Then I ordered my driver to bring me straight here."

Ryuk pursed his lips and turned toward Yin. "You've read Mawro's brief?"

"Just the abstract. But our own prior calculations and experiments appear to be in line with his conclusions. Distillation and reproduction of this youngling's DNA ought to yield sufficient quantities of catalyzed reversed-enzyme transcriptase. With it, we can begin large-scale production of the ailuranthropazine we'll need for..."

Yin's voice trailed off after Ryuk held up one hand. "The same material in quantities Captain Mawro originally sought out the MGS to replicate?"

"That is correct, honorable Chairman," Oh answered before Yin could reply.

Ryuk leaned forward and steepled his fingers. "Suppose we discuss how we might effect such a procurement then, hm?"

Oh rose and shot Yin a look. The scientist gulped and looked down at his feet. Oh knew that the other man knew who was really in charge of this enterprise. "Mawro is sure that he can lure in Katczynski and his family with these catalyzation proteins he's cooked up, so long as we broadcast it via our subterfuge networks."

"That represents a sizeable investment of material, compounds that ought to have gone to our on-shored psychotropic drug production facilities in the US." Yin took his cheek in one hand and rested his elbow on the conference room table in front of him. "Our contracted operators there may not be able to keep to their production schedules given such an interruption in their supply chain, temporary or no."

"I expect it to be but a momentary one. Mawro and I will allow Katczynski's people access to the ship before docking so they can see the container with the catalyzation proteins inside is indeed aboard. Then we'll toss the container overboard at a set of predetermined coordinates and put ashore an empty decoy for them to chase down."

Ryuk snorted. "I thought you said the supply chain interruption would be only momentary, General."

"But it *will* be, honorable Chairman," Oh replied, his open palms at his shoulders. "We will dispatch another vessel to fish the container from the water under cover of darkness, one already outbound from Chicago so as not to arouse suspicions. Put the container ashore at Detroit or Cleveland and a private drayage provider can have it back to Chicago in under a day's time."

"But what about the samples we need?"

Oh sighed and rubbed his forehead. "I would have thought that would be obvious, Director," he said as he met Yin's gaze. "But, anyway. With the family caught up in our fire drill, Hana moves in and subdues the youngling. Then she spirits her away so Mawro can collect them."

Park, Office 35's head of counterintelligence, rubbed at his chin. "We just saw Hana go feral during her previous encounter with the girl. If she takes point on this operation, won't she be at risk for doing so again?"

"Captain Mawro showed me a prototype breathing unit he'd rigged up from what he could scrounge in his ship's firefighting locker. Hana will wear it whenever she's in theatre." Oh covered his mouth with his fist. "The fitted face mask is connected by a hose to a small tank in a pouch on her utility belt," he went on, tracing an invisible line with his finger between his mouth and his waist. "Most of the time, it vents in air from the surrounding atmosphere. But Mawro has coined a way to sense the youngling's scent in the air. The apparatus will blink an indicator light inside Hana's field of vision to indicate it has detected the youngling. Then it will switch over to cannister air."

Ryuk rubbed at his chin. "How long will that last her?"

"Right now, about five minutes. Any larger cannister would likely encumber her too much. But Captain Mawro is working on a belt pouch-sized reactor to produce oxygen and nitrogen chemically, enabling Hana to sortie longer."

"For what we need her to do, that will be plenty."

Oh cocked an eyebrow. "I'll grant you that she's fast, honorable chairman, but five minutes is barely enough time for her to deliver the youngling to Mawro. He'll surely need more time than that to collect the samples before she takes the youngling back to—"

"The youngling isn't going anywhere, once we have her."

Oh blinked. "I'm not following you," he said, turning to face Yin. "You made it sound like your people could synthesize whatever we would need from mere samples of the youngling's genetic material."

"We're not keeping the youngling for the Director's benefit," Ryuk said before Yin could answer. He waved toward a man sporting a graying mullet, seated opposite the table from Park. "Isn't that right, Chong?"

"I don't understand," Oh replied as he glanced over toward Office 35's propaganda director.

"The girl will be a sensation! We're going to invite representatives from sovereign states and NGOs from around the world to show off our ailuranthropic stock."

"Which we'll be glad to share with anyone," Ryuk added. "Anyone who places the high bid at our auction, that is."

Oh drew back and eyed Ryuk and Chong each in turn. "You're going to parade the youngling around like some kind of show pony?" He waved an arm toward the remaining Party officials gathered around the conference room table. "Every man here knows that Captain Mawro would never go for that."

"We agree. Though, by then, he and Hana will both be extraneous. Which is why we need you to disposition them." He nodded toward a white-haired man seated to his right. "Befitting of honorable Li-Ok's replacement as Office 35's new director after his forthcoming retirement, don't you think?"

The corners of Oh's mouth turned upward. "Why yes, honorable Chairman. I indeed think it would."

Chapter Two

— • —

Naval Consolidated Brig, Chesapeake, Virginia. Days later.

Lenny snapped to attention and saluted sharply as soon as the Master-at-Arms attending him removed his handcuffs. He wasn't sure what exactly he had done to earn himself a trip to the Commander's office, aside from grousing about the barely edible chow. Nor was he looking forward to finding out, either. The guard gave the Commander a salute of his own and shuffled out the door, closing it behind him. All Lenny could do now was play along in hopes he wouldn't make a bad situation worse.

"At ease, Lieutenant." The man sat down heavily in his desk chair and rubbed at his face with both hands. "Please," he said at length, motioning toward another chair opposite the desk from him. "Sit."

Lenny did as he was told. He sat with his palms flat atop his thighs, twiddling at the fabric of his brig-issue brown trousers while the Commander leafed through the contents of an open manilla folder lying on his desk. "I've seen countless Sailors and Marines come through my office during my tenure, Reintz. Many surprise me by just how long they were out in the Fleet before finding their way here."

The Commander slid back in his chair and stood before clasping his hands together behind his back. "I read their files, ask them a few questions, quickly make up my mind they're nitwits or wanna-bes or ne'er-do-wells," he said and strode over to his office window. "Your garden-variety fupid stuckers."

The clock hanging on the wall opposite the Commander's desk ticked away the seconds while the man gazed out upon the recreation yard. "No accounting for you, you know?" he said at length without making eye contact. "From what I've read and been told you were a model Coast Guardsman before you shot your partner. So, the real question is this, Reintz—did you *really* shoot him under duress?"

"Yes...yes, sir," Lenny replied slowly.

Tick. Tock. Tick. Tock. Tick.

Lenny bit his lip, hoping the Commander wouldn't press him for details. Humanoid cats from rival states duking it out in some sort of cloak-and-dagger grudge match? Because even if he could have dished to anyone without a need to know, he was certain no one would have believed him.

"I've listened to a lot of people lie to me. And I have reason to believe you're telling the truth. It'd be a damned shame for this to scuttle your entire life, wouldn't it?"

That very question nagged at Lenny day and night in the weeks since he had left Poland in handcuffs, no matter how many books he borrowed from the brig's tiny library to try and keep from thinking about it. Over a year before, Pawly had gone on the run after their Chah Bahar operation ended in disaster. And only shortly before being taken into custody by the Marines from the embassy in Warsaw had Pawly herself told Lenny his command had sought to use him as their fall guy. Seeking to send him to lockup at Leavenworth for who knows how long by Pawly's testimony—but only if they could find her. Which Pawly made good and well sure they wouldn't.

Now, not only was Lenny's Coast Guard career surely over, but he also once again found himself staring down military incarceration's long barrel. How long would it delay his return to civilian life? Would Pawly wait for him? Would he even *have* a life to speak of with a dishonorable discharge on his service record? Would he ever be able to find a job paying more than minimum wage?

Not that any of it would matter to Latharo. Or to whatever family the man still had left. *I'm sorry, I'm so sorry, I...*

The snap of a finger jarred Lenny back to the present moment. He blinked and stared up into the Commander's face. "An old shipmate of mine wants to talk to you," the man said, nodding toward the door. "He's a civilian employee with one of the alphabet soup agencies now. Apparently, you and your background spark a fair bit of interest with his team. I'll send him in." He leaned forward toward Lenny and fixed him with a penetrating stare. "And I humbly suggest you take whatever deal he offers you. Unless you've come to *like* your three hots and a cot here while you learn woodworking."

Lenny's head swam. "Wait, just who is this guy?" He looked at his bare wrists and then back to the Commander. "And aren't you going to put my shackles back on before you let him in?"

"Nah, he'd rip a leg off the chair you're sitting in and shank you with it if he thought you posed any threat," he replied as he opened the door. "Besides, his security clearance is way higher than mine." He stepped through the door and pulled it shut behind him before greeting another man with backslapping, laughing, cutting up. A moment later the knob turned and a dark-skinned man wearing a leather bomber jacket entered. With a brown *ushanka* atop his head.

"I...I remember you," Lenny croaked, his mouth as dry as a cotton ball. "You're that Biggs guy from CIA! What the hell do *you* want?"

"You, Lieutenant Reintz, now that my employer and I have managed to track you down. Required no small amount of digging, I'll have you know."

Lenny stood and narrowed his eyes at the man. "And you want me for what exactly?"

"For starters, Bravo Zulu for that little trick you pulled back in Gdańsk," Biggs replied with a broad grin. "Pretty impressive what you did with that container's smart seal. My team and I were grateful for your help. Our tactical operator especially."

Lenny gasped. *Pawly!*

A smug look on his face, Biggs clasped his hands behind his back and strode over to the window. "My team is going to need a liaison with DHS for the next phase of our operation," he said, peering out into the recreation yard just like the Commander had a moment before. "Latharo was our first choice, but we can't wait on him."

Lenny blinked. "I...I don't understand."

Biggs turned away from the window and fixed him with a quizzical look. "You mean, no one's told you?"

Lenny cocked an eyebrow at him. "Told me what?"

"About your partner. He's alive, you know."

Lenny clasped his open palms to his chest. "He is? Latharo's alive? Where is he? Will he be okay? When can I see—?"

"Whoa, whoa, slow down, high speed," Biggs replied as he waved his arms back and forth in front of him. "He was injured pretty bad from the gunshot, so he'll be some while mending. But the doctors tell us that he ought to recover well enough given time. He's holed up back in Peru, at some woodland retreat in the Andean foothills." The man crossed his arms across his big chest. "You mean to tell me you didn't know *any* of this already?"

Lenny shook his head. "The embassy's Marine detail handed me off to the Inspector General's office. Once stateside, they handed me off to CGIS, who brought me here to Chesapeake. Without even so much as a courtesy call to the JAGs." He rolled his eyes. "In fact, no one's said two words to me outside normal drill and inspection for the last three weeks," he went on, rubbing at his chin. "Except for a couple of the other guys and me bitching about the cafeteria food."

"All the more reason you ought to come with me, then. My team and I can make good use of your talents, what with Latharo laid up for the foreseeable future." Biggs nodded toward the door. "If you'd like a more comfortable bed and some far better eats, you're welcome to come roll with us."

"I didn't think that was your call to make," Lenny replied, narrowing his eyes. "Last time we met, you were just somebody's lap dog."

Biggs crossed his arms over his chest. "At the time, I was. But now I'm the *top* dog, you see. Bad pun not intended."

Lenny's brow creased. "I don't understand."

"Only people who still call me 'Christopher' are my two sisters and our mother. Nearly everyone's called me 'Top' since my first week at boot camp." Biggs shrugged. "Regardless, my old boss is a wanted man in Poland now. The brass at Langley thought it'd be bad optics to the people we have to work with there if he were still running the show." He made a sweeping gesture with one hand, as if to suggest a plane taking off. "So, they sent him to Peru to make sure Latharo is all squared away. He ought to be on his way back to Chicago by now, because he wants to brief us before we deploy on our Lake Michigan surveillance detail."

"The fact remains that you and your fireteam shagged my partner and I off that ship in Gdańsk Harbor on Christmas Eve at gunpoint," Lenny replied as he rubbed at his forehead. "We were there working within our jurisdiction, just doing our jobs. You *had* to have known that. Give me one good reason why I ought to trust you."

"Because I do," came the sound of a woman's voice from behind him, husky with emotion.

Lenny turned an instant before Pawly closed the distance between them. She threw her arms around him and glommed on, evoking from him something between a grunt and a cry as she expelled the air from his chest. He earnestly returned her embrace, not caring that he couldn't breathe.

H OLY SHIT, SHE'S FAST. Too fast. No one is that fast. No *human* could be that fast.

But...Pawly can't be human. Humans don't sprout tails and whiskers and ear tufts. I...I don't know what the hell she is.

And look at *that*, wouldya. Humans don't vault a four-high stack of containers either. As if she were hopping a backyard white picket fence or something.

That shit I saw that night in Chah Bahar? That was the gas. Them chemicals rat-fucked my brain but good. I was seeing things. Yeah, that's it. Seeing things.

But not tonight. Not on Christmas fucking Eve. Haven't even touched any egg nog yet. After seeing this goofy shit, gonna need something a whole lot stiffer anyway.

And now I'm thirsty. At least I can do something about that. Just kneel down beside this gantry crane here and take a swig from my...

What? There's another one? Pawly's mixing it up with some tiger-looking woman. And her sneak suit has stripes. Of course, it would. Why the fuck *wouldn't* it?

Oh, wait, here comes Pawly. What's she carrying? A child, a girl with long pigtails...and orange fur? Holy shit, how many of these fucking cat people are there anyway? And what are they all doing on a pier in Gdańsk Harbor? Do they gather like strays in a back alley for a night's caterwauling or something?

"Be right back."

Wait, what're you—?

Wow, that tiger woman is fast, too. Pawly parried her spear with some kind of bladed short staff thingy. Now she's gettin' all stabby with it, taking the fight to her like a mother bear defending her cub. More like a mother cougar.

Wait, what? That tiger woman, she freaked out or something. Screamed out in pain even before she plowed headlong into the hull of the ship. Damn, that had to hurt.

No sign of the tiger woman except for ripples spreading out from where she had fallen into the black water. "Be careful, she's known for her feints," Pawly says as I trot up beside her, my sidearm at the ready out in front of me. "She might pop out again when you least expect..."

But I don't hear her. I lean in, my gaze fixed upon the small silver bead dangling from a chain around her neck. I already know what I'll see—a lion and griffin above a scrolling banner with two words spelled out in tiny letters:

SEMPER PARATUS

Holy shit, Pawly had given that thing to me for my birthday year before last. And I'd lost it at Chah Bahar. She found it in the chaos? Had been keeping it all this time? For me?

"Pervert! We're on watch!"

I draw back after she swats me with the back of her...of her *paw*. Feeling fur brush the side of my nose is just eighteen different kinds of wrong. I glance up, watching Pawly scramble to cover herself with the scraps of her shredded sneak suit. "Nothing here you haven't seen before."

Except for the fur.

"Pawly, I..."

We both turn toward the sound of a man's groans from nearby. Beyond where Pawly had laid the cat girl lay Latharo, trying to prop himself up with his elbows.

A dull thump from behind me. I turn to see one of the blades topping Pawly's staff stuck deep into a wooden piling, her claws tearing a swatch of fabric free from her tattered uniform. "I...I have to go." She loops the fabric around her chest and knots the ends together between her bare shoulders. "Can't let anyone see Stuie in the shape she's in."

My jaw falls open. "Th-that's Stuie?"

But of course it is. The pigtails leave little doubt. Just chalk up one more fucked up thing I've seen tonight.

I follow Pawly's gaze toward Latharo. "I trust him," I say, nodding in his direction. "I believe you can too."

Pawly shakes her head. "No way. If you didn't know too much already, I would have never risked your safety seeing us like this. I won't risk his." She takes a step toward Stuie. And stops after Latharo stumbles to the girl's side.

"*¿Salvación? ¿De veras...que eres tu, mi hijita?*" Latharo pushes Stuie's hair away from her face, his service piece lost in his trembling hand.

Until the instant Latharo spots Pawly. He jumps to his feet and takes aim. *"¡Déjala en paz, la mujer gato malvada!"*

Oh, shit.

I'm already off in a full sprint toward them as she takes to the air, tracing an arc over my head. "No!" I cry as I brandish my weapon back and forth in front of me. Latharo looks my way with wide, wild eyes, drawing a bead on me with his own weapon.

"Lenny! Don't!" Pawly shouts as she touches down.

I glance at her and smile an instant before the *pop* and everything goes dark. Pain explodes across my face and neck as I'm falling. Falling, falling, Pawly's screams ringing in my ears.

"**T**HE HELL IS INTO you?"

Lenny blinked his eyes open and groaned. He lay on his side on the floor of the RV, his face pressed up against the bottom of the kitchenette's tiny oven. He kicked his legs back and forth in the space beneath the kitchenette's bench seat, trying to find purchase. Darkness surrounded him save for the dim glow of the dashboard beyond the end of the aisleway.

"Quit squirming around," Pawly hissed into his ear. "Don't know what was going on a moment ago. Calm down, you're okay."

He opened his mouth to say something and immediately began to gag.

"What's going on back there?" Top said from where he sat behind the RV's steering wheel.

"Lenny and I were asleep until just now. He started wigging out for some reason and fell out of his seat onto the floor," Pawly answered for Lenny while he coughed and wheezed. "Like he was having a nightmare or something."

She brought her face close to his. Her *human* face. "Is that what this is all about? You...you all right?"

He turned his head away and spat out what felt like a cross between a hairball and a dust bunny. "I will be. Now that I'm not trying to inhale whatever crud was stuck to the floor beneath the oven."

"Sorry. Top tells me he and the others have logged a lot of miles in this RV working. Guess the rig's not the cleanest."

"Going to be pulling off at the next exit to refuel. Get yourselves put together so you two can switch off driving afterward. I'm about beat." Top let out a long yawn and smacked his lips. "Dory texted me saying he'd meet us there. We'll have a few minutes if you want to grab a shower or get something from the café. But Dory said forget about the diner. Molasses this time of year moves faster than their wait staff and kitchen crew."

Their RV rumbled down the exit ramp ten minutes later. Not long afterward, Top brought the rig to a stop in a line of semi trucks awaiting their turn at the pumps. "All right, lovebirds, go on inside and tend to your business. I'll come inside once I top off our tanks. After I use the head, I'll come and find you."

Pawly replied in the affirmative and grabbed a pair of duffel bags—a white one and a navy blue one—from the rack above the kitchenette's dining table. "We went shopping on our way to come get you," she said as she handed the blue one to Lenny. "There's a shaving kit and a couple changes of clothes in there, much like the ones you're wearing now." She glanced out the window toward the truck stop and nodded. "C'mon, this time of morning we ought to miss the line for the showers."

Lenny motioned past Pawly toward the rear of the RV. "But there's a bathroom with a shower right there. Why would we need to take one inside the truck stop?"

Pawly arched an eyebrow at him. "Clearly, you've never tried to shower in a moving RV. Do *not* recommend. And the thing I hated most about sea duty was having to take Navy-style showers all the time. Without hookups, you and me would both have to take one. And the puny tank on this rig might well run dry before you'd be finished."

She hopped down the steps to the RV's side door and stepped outside. Lenny followed behind. "Looks like there's a bunch of construction cones and yellow tape over the glass doors," Pawly said as she squinted across the parking lot toward the entrance.

Lenny slung his duffel's strap over his shoulder and he closed the door behind him. "Let's go around to the other side, I don't mind. Being cooped up in that cell at Chesapeake for the last three weeks, I'm grateful for any chance to stretch my legs."

Pawly shrugged and took his hand. Together they strode off across the parking lot. "So, what *was* that all about anyway? Were you having a nightmare or something?"

The muscles in Lenny's neck tensed. "Yeah. Yeah, I was," he replied, his eyes fixed straight ahead.

"I've spent a night or two in the brig myself, you know."

He snorted. "Yeah, Tommy told me about your C-school escapades while he and I were on watch together. Passing time during many a long night aboard the *San Jac*."

"And aside from being bored out of my mind, it wasn't all that big of a deal." Pawly looked up at him. "Was Chesapeake really that bad?"

Lenny glanced her way for a moment, then turned to face forward once more. "Oh...oh, no. It wasn't about the brig. In the dream...I...I lived through it again. That night in Gdańsk." He screwed his eyes shut and shook his head. "When...when I shot..."

She drew up beside him and wrapped her arms around his. "You said Latharo would've surely shot *me* had you not intervened. I'd likely be dead if it not for you."

"But...I'm not sure I can ever face Latharo again," Lenny said in a small voice. "And how could I be trusted with another partner at all? Even while on some batshit crazy detail like this."

"Well, you're stuck with me now, like it or not, until we manage to catch Mawro with his pants down and take him out." She pushed open the plaza door and stepped inside, holding the door open for Lenny with her shoulder. After a glance back and forth to confirm they were alone, she went on in a low voice: "By now Grandpa D's people have surely gotten word to Latharo he was hallucinating."

Lenny turned and cocked an eyebrow at her. "You think he'll forgive me?"

"Of course, he will. He's a professional. He'll surely realize the danger he posed to himself and others. Like me."

He snorted. "Same sort of danger I'm only now coming to realize."

Pawly reached up under his hoodie and T-shirt and began stroking his chest. "Let me see if I can make it worth your while," she whispered into Lenny's ear. "What say you and me share a shower, hm? We could..."

Lenny gasped after Pawly's fist clenched around a clump of his chest hair. "What? What's wrong?"

She said nothing, sniffing at the air for a moment. Then she withdrew her hand and tugged the hem of Lenny's hoodie down past his waist. "Change in plan." Pawly nodded toward the intersecting corridor in front of them, just before the entrance to the shower rooms. "We've got company."

An instant later, a leathery-faced older man rounded the corner. His eyes went wide at the sight of Pawly. "There you are, lil' fighter!" The man approached and drew Pawly in to an embrace. "So, you're the beau, huh?" he said, looking Lenny up and down over Pawly's shoulder. "A fine specimen. Just what I would expect from a fellow Coast Guardsman. Lenny, is it?"

"What are you doing here anyway, Grandpa D?" Pawly answered as she drew back from him, an edge in her voice. "Top said you would brief us in Chicago once you got back from Peru. Not at some truck stop east of Bumblefuck."

Lenny's head swam. *'Grandpa D'? Peru? Wait, so Pawly's grandfather was tending Latharo? Was the guy running the show in Gdańsk until—*

"The attendants had closed down the showers for cleaning before the morning rush," he replied with a nod toward the yellow folding signs at the end of the corridor. "I grabbed the last one open before they did." He held out a slip of paper toward Pawly. "Here's the door code. Milda is expecting you. She should be finished momentarily, then you can shower while she's getting dressed and putting her hair up. Wash out that potty mouth of yours while you're at it and then come greet this old man with a proper kiss."

The man's face broke into a Cheshire cat grin as he ran a hand through his graying, close-cropped hair. "C'mon, shipmate. You and I can catch a shower this evening after we get to town." He clasped Lenny on the shoulder then motioned for him to follow. "Right now, I could use some help lugging our food out to the RV."

Lenny's gaze darted back and forth between Pawly and her grand-father. She rolled her eyes and nodded toward the corridor beyond, as if encouraging him to just play along.

CHAPTER THREE

DOOR COUNTY, WISCONSIN. WEEKS LATER.

NIKO BLINKED AWAY TEARS as he stared out through the boat's windscreen hatch toward the horizon. There angry gray clouds blotted out the setting sun, heralding the coming storm as surely as NWS forecasters had over the weather marine band minutes before. Dory's retired Coast Guard motor lifeboat was a swift and sturdy craft; engines both at wide open throttle they would arrive at their Pilot Island mooring before long. And, despite Lake Michigan's growing chop, without anyone aboard being more shook up than they already were.

He tugged the windscreen hatch shut with a grunt before retaking his seat at the helm. After a momentary glance down at the compass, he peered through the tiny round window in the forecastle hatch. Stuie sat at the chart table, her head down on one arm, banging on the table with her free hand while her shoulders shook. Niko turned his head her way to try and listen, but the roar of the engines from beneath the deck plates drowned out any of her crying he might have heard.

Nat and Annie labored over Alex behind him in the aft cabin, trying frantically to stabilize Niko's daughter. Leaping treetop to treetop all afternoon to guide Stuie toward her prey had taken its toll on Alex. The deer hadn't even completely bled out before she collapsed.

A hatch slammed shut behind him. Niko turned to find Nat trudging his way forward into the wind. "How is she?" Niko asked a moment later when his son joined him next to the helm.

"Stable. Annie and I think it was just a routine case of overexertion, though we still want to examine her more closely when we get back to the lighthouse."

Niko pursed his lips. "Will you draw samples too?"

"We were planning on it," Nat replied. "If Top and his team deliver us those catalyzation proteins on schedule, then they should still be fresh enough for us to work with."

"We can't steal everything we need from the North Koreans, you know." Niko drew his free hand to his chin, gripping the boat's helm tightly in the other. "You'll need samples from Stuie, too."

"And we just had to abort right after Stuie took her kill." Nat shook his head. "If we'd gotten a cheek swab right afterward, then maybe this wouldn't all have been for naught. We'd've been able to get a snapshot of all of Stuie's ailuranthropic markers at their peak."

"We might be able to yet. The sublingual glands ought to manifest the ailuranthropic markers too, right?"

The corner of Nat's mouth turned up. "So, we should be able to harvest a sample from the saliva Stuie left on the carcass she devoured."

Niko patted his son's shoulder. "Couldn't have said it better myself."

Nat looked out over the choppy water toward the horizon. "It'll be dark soon. And that storm is blowing in fast."

"Yes, but Dory's seen to it that this ol' gal is faster," Niko replied, patting the helm's console. "And I'll make sure to monitor the weather bands so the storm can't get the drop on me." He waved his free hand toward the forecastle. "But let me worry about that. Stuie blames herself for Alex's condition. Right now, we've got a scared little girl in there who needs her Papa."

Nat sighed and hung his head. "Yes, you're right," he said before opening the hatch and ducking inside. The heartbreaking sound of Stuie's sobs went mute after Nat pulled the hatch shut behind him. Niko peered through the hatch window into the forecastle again. Stuie's orange-and-white fur-covered hands clenched together tightly in the small of Nat's back, trembling as she clutched her father to her.

Minutes later their boat ducked behind the lee side of Pilot Island and motored up the tiny inlet that led to the family's cabin. Nat popped up from the forecastle's deck hatch and tossed out the hauling line around one of the mooring bollards. Niko pulled the throttles back to him and turned in time to watch Annie do likewise with their stern line. How long had she been standing there? He hadn't even heard her emerge from the aft compartment.

Niko stepped over to the open hatchway. "Hiya, Pops," Alex said, whiskers twitching, the low growl of the boat's twin diesels nearly drowning out her weak voice even at idle. Before he could chastise her for trying to move about, Annie pushed her way past Niko and drew up beside her. "Take it easy. Doctor's orders," Annie told Alex while Niko came alongside, helping coax Alex up into a sitting position. "And keep quiet," Annie told her, a stern look on her face. "Can't deal with any of your sass right now, girl. You get me?"

A sheepish look came over Alex's face but she said nothing. Niko and Annie both took an arm over one shoulder and hoisted Alex to her feet. Alex remained quiet as Niko and Annie carefully sidestepped out of the aft compartment and shuffled across the Forty-Four's deck to the pier. Nat was already there, both hands rubbing at the black-and-white fur covering Stuie's small round ears, perched atop her head of long black hair. He gently nudged his sniffling daughter aside and knelt down beside the rail. Niko handed Alex's arm over and Nat placed it on his own.

"Could you get the door for us, kiddo?" Nat asked. Stuie nodded solemnly and strode off down the pier toward their cabin's back door. Annie resumed her station under Alex's other shoulder. "We've got this," Nat told Niko as he turned back toward him.

"Good. I don't expect I'll be over long." Niko worked the stern line free of its bollard while Nat and Annie shuffled along the pier with Alex between them. Then he shimmied around to the bow and freed the line there. Nat turned after Niko goosed the throttles, flashing his father a wan smile. He tossed Nat a lackadaisical salute and steered the boat back toward open water.

Niko had hardly cleared the breakwater before the boat's satellite phone began to ring. He peered down at the thing, seated in its charging cradle beside the helm, and knew from the number he needed to answer. "*Słucham, Pan Teodor,*" he shouted over the crashing surf after picking up.

"There's a storm coming, fool," Dory replied in Polish, his voice booming through the handset's earpiece. "Why are you putting back out? I've got too much into you and that boat to risk losing either of you."

"I figured you'd be calling," Niko said as he throttled back so as to hear him better. "You've got that pesky tracking device well-hidden, have to hand you that. I know it's nowhere topside. Couldn't find any trace of it earlier today when I was down in the engine room topping off your oil."

"Its location is for me to know and you not to," Dory replied with a chuckle. "Nor anyone else. Got me?"

"One of your many secrets I keep in all due confidence, my friend."

Niko went on about Nat's suggestion and the errand he'd volunteered to take on, then said goodbye to Dory. After hanging up and replacing the handset in its cradle, he aimed the boat's bow toward the rocky shore of St. Martin's Island and mashed the throttles as far forward as they could go.

HUFFING AND PUFFING, MAWRO approached the deer's carcass and knelt down. He brushed aside the reddish-brown fur covering his watch and frowned. Had Hana really put him ashore nearly a half an hour ago already? He had tacked back and forth the length and breadth of St. Martin's Island for some while, desperate to catch a whiff of Stuie's scent. Though Hana was by far the better tracker between them, he didn't dare risk exposing her Stuie—even indirectly. He needed Hana to remain lucid in case they needed to effect a hasty escape. If, for no other reason, so he wouldn't have to try and squeeze his oversized body into the confines behind their boat's helm.

Mawro tugged at the flap covering a pocket in the makeshift cargo shorts he had stitched together from canvas scraps weeks before aboard their ship. From it, he pulled out a bag like one might rake leaves from the lawn into come fall, made of sturdy black plastic. Taking care not to puncture the bag with his long claws, he rolled up its edges and sat it down on the ground next to the deer's head. Then he used his claws to slash away at the flesh surrounding the bite wound through which the deer bled out after Stuie snapped the thing's neck. He sniffed carefully at the carcass as he worked to make sure he retrieved as much of Stuie's saliva as he could. Once back aboard the boat, he would put the samples on ice until he got them back to the ship. Then he would extract Stuie's DNA so he could finish constructing and calibrating Hana's self-contained breathing apparatus. She could sortie the next time, confident her SCBA would switch over to cannister air quickly upon detecting Stuie's scent, which would prevent Hana from raging out of control again.

Satisfied he had indeed harvested all he could of Stuie's DNA, Mawro fumbled with his big hands to carefully knot the bag above his collected samples. Then he stuck the bag back into his pocket and snapped the flap closed. He stared up at the clouds, running numbers in his head as storm cloud swirled in the gray sky above the clearing. And smiling as he realized he might just well extract enough of the girl's DNA as to render frivolous the rest of their operation.

But his smile faded after he turned to head back toward shore. The shifting winds brough with them a new scent, a familiar one. A horrifying one—that of his sister Alex. Or, more specifically, the putrid tinge of rot and decay. Unmistakable, even to his handicapped olfactories.

He swore and bit his lip. Damn her anyway. Was Alex helping Stuie take her kill or something? She knew better than to go and overexert herself like that. Which served only to make her body break down all that much faster.

His watch began to vibrate. Mawro sighed and drew the thing close to his mouth. "Open channel." The thing chimed in reply. "Go ahead, Hana."

"I have spotted the Katczynski family launch," came her voice through the watch's tinny speaker. "Coming this way. We ought not dally. Where shall I pick you up?"

Mawro raked his claws through his ruff. "You shouldn't yet," he said after a moment. "Hold station but see to it you keep out of sight.

I have...business to attend to with who I think ought to be aboard that boat. When you see me emerge from the tree line, beach the boat next to the dock and stand by."

"Under...understood," Hana replied before cutting their connection. His watch vibrated twice in response and went still. After dashing across the clearing, Mawro tiptoed into a thicket and crouched down to wait.

S PUME AND SPRAY BLASTED overtop of the rickety dock as Niko and the boat neared the windward side of St. Martin's Island. Winds drove the water with nearly gale force strength already, and the day's light had all but deserted him. Niko stood beside the helm, bow line in one hand, goosing the throttles with his other while managing to hold the helm steady with his elbow. Slowly he tacked back and forth into the choppy surf, deftly avoiding presenting the boat's flank to the wind. Once alongside the dock he tossed out his bow line, and with a flick of his wrist managed to snag the tiny bollard there. He looped the line around his waist and threw the rudder hard over before hauling the line in. A half hitch around the cleat beside him held the line taut until Niko managed to hook another bollard and pull the boat's stern toward it. Huffing and puffing, he tied off the lines and killed the engines.

Niko ducked down into the forecastle and pushed the chart table to its raised position against the bulkhead. He plucked the handheld marine band radio from its charger and flicked its "on" switch. It chirped to life, the NOAA Weather Radio marine forecast blaring out through its tiny speaker until Niko silenced it with a poke of a button.

He clipped the thing to his belt and grabbed a collection bag from a locker beneath one of the bench seats. Then he went topside.

He scanned the windblown shoreline while he doffed his flotation vest. Then he pulled a small silver flask from the chest pocket of his windbreaker and took a swig. "Not a bad batch at all," he mumbled with a smile and shoved the flask back into his pocket. He smacked his lips together, savoring the warm, soothing sensation washing over him. "If I do say so myself."

After double-checking each of the lines with a good tug, Niko tossed his bag onto the dock and hopped over the gunwale after it. Dory's boat would await him like a cowboy's trusty mount—just like the ones he'd read about in all the Zane Grey novels he'd checked out over the years from the Loyola student library. He made his way a short distance down the shoreline until he came to the path that led inland. Though their foliage wouldn't fully deploy for a month yet, the knotted masses of budding branches above Niko's head were plenty enough to blot out any trace of remaining daylight. He pulled a small flashlight from another pocket and twisted it on. With its beam to guide him along the path, Niko quickly made his way to the clearing where Stuie had finally managed to take her kill. Right before Alex collapsed.

He gasped as he approached what remained of the deer's carcass. After taking a knee, Niko poked at the edges of the gaping hole where the base of the deer's neck had once been. Muscle and bone and connecting tissue surrounding the small bite wound Stuie inflicted while taking her kill had all been cleanly cut away, as if by some giant-sized surgeon wielding a machete like a scalpel.

And, with it, every trace of Stuie's saliva.

A piercing tone blared forth from the tinny speaker inside the marine transceiver clipped to his belt, giving Niko a start. "THE

NATIONAL WEATHER SERVICE IN GREEN BAY, WISCON-
SIN HAS ISSUED A SPECIAL MARINE WARNING FOR ALL
NEARSHORE AND OPEN WATERS ACROSS NORTHERN
LAKE MICHIGAN," the thing blared while he poked at the buttons
on the transceiver's faceplate. "AT FIVE FORTY-FIVE P.M., NOAA
WEATHER RADAR INDICATED A LINE OF THUNDER-
STORMS CAPABLE OF PRODUCING GALE FORCE WINDS,
FREQUENT CLOUD-TO-WATER LIGHTNING AND LARGE
HAIL LOCATED NEAR A POINT EIGHT MILES OFFSHORE
DUE WEST OF WASHINGTON ISLAND TO A POINT—"

The weather radio fell silent as Niko got to his feet. The deer's
carcass had clearly been carved up by someone using some kind of
knife. Or, he realized, by some sort of animal with very long, very sharp
claws. And whoever it was—whatever it was—he wasn't about to wait
here for a face-to-face encounter. But before Niko got more than two
steps back toward the boat, a ragged snarl, low and long, reverberated
through the clearing,

He froze. Another snarl came a moment later, nearer-by than the
first. Niko shone his flashlight all around until its beam fell upon the
deer carcass. Or, at least, fell upon the spot where he had last seen
it. Beside the carcass now crouched an enormous creature covered in
mottled brown fur, the reflected light giving its eyes a sinister green
glow. Time slowed while Niko and the thing stared at one another,
heart pounding in his chest. After untold seconds Niko slowly took
a step backwards and unknowingly placed the toe of his boot directly
atop a dry twig.

Ka-snap.

The thing belted out a blood-curdling roar and pounced. Niko
turned and bolted, his flashlight's beam flitting wildly across the path
back to the shoreline. He stumbled over roots and decaying logs as

he ran but by Providence managed not to fall. Beyond the darkened forest, Niko dashed toward the shoreline and swung right short of the breakers crashing ashore to avoid the larger rocks. The boat bobbed up and down at its mooring mere yards away.

An instant later the growling thing burst forth from the darkened forest and into the murky twilight. Niko stole a glance over his shoulder, gasping at the sight of his pursuer's towering silhouette. Giving chase on *two* legs. And closing in on him.

His head swung around back to center by reflex, his body responding to a metallic screeching directly ahead. A wall of gray flashed past an instant before a surge of water knocked him backwards. He tripped and landed flat on his back upon the rocks. Niko shook his head and blinked for a moment before gazing up at what appeared to be the side of a boat's hull. He glanced to his left and realized indeed a boat had driven itself up on the shore before him, as if trying to cut off his escape route. Which, he understood after his gaze met that of the Korean woman glaring down at him from the boat's helm, was precisely what she had had in mind.

Hana? How did she get here? Niko thought as he sat upright. *So where is…?*

Niko glanced over his shoulder to find the creature standing by a stride's length away with a puzzled look on its face. He held his arms out at his sides, trying to demonstrate to the thing he was no threat. It simply knelt forward and sniffed at the air around him before its eyes went wide. "Maurycy?" Niko blurted out as the thing drew close. "Is…is that you?"

With a hiss the thing reared back and bared its dagger-length fangs. Then drawing back one massive paw, it swung directly for Niko's head.

Chapter Four

MEANWHILE, AFLOAT SOMEWHERE ON GREEN BAY...

TOP GAZED OUT OVER the water's choppy surface. Ice chunks bobbed to and fro all around their boat, but he paid them no mind. Bobby Katczynski sat to his right, seated at the helm, deftly navigating around them with practiced ease after decades of piloting boats large and small all over the Great Lakes. Top raised his field glasses and peered through them toward the superstructure towering above the stern of the ocean freighter off their port side. Another pair of field glasses stared back at him, lowering an instant later to reveal the scowling face of the ship's master. Top cracked a smile and waved in salute, but the captain just ignored him.

Which was exactly what he had wanted the man to do. Top had been counting on Bobby's non-descript work launch arousing no suspicions while Pawly accomplished her task. If the ship's master dismissed Top and his crew as just another salvor's boat trolling these waters in search of sunken vehicles and ice shanties, that suited him just fine.

His earbud began to warble, announcing the incoming call to his satellite phone he had been expecting. He let his field glasses return to the spot on his chest where they dangled at the end of the strap around his neck and poked a button on his earbud. "Completed your sweep already?"

"And I took my time. This place is pretty tiny, you know," Lenny's voice crackled through the earbud in reply. "Could almost throw a rock from one side and hit the fence at the other."

Top glanced down at his chronometer. "Stay frosty. Traffic might pick up as zero hour approaches."

"Or it might not," Lenny answered, an edge in his tone. "This is the fourth fire drill we've been through in not even two weeks."

He swallowed his lips and stared out over the open water. The guy wasn't wrong, despite Dory's imploring Top to keep the team in-theatre. Langley's intelligence wonks had checked and double-checked reports the North Koreans planned to put a container full of the stuff ashore to their mobile "shroom factories" inland. Most likely delivered by a Chinese-flagged freighter, just like the one they were pacing now.

"Look, Dory's sources are sure DPRK will try to put their container ashore at a Lake Michigan port. Which is why we need to keep Pawly in the water and you ashore to scope out every saltie west of the Mackinac Bridge, now until summer if need be. Mawro might be planning to avoid Chicago, and a port within drayage distance might offer him a—"

"Hey, skipper, you should see this!"

Top turned to find Tommy waving to him from behind his console in the boat's tiny forecastle. "I gotta go," he said, acknowledging Tommy with a nod. "Jakub dropped the MGS and its trailer at our safe haven in the U. P. about an hour ago. He should be bobtailing your way now. Call me when he gets there." With that he ended the call and poked his head through the companionway. "What you got, Tomcat?"

The younger man waved at the screens to his left. One contained a reproduction of the real time chat window between Tommy's console and the military-grade electronic slate Pawly wore strapped around her wrist during her dive. The screen was blank except for the bottom line: APPROACHING HULL

Top glanced over at Tommy. "She's been in this icy water for over a half an hour now. You're *sure* Pawly's not at risk for hypothermia?"

"Our undercoats don't normally start to blow out for a couple more weeks yet," Tommy replied, tugging at the ruff of white fur beneath his chin. "Between that and her wet suit, she ought to be good for as long as her air holds out."

"Tell her to commence observation. And to stay out of sight."

"Aye, Cap." Tommy tossed Top a sloppy salute and turned back to his screen. He tapped out a response and sent it on its way to Pawly: OBSERVE AND REPORT

A chime announced her incoming reply a moment later: ROG UP PERISCOPE

P AWLY PILOTED HER SCUBA scooter alongside the saltie, just fore of its superstructure at the stern. With a flick of a switch on her dash, the thing matched the ship's speed and bearing. Pawly plucked a small metal box from a pouch on her tool belt. After poking a button on its top, the thing began to glow. She tugged at the tether holding it to the climbing harness over her wet suit to make sure it was secure. Then she held the box with both hands out in front of her and pushed off with her legs straight ahead of her.

She angled her hands toward the ship. Just before the wake's powerful current broadsided her, she slammed the box in her hands against the ship's hull just below the waterline. The tether connecting it to her harness snapped taut, fixing her in place.

A couple of solid tugs to the tether assured Pawly she wasn't going anywhere. She reached over her shoulder into her backpack and pulled for the little rover Tommy had fixed to the end of his antenna cable. Pawly set the thing wheels down on the ship's hull, pointed its front upward toward the deck, and flicked a switch. An indicator lamp above the switch's toggle flashed twice in reply. Pawly let go and the thing held fast. She wiggled at it but it didn't move; she wreathed on it with both hands but the thing didn't budge. Good, the electromagnet appeared to be holding. Just as Tommy had said it would.

She toggled another switch and the rover began to move. After breaching the waterline a moment later, it continued rolling slowly up the side of the ship's hull while Pawly played out the remaining antenna cable from her backpack.

The LED at the top right corner of her slate blinked red to announce an incoming message. FEED OK popped up on its screen an instant later, indicating the sonar data link between her scooter and her Great Uncle Bobby's boat was functioning in good order.

Before long, the jacket of the antenna cable playing out from Pawly's backpack changed from black to red, indicating it was near the end. She took the cable in both hands and gave a couple of quick jerks to signal to the rover to stop.

Pawly pulled the rest of the cable free and took hold of the magnetic mount at its end. She placed the mount atop the red circle painted onto her scuba scooter's fuselage, just ahead of its instrument cluster. Another indicator lamp flickered to life, this one indicating the data link between the inductive antenna inside the magnetic mount and the scuba scooter had been successfully established. PERISCOPE DEPLOYED Pawly scribbled on her slate, knowing her scooter would already be relaying data to Tommy in real time.

Her brother wrote back a moment later ACCESSING CAMERAS STAND BY

She swiped her finger across the slate's surface to call up the video feed. A chunky, pixelated image appeared, wavering in and out of focus as Tommy durdled around with his filtering algorithms. Before long, the raw data being intercepted from the ship's cameras yielded a crisp, clear image of the ship's main deck.

Tommy panned the view back and forth before the screen went dark. Another image appeared, this one from what looked to Pawly to be inside the engine room. Then one from behind the pilot house looking astern toward the lifeboat. He scrolled through several more views of the ship's common areas before stopping at a pair of images from inside the hold.

SHIT NO PTZ he messaged Pawly as he toggled back and forth between the two images.

Pawly clenched her teeth around her regulator. Apparently, the cameras in this particular ship's hold lacked any pan-tilt-zoom functionality. Which, she knew, would make it just that much more difficult to confirm the container they were looking for was actually aboard this ship. And which would surely require her sending up the damn drone. Pawly hated deploying the thing, believing they might as well hail the captain on the marine bands to request permission to come aboard. The drone could easily alert the deck crew to their presence if any of them spotted the drone in-flight.

But she knew it needed to be done. Grandpa N had said locating the container carrying the catalyzation proteins Grandpa D's contacts told him about was imperative for effectively treating her mother. Breaking the teeth of their Affliction before it, one by one, broke *them*.

P REP FOR FLIGHT

Pawly and her scuba scooter had already breeched the water's surface by the time Tommy's message arrived. She spat out her regulator and breathed through her mouth while flipping open the scooter's rear hatch. The drone's blades began to spin up hardly an instant after Pawly poked the "thumbs up" icon on her slate. She had no reason to doubt whether Tommy shared her sense of urgency.

With a *bzzzzzzzzzt!* and a *whoosh!* the drone was airborne. Pawly slammed the hatch shut and coaxed her scuba scooter into a dive, jamming her regulator back into her mouth an instant before her head dipped beneath the cold water's surface.

She called up the drone's camera image just after the thing crested the ship's railing and disappeared. Tommy piloted the thing into the first cowl vent he could find. Now out of sight of anyone above deck, he took his time negotiating a series of sharp turns around the baffles. Before long the drone emerged from the vent's air inlet into the wide-open space within the hold proper. It made a beeline for the bow and then began making its way sternward, sweeping back and forth the width of the hold as it went.

The reporting marks of the containers in the ship's hold flashed by faster than Pawly could possibly ever read them. But she knew Tommy's Eyes would be able to make them out just fine.

JACKPOT

A container atop one of the stacks loomed into view, sporting a dingy coat of navy-blue paint. He maneuvered the drone back and forth above one corner, allowing Pawly to make out the reporting marks.

CORRESPONDS TO THE MANIFEST GRANDPA D GAVE US

GOOD NOW LETS GTFO, Pawly replied.

WAIT WHATS THIS THING?

Pawly squinted through her facemask at the image on her slate. It was some sort of spindly structure, appearing as though someone had hastily slapped it together from scrap dimensional lumber and metal gusset plates. DOLLY? she swiped back, taking note of the rubber-tired wheels at the four bottom corners and midway along the lower sill on either side.

RIGHT TOP SEZ CRADLE FOR A SUBMERSIBLE

WHERE IS THE SUB? Pawly replied.

OUT S/W MAYBE BUT HOW COULD THEY LAUNCH IT?

CRANE DUH

NONE ABOVE DECK DUH

MUST BE ONE IN HOLD S/W

Pawly watched as Tommy piloted the drone over beside a large wheeled hydraulic crane. The drone's headlight glinted off the thing's gleaming yellow paint. The thing was practically brand new.

LIKE THIS ONE?

Before she could answer, Tommy flew up and over the thing as if to afford Pawly a better look. She'd seen several like it in action while providing force protection ashore for a detachment of Navy Seabees. Via an open hatch cover in the deck above, a rig like this one could easily play out its telescoping boom enough to lower a submersible into the water at the end of its whip line. And then, upon its return, reel it back in. Deploy the sub under cover of darkness while under way miles from shore, stick the sub back in the container when it's not needed. And no one would be any the wiser. Even if the Coast Guard did come aboard for an inspection, the crew could always hand-wave away the crane and even the submersible itself as simply cargo.

DON'T NEED SUB BAY PRETTY TRICKY

NOT TRICKY ENOUGH FOR YOU AND ME SIS

GTG TTYL

The drone flew back up into the air vent through which it first entered the hold. After tiptoeing around the baffles again, it popped out of the cowl vent above deck.

Then it stopped moving, hovering near the vent. Surely within view of anyone who might happen to be standing watch on the main deck.

Pawly glanced over at the console of her scuba scooter. The link light was still lit, indicating the virtual circuit via sonar signal between her and Bobby's boat was still intact. Then why had the stupid drone stopped responding?

WTF OVER

The seconds following her message dragged on, each one seeming to tick by slower than the one before it. None yielding an answer from Tommy.

She would coerce an explanation out of him later. Right now, she needed to move. After taking the antenna cable in both hands, she heaved on it with all her strength. After the rover's magnetic wheels broke free from the side of the ship, its antenna cable slipped freely through her hands. She reached over the dash of her scuba scooter and tugged the other end of the antenna cable free from its mount. Then she goosed the accelerator on her scooter's handlebar grip and piloted the thing into a dive. After passing the end of the sinking antenna cable, she spun the thing around and made for the surface. She was on her feet as the scooter broke the water's surface. Like the diver at Sea World's killer whale exhibit from a family vacation long ago, she took flight from the scooter as the thing plunged back into the water.

Pawly vaulted the ship's deck rail and dropped into a low defensive stance. She whirled back and forth, claws bared, ready to rip out the throat of anyone who might have spotted her, to prevent them from raising an alarm. Seeing no one, she stood and looked around for the stalled drone. She found it hovering motionless in front of the cowl vent, right where she'd expected from viewing the drone's video feed.

And in the line of sight of a sentry carrying an automatic rifle in his hands, to boot. That is, the drone *would* be presently, just as soon as the sentry completed his march and about-faced. Which Pawly estimated would be in about three seconds, seeing the man approach the bow.

She coiled and sprang. Her momentum carried her across the deck as she thrust out her arms wide to her sides. Pawly snatched the drone mid-air, bear hugging it to her, clenching her teeth as its blades ripped through her wet suit and dug into her pelt. Pain exploded across her chest and back as she slammed into the deck with one shoulder. With a grunt, she managed to marshal her reserves and propel herself over the deck railing just as the sentry's gasp registered. A moment's weightlessness afforded her the opportunity to suck in a lungful of air before she splashed down into Lake Michigan's frigid waters.

Once below, she thrust the now terminally disabled drone away from her. *Good riddance,* she thought as the thing disappeared into the depths. She rolled onto her back and stared up through the water toward the ship's railing. There stood the sentry, frantically scanning the water's surface, as if trying to confirm whether or not he had indeed just seen a stowaway jump overboard. Content for him to go on wondering, Pawly swiped at her slate to summon her scuba scooter. North Korean special forces commanders didn't take kindly to reports of spectral sightings, she knew. Likely as not the man would simply shrug it off and say nothing. That was the delusion Pawly labored under, at least, though little else she could do about it now. Once back aboard their boat, however, she would slash away at whichever part of her dumbass brother she could sink her claws into first until he fessed up as to *what the absolute fuck* had just happened.

Seeing her scooter approach, Pawly surfaced just long enough to expel the stale air from her lungs and jam her regulator back into her mouth. Then she climbed atop her scooter and piloted it into a dive, ducking beneath the hull of the ship before making a beeline back to Bobby's boat. Surfacing minutes later as she approached the boat's stern, Pawly spied Top leaning out over the water stabbing downward with his fingers. With a nod of acknowledgement, she poked at a button on her scooter's console and bailed off. A line blew out from the back of the scooter with a *whoof!* an instant before the scooter began to sink. Pawly paddled toward the boat, glancing over her shoulder in time to glimpse a yellow-and-blue buoy break the water's surface to mark the scuttled scooter's location.

She only noticed the incoming message light on her slate blinking when she snatched hold of the dive platform handle bobbing up and down above her head. Top reached down and hauled her aboard, saying nothing as she spat out her regulator. Maybe he could see the steam rising from her forehead? Beyond him stood her Uncle Bobby, the pair of field glasses he held to his eyes trained on the gray horizon ahead of the saltie.

"Where is he? I'll kill him!" Pawly fumed while she pulled off her goggles. But then a new scent registered, one tinged with pain and fear and anguish. She turned to Top, her anger instantly morphing into worry. "Is...is Tommy—?"

"I'll...I'll be fine," came her brother's voice from beyond the companionway before Top could answer.

Pawly shucked her air tanks and let them drop to the deck. She darted through the companionway, nearly tripping over a part of Tommy's exo. Her brother lay flat on his back on the bunk opposite his console. "What...what happened?" Pawly asked as she knelt down beside him, her voice barely a whisper.

"I...I don't know, sis." Tommy's eyes remained closed as he slowly shook his head back and forth. "Stabbing pain in my back, just above my waist. Tried to stay on task...couldn't focus anymore..."

"You can blame me all you want for the drone going wonky."

Pawly glanced up and behind to where Top stood above her, his arms resting on either side of the companionway hatch. "His exo is a prototype, so I thought maybe something shorted out inside of it. I pulled it off of him when he started screaming. Must've cut the connection to the drone in the process."

He dropped into the compartment next to Pawly and tapped Tommy's cheek with his fist. "You lay here and rest, sailor. We need you shipshape and seaworthy when we catch up to that ship." Top turned and shouted back up the companionway. "Can you make that happen, Bobby?"

"Sure can! All of you best hang on to something, now..."

Pawly and Top both reached up and gripped the handrail bolted to the cabin ceiling an instant before Bobby threw both throttles wide open. The bow of their boat pitched skyward as its engines screamed in response.

Chapter Five

Back on St. Martin's Island...

M awro lunged with a roar. The backside of his paw clipped the top of whatever Dr. Opoworo clutched in his trembling hand, sending it flying. It crashed into the hull of Mawro's boat with such force as to shatter into a thousand pieces.

"What are *you* doing here?" Mawro barked in Polish, his forearm barred across the other man's chest. "And in Katczynski's boat, no less. Is that why you were on the radio? Where is he?"

The trapped man grunted as he pushed impotently with one hand against Mawro's forearm. "I was only monitoring the weather bands. To know if the coming storm changed direction so as to best maneuver around it upon my return to Pilot Island," he went on, narrowing his eyes. "I *know* you know that, Ritzi."

Hana popped her head up through the canopy hatch and bounded over to where Mawro held his father pressed against the hull. "Honorable Opoworo speaks truth with regard to the storm," she called out in her native Korean. "It grows stronger by the minute."

"And I came alone, if that's what you're worried about," the elder man assured him. "Dory's been in Chicago all week, giving his reports."

Mawro snorted. "And giving that Milda woman a whole lot more than that, I'll bet," he mumbled before letting his arm go limp. His captive let out a yelp and fell to the rocky shore, landing on his hands and knees. "I scented Alex, Papa. Scented her scouting around before you arrived. She's in trouble, isn't she?"

The other man groaned and sat upright. "Alex has managed to help Stuie remain lucid whenever the girl morphs, but it's taken a toll," he said, rubbing at his bruised knees. "She collapsed today, right at the conclusion of Stuie's hunt. I'm here to collect whatever remnant I could find of her sublingual gland expressions. Everyone else is back on Pilot Island, tending Alex."

Mawro knelt down and met his gaze. "You and Nat have had the MGS back in your possession for nearly four months now, Papa. By God, why haven't you healed her already?"

He turned his head aside, saying nothing.

"It's not *with* you, is it?" Mawro asked, his eyes growing wide. "Katczynski has been ferrying it around the countryside to keep my people or the Nohs from finding it, hasn't he?" He bared his fangs and drew close to Opoworo's ear. "Do you have any idea how much time you're wasting with such games?"

"Dory believes we need more time to—"

"I know I need not tell you, Papa, just how little of that we have."

The elder man crossed his arms over his chest. "And I know I don't have to tell *you* just how painstaking this work is. Nat and I have replicated tissues from Stuie with the MGS, to be sure, though so far only in small amounts so far."

Mawro cocked an eyebrow at him. "But why?"

"We made a critical miscalculation," he said, his chin drooping. "Stuie being a different species from the rest of you, we've only been able to transfuse small quantities of her DNA into Alex to try and stabilize her. Today, we found out the hard way such amounts are indeed insufficient."

"Can you make more? Can she accept more?"

Opoworo looked up at Mawro. "Yes, and I don't think so. But Nat and I anticipated this. We knew the limited doses we've been giving Alex would only serve to buy us time until we can produce catalyzation proteins on a large scale. Which is why we've been administering Stuie's replicated DNA to Tommy as well."

"I don't understand," Mawro replied as he shook his head. "To what purpose? Especially given Alex's condition."

His father tapped at the side of his head with one finger. "Think about it. Introducing the morphogens from one species into another ought to..."

"...ought to induce the host body to begin producing morphogens for its own native species, right. So, you're injecting Tommy with tigrine cells so his body will begin producing lyncean ones?"

Opoworo nodded. "Exactly. Which we can then harvest from Tommy and put right back into Alex while we ramp up production." He waved an arm toward the tree line. "That's why I came to collect Stuie's sublingual gland expressions from after she took her kill. Nat and I are hoping they'll push the cellular reproduction processes underway within Tommy's body into overdrive."

Mawro's eyes went wide. "Do you think his spinal injury might begin to repair itself if it does?"

His father shrugged. "Only time will tell, son. Tommy is young and virile, and his body might already have a head start. He's been experiencing occasional pain and numbness in his lower back recently.

Nat and I had been handwaving it away as biofeedback from his exo, to keep anyone from getting their hopes up..." He reached up and clenched one of Mawro's enormous fur-covered fingers. "We could really use your help to heal Alex and the twins. And...and your mother and I miss you terribly. We all do. Come home, and...and let us be your family once more," he said in a creaky voice as he glanced over at Hana. "You would be welcome, too." He sniffled and dabbed at the corners of his eyes with his thumb and forefinger. "Dory would certainly run interference for you both."

Mawro shook his head. "Don't be foolish, Papa. You and I both know neither Katczynski nor his family would tolerate that. Surely, they must know I'm responsible for...well, you know." He furrowed his brow before breaking the heavy silence. "And besides, I've seen firsthand how Hana and that girl Stuie react to..."

Ears twitching, Mawro cocked his head to one side. "The wind has changed direction and is picking up speed," he said after a moment, his eyes fixed upon the choppy surf beyond the shoreline. He tugged open the flap on the pocket of his cargo shorts and pulled out the plastic bag containing the samples he had harvested earlier from Stuie's kill. He took one of the bloodied strips of venison from inside and wrapped it with a corner of the open bag's top. Then he slit the plastic with one claw and handed the meat to his father. "This is one of Stuie's sublingual samples. I will see to it you get the rest of what you need to help Alex." Thunder rumbled in the distance. "But now...now you should go."

Opoworo took the wadded-up meat into his hands and mumbled "Thank you, son." Then he scampered off toward the dock.

Mawro wrapped the samples from Stuie back up and returned them to his pouch. "We should be away soon too, my dear. Otherwise, we might have to return to the ship via the lee shore instead of heading straight across the lake," he said as he lumbered over to the bow of their boat. "Get to the helm, then goose the throttle twice to tell me you're ready."

Hana nodded and disappeared down the open hatch. After the engines revved up and down and up and down a moment later, Mawro belted out a roar and jammed his shoulder against the boat's bow. He grunted and groaned in time to the boat's hull screeching and scraping across the rocks. With enough water beneath the boat's keel to right itself, Mawro bounded ashore and thrust himself high into the air. He landed atop the canopy with a hollow thump, then set about to squeezing himself into the compartment behind Hana. She opened the throttles halfway while Mawro fumbled at the hatchway above his head. Once secured, she flicked a switch beside the helm and their boat began to slip beneath the waves.

"Looks like Agent Katczynski has been successful keeping the Honorable Opoworo hidden from the other American government agencies," she said once their craft had reached cruising depth.

"Thus far, perhaps. But his luck will run out sooner or later." Mawro shrugged his shoulders as best he could in the compartment's cramped confines. "Katczynski and Papa and I all know it, too. Papa was deported from this country years ago and is now a fugitive from justice in another. My being anywhere near him would only hasten his capture." He turned to gaze out the porthole window beside him and sighed. *And any group or government willing to offer safe haven, Papa, would certainly seek to exploit your talents for their own ends. I should know.*

Hana clicked her tongue. "You worry after your father still? Despite Katczynski's strong ties to CIA?"

"I do. Which is why I need Katczynski to trust me."

Her brows knit. "I...I don't understand. Would he not still blame you and Blaznikov's people for the death of his son?"

"I'm sure he does. But I'm going to make him a peace offering."

Hana's eyes went wide. "And just how do you plan to do that exactly?"

"Set course for Northport," Mawro replied, stroking at the fur covering his chin. "You shall see soon enough."

CHICAGO'S MAGNIFICENT MILE. MOMENTS LATER.

OH LEANED BACK INTO the plush leather covering the back of his chair and savored a pull from the hand-rolled cigar. Seated opposite the table from him, his host Noh Myung-Duk lifted his own lit cigar he held aloft. "Complements of our friend Rodrigo, who brought these with him on his last trip from Panama. Requesting we share them with you next time you were in town, General."

He blew out a mouthful of savory smoke before taking a sip of single-malt Scotch from the tumbler in his other hand. "That has to be some of the tastiest crab I've ever had. Thank you to you and your family for your hospitality," he said, motioning his consent to the waiter's silent inquiry whether he could take his empty plate away.

"This place flies 'em in fresh from Florida nearly every day of the year. Esteemed guests such as yourself, a representative of our dependable and honored partners from the Motherland, deserve no less than our best."

Oh smiled at the young patriarch and tipped back the last delightful swig in his glass. Only a year or so into his tenure, despite being groomed by his father Sung Jin for over a decade before his death, he appeared to err on the side of caution. Better to kiss more ass than less. Oh was getting used to living the high life, the perks of his position. The Chairman's assurances he would succeed Li-Ok as the director of Office 35 promised to make luxuries such as these, commonplace. He was eager to find out just how quickly he would tire of them. No time soon, to be sure.

He winced as he turned to set his empty glass down on the table in front of him. His inspection tour of the *Morning Glory* earlier that day before it put out from Chicago had helped him work out most of the kinks in his back, but apparently not all of them. Tossing and turning throughout his thirteen-hour nonstop flight between Beijing and Chicago left him with more than a few. He yawned and smacked his lips, allowing the peaceful easy feeling brought on by the nicotine and the alcohol to wash over him. Soon he would retire to his lavish suite on the seventeenth floor of the five-star hotel above them, where he planned to sleep soundly until whenever he damn well felt like getting up the next morning.

Bzzz-bzzz-bzzz. Pause. *Bzzz-bzzz-bzzz.* Pause.

By his cell phone's third ring, Oh had snuffed out his cigar in the ashtray beside him and was up out of his chair. He yanked his phone from the inside pocket of his suit coat and swore under his breath, confirming the name and number on its display as one of Min Soo's many aliases. "Excuse me, I need to take this," he said, turning to Myung-Duk.

"Yes, yes, of course," he replied. "Duty calls and all that." Myung-Duk waved a hand toward the open bottle of Macallan Signature Reserve at the center of their table. "We'll make sure to save you some. And we'll have another bottle waiting for you at O'Hare's duty-free shop for your return trip."

Oh nodded and strode quickly to the front of the restaurant. He barged his way through the waiting area and out onto the sidewalk. After rounding the corner, he plucked his phone from his pocket and glanced down at the display. Though he had missed Min Soo's call, the man had already sent him a text:

at the lake cottage call me

He swiped through the list of phone numbers Min Soo had uploaded to his phone earlier that day. Standard practice for whenever Oh was abroad, to help ensure neither Katczynski nor anyone else could use call histories to monitor their movements. After poking the entry labelled "Lake Cottage," Oh leaned back against the building's brick wall and stared up at the night sky above. "This had better be good," he growled after Min Soo picked up on the third ring.

"Mawro has tipped his hand. I hope that will suffice."

"Hold on. One moment."

Oh darted down the alley, certainly out of sight from passers-by on the sidewalk. "Tell me how," he said as he drew into a crouch behind a dumpster.

"Jin-Ho reports Captain Mawro has ordered his crew *not* to throw the container containing the catalyzation proteins overboard after all. He told them to put it ashore at Green Bay and to maintain radio silence until they put back out."

"What? You are sure?" Oh cried before cupping his hands together over his phone.

"He was quite sure, and so am I. Especially seeing Captain Mawro together with Agent Katczynski on a deserted island in the middle of Lake Michigan. I *told* you hacking the AIS transponder code of Katczynski's private launch would come in handy."

"Did Office 35 authorize Mawro's sortie?"

"I contacted them already. The operator on duty said he was aware of no such request nor authorization. In fact, he asked me if *you* had given the captain one."

"I most certainly have not." Oh pursed his lips. "Do you have any reason to believe Mawro has gotten wise to your surveillance?"

"He surely knows I routinely track his crafts' movements on behalf of the Committee's operations advisors. But you and Jin-Ho are the only other people alive who know I'm also keeping tabs on Katczynski, General."

"See to it you keep it that way," Oh replied, tugging at his chin. "Does any of the crew suspect Jin-ho?"

"Doubtful. Usually, he composes his messages to me while sitting on the head. Then presses the 'send' button through his shirt pocket once he's topside again. He knows full well Mawro's people would haul him below deck and feed him feetfirst into their brush chipper if they suspected anything."

"I see. What were your last instructions to him?"

"That he keeps his head down and his mouth shut until we instruct him further."

"Good. I'll handle the rest of this myself. The Nohs are eager to be helpful, and I'm glad to oblige them. I'll be in touch." With that, Oh terminated the call and shoved the phone back in his pocket. Then he tugged the lapels of his suit coat back into place and sauntered off toward the sidewalk.

Aloft somewhere over Green Bay.

Someone shook Oh's shoulder, rousing him from his fitful sleep. "We're nearing the ship, Honorable Oh."

Oh blinked toward the fellow Myung-Duk had sent to accompany him. He struggled to remember his name but could not; it wasn't important anyway. "Thank you," he said as he yawned and adjusted his headset. Out the window, he spotted the lights of a single freighter, surrounded by eerily calm water. It was surely Mawro's ship, Oh himself having given the pilot the ship's AIS ID prior to lifting off.

He glanced down at his watch and smiled. They had made good time, lifting off from Chicago hardly an hour ago. "Maintain an altitude even with the bridge," he spoke into his boom mic.

"Understood," their pilot replied.

"Good." Oh smacked his lips and stretched out his arms above his head as far as he could without smacking the ceiling of the helicopter's passenger compartment. "You are familiar with International Morse, yes?"

A pause. "Pardons, Honorable Oh. I was fluent during my Navy days, but it has been some while."

"I'll be brief. Flash your landing light as we approach with the message 'The General requests immediate landing clearance.' Follow whatever instructions they reply with. And under no circumstances break radio silence."

Another pause. "Understood."

The corner of Oh's mouth turned upward at the sight of the bridge crew's frantic response to his request. "Do you have the *Morning Glory* on your screen?"

"Yes, I do," their pilot replied. He pointed to a yellow arrowhead shown near the middle of Lake Michigan, veering north-northwest toward Door County. "Right there, in fact."

"How are you on fuel? Enough to get me there from here and for you to make it back to Chicago?"

"Only if I set down at Mitchell in Milwaukee for a refuel," the man said before banking toward the freighter's bridge.

"Do that. I shall see to it that your employer is reimbursed." Four crewmembers fanned out across the deck below them, marking out a landing zone with orange flashlights. "Now, once you touch down on deck, I must go below to attend to important business. Stay spun up and ready to lift off just as soon as I come back aboard."

"Understood, Honorable Oh."

The pilot called out upon their landing, indicating it was safe to disembark. Oh emerged from the helicopter's passenger compartment to find himself face-to-face with the ship's captain, a tall and willowy man named Ping—one of the Han Chinese nationals secretly in Pyongyang's service as mercenaries. "You will take me to the container," Oh hollered in halting Mandarin as Myung-Duk's man handed him his briefcase. "Right now."

Ping cupped his hand to his mouth and shouted something into his first mate's ear which Oh failed to make out above the surging rotor wash. The man nodded and pointed toward two crewmen armed with automatic rifles. The two of them flanked Oh before the first mate led them all toward a sea door situated near the bottom right of the superstructure. Minutes later, Oh recognized the container he sought.

"Open it."

The first mate nodded toward one of the men with him. He slung his rifle across his back and pulled a tool from his utility belt. After freeing the seal, he pulled up on the door handles and tugged. The door creaked open, the dim lights above their heads illuminating one of the concrete weights he and Mawro had watched their men load back in Chŏngjin. "Light, please."

The second man handed Oh the flashlight he'd been using to examine the reporting marks of each container they passed on the way. He stepped inside the container and set his briefcase atop one of the concrete weights. He opened it up and pulled out a piece of white cardboard with a downward pointing arrow on it with the words *FOR PAWLY* printed above in black block letters. After plucking two small magnets from the side of his pencil case, he turned and stepped over to the wall opposite him. There he fixed the sign into place using the magnets, oriented so that its arrow pointed downward toward the wooden crate pushed up against the container wall beneath.

"This is the container you shall put ashore," Oh said in a loud voice as he slammed his briefcase shut. He emerged through the open door and pointed toward the container beside it, the one Mawro had told him earlier contained the catalyzation proteins. "And *not* that one."

"But, General, Captain Mawro's instructions—"

"*Captain* Mawro's instructions have just been countermanded," he spat back. "By me. Are we clear?"

The first mate pursed his lips. "Yes, General."

"Good. And I further order you to maintain radio silence on our tactical channel. No communication except for mundane marine band traffic until your rendezvous with the *Morning Glory*." He waved his arms around the hold in a circle. "Because if you don't, or if you don't put off the correct container, each and every one of your families back in Korea will be sent to the nearest reeducation camp.

And each and every one of *you* will surely be whisked off to join them the moment you step ashore."

The first mate gulped. "Yes...yes, General."

"Close this back up," he said waving toward the container's open door, "and reapply the seal." Oh met eyes with the first mate and nodded toward the deck above their heads. "You and I are done here."

Moments later, Oh was back topside. He approached the helicopter, tossing his briefcase to Myung-Duk's man standing next to the helicopter's passenger compartment door. "Let us be away," he shouted to their pilot as he pulled himself inside. "The crew aboard the *Morning Glory* will be expecting us to approach them the same way. Notify me when you sight our landing zone."

"Understood, Honorable Oh."

He strapped himself into his seat and closed his eyes. Sleep overtook him even before the helicopter's landing gear came up.

CHAPTER SIX

GREEN BAY, WISCONSIN. LATE THAT SAME NIGHT.

PAWLY BOUNDED FROM ONE stack of containers to another, cursing not quite under her breath. She had crisscrossed the port's grounds twice already and still no sign of Mawro or Hana. How could that be? The North Koreans would want to keep things on the down low, to be sure. But shipments of catalyzation proteins like these were part and parcel of the supply chain for their illicit psychotropic drug trade. Given this ought to have been Mawro and Hana's top priority, why were neither of them to be found? Was this all some sort of elaborate ruse?

"Polecat, copy?" erupted Lenny's voice into her earpiece.

"Copy, Lemony Rinse." She adjusted the throat mic encircling her ruff, making her whiskers twitch. "Go ahead."

"Just found out someone'd pulled the strings with Customs before that damn container even made it off the ship."

Pawly snarled and bounded off. A moment later she stared down at the tractor and trailer she had last seen on the pier beside the Chinese freighter. It had a dingy dark blue box on it now, indistinguishable from dozens of others among the hundreds stacked up across the port grounds. Or from the hundreds headed up and down the expressways between here and Chicago.

She reached into the pouch at her belt and pulled out the tracking device Tommy had given her as Uncle Bobby's launch tied up at the port earlier that evening. "Tomcat, copy?" Pawly said as she poked the button on the thing's top. It beeped once and blinked red, yellow, and green through its boot sequence.

"Copy, Polecat. Where are you—?"

"Are you receiving signal from the homing beacon?"

Clacking keys. "A-firm, Polecat. Three nines."

"Good. I'm going in."

"Wait! There are too many luminaries within the fence. Someone's sure to spot you making the drop."

"A-firm, Lemony Rinse," Pawly answered him without breaking stride. She stopped atop the container overlooking the chain link fence beside the facility, next to the road leading to the port's entrance. "Which is why I'm sneaking out the back door."

She crouched on the edge of the container and watched the tractor trailer approach. At the right moment, she sprang, launching herself at an angle in the direction of the thing's movement. She rolled through her landing on the container's roof and jammed her arms out ahead of her to arrest her forward motion. As the vertigo passed, Pawly panted for breath, then looked up toward the front of the rig. In the distance she spied a low overpass. She knew better than to dally.

"Beaconing activated, Tomcat." Pawly slid the homing device into a trough in the container's ribbed metal roof and sat back on her haunches. "Your signal strength okay?"

"Clearing the threshold by a good twenty dee-bee."

"I'll take that as a 'yes,' then." Pawly stood up on the moving container's roof and paused a moment until she got her sea legs beneath her. "Lemony Rinse," she said, making her way to the rear of the container, "can you please pick me up near the...?"

Her voice trailed off while a van drifted around the corner and roared up to the back of the truck. She had made the trip into Green Bay with her Grandpa D many times; aside from the occasional tractor trailer calling on the port, this street was normally deserted this time of night. What features she glimpsed of the driver and passenger suggested they were Korean. Likely the rest of the van's occupants were too. Clearly the Noh family's strongmen, there at their boss' insistence to ensure his DPRK "partners" kept their end of their bargain.

"Polecat? Please repeat? You cut out on me."

Lenny's voice jarred Pawly back to the present moment. She whirled around and stared at the overpass bearing down on her. Instinct taking over, she dashed for the front of the truck and dove over the edge of the container. She landed roughly on the grating behind the tractor's cab an instant before the diesel engine's moaning crescendoed into a roar. The sound returned to normal a moment later after the rig emerged from the tunnel.

Now what the hell do I do?

She glanced around and took inventory of her situation. Behind the blind face of the truck's sleeper cab, out of sight, no sign of a backup camera. Good, both she and her mission were secure for the moment. The truck rumbled over a pothole; Pawly shot out a hand to grip the grab iron beside the air hose hookups to steady herself. She bent her knees and bowed deeply...

"Negative, Polecat!" came Tommy's frantic voice through her earpiece.

Pawly swore through gritted teeth. Though others observing the manifestations of her seemingly psychic link to her twin brother found it unsettling, to her it was just *annoying*. "I'm sure I can clear the top of the trailer in one bound!"

"I'm sure you could. And given the truck's current speed, I'm sure you'd end up in the driver's lap of the van behind you. Unless maybe you *want* to lie prone for hours while we all take turns picking bits of tempered glass out of your ass with a pair of tweezers…"

She clicked her tongue. Tommy could've plotted her trajectory in his head, even without the computers and monitors she knew sat all around him in the forecastle of their great uncle Bobby's work launch. She knew better than to doubt him. "All right, Tomcat, what do you suggest?"

"I'm scanning the satellite imagery on ahead of the truck looking for a traffic light cantilever or a big tree limb. When I tell you, jump straight up and grab on to whatever looks like that above you. The van full of mooks ought to drive right on beneath."

"How will I get down without being seen?"

"I'm coming up behind the mooks' van now."

"Negative, Lemony Rinse," Tommy said, replying to Lenny's call. "If you stop, there's a chance someone might see Polecat."

"I'm not *planning* to stop. I've got a ladder rack on this van and a moon roof. Drop right on in, babe."

Pawly rolled her eyes. *My hero.*

"All right, you two, quit clowning around," came Top's voice over their channel. "Our brain trust needs Tomcat back on the island ASAP, so we need to wrap this up."

She blinked. "Is…is everyone okay?"

"Big Top here insists G-Nik check me and my exo over following that episode aboard the boat," Tommy replied with a snort. "But I keep telling 'em it's—"

"I *said* you are off the fire line until Niko says you blow clean!" Top said in clipped tones, as if through his gritted teeth. "*Not* entertaining further debate. And as for you, Polecat, you and Lemony Rinse need to rendezvous with Cubby right away. He's at the muster point already."

"Roger that, Big Top," Pawly and Lenny said as one. Appeared Jakub had pulled his hitch already, had made good time back here after dropping the MGS' container. Now it was their turn to stand and deliver.

"Over to channel two, Polecat," Tommy said. "Lemony Rinse, stand by."

By the time Pawly switched frequencies on her earpiece, Tommy was already murring into his mic. As the truck progressed his pitch increased. When the pitch abruptly fell off, Pawly growled and launched herself toward a stout-looking tree branch above her head. Her claws sent tiny chunks of bark flying in all directions as she twirled around the branch like a gymnast on the uneven bars. She curled herself into a ball as the truck rumbled past, hoping the dark hues of her sneak suit would blend in well enough with the branch. If anyone in the van following behind the truck had indeed spotted her, they gave no indication. The van sped along after the truck without its driver once tapping the brakes.

Before Pawly could switch back to their tac net, she spotted Lenny's cargo van approaching. No longer needing Tommy to guide her, she launched herself toward the van and curled her arms and legs around the rungs of the ladder on top as she landed. With a groan she jerked to a stop. For several moments she stayed there, slowly working her legs and arms one at a time to get sensation back into her hips and knees and shoulders. "Are you okay?" Lenny hollered to her through the open moon roof when they stopped for a deserted intersection's red light.

"Yeah," she replied before slowly pulling herself through the opening. She curled up on a foam pad spread out across the cargo area behind Lenny's seat, surrendering to unconsciousness' sweet embrace before the light even turned green.

L ENNY DROVE HIS VAN up beside the rear of the tractor trailer and parked. Luminaires mounted atop tall poles dotted the parking lot's perimeter, lighting up the area around the casino almost like daylight. He exited the van and stepped toward the container, waving a transponder wand back and forth as he came alongside. His shadow flashed across the windshield of another van idling behind the tractor trailer and two men with black hair and tan skin got out. "I'm Lieuten—I mean, I'm Lennart Reintz. With Inland Seas Security Consulting," he said as the sour-faced men approached. "My employer is under contract to the US Coast Guard to monitor performance of containers equipped with smart seal transponders."

The other van's driver crossed his arms and narrowed his eyes. "Yeah, so what about it?"

"That one there is continuously squawking its GPS position, which will quickly deplete its internal battery and make this container untraceable." He indicated the container's doors with his wand. "Normally we would have caught such a thing on an incoming international shipment during a routine gate inspection, but for some reason this unit was allowed to come ashore without one."

Lenny lowered the wand to his side and nodded toward the tractor trailer. "I know it's chilly out still but leaving a tractor's engine running with no one in the cab poses a security risk. Are either of you the driver?"

The van's passenger stepped forward, cracking his knuckles. "No, we're not."

He smiled sheepishly and held out his open palm toward the casino's entrance. "Well, could one of you fellows go on in and get the driver? I'll need to see a copy of the papers they received from ICE pier side before they—"

The sound of the men's skulls knocking together cut Lenny off. The pair planted their faces into the pavement as Pawly rolled through her landing and sprang back up to face them. Each man groaned a moment, then lay still. Pawly smirked and dusted her hands together. "These two will be sleeping on the job for a while yet."

Lenny reached into a pouch on his belt and pulled out a roll of duct tape. "Thanks, love."

The rumbling of an engine and crunching of gravel nearby drew his attention to a brown-and-tan tractor approaching from behind. It stopped beside the van long enough for Top to jump out before motoring off across the parking lot and disappearing around the corner. "I'll need you to disable their van," he said to Lenny. "Then secure these two inside so they can't go any—"

A series of loud pops cut him off, followed by the sound of air hissing from the van's tires. "This thing's not going anywhere fast," Pawly proudly proclaimed as she landed beside them and brandished her claws.

Top groaned and pinched the bridge of his nose. "Stick to plan, sailor. And stay the hell out of sight of these security cameras, got me?"

"I'm on the shady side," Pawly countered, her whiskers twitching. "And most of my sneak suit is the same color as Lenny's van, so I'm sure no one will be able to pick me out lying on top of it." With that she threw Top a quick salute and trotted off alongside the container.

"We'll be down the street with Jakub, swapping out tractors." Top stabbed his finger toward Lenny. "Meet us there after you get these two tied up. And don't waste any time." He turned and grimaced toward Pawly as she took up station behind the tractor's cab next to the air hose connections. "I think she's trying to hurry us along, but we can't afford either of you getting sloppy. Whether you two have a hot date or something planned for later is none of my business, but you both need to keep your heads in the game until then. Understand?"

After Lenny nodded in reply, Top turned and strode off to the tractor's cab. A moment later he jammed the thing into gear and sped away toward the street. Lenny watched as the rig disappeared around the corner, following the same route Jakub's had taken after dropping Top off.

Once he had dragged the two men one at a time beside their van, Lenny bound their wrists and ankles together with the duct tape and slid open the van's side door. He heaved the men onto the floor between the bench seats and reached over beside the steering wheel to the ignition switch. After killing the engine, he yanked the key free and scrambled out of the van. After slamming the sliding door closed, he clicked the "lock" button on the key's fob. The van's lights flashed in response as he hurled the fob and key over the fence into the woods beside the parking lot.

Then Lenny hopped into his own van, fired up the engine and sped off. Within minutes he drove up to their rendezvous point. Top had already pulled his tractor away; it sat beside the curb up the block from them with its engine off and all its tires slashed. Jakub's own tractor now sat hitched up to the trailer bearing the container. Lenny made a U-turn and parked behind them, grabbing his tool pouch as he exited the vehicle. He stepped up to the rear of the container and reached into his bag for a screwdriver. "No, wait," Top said, trotting up beside him as Lenny put his hand on the smart seal.

Lenny cocked an eyebrow at him. "I made up that part about the seal continuously squawking, you know. But it is still squawking at its normal rate. It'll give away our position within minutes if I don't disable it."

"Yes, I know. This whole operation has gone way too smoothly so far, and I don't like it." Top nodded his head toward the container. "This thing might be booby-trapped for all we know. Jakub and I swept the area around the fifth wheel before we pulled the tractor away and our assholes still puckered up. Any part of this thing is as likely as not to blow up in our faces if we fuck with it."

"Well, we can't hardly take this thing to Door County with us with it still squawking," Lenny said, putting his hands to his hips.

"Brain trust's got us covered," came the sound of Pawly's voice. Lenny turned as she landed beside him and slapped a small metal box onto the steel panel next to the container's door latches. "Problem solved. Tommy reprogrammed our homing device's frequency right before he and Bobby put back out. It's set to continuously transmit."

A smile spread over his face. "So, it'll jam the smart seal's signal!"

"Right, for a while, anyway," Pawly replied with a nod. "The thing's battery will run down soon enough. But Tommy believes we ought to make it to the safehouse in Northport well before then.

"So long as we keep moving. Now stand clear." Top stepped up beside the container and thumped on its sidewall. He met Jakub's gaze in his rear-view mirror before the man put his tractor in gear and rolled away from the curb. "Okay, let's go."

Lenny stuck his thumb toward Jakub's rig. "I thought you were going with him. 'Stick to plan,' right?"

"Yes, but I want to keep my eye on you two," he replied, climbing into the passenger side of Lenny's van. "The rest of the team is *en route* to the safehouse. Bringing their CBR gear so we can figure out just what's what with that thing," he went on, nodding toward the container as Jakub took the corner. "We can't afford any delays, shipmates. Because we're not out of these woods yet."

CHAPTER SEVEN

MEANWHILE, ON PILOT ISLAND...

MAWRO FLOPPED OPEN THE hatch and scanned back and forth along the dark shoreline. As he had directed Hana, their boat approached Pilot Island from the lee side. "Depth, two meters," she said in a shaky voice from her place at the helm, below and to the right of him.

"Hold our position. This should be close enough."

The Katczynski's family cabin lay opposite the woods from them, fashioned from the former lightkeeper's quarters. He gazed up at the periodic glow above the tree line, emanating from the flashing beacon atop the new structure the Coast Guard erected not far up the shore from the original lighthouse decades before. Agent Katczynski's father purchased the aging building at auction soon after it had been decommissioned, immediately following his retirement as commandant of the Green Bay station.

From the dim glow, Mawro made out a large tree lying on its side across the rocky shore, the inlet's calm water lapping at its withering branches. "Mark these coordinates. Return here when you've finished on the mainland." He ducked down and nodded toward the shore.

"Be looking for me beside that fallen tree there. If I have cargo, I'll wave you in. Beach the boat near the tree so I can haul it aboard. Otherwise, I'll just swim out to you."

"Yes, Papa," she chirped.

Mawro replied with a nod and pulled himself through the hatch. He tugged at the canvas bag clipped to the back of his web belt then slammed the hatch shut behind him. After a bunny hop over the windscreen, he sprinted to the bow and thrust out his legs. He smashed his forepaws together in front of him and drew in as much air as he could manage before plunging headfirst into the frigid water.

Thick fur warded the ferocious cold away from his skin as he kicked and clawed. By the time his head broke the surface, Hana had already come about and was headed back out toward open water. The boat's running lights flashed twice in salute and went dark again a moment before it sank out of sight.

Once ashore, Mawro pulled off his web belt and bandolier and laid them both aside. He crouched down on all fours and shook like a dog to rid his pelt of excess water. After a moment's fumbling, he managed to work the canvas bag free from his belt. Something was moving around inside!

He gingerly tugged at the drawstrings and peered into the bag. There he found several perch flopping around atop a black plastic enclosure about the size of a box of greeting cards. He pulled out the box and jammed it beneath his armpit, careful not to let the ends of two steel straps, one riveted to each of the box's long sides, poke him in the ribs. Then he reached back into the bag and gathered all the fish together in his clenched fist. He had been feeling a little peckish, and some fresh fish would certainly hit the spot.

Heads and tails wriggled about as Mawro shoved the fish into his mouth. He clamped his teeth down around them and gave a tug, their bodies tearing in half one by one as he pulled. Gazing offshore as he chewed and swallowed, he thought of Hana. It would be selfish of him not to allow her to share in his abundance, no? So, he shoved his hand back inside the bag, dropping what remained of the fish. Then he cinched up the bag's drawstrings and clipped it back securely to his belt, so he might offer Hana a light snack upon his return.

He retrieved the box from beneath his armpit and turned it over in his hands. After all, Hana had performed final assembly of this unit herself—under his watchful eye, of course. During their weeks-long voyage to the Great Lakes from the Korean Peninsula, Hana had proven herself more than capable of serving as his pair of hands whenever a job like this one called for it. Providing a tasty treat for her to enjoy as they made their way back to the freighter was the least he could do to show his thanks.

A single large green button sat in the center of the device. Gently, carefully, lest he trip the thing's anti-tamper sensor, he poked the button with the pad at the tip of his thumb. The box flashed brightly three times as it went through its boot sequence. Then it began to flash, dimly, in an alternating pattern consisting of a pair of bursts followed by a single one.

Mawro cocked an ear in the direction of the Katczynski family cabin. Tommy ought to have been ashore, Papa and Nat laboring away in the basement, Alex out cold, and Annie comforting Stuie. Hearing no commotion, he concluded no one had yet noticed his jammer's interference.

That he planned to remedy. After donning his belt and bandolier again, he tucked the device under his arm. Then he made his way inland.

Minutes later, Mawro emerged from the tree line. The night sky over the lake's roiling surf lit up once every three seconds, courtesy of the powerful strobe light topping a towering steel lattice column situated about thirty yards from shore. He pulled the canvas bag from his web belt and set it aside near the water's edge. Glancing back and forth, he clipped the jammer to his belt in the bag's place. Mawro soon located the tops of the limestone boulders which Dory and his brother Bobby had placed years before in a soon-aborted attempt to construct a new breakwater. Now they were barely visible, disappearing momentarily whenever a breaker of any size crashed over them. Was the lake level higher these days or was it just his imagination? He shook the stray thought away. It mattered little now.

Mawro took off running toward the water's edge. Timing the waves, he thrust himself into the air and landed atop one of the boulders. He pushed off, aiming himself in the opposite direction. Back and forth he parkoured, building up momentum until he approached the rock closest to the light tower. The water receded from around it an instant before he touched down. With a grunt, Mawro launched himself toward the top of the tower.

He looped his arm around the tower and locked his two hands together near his waist. Momentum carried him around to the back of the tower but he grunted and held on, managing to secure a footing with his toe claws. After allowing a moment's vertigo to pass, Mawro let go of his arm and reached for the lattice above his head. Moving but a single arm or leg at a time, careful to maintain three points of contact, Mawro made his way up the tower toward the radio aerial at the top beside the strobing beacon.

The *reeeeeeeeeee!* of buckling metal stopped him cold.

He thrust himself away from the tower with both hands. Somehow, Mawro managed to avoid splattering himself all over one of the boulders. But the surrounding rocks proved hardly any less hard or sharp. The punishing surf smashed him into the boulder nearest him three times before he managed to scramble atop it. After instinctively shaking the frigid water free from his pelt, he stared back up at the tower and swore. It still stood, its beacon continuing to flash, but the lattice column now had a noticeable dog leg in it. His calculations had led him to believe even with the wind and his increased bulk, he ought to have been able to scale the tower without damaging it.

Fucking low bid contractors anyway.

Trying to scale the tower again would well be a fool's errand, if not an outright death wish. Had the concrete used by the crews to construct the tower's foundation also been of substandard quality, like the steel used to fabricate its superstructure? He couldn't risk finding out. If the tower fell, either because the lattice snapped or the foundation gave way, he would have no way of mounting the jammer at a sufficient height as to be effective over the entire island. That is, if he survived the fall at all.

Then he remembered the canvas bag he'd left onshore. Between waves, he bounded across the top of the rocks until he made his way back to the water's edge. *Sorry, love,* he thought as he picked up the bag and dumped out what remained of the fish which he had planned to offer Hana upon his return. Then he unclipped the jammer from his belt and stuffed it inside. He pulled the drawstrings closed and spread the fingers on one hand wide open, palm up. Then he set the bag into his open hand, flexing his arm up and down gently to guestimate the bag's weight. He gazed back up at the light tower and fixed his eyes on the radio aerial. Narrowing his eyes, he looped the bag's drawstrings through the crook of one arm.

Yeah, he could do this.

Timing the waves, he parkoured once again back and forth between the boulders. He touched down beside one of the lattice foundations and thrust himself skyward. As he flew, he flexed his arm back and forth to coax the bag's drawstrings into his hand. "Gotcha!" he cried as he snagged them on a radio aerial sprouting out from the solar panel fixed to the top of the light tower. He splashed down a moment later, kicking and pulling as hard as he could to avoid being swept away out into open water.

Minutes later, his reserves nearly exhausted, Mawro managed to pull himself up onto the rocky shore. He laid there for some while, sucking in air and blowing it out in a rhythmic pattern so as to get his breathing under control. Finally, he rolled up onto his haunches and stared up at the light tower. His face broke into a grin of weary satisfaction, spotting the jammer's dim light flashing through the bag's fabric. Two bursts and then one, with a second or so in between.

Enough farting around. It was time to get to work. With any luck, he and Stuie would be long gone by the time anyone noticed the jammer. Or before the Coast Guard dispatched a crew to investigate reports of the tower's malfunctioning radio beacon.

NIKO FLICKED ON THE porch light and pulled the cabin door shut behind him. He waved toward Bobby's boat as it motored through the harbor's calm water. Its spotlight shone back and forth along the pier beyond the boathouse, fixing on the large wooden piling which marked the *Wenceslaus'* usual berth. Angry surf crashed over the jagged, rocky outcrop behind the boat. Almost as if the lake itself were grasping for it, sore at having being cheated out of its due. Through the years countless craft small and large had sought refuge in the natural breakwater here, their pilots sheltering in the lee side of Pilot Island to wait out scores of Lake Michigan storms. Much like this one, in fact, through which Bobby and Tommy had tacked their way back and forth across Porte de Morts for nearly an hour already.

A door slammed behind Niko as he trotted up the pier. Nat's silhouette shone against the wall of the Delco house, illuminated by the sodium vapor lamp mounted on a pole high above the cabin's back deck. When he turned the corner, Niko saw Nat wheeling Tommy's chair in front of him, down the ramp toward the sidewalk. "Thought we might want this, just in case."

Niko stopped at the spot where Bobby normally tied up whenever he came for a visit and glanced down at his watch. Tommy and the others had put out at dawn to go and find the Chinese-flagged freighter. His grandson was a smart lad; surely, he had topped off his exo's batteries beforehand. Likely he hadn't had occasion to be up and down and all around while aboard Bobby's boat, either. But if Tommy had indeed been experiencing biofeedback, any one of a number of things might have gone wrong with the exo itself. Better then not to risk exposing Tommy to further injury by allowing him to...

"Where's Bobby?"

Tommy, seated at the helm of Bobby's boat, coaxed the throttles into reverse to slow their approach. As the boat nudged up against the piling nearest Niko, Tommy chuckled and pointed toward the companionway. A loud *kuh-floosh* came from the head below, followed by a relieved whoop. A moment later Bobby emerged, proclaiming "Hoo*wee*! Been holding *that* ever since Sister Bay!" as he stepped to the stern and picked up a mooring line. "But I knew I could trust our boy here to spot me at the helm once we cleared the breakwater."

Tommy closed the throttles and leaned out over the side of the boat. "Learned from the best even before enlisting in the Navy, B-Grunk," he said as he threw an arm around a piling. He pointed toward a cleat just fore of the helm's windscreen. "Could you tend our bow line,

G-Nik? My exo's batteries are *kaput,* so it's not easy for me to get around."

"Gotcha covered!"

Niko turned to find Nat striding up the pier, pulling Tommy's chair behind him by the top of its backrest. "Here you go, T-neph," he said as he parked the chair beside the boat's helm and set the brake. Then he sat down on the edge of the pier and let his legs dangle over the edge. "Now give me your hands."

Tommy swung around in his seat and let Nat take his wrists into his hands. "Alley oop!" Nat said before he leaned back and pulled Tommy up into his lap. It had been nearly two years now since the explosion in Chah Bahar had robbed Niko's grandson of the use of his legs, and almost a year since the CIA's tech geeks released him from their care with his shiny new exo. Seeing Tommy scrunch up his face as Nat hauled him onto the pier made Niko all that much more resolved. Resolved to determine just what had sent him into seizures earlier.

Nat must have caught on to Tommy's embarrassment. "You good?" he said, extracting himself out from underneath of Tommy. Tommy pursed his lips and nodded before pulling himself up into the seat of his chair. "I figured you would be." He turned and hopped down into the boat. "Oh, and don't forget this," Nat said as he picked up Tommy's sea bag from where it had been wedged in between a pair of seat boxes.

Niko reached out his arm and took the bag, stumbling forward as Nat let go. "Oof. What is *in* this thing?"

"My dead exo for you to look at. Along with a couple changes of clothes and my shaving kit," Tommy said as he rolled up. "Thank you both, but I can take it from here."

He shrugged and laid the sea bag across Tommy's lap. "If you insist, my lad." Then he turned back toward the boat. "Suppose you and Nat best be going then, *Robercik*."

"We will be as soon as he stows his pack and sits his ass down. Better hang onto something too, son. Plenty good chop out there today, oy." Bobby waved one hand toward the bow as he took his place at the helm. "If one of you fellas could tend that line for me..."

"On it, B-grunk." Tommy wheeled his chair up to the cleat before Niko could protest. He reached down between his legs and tugged the line free, then tossed it to Bobby.

"We'll radio when we make the harbor in Northport." With that, Bobby cracked open the throttle and came about. A moment later the boat's engine opened up into a roar. It sped across the inlet and rounded the breakwater, then charged into the raging surf beyond. Within seconds Bobby's boat disappeared into the gray spume.

"How's Mom?" Tommy said over his shoulder as he wheeled off toward the house.

"She's stable. But out of it. Likely to stay that way until we figure out just what's going on."

Niko caught up to Tommy near the back door. Tommy sat slumped forward in his chair at the top of the ramp, huffing and puffing. "You've got to pace yourself, lad. I'd've been happy to push you if you'd been patient. I'm no invalid, you know."

"And neither am I," Tommy spat back. "Which is why I don't want any of you babying me, understand? Just figure out what the hell is wrong with me and the others so we can all get back to—"

The patio door slid open and Annie emerged, glaring at her nephew. "Pipe down, both of you," she hissed through gritted teeth. "Patients are inside trying to rest."

"Sorry, A-squared," Tommy answered her, his eyes cast downward toward the deck beneath his feet. A moment later he blew out his breath and met her gaze. "How's Mom? And Stuie?"

"They're fine, for the moment. Alex has been asleep for hours, and I was just about to go upstairs and look in on Stuie." Annie stared down at the threadbare rug covering the pockmarked wood floor around her feet. "She might have cried herself to sleep by now after she...well, you know..."

Tommy sucked in his lips. "Poor kid. Send her my way when she wakes up. I know exactly what she's going through."

"Thank you," Annie replied, the hard lines on her face melting away. "That would mean a lot to Nat and me." Then she turned an disappeared up the narrow staircase.

Niko drew up behind Tommy and grabbed the back of his chair. "Your mom's this way," he said as he rolled his grandson through the kitchen toward the sitting room. "We brought her down here and made her comfortable because we knew you were coming."

He pushed Tommy's chair up beside the old futon and flipped its brake handle. "I just remembered," Niko said as Tommy leaned over to kiss his mother on the forehead. "Could you do me a favor, lad?"

Tommy drew his sleeve across his lips, as if trying to wipe his mother's shed fur away from his mouth. "Sure, G-Nik. What is it?"

Niko strode back into the kitchen and picked up Tommy's bag. "Could you call Top on your satellite phone and tell him Bobby and Nat are on their way?" He walked back to the futon and held Tommy's bag out at arm's length in front of him. "I just remembered Dory asking me to ask you to do that as soon as you came ashore."

"Oh, sure. Be glad to. Just give me a moment."

Tommy took the bag from Niko and set it in his lap. He unzipped it and took out the pieces of his exo and set them aside. Then he rummaged around and produced a clear plastic bag from beneath his shaving kit. Niko couldn't help but chuckle as Tommy opened it and pulled out a second plastic bag, from which he produced his CIA-issue satellite phone. As the phone powered up, Niko thought back to Tommy's father years before lecturing both his children to double-bag everything in advance of a family canoe trip. Surely, he learned an important lesson while shivering around the fire wearing a damp change of clothes. Memories of his ruined cell phone after he and his sister had tipped their canoe over arguing had clearly stayed with him.

His grandson's brow furrowed as he scrolled through the phone's menu. "I...I don't understand."

Niko blinked. "What's wrong, son?"

"Says I have no signal. But my phone's never had a problem connecting to the satellites from here before..."

Tommy reached into the side pocket of his sea bag and pulled out another plastic bag. After shucking the double layers of plastic protecting it, he powered up his tablet computer. He swooshed at the screen for a bit and frowned. "Huh," he said, squinting across the room toward the wireless router situated below the wide-screen TV on the credenza. "Looks like my setup here at the house can't ping the satellites either. But all the connections *inside* the building ring out okay." He glanced down at his watch, then outside through the sitting room's picture window. "This time of day, I ought to be able to uplink easily with both the Globalstar and Iridium satellites. Right now, nothing I have here seems able to connect to either of 'em."

"I...I just remembered. Something I left in the boathouse. Yes."

Niko was out the cabin's back door and down the deck steps to the sidewalk before anyone could ask any questions. The wind still carried plenty of bite, but at least the rain had blown on out. After dashing up the pier, he ducked into the boathouse and closed the door. He flicked on the light switch and pushed the button to raise the roll-up door behind where Dory's boat sat at its mooring. The door rattled its way open, clanking to a stop just before Niko keyed the boat's ignition. But he didn't turn the engines over; instead, he flicked on the marine band rig mounted on the bulkhead beside the helm.

The thing chirped twice before static began blaring out through the speaker mounted into the overhead. Niko winced and turned the volume down, then adjusted the squelch. Or, he tried to, at least. White noise continued to emanate from the speaker through the squelch knob's full range.

Niko pursed his lips then keyed his mic. "*Wenceslaus, Wenceslaus, Wenceslaus...Forty-Four* hailing *Wenceslaus* on channel sixteen one-six, over."

No reply, just static. He tried the call again. More static. A boat like Bobby's could make Northport harbor in about twenty minutes at wide-open throttle with anything less than a walleye chop out on the water. Hard to the wind in a storm like this, he might be more like forty-five to an hour. No way Bobby and Nat could have been out of radio range already.

With a growl he switched off the radio and shut off the ignition. Then he jumped out of the boat and smacked the switch to close the boathouse's roll-up door. Not waiting for the door's groaning and creaking to finish, he darted out the boathouse door and slammed it shut behind him.

A wave of relief washed over Niko after he stepped through the cabin's back door and into their kitchen. "Jakub should have the container here by the time Nat and Bobby tie up," came Top's voice from a speaker positioned on the breakfast table next to Tommy.

Tommy waved Niko over to the bench next to his wheelchair. "But how is *that* going to help her, exactly?"

"That North Korean mobile drug production unit is sure to be packed with catalyzation proteins," Niko answered as he took a seat, raising his voice to ensure Top could hear him. "Those should help us perk Alex back up."

"We need a moment here, boss."

Tommy muted the speaker's microphone with the poke of a button. "Don't get your hopes up."

Niko cocked an eyebrow at his grandson. "Why not?"

"Uncle Nat will need to stream markers from the catalyzation proteins' chromosomatic signature so you can synchronize them with the ones you've already injected into Mom, right?"

He blinked. "Well, yes, but Nat and I have done this before. Remotely, in fact."

"And did you do it *without* a real-time video and data connection?"

"Now, hold on." Niko waved a hand toward the speaker on the table. "Right there you have—"

"A shaky connection at best. Can't you tell?" Tommy gestured toward the speakerphone. "This audio has more 'snap-crackle-pop' going on than a bowl of Rice Crispies. But that's the best I can do patching in to the Coast Guard's submarine cable between the light tower and the mainland."

Niko set his elbow on the table and rested his chin in his hand. "Isn't that a POTS line? I thought you'd've had at least enough bandwidth for a VDSL connection."

"Oh, sure, that and then some. But whatever is rat-fucking our VHF and microwave connections also appears to be inducing interference on the copper, too. So much, in fact, that I can't get a connection to stay up at anything greater than dial-up speed."

"I...I see," Niko said as he stood. Biting his lip, he stepped over to the back door and stared out through the window toward the tree line. *Jamming our radios? Really? Just what the hell sort of games are you playing, Ritzi?*

"That's all I had to tell you, G-Nik. Should we continue?"

He met his grandson's gaze and nodded. Tommy reached over and poked the flashing button on the speaker. It went solid before he said "Aaaaand we're back."

"Niko, are you still there?"

"Yes, Topper, I am. Go ahead."

"Good. Do you think Nat will need to do any wet work?"

"I suppose so. Why?"

"Because our hazmat suits are still in the RV Dory took to Chicago. He and Milda are on their way here now."

Tommy groaned and scratched at his scalp. "When do you expect them?"

"They were on the road already when they called about an hour ago. But this storm is dropping ice down there and snarling up traffic, so I can't say how long they'll be."

"Might well be a blessing in disguise." He opened the cupboard beside the door and drew out a bottle of Polmos Szczecin 15 Year, along with a pair of shot glasses. "I can use that time to set Tommy up here with a data visualization scheme. That way, we may still yet be able to synchronize the chromosomatic signature remotely."

"Very good," Top replied. "I'll leave you to it, then. Ping me when you're ready on your end. I should have an update for you by then."

And with that, the line went dead. Tommy poked a button atop the speaker in front of him and creased his brow. "You really think I can do that, G-Nik?"

Niko finished pouring and handed one of the shot glasses to Tommy. "If anyone can do it given a vastly limited dataset due to bandwidth restrictions, it would be my grandson here." He held his glass aloft. "To your Eyes of the Lynx. *Do sukcesu!*" he said before downing its contents in one gulp.

CHAPTER EIGHT

M awro made his way through the woods to the edge of the clearing surrounding the family's cabin. Light shone through the blinds covering the main floor windows. Most of the upstairs was dark, except for one window on the end of the house opposite him. A dim glow punctuated with bright flashes emanated from the tiny basement windows, situated just above grade level. *Shit, they're at work already.*

He knew his thick fur would camouflage his movements from regular cameras. But in light of the family's frantic flight from Poland weeks before, by now their CIA handlers had likely installed infrared ones on the building—which he knew Tommy or one of his AI apps would be monitoring. Emerging from the tree line to approach the cabin directly would be too risky.

Mawro vaulted up into the canopy and made his way carefully, cautiously, from one tree to the next. His movements were slow and deliberate to prevent his considerable weight from snapping a limb or even laying a tree right over. Upon reaching the water's edge he spotted a line of limestone boulders jutting out from the shoreline in front of the old lighthouse.

Of course!

The lighthouse lay mere steps beyond the shoreline behind the boathouse, situated opposite the breakwater from him. Approaching the shore from below the water's surface would allow him to remain hidden from the infrared cameras until he was within striking range. By the time anyone spotted him, it would be too late. Making it impossible for anyone to leave the island would buy him more time to flee with Stuie.

After drawing a deep breath, Mawro dove from the treetop and into the raging surf. He powered himself toward the breakwater, a thousand tiny needles lancing his nose and paw pads. Just as he thought he could stand the burning in his lungs no longer, he managed to latch on to one of the slippery, algae-covered rocks. He scrambled atop it with barely enough time to refill his lungs before a massive roller came crashing down, making him give it all back.

Mawro groaned and shook his head. *No! You can't black out now!* He gulped down more air and pushed off from the rock just as another wave rose up to meet him. With his arms stuck straight out from his sides, he rode the wave past the end of the breakwater and into the lagoon beyond.

He floated there for a moment to get his breathing back under control, then glanced around to reorient himself. Upon spotting the boathouse, he gingerly paddled over to it and ducked beneath the rollup door. After surfacing, he cocked his head and listened. Silence but for the gentle lapping of water against the hull of Katczynski's private launch. He hoisted himself atop the platform fixed to the stern of the old motor lifeboat and stood—carefully, cautiously, until he was certain the platform could indeed bear his weight. After a quick rub down, Mawro lumbered over to the helm. With a cry he smashed both of his fists down upon it, crumpling the boat's wheel and throttle housings. He wrapped one hand around the shipboard radio and ripped it from its mount, then tossed it into the water beyond the boat's stern.

He turned back toward the ruined helm with a satisfied snort to examine his handiwork. This boat wouldn't be going anywhere anytime soon. Nor would anyone be able to call for help, even after his jammer was discovered or its battery gave out.

Mawro tugged his canvas shorts up on his hips and hopped over the boat's gunwale. After squeezing himself through the boathouse door, he peeked around the corner toward the Katczynski family cabin. No more lights had come on, no more windows or doors had opened. Suggesting that no one had heard him.

Though all odds lay in his favor, Mawro knew better than to squander any opportunity his planning and execution afforded him. The rest of his plan seemed straightforward enough—grab the girl without being seen, subdue her, get her aboard ship, take the samples he needed, then get her back to her family before anyone in Washington even knew what was going on. But to do that, he would need to wait, need to seek his ideal opening. Or the closest thing to it, whenever it saw fit to present itself.

He slipped back into the water and ducked underneath the boathouse door. Then he thrust himself up beneath the pier, following it until he reached the shoreline.

Mawro waded ashore and shuffled to over to the edge of the cabin's unkempt lawn. Glancing back and forth, his keen eyes quickly pinpointed the cameras mounted beneath the house's eaves. Icy water saturating his outer pelt would serve to camouflage his movements from their infrared, but not for long. He dashed to the side of the house and froze in place, arms outstretched and back to the wall beneath the living room windows. *This* was the moment, in all the Warner Brothers and Tex Avery cartoons he had seen on television after arriving in America with Alex and their adoptive parents, where the sirens would begin blaring. Followed by spotlights swinging back and forth until they finally focused on the bad guy.

The tufts atop his ears twitched as he listened all around. He forced himself to count to thirty, though it felt more like three hundred. But no cry of alarm came, nor any other indication anyone had spotted him.

Mawro plucked a tube-shaped folding periscope from his bandolier and carefully pulled it open so as to not allow his big and clumsy paws to drop the thing. No one was in the room as far as he could see. But the sound of someone snoring quietly emanated from a window apparently left cracked open for ventilation.

He rolled back on his haunches then slowly stood. He peered through the screen covering the window and gasped. A lanky blonde-haired woman lay there on the futon covered in red vinyl, sleeping peacefully with her hands crossed atop her abdomen. "Oh, Alex, it's you…it's really you," Mawro whispered, a lump in his throat.

A piercing squeal belted forth from the basement stairwell in the corner of the room opposite the futon, setting Mawro's teeth on edge. "Sorry, U-Nat, that's all the gain I can give you. Any more and neither you nor G-Nik will be able to hear a damn thing."

Tommy? What the hell is he doing here? He's supposed to be ashore!

"It would be better if I just could show Pops what I have in mind rather than you trying to talk him through it, Tommy." Nat's voice sounded tinny, distant, as if coming over some sort of speaker. Likely he was ashore instead. But how the hell were they communicating at all? His jammer should have been—

"Best I can do under the circumstances, U-Nat. We've got barely more bandwidth than required for voice, so we're stuck with the ridicustupid low frame rates."

Nat *tsk*ed. "You managed to get Everquest to work over a dial-up connection when I was off at Champaign for my undergrad work."

"We'll just have to make do with what we've got, son," came his father's voice from elsewhere in the basement. "And but for Tommy here nailing up a connection over the lighthouse's old submarine cable, we'd *all* be S.O.L. right now."

So that was their trick. An unexpected development, to be sure, but one Mawro knew he would have to find a workaround for. He had too much vested to turn tail now. And no idea when another opportunity to gain samples from Stuie might be in the offing. Though Mawro knew would need to be all that much more vigilant. If Papa and the others were intent on Tommy's using his Eyes of the Lynx to decipher data delivered over a laggy connection, he would have to first assume his ailuran form—which would also afford him hearing just as sharp as Mawro's. At least the chemicals from Papa's lab ought would negate any advanced detection capabilities from his advanced olfactories.

"Fine. Whatever. I'm sending you the first image now."

"Okay..." Tommy answered Nat, drawing out his last vowel sound as his fingers flew over his keyboard. "There. Done. On screen now, G-Nik."

"*Dziękuję, Tomasz.* What are we looking at, Natan?"

"Spectral analyses of the binding agents," Nat answered after a moment's pause. "I took this one after deriving the lithium acetylide from the propargyl chloride I had on hand."

"Then we'll treat it with ethyl chloroformate," their father answered. "Or whatever other suitable reactant we can find in the container from the Chinese ship."

Mawro ground his teeth. The family had been so eager to chase after the red herring he had tossed out. For Alex and Tommy's sakes—now he knew why.

"Ethyl 4-chlorotetrolate would be better if we can lay hand on some. It'll condense with the hydroxylamine," Nat said, responding to his father's statement after a moment's pause, "yielding us chloromethylisoxazole."

"Right, which we can then convert using anhydrous ammonia."

Wait, are they making muscimol?

Nat whistled. "Whole lot of farting around, don't you think? Why not just use muscarine instead?"

"Because it won't work."

Mawro bit his fist to keep from crying out.

"How...how can you be sure?" Nat asked in a quavering voice.

"I took liberty with the MGS aboard the *Archer* one night while you and Annie and Stuie were asleep in your cabin, son. I decarboxylated what I *thought* would be enough muscarine to keep Alex going far beyond today. Being an acetylcholine receptor agonist, I had thought sure muscarine would effectively quash her autoimmune response."

Their father sighed and smacked his lips.

"I was insistent Ritzi use it as he developed the twins' in vitro treatments. He had wanted to use a GABA receptor agonist like muscimol right from the get-go. And...and I realized all these years later that Ritzi had been right all along." A pause. "Maybe if we had, Alex wouldn't be in such a state right now. Maybe Pawly and Tommy's Affliction might not have ever manifested."

London's Heathrow Airport. Years before.

"A rival hockey team jumped Pawly and Tommy tonight," boomed Barry's voice through the flip phone's speaker. "They were fighting them off...and...and she turned."

Mawro scratched at his temple. "'Turned?' I'm not sure I—"

"Oh Christ, Ritzi! She went fucking *feral*, okay? Claws, fur, whole nine yards. Same as you and Alex."

Ritzi's mouth fell open, the panicked realization his niece and nephew might be no more human than he or his sister clawing away at his consciousness. With a low growl he willed the red shadows back to the periphery of his vision.

"Hey! You there?"

He blinked and shook his head. "Oh, sorry. Yes, Barry, I'm still here."

"That's not the worst of it. She drew blood. Human blood."

Ritzi staggered forward and gripped the seat back from the row of chairs in front of him. His breath came in desperate gasps as he catalogued years of testing, decades of research, every assurance he had given his sister and her husband—his best friend long before becoming his brother-in-law. Telling them their kids would never...

He smacked his lips, feeling like he'd swallowed a cotton ball. "Where are you?"

"We're all *en route* to Pilot Island. Though God only knows what we're gonna do once we get there. Or how long we'll be."

Ritzi glanced down at his watch. "We should be seven and a half hours into O'Hare once we push back. I'll catch a flight to Green Bay from there then call Dory. He can cross over with the boat to fetch me as I'm cabbing it to Northport."

He heard mumbling in the background before Barry's voice came back on the line. "No, Dad says Northport is a fucking zoo with all the lookie-loos going to Washington Island. He'll meet you at Gills Rock. Which is where we're headed now."

Ritzi gulped. "Is...is Pawly *with* you?"

Barry let out a long sigh. "Yes, fortunately. She's right here in the RV. Lucky fucking break it's Halloween, though. Alex managed to chase Pawly down and subdue her without attracting attention. Or using her darts."

Ritzi crossed himself. Not having examined Pawly after her transformation, he could hardly have been sure whether the paralyzing agent tipping said darts would have even worked. Or whether it would have stopped his niece's heart. "And is she...secure?"

"Alex and Sheila're trussing her up with the cord they ripped out of the window blinds. Sheila figures if she can lash Pawly's wrists and ankles to the bedframe, she won't be able to claw her way through her bindings."

"Wait, who's Sheila?"

"Service buddy's fiancée. A nurse at a Navy hospital in Portsmouth."

Ritzi gasped. "She *knows*? No one outside the clan or the CIA can know, Barry! Does her fiancée know too? This is completely unaccepta—"

"Was kinda hard to avoid given the circumstances, you know! So sorry to monkey fuck all your precious calculations, *Doctor*. For as much good as they've done us."

Back on Pilot Island...

Mawro's knees gave out. He stumbled forward, suddenly faint, red haze momentarily obscuring everything until he willed it back to the periphery of his vision. But the horrifying realization remained.

...Ritzi had been right all along...maybe Pawly and Tommy's Affliction might not have ever manifested...

Barry might well still be alive today if the twins' Affliction had never manifested. And responsibility for their Affliction manifesting when it did lay squarely with Papa. Not him. It never had. Mawro had heard him say as much. Just now. *Oh...oh, Barry...*

His own ragged breathing echoed in his ears, drowning out the sound of everything else. Until Mawro noticed the vibrations emanating from the ground beneath him. Again and again and again.

Footsteps. Running toward him. Right behind him!

By instinct Mawro leaned to his left and lunged. He landed atop a stand of crocuses, crushing their delicate purple and yellow blooms into the dirt. Wood splintered and cracked above him, near the spot where his head had been a mere instant before. He turned to glimpse lamplight from the window above glinting off the head of an axe buried deep in the house's siding, Annie Opoworo's trembling hands gripping its handle.

Mawro leapt to his feet. "Annie! Annie, please! I need you to listen to me."

"It's 'Doctor Opoworo' to you, fleabag. And supposing you give me one reason I ought to, hm?" She put one foot against the siding and pulled the axe free with a grunt. "I don't care what intel those bastards in Pyongyang have on us," she said between gritted teeth. "Where do you get off trying to be familiar?"

"I remember your first date with Nat," Mawro replied, holding his open palms at shoulder height. "When he stopped off at my apartment to change his pants with a certain Annaleigh Rehbein in tow. And some story about a quadruple-scoop ice cream cone being upended during an impromptu make-out session."

Annie clutched her axe to her chest and leaned toward him. "R-Ritzi?"

"I suppose Tommy heard something no one else could and sent you out to investigate. Am I right?"

She narrowed her eyes and stepped toward him, brandishing her axe all the while. "And I suppose you're that freak the Poles saw fleeing Niko's lab after your troops got their asses handed to them!"

He held out his hands in front of him and took a step backward. "Wait, Annie! Give me a moment to—"

Belting forth a raging cry, Annie rushed him. Mawro retreated while the axe whizzed back and forth, narrowly missing his abdomen each time. "Don't you *dare* toy with me!" she shouted between swings, meeting his gaze with murder in her eyes. "Alex told us Ritzi was dead." *Whoosh!* "Told us Mawro himself had told her." *Whoosh!* "Did Mawro spring you from his lab so you could do his dirty work for him?" *Whoosh whoosh!* "Is that woman here with you?"

Mawro started as he backed into something solid. He glanced behind him, discovering he had managed to work himself into a corner between two of the cabin's exterior walls. He turned back toward

Annie just as she drew the axe behind her head for a two-handed over-the-head strike.

Aimed straight for Mawro's chest.

With a grunt, Mawro snapped his forearm out to one side, striking the head of Annie's axe with the back of his hand. It whirled end-for-end until it embedded its head into the soft ground nearby with a dull *thud*.

Annie roared and began pounding on Mawro's bare chest with both her fists. "Nat and I" *huff* "brought that child forth" *puff* "into the world" *huff puff* "with our own hands!" *huff*

She yelped after Mawro bear-hugged her and drew her close to his chest. "I know you're upset. I know you have no reason to trust me. But hear me out, would you? A couple of tissue samples from Stuie are all we need and then we'll be gone. None of you ever need see us again, I promise."

Annie squirmed around in Mawro's grasp like a stream-caught salmon might between a bear's paws. "We raised Nastusia...like our daughter...Hana will never have her back...do you hear me?"

A thump drew Mawro's attention to the back porch. He and Annie turned their heads toward where Stuie lay there, storm door propped open by her prone form. As if she had been leaning up against the door jamb this whole time with the door cracked open, listening...

Oh, shit.

Stuie turned to look their way, a panicked look in her eyes. "Mom, is...is it true? Mom?" she managed in between gasps. "Is it *really*...true...?"

Annie wriggled her shoulders free and craned her neck over top of Mawro's arm. "Ow!" he cried after Annie bit down deep into his tricep. The muscles in his arm began spasming immediately, causing his arm to go limp. Annie grunted and freed herself from Mawro's grasp, taking off in a sprint toward Stuie just as soon as her feet touched the ground.

"No, Annie! Don't!"

But she paid Mawro no mind. He gasped seeing Stuie's face going blank as Annie approached. Her eyes glazed over, replaced an instant later by a wild, feral look. Just as Mawro would have expected from the girl getting a snootful of Hana's scent. Which he had had all over him. And now, Annie had all over *her*.

Then Stuie charged her mother—claws out and fangs bared, her face contorted into an orange-and-white mask of rabid fury. Mawro sprinted toward Annie, screaming, desperate to keep Stuie away from her when something drilled him square between his shoulder blades. The force of the impact made him trip over his feet and he tumbled forward.

He saw stars even before his head hit the ground.

CHAPTER NINE

MEANWHILE, NEARSHORE OF NORTHPORT, WISCONSIN…

THE CORNER OF HANA'S mouth turned up as she peered through her monocular toward where the tug *Casimir* lay at its berth. After having spotted the werecat woman known as Pawlina Katczynski leaping aboard minutes earlier, she now glimpsed the other woman pass the porthole window aft of the boat's stateroom with a towel draped over her shoulders. Clearly, she was making her way to the head. Good.

Hana glanced down at the chronometer strapped to her wrist, quite ready to be done waiting around. She had laid atop the seaward side of the harbor's breakwater for nearly a half hour already. But howling wind, plummeting temperatures, and frigid spray from the punishing Lake Michigan surf crashing into the boulders all around her made it feel much longer than that.

Hana returned her monocular to its pouch on her web belt and slowly got to her feet. Numbness from the cold and damp and inactivity soon gave way to pins and needles. After turning to face away from shore, she jogged in place to get blood flowing to her legs again.

No one would be able to see her given the wet suit covering her body wholly, except for the small cutouts for her face and the very tip of her tail. And with the wind blowing offshore at a steady clip, no one would be able to hear her, either.

She sucked in her breath and bounded atop the breakwater. With a loud *ki-ahp*, she launched herself toward shore. Three giant leaps later, Hana landed on the pier beside the tugboat. She stuck her tail straight up in the air behind her, using its tip to confirm the wind's direction as she sniffed at the air. The sound of running water from within the boat's head accompanied only the faintest trace of lyncean scent, suggesting Katczynski was taking a shower. Just as Hana had hoped she would. The other woman would be some while sloughing off her shed and cleaning up afterwards, as she well knew.

Hana tiptoed aboard and peeked through the porthole window in the first hatchway door she came to. Seeing no one, she tugged gently at the handle. It came easily. Hana grinned as she worked the handle to the end of its stroke. Then she slowly pulled the door open just enough so she could squeeze her way inside and quietly closed it behind her. She glanced around and realized she was in the boat's galley. The engine room would be one deck below, so Hana made her way forward to the ladderway amidships. Just as Mawro said to during their briefing before he disembarked for Pilot Island.

She cocked her head and listened, but could discern no footsteps, no movement, no breathing. At least not over Katczynski singing to herself in the shower, loudly and decidedly off-key. All the more reason to believe no one else would be aboard.

After planting her hands along the railings lining either side of the ladderway, Hana pushed off with one leg and slid down until her feet came to rest silently on the engine room's deck plates. She squinted in the dim light coming from the annunciator panel beside her until she found what she was looking for.

In a moment's time, Hana knelt down beside a large wheel valve tucked away in one corner of the compartment beside a workbench. A padlocked chain dangled between the valve's handle and a stout-looking cleat bolted to the bulkhead. Taking the padlock in her left hand, she extended a claw from her right-hand pinky finger and wedged it into the lock body against the inside edge of the shackle. She stuck out her tongue and wiggled her claw tip back and forth until the shackle popped upward with a satisfying *click*. After pulling the chain free of the wheel valve handle, she took it between her hands and twisted with all the strength she could muster. Once she had grunted two more times through whatever rust had built up inside the valve's mechanism through decades of disuse, the valve handle began to turn freely. Soon a spray of water hissed forth from the sea cock's opening, followed by a gusher. Hana kept turning the wheel until it stopped. By then the water in the compartment was already ankle deep.

Hana stepped back and nodded, admiring her handiwork as water continued to jet forth from the sea cock. Right up until she heard footsteps shuffling across the floor above her. "Brought us coffee and a cheesecake from town, love," a man shouted after pounding on the wall shared between the galley and head. "How about you give it a break so's I'll have some hot water later?"

Shit, hadn't expected Loverboy to come calling!

She darted over to the wheel valve and spun it partway closed, enough to silence the flow of water. But doing so would slow the flow rate down considerably. Hana glanced at her chronometer and knit her brow. If she left now and her sabotage was discovered, the family might be able to pump out the boat and get underway before her and

Mawro were away with Stuie. But if she stayed, it would certainly delay her rendezvous with him.

She pursed her lips and crouched down against the bulkhead, deciding after a moment's consideration to wait them out. Besides, who knew what Katczynski and her lover might get up to? Maybe, after having their dessert, the two of them would afford her an opportunity to likewise have her cake and eat it, too.

"**L**OOK AT YOU, BEING all domestic! Might be able to find an apron around here somewhere to dress you up in."

Pawly emerged from the passageway into the tugboat's tiny galley toweling at her hair, dressed in one of Lenny's old button-up shirts and a pair of denim cut-offs. "I might have to change out of my tactical gear first for it to fit, though," he replied, pulling out a chair for her at the end of the breakfast table.

In an instant Pawly was on him, hands pressed up against his cheeks, lips pressed up against his. He started, clearly surprised by her eager advance. But quickly he was fully engaged; their hands and tongues greedily consumed as much of one another as they could. "Where's the fun in that? I'd rather rip your boots and gear off piece by piece," Pawly said when she finally allowed Lenny to come up for air. "And then all your clothes. You could put the apron on after that." She waved her hand like a cat might swat at a toy dangling from the end of a stick. "Mee-*yow*."

Heat rose to Lenny's hairline as she nodded toward the cardboard box on the table, next to a stack of paper cups and a clear plastic container with a strawberry-topped cheesecake inside. "But you went through so much trouble to bring me all this," Pawly purred as she batted her eyelashes at him. "It'd be a *shame* if we allowed our coffee to get cold, don't you think?"

That's not the only thing it'd be a shame to let grow cold...

Pawly chuckled, seeing the pained expression on Lenny's face. "Don't worry, we ought to have plenty of time to kill. Especially once the brain trust links up the warehouse with the island and they start doing their thing."

Lenny smacked his lips and pulled a pair of paper cups from the top of the stack. Then he twirled open the lid of the box and began to pour coffee into one of them. "We might be too late, though," he said with a frown as he sat the box down.

Pawly reached over to a drawer beside the galley sink and opened it. "Yeah, I noticed a decided lack of steam, too." She held the cup to her lips and took a sip. Her grimace confirmed his suspicions.

"I don't know what to say, love. The gal behind the counter told me they'd just brewed it."

She snorted. "People here around closing time are likely to tell you whatever they think you want to hear if it'll get you out the door quicker."

"Well, they've surely locked up and left by now, so it's not like I can take it back and complain—hey, no need to be *that* way about it!"

Pawly glanced at the chef's knife in her hand before cocking an eyebrow at him. "This is for the cheesecake, dumbass." She held up her free hand to his face and flexed her fingers back and forth. "Besides, I can good and well make you bleed any time I want. Without having to worry about anyone finding some bloodied knife lying around afterward."

"I'll, ah, keep that in mind," Lenny replied with a nervous laugh.

With a satisfied smirk, Pawly popped the lid on the cake's plastic container and set it aside. Then she sliced into the cake. "What the hell?" she said, her smile turning downward into a frown. "This thing is still half frozen!"

"Before you ask—yes, I did get it out of the bakery's refrigerator case and not from the frozen foods aisle." He sighed and leaned against the galley counter. "Suppose we'll have to wait a while before trying to eat it, then. Wouldn't want you to chip a fang or something."

Pawly blew a raspberry at him. "You're a funny little man. Might just have to keep you around then." She flipped the latch open on a cupboard beside the galley sink and drew out a drip coffee maker. "Here," she said, handing him the carafe. "Fill this up with water while I look for the coffee and filters. We can brew ourselves a fresh pot while we're waiting for the cake to thaw."

"I doubt the thing will be ready for us to eat even then, the way you made it sound."

"I agree," she replied as she reached for the buckle of his web belt. "Which is why I thought you and me might play 'good cop/bad cop' until it is." The corners of her mouth turned up into a sly grin. "You said we've got nothing but time, didn't you?" she breathed into his ear, right before his web belt tumbled to the galley floor with a tinny *clunk*.

"**Y**OU...YOU'D BETTER...TAKE THAT," PAWLY said breathlessly after she broke Lenny's lip lock.

Lenny swore under his breath, then looked back into Pawly's eyes. Deep, carnal, *primal* longing lay within them, framed by trails of sweat connecting her forehead and chin. Panting, heat rolling off their near-naked bodies, mere inches between their faces—surely, she could see the same in his.

"Only reason anyone would be calling that phone now is if something's off the rails, dumbass," Pawly said after Lenny's satellite phone rang for the third time. She glanced back and forth between her wrists, both shackled with a pair of handcuffs to either end of the stateroom's metal coat rack. "I *would* offer to answer, but, well…"

Lenny drew back from Pawly's face and let out a disgusted sigh. He stomped across the stateroom to where his gear lay in a heap beside Pawly's and rummaged about until he found the pouch containing his phone. "Looks like you were right," he said, squinting at the number. "Top's calling me."

"And likely as not to send you straight back to Chesapeake if you don't answer." Pawly's desperate gaze morphed into a bemused grin. "Not a chance I'd care to take, unless maybe you get a bigger thrill out of woodworking."

"You make me sound like my father," Lenny muttered, side-eying her as he took the call.

"Put Pawly on the line," said a voice that was decidedly not Top's.

"Wait…Tommy? Don't you have a satellite phone of your—"

"No time, L-Rinse. I need to speak to my sister, right fucking *now*!"

"Okay, okay," he said, poking the phone's speakerphone button as he turned back toward Pawly. "But I'll have to put you on speaker. Pawly's a little, well…tied up at the moment."

"Fine, whatever," Tommy replied while Pawly rolled her eyes. "Hey, Sis!"

Pawly swallowed her lips as Lenny raised his phone to her face. "This had *better* be good, Tommy. I know where you sleep!"

"The North Koreans are here. Good 'nuff for ya?"

Pawly's eyes went wide. "What? Are you sure?"

"*Deadly* sure. Annie's spotted some big hairy thing walking around on two legs. Looked too much like what the Poles saw fleeing G-Nik's lab in Szczecin for us to think it was a bear. Then Stuie went feral again and all hell broke loose."

Pawly bit her lip. "Have you seen Hana anywhere?"

"Negative. But they've been jamming our radio traffic, so I've been busy—"

"Wait, if the North Koreans are jamming your radio traffic, how are you calling us now?"

Tommy sighed. "I nailed up a connection through the lighthouse's old POTS line, but it took some doing. Dialed your cell phone as soon as I could, but it went right to voice mail. So, I called Lenny's satellite phone instead."

Lenny snorted. *Spoofing Top's number so your sister would goad me into picking up? Well played, Tomcat.*

Pawly's gaze fell to the floor. "If the North Koreans are there already..." She gasped and looked up at Lenny. "Then Hana might be around here someplace." She yanked at her cuffs and swore. "Hurry up and get me out of these things. I gotta go!"

Lenny dashed back over to his gear and grabbed his left boot from atop the pile. He jammed the thing under his arm and trotted over to Pawly.

"This is no time to be fucking around," she said, narrowing her eyes at him. "What do you think you're gonna do with that anyway? Club me over the head with it?"

"Oh, ye of little faith," he replied as he threaded his bootlace through his fingers. "Now stop squirming around."

Lenny took the metal eyelet of his bootlace between his thumb and index finger and stuck it into the hole on the cuff around Pawly's wrist. A half-turn and the cuff popped open. "Okay, so where's *your* key?"

She pointed over to her own gear, heaped up into a pile beside Lenny's. "There's a key pen tucked away in the seam of my left bracer."

"Your what?"

"Those thingies I wear around my forearms while I'm in my sneak suit, dumbass. Bracers. I need the left one." She reached out her free hand and made a *gimme!* gesture. "Toss it here and I can get it out. Hurry!"

Lenny knelt down and started rooting around in the pile. "Found it!" he cried before tossing the bracer to Pawly.

She caught the thing and drew it near to her face. "No, no, dumbass. This is the right one. I need the *left* one."

"Right!" Lenny said as he dove back in.

"No, left! The left one, do you hear…?"

Lenny looked up in time to glimpse a black blur, streaked with orange, pass by the stateroom's porthole windows. A ragged snarl drew his attention back toward Pawly. She breathed in, breathed out: once, twice, three times while reddish-brown fur erupted from her skin, all over her body, right before his eyes.

"Aw, fuck it," she said, baring her fangs as she set her feet. The fur on her forearm stood on end as she flexed her bicep. The handcuff holding her fast to the coat rack's metal bar snapped taut, followed by a tinny *pop* two seconds later when the coat rack pulled free of the compartment wall. "Get ashore and warn the others!" she cried before reaching down to yank up her cutoffs to her waist.

Lenny blinked as Pawly dashed over to the door. "Where…where are you going?"

"To find Hana," Pawly replied, buttoning her shirt. "If she's skulking about, no telling what might actually be in that container. It could be booby-trapped. Or some kind of a Trojan Horse." She bared the claws on one hand and curled her fingers one by one into a fist. "And I want me some answers. So, you get everybody out of the building and *keep* them out until I give you all the 'all clear,' you hear me?"

With that, Pawly darted out into the passageway and disappeared. Lenny scrambled after her, bursting through the hatchway an instant after it closed behind Pawly. He reached the railing of the tug's main deck in time to spot her, leapfrogging the pier's wood pilings beyond *Casimir*'s mooring two at a time. With her handcuffs still dangling from one wrist.

THE WIND CHANGED DIRECTION as Hana made her way toward shore, carrying to her the all-too-familiar scent. The decidedly unwelcome one of that werecat woman Katczynski, surely following her. Hana swore, hopes dashed that making a break for the warehouse would prevent anyone from spotting her.

Landing atop a piling, Hana turned and pushed off with a grunt toward the deck of a nearby dump scow. She touched down and sniffed at the air around her before taking flight again, invoking evasive maneuvers in the hope she might shake Katczynski. After bounding from the roof of a pilot boat to the wheelhouse of a derelict dredge, she ducked down behind a massive drum coiled with wire rope.

She cupped her hands to her mouth, lest her panting give away her position. It was right to stay aboard the tug and monitor the rising water level, she repeated silently to herself. Yet *something* had caused a stir between Katczynski and her lover while they noisily made out in the compartment above her head. Though she suspected it had more to do with the pair's phones ringing than with her. Surely the other werecat woman becoming wise to Hana's presence was merely an unfortunate coincidence.

That didn't excuse her from accomplishing the task Mawro had sent her here to perform. Whether the tug ended up shoaling out on the bottom of the harbor or not didn't much matter. What did matter is that it had plenty of water in its bilge, enough already to delay its crew for hours if not days while they pumped it out and made repairs. The closest alternate vessel with means to transport the container to the island was a day's sailing away at best, if it had even been made seaworthy yet this early in the season. That meant the container would remain here, in the warehouse, with the skeleton crew already tending it tied up until someone came from the island to relieve them. The second part of Hana's mission was equally as important as the first—to see to it that *that* could not happen either.

Having managed to catch her breath, Hana emerged from behind the coil and hopped over the gunwale of a fishing trawler moored alongside. But when she glanced back over her shoulder, there was Katczynski, bounding her way. Dressed only in a flannel shirt and a pair of shorts?

With a chuckle, she sprang atop the trawler's net boom, wondering just what sort of goings-on she had interrupted. Then she launched herself across the slip to the pier on the other side. Zigzagging left and right across the harbor as she neared the shore, Hana managed to keep some distance between her and her pursuer. But whether courtesy of pure adrenalin or spirit-world intervention, Katczynski was closing the gap, slow but sure. Ordinarily, the other woman would have caught up to her by now. But Hana knew morphing more than once in a day took a mental and physical toll on any ailuranthrope. Her opponent was clearly no exception.

Landing atop a sailboat's mast, Hana dove for the ground then launched herself toward the spar of the one beside her. She gasped, spotting Katczynski, bearing down on her like a dive bomber.

The other woman reached out her arms, as if intending to tackle Hana. But then she yelped, one arm drawing taut behind her. Katczynski flailed about as she fell, twirling round and round about the mast by the handcuff fixed to her wrist. Down she went until she bellyflopped atop the boat's cabin roof with a hollow *thud*.

Hana touched down atop a bandshell across the street from the marina. She couldn't help but flash a smug smile toward her would-be pursuer before bounding off. She traced a wide arc along the shoreline to the opposite side of the harbor. Then Hana made her way back to the shabby-looking workboat which had brought the younger Doctor Opoworo here from Pilot Island.

She poked at the display on her chronometer with one finger. Its display changed to show her position relative to where their submersible lay at anchor beyond the harbor's breakwater. Some quick math in her head allowed Hana to conclude that though it would be a bit of a swim from here, she could make it nevertheless. And if she avoided coming up for air too soon, she would prevent anyone else from spotting her.

After taking up station atop the dive platform at the workboat's stern, Hana drew an incendiary grenade from a pouch on her web belt and pulled its pin. She drew in a deep breath and tossed the grenade underhand through the boat's companionway. Then she turned and dove headfirst off the dive platform into the frigid water.

Chapter Ten

W ITH A GROAN, PAWLY sat up and looped her arm around the sailboat's mast, hoping it might stop the world from spinning. When she finally managed to blink her surroundings into focus, Hana was nowhere to be seen.

Pawly snarled and swiped her claws clean through the halyard beside her. The metal hasp which had snagged her handcuff—the one dangling from its mate still cinched up tight around her wrist—fell free and bounced off the cabin roof, disappearing from view. She inwardly cursed Lenny for handcuffing her. Cursed herself for not securing the stupid cuffs better before giving chase. Cursed Hana for being here. Cursed Mawro for having dispatched her in the first place.

After the conclusion of her silent rant, Pawly pulled herself to her feet and hopped over the rail. From the sailboat's deck, she noted her position relative to the warehouse. She cocked her head to one side, her tufted ears twitching, but heard no voices coming from the warehouse's direction. Was everyone out and they were just laying low? Did they ignore Lenny's warning? Did Lenny ignore her when she told him to tell them all to evacuate?

Pawly scrambled atop the pier and sprinted ashore, making a beeline for the warehouse. Regardless of just where the other woman had gotten herself to, Hana would just have to wait. If the container they'd lifted from the Chinese-flagged ship was indeed booby trapped, if it was some kind of Trojan Horse, Pawly knew she would be the one to have to deal with it. Being the only one ashore having lightning-fast reflexes, a rhino-tough hide, and the ability to hold her breath for several minutes at a time, she was the only one who *could*. She would not permit anyone else on her team to put themselves in harm's way trying to open the—

A loud *bang* from behind Pawly drew her attention toward the pier opposite the harbor from her. She gasped seeing what looked to be some sort of metal canopy high above the harbor, falling end for end, propelled by the driving winds blowing ashore. It splashed down in the middle of the channel a moment later. Beyond lay a flaming hulk, tied up where Pawly had last seen her Uncle Bobby's runabout.

She gasped. Had he been aboard when it...? *Oh, God, please, let him be...*

A rash of Polish expletives rose up from beyond the full-height landscaped shrubbery forming the perimeter of the marina. Pawly breathed a sigh of relief after her great uncle Bobby darted through the portico and stopped. He gazed upon the smoldering remnants of his venerable workboat and gasped, clutching at his chest. Pawly crossed herself, hastily praying he didn't have a heart attack then and there.

"You're with me, young man," came Top's booming voice before he trotted into view, her uncle Nat right behind him. "Nat and I will go check out the *Casimir* for you, Bobby," Top said as drew his weapon from its holster. "Wait here for Lenny, then tell him I told you two to scope out whatever's left of the *Wenceslaus.*"

Uncle Bobby let out a long sigh and nodded, allowing his chin to sink to his chest afterward. Though still heartbroken, he no longer looked like he was going into cardiac arrest at least. *Thank you, Top.*

"I want everyone to rendezvous here in ten minutes to compare notes. If anyone hears shots fired in the meantime, we'll meet back here on the double. Got it?"

This was Pawly's chance. Bobby and the others would have only made it to the marina so quickly if they were already outside when his runabout blew up. Lenny had kept up his end of the bargain. Now she needed to follow through on hers.

The thick fur covering her toes and both heels allowed her to make her way silently toward the border hedge. She vaulted it easily, glancing back over her shoulder in time to spot Top and Nat running along the pier near the *Casimir*'s berth. With no sign at all of Hana. Eyes forward again when she touched down, she barely had time enough to bellow "Look out!" before plowing headlong into Lenny.

Momentum carried the two of them end for end three times before they slammed into the side of a park bench. Having ended up on top of her, Lenny managed to scramble to his feet first. He whirled around to face her, brandishing his service piece. "Hold it right there! Don't make any sudden...oh. Sorry, I—"

"You can't be half as sorry as I am. Hana managed to give me the slip." She held up the wrist with the handcuff still attached and jiggled it in front of his nose. "All thanks to *these* fucking things. Think your bootlace key will work on 'em?"

Lenny nodded and reached down into a pouch on his web belt. "I'll do one better." He pulled out Pawly's key pen and jammed it cap-first into his mouth. "Givve yer hann 'an hol shill," he said around the cap as he reached for Pawly's wrist. "Fown ih aher oo lehd." The cuff popped open an instant later.

Pawly rubbed at her wrist and noticed it was damp. She eyed Lenny up and down in the dim light and realized his uniform was soaked head to toe. "How did you get all wet? Did you swim ashore or something?"

"I thought I might have to," he said after snapping the cap back onto Pawly's pen key. "Hana must've been lying in wait already when you came aboard. Then took her sweet time sabotaging the boat while we were...uhm...you know..."

Pawly clenched her fists. "And right beneath our damn feet!" *Never mind my nose.*

Lenny met eyes with Pawly and smacked his lips. "Yeah, she must've managed to open up the sea cock and waited while the water level rose until just before you spotted her. I went below right after you took off to check things out. Water level was up to my waist already."

Pawly's eyes went wide. "Top and Nat were about to make their way aboard just now. You don't think they're in any danger, do you?"

He shook his head. "I dove under and worked the sea cock shut before I came ashore. But *Casimir* is not going anywhere until after its pumps are back online." He tut-tutted with a wave of Pawly's key pen back and forth before handing the thing back to her. "And as deep as the water is in the engine compartment right now, I doubt Bobby would dare turn over his prime mover. Even after the water's all pumped out, I'm sure he would insist on ringing out his electricals and bleeding out all his fuel lines."

"I...I'd better go," Pawly said, glancing over her shoulder toward the warehouse. "Remember what I told you. None of you go back inside until I give you the 'all clear.'"

Lenny nodded. "If you don't spot us on the pier, we're likely below deck aboard *Casimir* getting a bucket brigade going."

Pawly gave him a quick peck on the cheek, then bounded over to a streetlamp near the marina's deserted entrance. She hopped atop it and then thrust herself toward the roof of the warehouse. After rolling through her landing, Pawly darted over to the roof's adjacent corner. The warehouse, a leftover relic from the region's shipbuilding heyday, towered over the nearby buildings. Every street, every rooftop, every direction: deserted. With Hana still nowhere in sight.

She found much the same after sprinting to the next corner. And twice again as she completed her circuit of the building's roof.

The wind changed direction, rustling the tips of Pawly's whiskers. She tipped back her head and took a whiff. No trace of Hana's scent in the air now either. But a strong smell like rotting cabbage nearly made her gag. Pawly wrinkled her nose and looked back over her shoulder. At the end of a deserted cul-de-sac beyond the warehouse sat a wastewater treatment plant. *Yeah, I probably smell like shit now, too.*

Pawly stepped over to a skylight and plunked down atop a ventilation hood. Panting heavily, her energy now nearly depleted after having morphed twice in the same night, she peered down through the skylight into the cavernous high-bay area below. Good, Lenny had thought to make sure they left the lights on as he was hustling everyone else out of the building.

She rose and shuffled over to the open skylight on the other side of the building and stepped through. Within moments, Pawly stood before the container she and her team had swiped from the Nohs earlier that evening. She reached for the door latch and looped her finger through the metal strap seal. With a grunt, she pulled the strap taut against the inside of the hasp, then worked it back and forth until it snapped. After tossing the now useless seal aside, she pulled the latch handle up and threw open the door.

And then...nothing. No "boom," no ticking, no hissing, no klaxons. No sound at all, save for the creaking of the door's rusty hinges. How disappointing!

After a moment, Pawly emerged from behind the door and stared inside the container. The dim light all around was more than enough for her to make out the front, the sides, the floor. They were all bare.

They had been *played*. Each and every one of them.

She hopped up on the trailer's bumper, gulped down a great lungful of air, and stepped inside the container. Low on the front wall near the center, she spotted a sign about the size of a sheet of notebook paper which read "FOR PAWLY." Below the words, an arrow pointing downward to a wooden crate, about the size of the old steamer trunk in *Halmonim*'s attic.

Pawly exhaled and knelt beside the thing. She extended one claw and wedged it underneath the lid, shrinking back by reflex as she flipped the lid open. After it clattered to the container floor, Pawly blinked and peeked inside. There she found what looked like a combination TV monitor and VCR, similar to the one on which she and her brother had watched *TaleSpin* and *Darkwing Duck* on many a rainy Saturday afternoon growing up. Beside it sat a car battery, hooked up to a box fashioned from metal grating. Some kind of inverter, maybe?

The VCR whirred to life, causing Pawly to flinch. She opened her eyes just as static gave way to a grainy, black and white image. She watched as the silent video played, appearing like a closed-circuit TV recording from inside of some sort of commercial facility. No, a medical facility? All sorts of instruments and glassware and a pair of examination tables. Atop one sat a lanky, fair-haired woman in a hospital gown, screaming toward something off camera with a bald, muscular man sporting a goatee clutching her shoulders...

Mom? And...and Dad?

Pawly gasped as an enormous, fur-covered creature burst into the camera's view, looking like the artist's rendition of a sasquatch but for its lynx-like face and ears. *Holy shit! That's the monster I found trashing Uncle Ritzi's lab.*

Another lyncean appeared in the frame, its petite gamine form leaping to and fro about the screen. Pawly drew a sharp breath and clasped both hands over her mouth. *And that...that's me!*

Her mind struggled to comprehend what she was seeing as the monster punched through walls and flipped over heavy wooden workbenches like they were foam cutouts. She remembered none of it, having been consumed wholly by her rage at the time. Pawly's past self appeared to have managed to stay one step ahead of her opponent's attacks—right up until she tore open a gas line. Then, amazingly, her mother pulled free from her father's grasp and rushed the thing. Despite being in human form, Pawly could tell from the lines on her mother's face she was consumed by her own rage. The monster side-stepped to the right, outside of the camera's field of vision. Pawly followed, her mother and father right behind.

A moment later the thing lumbered back into view, stepping away from the camera toward what remained of a shattered floor-to-ceiling window. Pawly emerged from behind the cabinet, her back to the camera, and leapt at the monster with both hands wide open, claws out. Right before her father stepped between them.

"No, Dad!" she screamed. "No!"

Pawly clutched at her stomach, feeling like it was going to turn itself inside out at the sight of her own claws raking across her father's middle, right before she drove her head into the monster's solar plexus. The shaggy thing stumbled backward through the broken window and disappeared. Her father's eyes went wide as his hands grasped at his abdomen, blood oozing between his fingers. He shouted something toward the younger Pawly, then dropped to one knee. He attempted to stand but fell forward instead, arms flailing. His entrails reached the floor before him, covered again by his own body as he flopped atop them an instant later.

Her world imploded. The human part of her brain shut down, her feral instincts all too willing to assert themselves anew. Her screams became pained yowls as blood-red madness consumed her.

Chapter Eleven

BACK ON PILOT ISLAND...

MAWRO ROUSED WITH A start, sensing something pressed up against the back of his neck. By instinct, he reached up and felt the edge of a rolled-up piece of metal. One, he realized an instant later, encircled his entire head.

He propped himself up onto his elbows, sucking in his breath as his head began throbbing anew. Grabbing the metal edge with both hands, he worked whatever was covering his head back and forth and up until it slid free. The cold night air immediately caused him to start coughing and sputtering.

Turning the object over in his hands, Mawro recognized it instantly. An ancient coal hod Teodor Katczynski kept by the fireplace in the old lighthouse keeper's quarters, original to the place as he had been told. Like generations of inhabitants before him, Dory used the thing to transport ash from the sitting room's fireplace outside to the fire pit before retiring for the evening. Paranoid for his family's safety, just as his father had been after buying the place decades before, that a stray ember might burn them all up while they slept if the last person to bed did not.

How did this *thing get out here?*

A loud cry drew Mawro's attention forward. Annie was there, barreling toward him, her axe held high above her head with both hands.

Immediately he tossed the hod aside and wrapped both arms over his head. "No, Annie! Don't!"

Whack!

Mawro peeked through his fingers as the sound of tinkling metal died away. He glanced over his shoulder toward the huffing and puffing going on behind him to his right. There stood Annie, bent at the waist, leaning on her axe's handle as she gasped for air, its head upon the ground. Beside her, next to the concrete footing beneath the cabin's fuel oil tank, lay two lengths of chain with a shattered link in between them. One was secured around one of the fuel oil tank's support braces. The other looped around his ankle.

"Get up."

He looked up at Annie and slowly got to his feet. She remained there, her gaze turned toward the ground, trying to get her breathing back under control. "Annie, I—"

"I believe you." She let the axe handle fall to the ground and raised herself up to her full height. "The Ritzi I knew agonized having to kill a live rabbit every week or two to stave off his bloodlust. The Ritzi I knew would rather take a blow from an axe himself than hurt someone he loved. Anyone *but* the Ritzi I knew would have surely attacked as I charged just now," she said, flashing him a sad smile as she looked up at him. "So, help me bring back Stuie and Alex then."

Mawro glanced back and forth. Sure enough, the other two were nowhere in sight. "Where...where did they go?"

"I don't know, which is why I can really use your help finding them. Good thing this island is only so big, though. They're both in danger."

Mawro felt his heart skip a beat. "But Papa didn't say anything earlier about—"

"You mean, you've met with Niko already?" Annie rubbed a hand over her face and groaned. "Whatever. Look, Stuie went feral just now, concluding Nat and I aren't her biological parents hearing me scream at you about Hana. And then...then she tried to..." She closed her eyes tight and shook her head. "Or maybe she just scented Hana on me from you being all grabby hands earlier. Maybe both. I dunno."

Annie waved one arm toward the woods. "Stuie is raging right now, but it'll pass. Just as well. Maybe by then I'll have figured out...how to tell her how much I..." She sighed and shook her head. "Right now, Alex is my bigger worry," she said after a moment.

"Let me guess. The girl took off and Alex went after her to make sure she wouldn't shred anybody."

She nodded. "That's about the size of it. Alex collapsed earlier in the day on St. Martin's Island trying to do exactly that, in case Niko hadn't told you already. She's been all loopy since."

Annie pointed at the coal hod lying on the ground beside them. "But now she must be running on auto-pilot or something. Bowled you over from behind and shoved that thing over top of your head without even breaking stride. Acting as if she didn't even recognize you, which is why I had to find out for sure for myself." She stepped around behind him, sliding her hand back and forth over the strap slung over her shoulder holding her kit bag to her waist. "Alex likely doesn't realize just how frail her condition is right now. If she exerts herself even a little bit, I fear she'll keel over. So, I ran back to the house and grabbed a portable AED and several shots of Rythmol."

"Better to have it and not need it than to need it and—ow! Hey, what're you doing? Ow, ow! Stop it! Ow!"

Mawro cried and winced each time Annie grabbed a handful of his fur, working her way up his back like a squirrel climbing a tree. "We gotta find Alex before it's too late," she said as she straddled his shoulders and looped her legs together across his chest. Then she grabbed the tufts of his ears and tugged, like a rider might their mount's reins. "Now giddyap, horsie."

M AWRO RAISED HIS FOREHEAD from its resting place atop his arms folded across his knees and sighed. On Annie's orders, he peered through the window to his right for the umpteenth time, into the kitchen of the lighthouse keeper's quarters. Strapped to a gurney, beside the kitchen table, lay Alex. Annie had asked him to watch over her before going downstairs to talk with Niko and Tommy, and with Nat whenever he came back online. Alex's chest continued to rise and fall as she breathed in and out, slow but steady. Good. Annie had instructed Mawro to cry out for her if he noticed any change in Alex's breathing. Like, say, that it had stopped...

He and Annie had found Alex, unmoving, unresponsive—mere minutes from death from what Annie could figure after her frenzied examination. Tense moments passed as Annie injected Alex with dose after dose of the drugs from her kit bag. When Annie determined Alex was stable enough to travel, Mawro scooped her up into his arms while Annie resumed her place atop his shoulders. By leaps and bounds they made their way back to the cabin, arriving quickly thereafter. Niko had been in the kitchen, anxiously awaiting them, and helped Annie haul the unconscious Alex into the kitchen and secure her. At the time, Mawro could do little more than watch. Even if he had managed to squeeze his way through the kitchen door to help them tend Alex, he would certainly have only been in their way.

Mawro leaned the back of his head against the brick wall behind him and closed his eyes. Before long, his thoughts wandered back to Stuie. Annie's revelation earlier that evening of the girl's true parentage now brought back vivid recollections of the night he—or Ritzi, rather—had snatched Lim Young-Hee out from under the noses of the Chinese security forces storming Katczynski's camp along the swollen Yalu River. The same young woman Blaznikov would rename as "Hana" before presenting her to the Party apparat. Because she would be their "first."

He clasped his hands to the sides of his muzzle and rubbed at his temples with the tips of his fingers, his mind a maelstrom of thought. Annie's heady and heartbreaking revelation confirmed over a decade's worth of his nagging doubts, his sinking suspicions, his waking nightmares. Not only had Hana's stillborn baby survived, but the girl had been living with his own family the entire time since. Blaznikov, he had to have known. Yet the elder man had kept it all from Mawro, had taken those secrets to his watery grave. It was all...all too much...

Footsteps from the basement drew Mawro's attention toward the bi-fold cellar doors beside him. A moment later they flopped open and his father emerged, his face flush. He turned and fixed Mawro with a withering stare. "If this is your idea of a joke, I'll have you know that I am *not* laughing."

He blinked. "I...I don't understand, Papa."

"You said you'd get us the rest of what we'd need to help Alex, didn't you?" his father asked, narrowing his eyes at him.

"Yes, I did. That container from the ship. The shipment of catalyzation proteins inside should be enough to—"

"There was nothing in that container from the ship but a video player, rigged up to play the tape from your lab the night Barry died. Which Pawly was the first to see."

Oh. Oh, no. No no no no no.

"She went feral, Ritzi. All this time, her and me and everyone else thought...thought that *you* had been the one to..." His father sighed and shook his head. "Son, I'm sorry. I didn't know. None of us did. And I'm sure Blaznikov saw to it you'd never have opportunity to tell us your side of the story."

"Yes, Papa, that's right," Mawro replied, his voice barely a whisper. "He told me I couldn't. Told me I was too important to our race."

Opoworo leaned over and patted Mawro on the thigh above his knee, just below his canvas cutoffs. "You'll always be important to me, Ritzi. You're my son and I love you."

Mawro reached over and laid his hand atop his father's, covering it nearly to the elbow. "Thank you, Papa. But all of our lives are in danger, now."

His father pulled his hand free and held it and the other both up, gesturing confusion. "What do you mean?"

"Our plan originally called for an empty container to be put ashore to distract all of you. Then Hana and I would harvest samples from Stuie to complete DPRK's human augmentation program. After you and I talked last, I had ordered the container full of catalyzation proteins be put ashore instead." Mawro placed his hands to his temples and shook his head. "Papa, please believe me, I had no knowledge that tape was even in there. Not that the thing was on our ship, even. I hadn't seen it since Blaznikov first showed me in the days following the explosion."

His father pursed his lips. "So, you think someone countermanded your order? Who would do such a thing?"

"Someone who has deemed me superfluous. And I have a pretty good idea as to who." Oh's sneering face came to mind, an instant before Mawro pictured cleaving the man's smarmy smile clean off his face with his own claws. "And if he manages to kidnap you and Stuie and anyone else he thinks DPRK needs from our family, he'll have no more use for Hana, either."

The elder man waved a hand toward the mainland. "Well, if he'd wanted to send everyone ashore into disarray with his little bait and switch, he succeeded. We just only now managed to get Nat back on the line from the warehouse. Everyone else is out looking for Pawly."

Mawro wagged his chin toward the kitchen window. "Then what about Alex?"

"Nat believes he can talk me through synthesizing the catalyzation proteins we'll need to save Alex with what I've got on hand here." *Because she wouldn't survive a trip ashore*, Mawro knew his father was saying without specifically saying so. "It'll be a dicey proposition with the rudimentary setup I've got, though. One wrong move and the whole thing could blow up in my face. But it's our last and best hope for Alex's survival," he went on, folding his arms across his chest. "And it'll only happen if Tommy can establish a real-time data connection via satellite uplink. Which, right now, he *can't*." He narrowed his eyes and drew his fists to either side of his waist. "Supposing you remedy that, hm?"

Mawro bit his lip and nodded. He stood and bounded off toward the tree line without another word.

B EFORE LONG, MAWRO ARRIVED back at the light tower. He leapt from rock to rock, tracing the same path he had earlier, before thrusting himself upward upon the boulder closest to the tower's base. As he flew past the top of the tower, he snagged the canvas bag containing the jammer with one claw and slashed through its drawstrings with the other. But the snap which had previously held the bag securely to the base of his belt came free with them. It tumbled into the surf below, quickly disappearing from sight.

Mawro cursed. With the drawstrings torn and the snap missing, he had no way to secure the bag to his waist. And if he tried swimming with the bag clenched in one hand, he might well lose the bag in the crashing surf. *If* he somehow managed to not drown.

So Mawro resorted to twirling the bag over his head as he plummeted toward the water's surface. Hoping the thing's momentum would suffice, he let the bag fly toward shore. He breathed a sigh of relief as it landed on the rocky shore a few feet from the water's edge. His splashdown caught him off guard, causing him to suck in far too much water.

With a few kicks of his powerful legs, he made his way back to the surface. He trod water there for a moment, coughing and hacking while he got his bearings. After sighting shore, he hacked once more and then dove beneath the waves. He surfaced once, then submerged again, powering himself through the water until he reached the partially completed breakwater. He hauled himself up with a groan and lay there, panting, trying to get his breathing back under control. At some length, he raised his head and squinted toward the shoreline. To find Stuie, nudging what remained of the canvas bag containing the jammer with her nose.

"Hey!"

The girl started and drew back into a crouch, her eyes wide. Mawro got to his feet and lumbered toward shore. She hissed at him a moment, then snatched up the bag between her teeth and dashed off into the woods.

No no no no no!

Mawro tore off after her. Though not even three of the girl's strides could match his one, what she lacked in size she more than made up for in speed. The amount of scent she was leaving behind—brushing past this, ducking under that—ought to have been as effective a means to follow her as a radiotelemetry device would. And, in fact, he caught wisps of it here and there, now and again as he gave chase. So much like Hana's, yet not quite as earthy. For years before meeting Mawro in the shadow of Mt. Paektu, Hana had slept rough. Likely the only time Stuie had come even close to doing likewise was on the occasional family camping trip. Another werecat would certainly be able to make the same distinction between them. And be able to follow the girl's scent from halfway across the island.

But his own heightened sense of smell had been compromised years before, during the melee in his lab the night Barry died. So, if he were going to have any hope of recovering the jammer, he would need to keep his eyes fixed on Stuie. If Tommy was to have any hope of establishing the high-speed satellite connection Nat would need to help Papa save Alex's life, the jammer would have to be deactivated. Or destroyed.

For her part, Stuie was hardly making his pursuit easy. Her small size allowed her to duck and weave her way through the thick underbrush far faster than Mawro could plow through it. She could hop through the gaps that he had to muscle through. Slowly but surely, she pulled away from him. Mawro kept on, only realizing she had eluded him when he at length reached the island's opposite shore.

He looked left, right, all around. Finding no trace of her, he roared in anger and bounded atop a pile of dredging spoil dumped here decades before from Washington Island's harbor. Just as the wind shifted direction.

That's her!

Mawro could hardly believe his luck. For his impaired olfactories to scent Stuie at all, the girl had to be close. He immediately dropped onto his belly and shimmied around, looking back and forth along the rocky shoreline. Behind a stack of recently-felled timber, he spotted her, kneeling down with the bag in front of her, sniffing at it then pawing at it then sniffing at it again.

He made his way forward all fours, stopping every few yards to spare a glance at Stuie. Keeping the wind to his face, he made his way along the rocks, camouflaged by the brush piles heaped up beside a recently clear-cut fire break. She paid him no mind, alternately scratching and gnawing at the bag, likely attracted to the remnants from the fish he had planned to take back to Hana. By the time he crept up behind Stuie, the bag was well and truly shredded. *So, maybe...*

He popped up, waving his arms over his head. With a roar, he lunged for Stuie, hoping that in startling her she might drop the jammer and dash off to find more food. He had not anticipated the girl would snap her head around to face him before she fled, flinging the jammer free of the bag. And straight toward his face.

By instinct, Mawro swatted at the thing. The force of the impact was more than enough to activate the jammer's anti-tamper device, instantly releasing the tear gas stored in a cannister strapped to its top. With the cannister pressurized so as to empty within a split second, the noxious cloud had fully enveloped Mawro before the hissing even stopped. He coughed and gagged and spat and swore.

With a frightened yowl, Stuie beat a hasty retreat, disappearing into the night. Or, at least, what of it Mawro could see through his watering eyes. Which wasn't much.

By pure force of will, Mawro kept his hands away from his eyes, lest they burn more and burn longer. Rapidly blinking to clear away the tears, he managed to glimpse the jammer lying atop a flat rock nearby. Growling with rage, he grabbed the thing and hurled it toward the rocks poking through the crashing surf offshore as hard as he could. Then he turned and stumbled his way ashore, groping and hoping until came to the tree line. Mawro then felt for the tree next to him to his right, then the one after that, then the one after that. He slowly worked his way along the shoreline back toward the family cabin—step by step, tree by tree, reciting the Rosary as he went. Anything he could do to keep his mind off of the chemicals stabbing at the insides of his eyes.

CHAPTER TWELVE

Niko entered the kitchen and quickly shut the door, but not quickly enough. Annie wrinkled her nose at the sickly stench wafting up the basement staircase from behind him, something like a mixture of chloroform and diesel exhaust. "Everything ought to be ready down there now," he said, apparently oblivious to the odor. "How are you two making out?"

She set the last of the plates into the drying rack beside the sink and grabbed a dish towel from the oven's door handle. "Alex was still out when I last checked on her," she replied, wiping her hands while she pointed with her chin toward the sitting room beyond the kitchen. "Vitals steady but still weak. I'll make sure to examine her again before we eat."

The night air blew in through the open window behind Annie, giving her a chill. Niko, apparently having felt it too, turned his attention toward Tommy. He sat beside the window, hunched over the kitchen table he had pushed over to the closet door earlier, tightening a terminal strip connector with a small screwdriver. "What's all this, son?" he said with a wave of his arm toward the mass of wires and electronic devices strewn across the table top. "And it's hardly spring yet. What's that window doing open?"

Tommy ignored him while he finished making his connection. "I'm able to ping the satellites now, but their current azimuth and elevation are less than optimal," he said when he looked up a moment later. "So, I feared I wouldn't have enough output power to get you the bandwidth you and U-Nat will need to help Mom." He patted at the terminal strip in front of him and slid it across the table beneath one of the equipment housings. "I fabbed up this rig here to boost our signal strength. It's running a little hot, though, so I opened up the window to let the excess heat in here out."

Niko stepped over to the table, his brow furrowed. "Where did you get this front end?" he said, pointing at one of the devices. "And this B-stage? And that chopper over there?"

"From your lab in the boathouse back in Chicago. Top's people took 'em down and hauled 'em all up here while everyone was aboard ship back from Gdańsk. They were squirrelled away up in the rafters of the Delco house, waiting for me to replace the power supplies in 'em."

Niko blinked and look back up at Tommy. "But they were built to run off of 240. Everything here at the house runs off of 120, doesn't it?"

Tommy pointed toward the panelboard recessed into the closet wall, its door hanging open and its front cover removed. "Almost. The oven runs off 240, so I ran that line there to the rig from the oven's breaker. That way, Annie and I wouldn't have to pull the oven itself out away from the wall."

"Just as well. We'd've had tuna salad sandwiches for dinner tonight if we had," she added. "With everything that's been going on, I thought a hot meal would help us keep our strength and our spirits up."

"Your lake perch in lemon butter would sure hit the spot, my dear," Niko said as he leaned over and kissed Annie on the cheek. "My son's truly blessed, having married a doctor who loves to cook when she unwinds. Along with the rest of us."

Tommy shoved his chair away from the table and stood, groaning as he straightened up. "Good thing we didn't have to move the oven, A-squared. I'm pretty sore from just shoving the kitchen table around."

Niko pursed his lips. "Or it could be neural interference from your exo again." He opened the door to the basement stairwell and waved Tommy over. "Here, let me help you down the steps. I'll need an assist from you once we get Nat on the line. Nothing you can't do from your wheelchair, though."

Annie made a face and turned away. "I don't know *what* is in that stuff you've got boiling away down there," she said as she glanced over at the oven timer. "Timer's just about to go off, so could one of you please take the fish out of the oven and set it on the stove top to cool?" She reached into the silverware drawer and pulled out a tablespoon. "I gotta go get some pink stuff into me. Then I'll go check on Alex while I'm waiting for the kitchen to air out."

"Sure, love," Niko said with a nod. "But could we trouble you to bring us each a plate down later then? Once we start introducing the reactants, Tommy and I will have to keep close watch over them until the procedure is complete. They're likely as not to go supernova if we don't."

She mumbled a curt agreement and bolted out of the kitchen, worried she might hurl if she stayed even a second longer. Her stomach began to unknot almost immediately, allowing her to make it through the sitting room and into the bathroom without incident. She pulled a bottle of Pepto-Bismol from the cupboard above the toilet and gave herself two spoonsful. Just to be on the safe side.

Then she sat on the toilet for a few minutes, her face in her hands, breathing in, breathing out, until she felt confident enough to stand again. By the time she returned to the sitting room, Niko and Tommy were just finishing thump-thump-thumping their way down the stairwell beneath her feet.

Which was why the *clunk* from beyond the portico between the kitchen and sitting room nearly made her heart stop. "Ritzi? Stuie?"

No answer. Instead came a *clunk-clunk-clunk*, followed by the sound of...*chewing*?

Annie padded over to the wall and peered around the corner toward the kitchen. She clamped her hand over her mouth to keep from crying out. Atop the kitchen counter knelt Stuie on all fours, face down into the baking dish Niko had set out on the stove to allow their dinner to cool. Greedily gulping down every morsel she could lap up.

She slid back behind the corner and glanced back and forth around the room. Beyond where they had rolled Alex's gurney into the sitting room, Annie spied her kit bag where she had left it on the buffet table beside the front door. She shuffled over to her bag and gently pulled out a small black plastic case. After popping open the latches, she laid the case open atop the coffee table and grabbed the air pistol inside. Then she picked up two of the tranquilizer darts Top had given her, fixing one to the end of the pistol's barrel and gently tucking the second one into her chest pocket.

By the time Annie peered around the corner into the kitchen again, Stuie was sitting back on her haunches, licking at the orange-and-white fur covering her hands and fingers. Quickly, silently, Annie stepped into the kitchen and took up a firing stance. Stuie looked up just as she let the dart fly, turning aside in time for the dart to impale itself into the wall above the backsplash, right where her shoulder had been an instant before.

Her daughter's lips drew back into a growl before the girl hopped atop the kitchen table and lunged. Annie drew the second dart from her chest pocket as the satellite signal amplifier's power supply tumbled over the edge of the table top. But before she managed to fix the dart to the pistol, Stuie slammed into her, sending the dart skittering across the floor.

In an instant, Stuie had Annie pinned like a predator about to take its prey. Annie looked up into her daughter's eyes, seeing not a trace of the girl's personality behind them. Seeing only feral rage and instinctual urges. To kill. Or to be killed.

"N-nastusia, don't. P-please," she stammered as Stuie gnashed her fangs.

"What the hell's going on up there?"

The sound of Niko's feet tromping up the stairwell followed his angry shout. Stuie turned and hopped atop the kitchen counter opposite the basement door. Annie rolled up onto one knee and plucked the dart up from where it had rolled beneath the kitchen table. Then she stuck it onto the pistol and took aim, just as Niko emerged through the basement door.

With an angry roar, Stuie pounced. By reflex, Niko crossed his arms in front of him and thrust them forward with all his might, sending Stuie sprawling backward. Right before Annie's dart struck him in the side of his neck.

Time slowed to an agonizing crawl as Niko whirled about and stumbled into the stairwell, arms flailing as he grabbed feebly at the railing. He bounced down the steps twice before landing with a sickening crunch at the bottom.

"Oh, God! Niko!"

She scrambled over the doorway and squinted into the darkened basement. "Holy shit!" came Tommy's voice from somewhere off to the right. "A-squared! Get Mom outta here before the whole fucking house goes up in—"

Annie's scream drowned him out an instant later as a fireball raced up the basement stairwell toward her.

CHAPTER THIRTEEN

THE WATERY DEPTHS SURROUNDING PILOT IS-
LAND.

OH GROANED AND TURNED away from the tiny video monitor
fixed to the bulkhead opposite the companionway from the
helm. "You okay, General?" the special forces commander seated behind the console asked over his shoulder.

"I...I just need a moment," Oh replied with his hands clenched
together against his abdomen. After the queasy sensations subsided,
he stood upright and turned forward again. And took care not to look
directly at the image of the island's shoreline wobbling up and down,
back and forth across the console's screen. "Have you located Captain
Mawro's boat yet?"

"Yes, General." The commander leaned forward and tapped the
screen with the knuckle of his index finger. "There, about fifty meters
or so starboard of the sled."

Oh frowned. "That's recklessly close, given we expect Lieutenant
Hana to be aboard. She possesses uniquely keen vision, in both her
human and ailuran forms. We cannot jeopardize our mission's success
doing anything which might alert her to our presence."

"SOP dictates we tow an array sled like this one whenever we're conducting littoral surveillance, General," the commander replied with a wave toward their stern. "Its instruments are molded into a dark-colored plastic housing formed to resemble the shell of a snapping turtle. Cruising at depth on a shoreside sortie like this, I doubt the lieutenant would pick out our sled unless she was looking directly at it. And she would have to know just what it was she was looking at." The corner of the skipper's mouth turned upward into a barely perceivable smirk. "Besides, all that surface chop makes the sled even harder to spot, bobbing up and down like it was. Which I see you noticed."

Oh shot the man a cross look. He shrugged in reply and grabbed a pair of binoculars from the cubby beside his seat. "The hatches topside were all closed, from what I could make out. And I spotted someone moving about in the cabin. She must have finished up her tasks ashore earlier and is likely now just lying low. Puttering around in the dark awaiting Captain Mawro's return." He tapped their helmsman on the shoulder and gestured toward the overhead. "Take us up, Kwang. I can get a better look at Katczynski's cabin from there."

"Aye, Skip."

Oh sat down on the seat box behind the commander. Moments later the submersible go-fast boat surfaced. Even before planing out, the commander popped open the topside hatch. "Steady as she goes," he said, propping the hatch cover open with his back while he raised his binoculars to his eyes. "And you can start reeling in the sled."

The sodium vapor lamp stood behind the lighthouse, fixed atop a wooden pole. Oh squinted toward it, unable to make out much from the gray pallor it cast over everything below. "What can you see?" he asked, glancing up at the commander.

"Not much more than you can, I suppose. Lights on inside, several subjects up and moving around. But nothing to suggest Mawro might have already made his—holy shit!"

Oh caught the flash from ashore out of the corner of his eye. He turned and winced as the shock wave crashed into them, the report from the explosion assaulting his ears an instant later. The commander groaned and shook his head while Oh gawked toward the burning lighthouse. Flames quickly obscured the lower level of the keeper's residence. After a moment, the commander bellowed down the hatchway, "Kwang! Take us in closer so I can see if—"

"No!" Oh cried as he reached up and took hold of the commander's belt. With a grunt, he yanked the man bodily down from his perch, causing the hatch to slam shut behind him. "Dive, man, dive!" Oh barked as he twirled the latch dog shut. "Hana will surely be on the move to see what's happening. We cannot risk her seeing us!"

Biting his lip, the helmsman complied, the boat's bow quickly dipping below the surface. "With all due respect, *General*," the commander said, picking himself up from the deck beside the helm, "while underway *I* am the only one authorized to issue—"

Beep. "Tonight...north winds ten to fifteen knots becoming northwest ten to twenty knots," blared the monotone, computer-generated voice in English though their marine transceiver's tinny speaker. "Waves two to four feet subsiding to one to three feet before dawn..."

Oh poked at the radio's channel selector to squelch the weather forecast. "I don't understand, General," the commander said, fixing Oh with a quizzical stare. "You *did* say during our briefing Captain Mawro would be jamming all shoreside communications frequencies, didn't you?"

"I did, indeed," Oh replied, pursing his lips. "If we can hear the weather band while in-theatre at this stage of the operation, then the captain has clearly gone off script for some reason." He waved toward the commander's console. "Can you detect jamming signatures with this equipment?"

"Only if they're directly overhead," the man replied. "With our antennae right down at the water's surface, we don't have much range at all. We would enjoy better reception of we deployed the aerial, but someone ashore might spot us if we did." He held up his open palms to his shoulders. "And you have made your position on *that* scenario quite clear already."

Oh waved his way in a dismissive gesture. "That will not do for what I need to know anyway. But I do have another idea to figure it out..." He pulled his satellite phone out of his pocket and flipped up its antenna. "Your sled can relay signals from devices aboard our boat, right?"

"Yes, General. One moment." The commander returned to his seat behind the console and poked at its touch screen. "There. You should be able to operate your phone now as you would normally."

After stealing a glance at his watch, Oh scrolled through his phone's contact list until he found the number Min Soo should be answering this time of day. He placed the call and waited for it to connect. Once it rang, then twice, then three times. After the fourth ring...

"I didn't expect hearing from you for hours yet, General. What's fucked up?"

"I don't know yet. Maybe nothing. Though I can't be certain until after you—"

"The shower won't stay hot for long," came a woman's voice via Min Soo's side of their connection. "Nor will *I*."

The hacker sighed. "Just give me a moment, love," Oh heard him shout away from the phone's mouthpiece before mumbling "Well, I'm in kind of in the middle of something, so let's hurry this up" into it. Oh bit down on one knuckle while Min Soo stomped across the floor. "What do you need, then?" he asked as he plunked down into a chair, the thing creaking under his weight.

"Bring up an RF emissions map of the island from our real-time satellite feed, please."

Clickety-clackety-clack. "Done. What am I looking for?"

"Can you detect any satellite phones in the vicinity?"

Pause. "None except for yours. Wait, how did you get all the way offshore to—?"

"Never mind that right now. Mine is the only satellite phone you can detect, right?"

"Yes. I detect no others anywhere on or near the island."

Oh stole a glance over at the wobbly image of the burning lighthouse on the boat commander's screen, streaming in real time from the sled's camera. Surely, anyone on the island equipped with a satellite phone would be scrambling to call ashore right now for help. Maybe Mawro had somehow managed to destroy or disable any others already? Or maybe they had already burned up in the fire. "Any additional signal sources?"

"Not that I can...oh, wait..." Clickety-clackety. "I didn't see anything on my first full spectrum sweep at low gain, but the second one just finished. Higher gain picked up a transmission with the same signature as Mawro's jammer equipment. But it's really faint."

Oh gasped. "Where? Where is it?"

"Extreme opposite end of the island from your current position, on a little spit of land."

"Is any part of the island within a shoreside cellular tower's coverage area?"

"Only that particular piece of land I just mentioned."

Oh grinned. Having surely by now disabled the family's boats, Mawro could well have set fire to the house to flush the family out. With their obvious escape route off the island cut off, he could herd them to where he knew they knew they could call for help. The one place on the island where Mawro's jammer was still active, its power output and frequency signature customized as if to avoid detection by the family's own hacker fellow.

A surgical versus a shotgun approach. Clever. Clever, indeed. But, as Mawro would soon learn, not clever enough. Because Oh and his strike team would get there first to snatch the youngling, the scientist, and whomever else he pleased right out from under Mawro's nose. Then he could dispense with Mawro and Hana at his leisure, and that would be that. "Then there is where we shall be heading. Min Soo, resume radio silence until I say otherwise. And get back to your more, ah, *pressing* matters."

Ashore on Pilot Island. Moments later.

ANNIE GROANED AND PUSHED herself up with her forearms. Flashes of orange and yellow played across the wall of the boathouse in front of her. She gasped and rolled up onto her butt before blinking up toward the towering inferno their family's cabin had become. "Oh...oh no!"

A moan rose from behind her. Annie looked over her shoulder to find Alex lying on the ground, wrapped in the afghan Annie had last seen draped across the back of the sitting room sofa. Instinctively,

Annie jammed two fingers up underneath Alex's jaw and drew an ear close to her mouth. *Pulse, okay. Breathing, okay.* She reached out toward Alex's forehead with the back of her hand. *Temperature, normal. Now to make sure the others are...*

"Good, you're awake."

Annie started and glanced back over her shoulder. Mawro hopped off the pier and trotted up to her, a coil of rope dangling from one shoulder.

"Alex is okay, but what about Stuie?" Annie said and clutched at a pair of Mawro's furry fingers. "And Niko? And...and Tommy?"

He reached down and hauled her upright by her shoulders. "Stuie came tearing out of the house right after the explosion as if her tail was on fire," he answered her, with a nod toward the woods. "I can go look for her later. Because I haven't seen any sign of Tommy and Papa yet either."

"Then they must be inside still. Trapped!" Annie flailed her arms toward the burning house. "Probably in the basement somewhere." An eerie groaning as the cabin lurched to one side made them both gasp.

"Then we've no time to waste," Mawro said and scooped up Annie into his arms. He bounded around to the other side of the house, then sat her down on the muddy ground beside a pair of steel doors covering the steps to the cellar. "Try them," he said, waving his hand toward the door handles. "These furry meat hooks of mine are way too big."

Annie nodded and knelt down. She yanked at both handles, trying to turn them, but neither would budge no matter how hard she pulled or how loudly she swore. "They're locked!"

"Very well then," he said, reaching across his chest to push the coil of rope off of his shoulder. "Take this," he said after it slumped to the ground. "Tie off one end snug around your waist."

Annie set to securing the rope around her middle. Mawro meanwhile straddled the doors and whirled both fists in the air above his head. With a yowl he crossed his arms in front of him and slammed his fists into the doors. The thunderclap made Annie wince; when she opened her eyes again, Mawro sat hunched forward halfway into the stairwell, panting. He reached up and grabbed the edge of the bent and torn remains of one door. Working the door from side to side, its creaking groans ceased after a loud *pop*. Mawro tossed the crumpled metal to one side and did likewise with the door's mate before turning her way. "Are you ready?"

She cinched up the knot above her belt buckle and handed him the free end of the rope. "Ready as I'll ever be."

Mawro stepped to one side and gestured to the steps beyond the cellar door. "Papa and Tommy might have been overcome by the smoke already. When you find them, tie yourselves all together."

She set her jaw and trotted down the steps. At the threshold, she ducked down and peered inside. Smoke completely obscured the basement's low ceiling. Toxic gases would be accumulating there too, and soon they would pollute what little breathable air remained. She would have to work fast. "Okay, I'll give two yanks on the rope when I've reached them," she cried, turning back toward Mawro. "Then you can pull us all—"

"Look! Look there!"

Annie followed the tip of Mawro's finger toward the furry figure emerging from the basement. With soot and dust covering the fur on his face, Annie barely recognized Tommy but for the light of nearby flames shimmering off of his wavy red hair. Niko lay in his arms, the tranq dart still sticking out from his neck.

Her doctor's training took over. "Get him up to level ground and lay him down. Quickly!"

Tommy nodded and shuffled up the stone steps toward her. She backed up into Mawro and nudged him along with her elbow to clear a path for Tommy. Just past the cellar door opening, the young man knelt and laid Niko out on the ground near his feet. Then he stood and backed away, leaving room for Annie to work.

In an instant, she knelt beside Niko's head. Annie yanked the tranq dart from his neck and threw it aside, then drew her ear near to his mouth. "Breathing's already really shallow," she muttered as she took his wrist into her hand. "And his pulse is weak." She snarled and glanced up at the raging blaze consuming their cabin. "My kit bag's surely toast by now, along with my stash of naloxone. If we don't get some into him soon, he'll...he'll likely..."

Annie closed her eyes and shook her head.

"I have some in my boat," Mawro said, gesturing toward the woods with his chin. "Hana ought to be in position by now—"

"No, we don't have time for that. Let's get Niko and Alex to Dory's boat here. He keeps his first aid kit there stocked with...hey, what're you doing?"

Tommy stood nearby, wobbling back and forth as he drew one knee to his chest then the other. "Trying to figure out just what's going on." He nodded toward the burning house. "My exo's still in there. Can't be much more than slag by now."

Annie glanced down at his legs, her mouth falling open upon realizing he was indeed not wearing his exo. "Then just how...how did you...?"

He shrugged, his eyes wide. "Beats the hell out of me," he said, jogging in place while Mawro approached with Alex cradled in his arms. "I don't know what to make of it, U-Ritz. No pain, no numbness, no trembling as before. Like I had Parkinson's or something."

"Papa and I thought something like...like this...*might* be theoretically possible," he replied as he eyed Tommy up and down, "but we had no idea how likely an outcome it was. Whatever discomfort you'd experienced earlier might have been your exo's neural signals conflicting with the connections your body was attempting to reestablish." Mawro knelt beside Niko and reached down, taking his father into his arms alongside his sister. "And we don't know whether regaining use of your legs is a temporary thing," he said as he stood. "Or whether any one or another negative side effects might develop. So, until we know for sure, young man, consider yourself on light duty. Now let's get these two to the boathouse like your auntie suggested."

"I'll run on ahead," Annie said with a nod. "Tommy, lean on him if necessary. Or maybe he can carry you too if need be."

"Annie, wait, I..."

She trotted off, Mawro's voice drowned out by the wind and waves.

A moment later she burst through the boathouse door and flipped on the light switch.

Nothing.

Mumbling and fumbling her way along the boathouse's inside walls, Annie inched toward the roll-up door. After tripping and stumbling several times, she managed to grab hold of the door's pull rope. With a grunt and a heave, she threw up the door. Flickering light from the blazing cabin flooded the space inside, allowing her to make her way aboard the boat without falling into the frigid water between the pier and gunwale. But she became disoriented upon reaching the helm; nothing felt familiar. No wheel, no throttle stand, no ignition switch. Just jagged edges and sharp, pointy bits where the boat's controls should have been.

"The boat's out of commission, Annie," came Mawro's voice through the boathouse door as he and Tommy approached. "I saw to it before I came ashore."

Annie reached around the helm, to where she knew Dory kept a flashlight stored. She grabbed hold of it and tugged its magnetic mount free, then flicked it on. Back and forth across the boat's console she shone its beam, gasping at the sight of the ruined helm. Looking all the world as if some great bird had dropped a boulder onto it from the skies above. "I guess so. This boat isn't going anywhere any time soon."

Flashing the light around back and forth across the console, Annie spotted a white metal box with a red cross painted on the top and sides. It sat at a rakish angle in what remained of the cubbyhole beneath the helm, its lid caved in, next to the smashed-up remnants of the boat's marine band radio rig.

Annie snarled and worked the box free, then yanked back and forth on the lid until it finally popped open. "Fuck!" she cried, spotting liquid sloshing around in the bottom of the box from several broken glass vials. She dumped out the box's remaining contents on the seat behind the helm. After rummaging about, she snapped up a pair of intact vials and the one plastic syringe whose needle had not been bent beyond what was usable.

By the time she poked her head up, Tommy had Niko laid out on the deck alongside the boat. "That dart was filled with enough carfentanyl to drop a bull elephant," she told him as she hopped over the gunwale. Approaching him, she held out the flashlight to him. "Here, hold this," she said before kneeling down beside Niko's head. "I've only got enough naloxone here to stabilize him for the moment," she said, taking the syringe's needle guard between her teeth. She pulled the needle free and jammed it into the vial's lid, drawing out nearly its entire contents into the syringe. After poking around beneath Niko's jaw, she injected him in his carotid artery. Annie repeated the process a moment later with the other vial, then carefully slid the syringe's needle back into its guard. "He'll need more than this before he's out of danger," she said in a raised voice as she tucked the syringe into her flannel's chest pocket. "A lot more."

Tommy hopped to his feet and stepped outside. "Where's your satellite phone, son?" Mawro asked Tommy before the younger man shuffled through the boathouse doorway, his mother Alex in his arms.

"Still inside, right beside where my exo was charging," he answered as he gently laid his mother beside Niko. "Fire's surely reduced them both to a puddle of slag by now."

Annie stood and jammed both hands into her back pants pockets. She gasped as her fingers rubbed against the case of her smartphone. "If we head to the point, we can likely get a cellular call through to the mainland from there, right?"

Tommy glanced up at the ceiling, tapping at his chin. "We should," he replied a moment later before glancing down at his watch. "Grandpa D and Milda were on their way to Northport in the RV. Which he keeps fully stocked for emergencies such as this, including naloxone by the crateful. But this storm was supposed to start dropping ice on the roads down south from where they were coming."

"I don't know if you or Papa or anyone else will want to wait here for a pickup, though," Mawro's voice boomed through the doorway. "The point is on the lee side of the island. With the wind and falling temperatures, I think it'd be better for you all to get there and build a fire. Lots of deadfall everywhere left over from that big storm last

November. And Dory ought to have some hand-held flares squirreled away somewhere aboard his boat."

Tommy nodded. "He's right, A-squared. Fire from the house might keep us warm if we got close enough, but it'd be risky. The whole thing could collapse on top of us at any moment. Or even explode."

Annie pursed her lips. "Hand me that light, would you?"

Tommy complied. She shone the flashlight's beam back and forth above her head until it landed on the hull of a fiberglass canoe tucked away in the boathouse's rafters. "There! Quick, Tommy, help me get that thing down. You and me can lay Niko and Alex in it, then we can drag them along behind us to the point."

Mawro snorted. "*I* can pull a canoe there overland far faster than even the two of you could."

"Nothing doing," Annie replied, turning to face the doorway. "Niko might not make it if we're camped out at the point for hours waiting for someone to come for us. Go get me that naloxone you said you had aboard your boat. We'll wait for you there." She stood and stared off through the open roll-up door toward the tree line across the harbor from them. "Then hopefully, Stuie," she said, her voice cracking, "she'll...she'll be able to..."

Tommy drew up beside Annie and rubbed at her back above her shoulder blades with one hand. "Don't worry, A-squared. Soon as U-Ritz brings us the naloxone for G-Nik, he and I will go looking for Stuie. We'll find her and bring her back to you safe and sound. Promise."

"Indeed, young man. Indeed, we shall," Mawro added, his voice husky. Then he bounded off up the pier, his footfalls shaking the entire boathouse.

Chapter Fourteen

ROLLING NORTH ON I-43. A SHORT TIME LATER.

DORY BLINKED AND CRACKED open one eye, confirming what he hadn't wanted to acknowledge.

His satellite phone sat on the RV's center console, ringing. Who the hell would be calling him *now*? Top insisted his team maintain radio silence from the outside world during an operation; in fact, Dory hadn't expected to hear from any of them until morning at the earliest. That included Tommy and Niko. Aside from them, the only other person who had this number was Milda. And she sat in the driver's seat opposite him in the RV's cab, the look on her face proclaiming *this can't be good.*

With a yawn, Dory reached over and picked up the phone. To his great chagrin, it was indeed Top's number flashing across its tiny display. "I'm here," he said, rubbing at his eyes with his thumb and forefinger. "What's wrong?"

"What isn't?" Top replied. "That container from the ship was some kind of plant. Now Pawly's raging out of control, I just got done restraining Lenny so his fool ass wouldn't take off after her, and Hana's managed to put both of Bobby's boats out of commission. Basically, everything's FUBAR."

Dory groaned and pressed the back of his head into his seat's headrest. "Where are you right now? Who's with you?" he mumbled into his phone, the palm of his free hand pressed up against his face.

"Lenny, Bobby, and Nat. Pawly's out there somewhere, though I doubt she's after Hana."

"Likely Hana has fled the scene already," Dory replied as he massaged his forehead. "But what could she have done to cause Pawly to rage?"

"I think Hana was just a decoy to allow Mawro to launch his psy-ops attack on Pawly."

Dory cocked an eyebrow. "'Psy-ops attack?' What psy-ops attack?"

"The one Pawly triggered when she defied orders and broke into the container before you and Milda arrived."

"I just woke up, Topper. Throw me a bone here, would you? I'm still not following you."

"The container was empty except for a video player," Top said after a moment's pause. "On its...on its tape was the surveillance camera footage from Ritzi's lab the night Barry was killed."

Dory's eyes went wide. "Oh. Oh no."

"And that's not the worst of it. The tape clearly showed that Ritzi wasn't Barry's killer."

"He wasn't?" He gulped. "Then...then who *was*?"

"Pawly. It...it was Pawly."

Dory let out a pained cry, drawing a look from across the cab from Milda. He answered her worried glance with a pained look and a sigh. "And Alex...she had to have known. Had to have known, all this time! Have...have you told her yet?"

"Negative. Right after Pawly began to rage, Nat cut the feed to Niko that Tommy had nailed up earlier. Now Nat can't raise anyone on the island."

Dory's mouth went dry. "Mawro might have been after Niko all along. Or maybe even Stuie. Alex is in no shape to fend Mawro or Hana off by herself and Tommy, well..."

"Shit, I hadn't thought of that! Maybe we can commandeer a boat from the harbor and then—"

"No, I don't want people around Northport getting wise enough to start asking questions. We're way compromised as it is and we need to keep things on the down low." He paused a moment after spotting a sign announcing the upcoming Denmark exit. "Look, you all lock down the warehouse and keep watch over our supplies and equipment. Make sure no one comes in or goes out until I say otherwise."

Dory ended his call and looked across the cab at Milda. "Take this exit, please," he said with a wave toward the RV's windshield.

Milda squinted up at the lighted signs beyond the off ramp, then back down at the RV's dashboard. "We've got over half a tank. And if you're hungry, I still have some sandwiches in the—"

"We're not stopping for food or fuel, dear," he said, pulling his cell phone out of his chest pocket. "We're stopping so I can call in a favor from an old service buddy."

Fifteen minutes later, Dory spotted the rickety wooden sign he had been looking for alongside the lonely county highway. "Slow down, slow down." Waving his hand toward Milda, he squinted to read the sign's wording by the RV's headlights. "Okay, this is it." He turned and looked across the darkened field toward a farmhouse situated on a small rise. Light streamed from the open door of the small barn beside it.

Milda made the turn and piloted the RV up the driveway and around the circle in front of the barn. After Milda parked, a mustachioed man approached and clambered up the RV's passenger side. Dory lowered his window halfway and the man flashed Milda a sloppy two-fingered salute.

"Ma'am," he said before turning his attention to Dory. "You sounded pretty worked up over the phone, Kat. Mind telling me what's this all about?"

"You know how it works, Mac. Agency business, need to know, yadda yadda." He stared past the man's shoulder at the tiny two-seater helicopter resting atop a rubber-tired dolly inside the barn and set his jaw. "All you need to know right now is that I need a lift. And that I'll pay triple your normal rate."

BACK ON PILOT ISLAND...

Mawro bolted through the woods en route to the inlet where he and Hana had agreed to rendezvous. His stride felt burdened and sluggish, as though the ground were covered with molasses. Seconds ticked by with agonizing slowness, Papa's words echoing through his mind over and over.

...we've been administering Stuie's replicated DNA to Tommy...

...he's been experiencing occasional pain and numbness in his lower back...

...push the cellular reproduction processes underway within Tommy's body into overdrive...

He skidded to a halt. Far above the clearing, countless stars twinkled in the night sky. He stared up at them, a cloud of steam forming around him as he caught his breath. Tommy could walk again. Far sooner than Nat or Annie or Papa or anyone else had ever thought he would. If ever.

Alex's peaceful visage filled his mind, having seen her earlier that evening lying on the sofa asleep. What would her prognosis be now, after fending off a feral Stuie?

...which we can then harvest from Tommy and put right back into Alex...

Now that Tommy regained use of his legs, maybe they could employ that very technique to bring Alex back from the brink. Maybe they could use it to spare the twins a similar fate. Maybe they could free the Forest Clan from their self-imposed isolation within Białowieża's ancient oaks.

Maybe they could save his entire race.

Ritzi had been right all along...

Recalling his father's affirming words reminded Mawro that *he* needed him the most right now. He shook his head and blew out his breath. Then he resumed his sprint toward the inlet, the place where Hana had agreed to meet him after scuttling the family's boats ashore. Approaching the tree line, he spied their boat's canopy bobbing above the surface of the gently rolling water. After making his way to a fallen tree near the water's edge, he waved his arms toward their boat.

Nothing.

He tried again a moment later. Still nothing.

Mawro squinted toward their boat's canopy. Hana was nowhere to be seen. Was she below? He stuck his fingers into the corners of his mouth and whistled loudly. And yet...still nothing. Was she asleep? Did she sustain an injury? Had she fallen overboard, somehow?

Fuck it.

Mawro darted across the rocky beach and plowed into the water. He paddled as hard as he could until he reached the boat, then hoisted himself atop the canopy on all fours. After shaking himself off, he peered down through the canopy hatch.

Neither Hana nor her staff were anywhere to be seen. Nor was the mask he had made to prevent her from raging should she encounter Stuie. He called out to Hana once and then again, hoping beyond hope against his effort's futility.

But the sound of water lapping at the boat's hull beneath him was the only reply he received. Surely Hana had gone ashore already, likely soon after the explosion at the lighthouse. Surely to look for *him*. Surely without any inkling Oh had turned on them. Surely unaware Oh would have them both shot the moment their usefulness to him was over.

Which would be about thirty seconds after Oh got his hands on Stuie. Just long enough for the man to gloat.

Grunting and cursing under his breath, Mawro squeezed his way through the boat's hatch. After managing to wedge between the helm and the foremost passenger's chair, he reached his arm through the companionway and patted around at the inside of the forward cabin. The back of his hand brushed against the latch holding the first aid kit in place. He flipped it up and curled his fingers carefully around the kit itself. Then he pulled back his arm gently so as not to risk the kit's contents spilling all over the deck. With the box secure in his lap, he opened the lid and peered inside. Yes, there was plenty of naloxone here still. Right beside a pair of autoinjectors, each filled with a werecat-sized dose of carfentanyl.

Now all he had to do was to get the naloxone to Annie to administer to Papa. Before...before it was...

Mawro shook away the horrible thought as he placed one hand over the box's contents and gently shook the box until the naloxone vials and a package of disposable plastic syringes slid out. He set the kit aside and stuck the vials and syringes into the pockets of his canvas cutoff shorts. Then he wriggled himself back through the canopy hatch and dove back into the frigid water.

MOMENTS LATER.

"**H**OLY SHIT."

That was the only thing Dory found himself able to say as the tiny helicopter approached Pilot Island. He and his pilot both stared straight ahead through the cockpit's windscreen at the flaming remains of the family's cabin, speechless. "Holy shit," he repeated a moment later, breaking the uneasy silence between them.

"Gee, Kat, I'm...I'm sorry. Is there something I can do to—?"

"Closer, Mac. Get me closer," Dory answered him, his gruff voice a monotone.

They flew directly over what remained of the cabin. Most parts were still on fire but some had burned themselves out already; by sunrise all of them certainly would follow suit. Dory reached down into his jump bag and pulled out his satellite phone. After sliding the small vent window open in the cockpit door beside him, he extended his phone's antenna and carefully poked it through. He tried Tommy's number, hoping against hope his grandson would answer, would tell Dory he and everyone else were safe.

He didn't.

"They might've been in too much of a hurry getting out to take their phones with 'em, Kat."

Dory gave him a curt nod. "How are you for fuel?" he asked, his gaze fixed upon the burning cabin beneath them.

"Enough to lap the island a few times before I'll need to head for Sturgeon Bay. Airport there's the closest place open to gas up this time of night."

Dory grunted his reply.

After passing over the woods, Mac doubled back over the island's far shore and approached the cabin from the other side. A high-beam light mounted below the cockpit shone down upon the scene as Mac hovered over the back yard, swinging the beam back and forth over the area with a button fixed to his cyclic's grip. Dory's gaze followed, desperate he might glimpse one or another of his loved ones. But not a trace of them was to be had. Not a hat or a glove or a mitten, not even so much as a swatch of fabric.

"Hey, Kat, do your people normally leave the boathouse open?"

Dory glanced toward where the shoreline met the breakwater. Beside the empty pier sat the boathouse, its door raised just as Mac had described. "Can you get me there?"

Mac chuckled. "Sure. Just hop off the skid and onto the pier."

Dory hiked the strap of his jump bag atop his shoulder and made ready, having all confidence in Mac's ability to deliver on his boast. His skill in handling his machine was unquestionable. In their Coast Guard days, this same guy and his winchman had hooked an illegal gill net and hauled it ashore during a sting operation before the suspected poachers could ditch the evidence. "I would like very much indeed. Then head ashore and fill up. Ring my satellite phone when you're done. I'll figure out in the meantime whether or not I'll need you back here."

"Oh, uhm, okay, Kat. Sure hope you know what you're doing."

I do, Mac. Making sure you never see what werecats are capable of whenever they're provoked.

A moment later, Dory alighted and stepped atop the pier. A moment later the little helicopter cleared the breakwater and sped off toward the mainland over the open water beyond, its skids barely clearing the tops of the rollers beneath.

Dory sprinted up the pier to the boathouse. As he neared the door, he noticed it slightly ajar. After reaching into his jump bag for a small flashlight, he tiptoed toward the doorknob and tapped at it gingerly with one finger. The boathouse door swung open at his touch. He clicked on his flashlight and swept its beam back and forth over *Forty-Four*, berthed snugly in its slip. An unexpected glint drew his attention toward the helm. He knew every square inch of brass and chrome aboard, having polished them to a mirror sheen countless times. And none of it was anywhere near the helm, so as to avoid glare obscuring his view of his instruments while underway at night.

A strained squeak emanated from Dory's throat when he finally laid eyes on his boat's ruined console. The cabin fire, whether it had been planned or unplanned, had certainly been part of a larger conspiracy. One with aims of sabotage at the very least. And, at the very most...

Seeing the contents of his boat's first aid kit strewn about the helm would have normally rankled him. But now it gave Dory hope his family got out of the cabin all right. Any enemy combatants responsible for putting his boat out of commission likely wouldn't have bothered ransacking it afterward. But Annie and Niko and Tommy would surely seek out provisions from the boat if they made a run for it with Alex and Stuie. Each of them would have known good and well what sorts of supplies Dory kept aboard. But they didn't know *all* of them.

He knelt down and felt around on the floor for the familiar seam line. After following it to the edge of the deck plate, Dory pushed down with his thumb on the corner. The corner popped up with a *click*, allowing him to wedge his hands beneath. A moment later, his secret stash lay open.

Dory drew from the cubby a long, black hard case and laid it on the deck in front of him. He popped at the case's latches and flipped its lid open to reveal a sniper's rifle and several loaded clips of ammunition. Carefully, he lifted up the rifle with two hands and leaned it up against the bulkhead next to him. After tossing in all but one of the clips into his jump bag, he zipped it shut. Then he stood, stuck the remaining clip into his jacket pocket, and reached for the rifle's barrel. He popped the remaining clip into the rifle and racked a shell into the chamber before looping its strap over his free shoulder. Then he darted through the open boathouse door and hustled ashore, not bothering to close the door behind him.

Chapter Fifteen

The sound of a twig snapping from somewhere up the trail in front of him set Dory's teeth on edge. He had made his way inland from the burning cabin along the most direct route he knew led to the point, following the freshly plowed furrow he had found while scoping out the grounds for clues as to his family's whereabouts. Given calls to Tommy's satellite phone had gone unanswered, the thing had likely been inadvertently left behind in the burning house while everyone got out. At least, that was what Dory kept telling himself, not wanting to accept the horrific ramifications any other explanation provided.

The furrow was puzzling, to be sure. But he knew if any of his loved ones had escaped the flames with their cell phones still on their person, then they would certainly try to put a call through to the mainland from the point. Cellular connectivity there was not a sure thing, however, under even the best of conditions. Regardless, with his boat's VHF rig deep-sixed, every Katczynski-Opoworo clan member understood the point would be the one place on the island where they had any chance at calling for help. He had hoped, beyond hope it seemed, that any bad guys involved with their current bad fortune would be unaware of that. Because one of them might well have him in his sights, even now.

Dory let his jump bag slide from his shoulder to the ground. Then he squared up his stance and drew the butt of his rifle to his shoulder. He swept the rifle back and forth along the trail in front of him, peering through the rifle's night sight scope. But he saw...nothing.

Tiny bits of debris tumbling to the forest floor drew his attention upward to the canopy. After spotting a fleeting trace of infrared signature, a *whump* came from along the trail beside him followed by *crunch-crunch-crunch*. He brought his rifle up to firing position in time to glimpse an orange blur blasting forth from the underbrush.

"Ohmigod! Grunkle D!"

Arms clamped together around his back in a vise-like grip just above his waistline before a head thrust itself into his abdomen. He stumbled as his breath left him in a surprised grunt. After managing to catch himself, he looked down to find a panting Stuie, shoulders heaving, her face crushed into his belly.

He reached down and scritched at the fur covering the tiny round ears poking forth from her long black hair. "I know you're scared, sweetie, but you needn't worry. I'll help you get you back together with—"

"No, you don't understand," Stuie mumbled. "We're...we're not alone."

Dory's mouth when dry. "Who else is here, then? Soldiers?"

"No, another werecat," she replied, shaking her head. "From outside our family."

He stared down at her, his eyes wide. "You're...you're sure?"

Stuie's whiskers twitched as she cast a bleary-eyed glance up at him. "I...I could *smell* her, Grunkle D. The woman I told you about from last Christmas Eve. The one who tried to kill me and Mr. Manny. I...I don't know if she noticed me, though." She rubbed one finger beneath her nose and sniffled. "Her smell got really strong and then it went faint. Like she was in a big hurry or something."

He swore under his breath and slung his rifle over one shoulder. "What's the last thing you remember?"

"Mom was screaming at that Mawro person. Everything went red after...after she told him..."

Tears began to dribble down the orange-and-black fur covering her cheeks. Dory gently coaxed himself free of her grip and tousled her hair. "Come on, let's get you back to your mother. I'm sure she's been sick with worry."

"No." Stuie turned her back to him and stepped away. "I don't want to see her *or* Dad," she said as she reached around behind her neck and unclasped her silver chain. Then Stuie pulled her pendant—one Dory knew contained a tiny photo of her, together with her parents—free from her blouse and hurled it into the woods. "I never want to see either of them. Ever again!"

Dory knelt down beside her and smoothed a lock of Stuie's long black hair away from her face. "Whatever would lead you to say such a thing, sweetheart?"

She snarled and fixed him with an icy glare. "How can I know they ever loved me in the first place?" she spat. "That *any* of you did?"

"Whoa, whoa there, kiddo," he said, raising his open palms to his shoulders. "I have no idea what you're—"

"Mom and Dad said my birth mother drowned during a flash flood after a dam broke somewhere in North Korea," she said, pain and rage flashing in her eyes. "If they ever loved me, why would they lie to me? Keep from me that my *real* mother is still alive?"

Dory flicked on his flashlight and shone its beam back and forth in the direction in which Stuie had thrown her pendant. Spotting the light glinting off its silver-finished surface, he stepped over to it and picked it up. "Annie and Nat have been lying to you all this time because your real mother tried to kill you," he said, turning to face her. "That's why."

Stuie gawked at him, her mouth wide open. "Wait...what?" she managed after a long moment.

"Twice, in fact. Before you were born, and then again immediately afterwards." His gaze met Stuie's wide-eyed stare as he strode up in front of her and knelt down. "She raged, trying to rip you and Nat and Annie to pieces moments after they'd delivered you via C-section," Dory said while he fastened the ends of the chain together around Stuie's neck. "Which they did to save your mother's life following a botched attempt to terminate her pregnancy herself. By rights, little girl, *you* should have died in the womb. And even for an ailuranthrope, your odds of survival after birth were staggering being you were born so premature."

Tears stung at the corners of his eyes as he tucked the pendant beneath Stuie's blouse. "You're our little miracle," Dory said, patting at her chest. "Why Nat and Annie named you 'Nastusia' in the first place. 'Stronger than death.'"

He stared off into the trees and puffed out his cheeks, his breath forming a cloud in the cold night air. "I pulled every string I could grasp to get the three of you into the best neonatal intensive care unit in Seoul, complete with armed guards providing 24-hour protection secrecy," he went on, his fingers tracing the outline of Stuie's pendant through her blouse. "For more than a month, the only time away from the doctors and nurses you weren't nestled snug in Annie's bosom was when she would get up to use the bathroom. Or whenever Nat insisted she take herself a shower."

"That...that was all *you*?" Stuie replied, her voice cracking.

"Yes, it was. Annie and Nat kept their mouths shut because I told them they had to. CIA already had its thumb on me and my grandchildren, and I wasn't about to let them put the squeeze on Nat and Annie too." Shaking his head, he stood. "And no one would be the wiser even now if Hana hadn't attacked you and Agent Latharo in Gdańsk before Christmas." Dory reached down and patted Stuie's cheek. "So, young lady, if you're going to hate on anyone for separating you from your birth mother, let it be me."

But she didn't answer. Instead, she stared blankly toward the woods behind him, wheezing as if unable to fill her lungs. Then, without warning, Stuie belted out a pained yowl and leapt up into the canopy above their heads. Dory's heart broke as the girl hurled herself from treetop to treetop, her flight driven by feral senses and human emotions. Trying to outrun her pain, her sadness, her grief, like a prey animal fleeing in vain from a hungry predator.

OTHER SIDE OF PILOT ISLAND. MOMENTS LATER.

HANA SWORE UNDER HER breath and yanked the straps at the base of her mask free. She was unsure just what annoyed her more—that this damn mask would not fit over her muzzle comfortably or that Mawro was down there daisy-picking.

Or, at least, that was what it looked to her like he was doing. Hana sat perched in the crook of a tall pine tree near the shore, staring at Mawro as he paced back and forth wringing his hands. She couldn't make out why, however. The offshore breeze made it difficult for her to hear anyone near the water's edge below even without her mask on. She had no idea just what to make of Honorable Opoworo lying unconscious in the bottom of the canoe beside Mawro. But surely it had something to do with Mawro's anxious state.

After crisscrossing the eastern half of the island twice, nearby to the lighthouse, she had chanced upon Mawro's scent about halfway through her a third sweep—heading away from their boat, not toward it. Desiring not to lose him, Hana had followed Mawro here, lagging behind some distance upwind. She didn't want her own scent alerting him to her presence or spooking the youngling, holding out the hope he was on her trail and would have her in hand soon.

With a disgusted sigh, Hana turned to one side and gazed out over the darkened forest canopy. The youngling was still out there, somewhere. All alone. Just like Soon-Bok had been, back when Hana had first...

She shook away the stray thought, then cinched her mask's straps as tight as she dared without snagging her fur. No time for sappy sentiment, there was work to be done. Mawro still needed samples from the girl. The sooner they got her to their ship, the sooner Mawro would have his samples. And the sooner they could put the girl ashore and lay course back to Korea. Let the Nohs figure out how to get her back to her family if they were so inclined.

Beep.

Hana gasped.

Beep. Beep beep. Beep beep beep. Beep.

Apparently, the youngling was closer than Hana realized. Much closer, in fact. Close enough for the girl's scent, wafting upward from somewhere below, to trigger Hana's mask to switch over to its cannister air supply. Which meant she had less than five minutes to subdue the girl, restrain her, alert Mawro. And then get upwind before her air gave out.

Sparing a parting glance below toward Mawro, Hana sprang from her perch and launched herself into the canopy. She made her way treetop to treetop, scanning the ground beneath her, back and forth until she'd worked her way inland out of sight of the shoreline.

No trace of the youngling. And no time to waste! She glanced down at her chronometer. Ninety seconds, gone. Poof.

Undaunted, Hana turned and repeated her sweep, at a right angle to her previous one so as to complete a grid-like search pattern. Upon reaching the island's north shore, opposite the southwestern corner where she had begun, she crouched down on a stout limb and leaned her back up against the tree's trunk. And listened.

The damn mask had seen to it she could scent nothing, but at least her hearing still worked. Well enough, in fact, for her to pick out the sound of leaves rustling in between wind gusts from within the top of a nearby tree.

Leaning forward, Hana fixed her gaze on the tree's budding leaf cover. She narrowed her eyes, spotting a trace of movement, by something far larger than a bird or a squirrel. She glanced to her right, making out Mawro and the others in the distance down the shoreline from her. Perfect.

With a yowl, Hana launched herself toward the nearby tree. As she had expected, something leapt from its leaves an instant before she landed. Something indeed large enough to be the youngling. It touched down atop a stout limb in the next tree over. In the blink of an eye, Hana did likewise.

Again and again, she repeated her maneuver, steering their course a little to the left here, a bit to the right there. Before long she had the object of her pursuit cornered. The canopy ended just beyond where Mawro and the others gathered below.

Playtime's over, little one.

She drew forth a handful of darts from her bandolier and let them fly. Regardless of whether the girl remained in a feral state, Hana's darts would surely herd the youngling in Mawro's direction. Allowing him to capture their quarry so they could both get the hell out of here.

"Careful, gorgeous," a man called out in Korean. "You could put someone's eye out with those things!"

Hana gasped and dove into the canopy, coming nose to nose with a lyncean male. "You have my thanks, regardless," he said in English as he ran one hand through his wavy red hair. "I haven't been able to stretch my legs like that since Chah Bahar!"

"You!" Hana cried in kind, raising a finger at him. "You use a wheelchair since then." She looked around and down at the ground toward Mawro. "No exoskeleton could jump this high. What sort of game do you play, Tomasz Katczynski?"

He shrugged and crossed his arms. "Oh is the only one playing games here. On you and Mawro both." He nodded over his shoulder. "Surely, if you ask him and my aunt down there, he'll tell you—"

"No! I won't do it!" came a woman's voice from below.

Katczynski's eyes went wide. "Wait, what?"

Hana turned and followed his gaze. "Annie, you must listen to me!" Mawro barked while he placed his massive paws over top of the woman's shoulders.

"No, you need to listen to *me!*" the woman cried in reply, struggling beneath his grasp. "Surely Dory and Top are on their way already. None of us are going anywhere with you, and that's final!"

She *tsk*ed and turned back toward Katczynski. "They are telling me a different story than the one you were just..."

Hana blinked toward the empty space beside the tree trunk where Katczynski had been standing a moment before. A *creeeeak* off to her left drew her attention upward to find him hanging upside-down like a bat, his toe claws sunk deep into the limb above him. "Sorry, sweets," he said between gritted teeth before letting go of the pine bough clenched to his chest. The branch snapped back toward Hana, striking her square in the face with force enough to rip her toe claws free of the branch beneath her. She tumbled through the air until she landed face first atop one of the limestone boulders lining the shoreline. With a *crack!* her mask's faceplate shattered. Her momentum rolled her to one side of the rock and she fell free the remaining distance to the hard ground.

She propped herself up on her elbows and groaned. Every part of her body hurt. Hana took small comfort knowing that meant she was at least still in one piece. She tapped at her ruined faceplate with one fist, then shook her head to expel whatever fragments had broken free. Pleasing images flashing through her mind of all the places she would sink her claws into Katczynski's bare flesh evaporated hearing the sound of hissing from in front of her.

Looking up, Hana spotted the youngling, cornered in the cleft of a rock mere yards away. Eyes wild. Baring fangs and claws at her. Ready to fight for her very life.

Hana breathed deep, all too happy to oblige. She moaned as the electrifying scent of the girl's fear set her body aflame with ecstasy. "*Jinguem jug! Jinguem jug!*" she mouthed in her native Korean. *Kill it now! Kill it now!*

The red haze flooded in from her peripheral vision, quickly obscuring everything else.

Chapter Sixteen

Annie pulled her fingers away from the side of Papa's neck and shook her head. "His pulse is getting weaker, Ritzi," she said, rolling back on the balls of her feet. "Breathing is growing shallower, too, even after administering the naloxone you'd brought us." She sniffled and rubbed at the corner of her eyes with her thumb and forefinger. "I had hoped that that would be enough."

Mawro grunted. He and Annie both knew little more than a coin toss decided whether his father's condition would worsen before it improved. He knelt down beside her and met her gaze. "Would a ventilator help? Buy him more time for the naloxone to work?"

"Yes, it would," she replied, looking up at him with misty eyes. "That and an AED. You know, just in case." She glanced around and sighed. "Hardly a chance of finding either of those around here, though," she went on in a husky voice. "Or getting ashore to find them before...before he..."

"Come with me, then. All of you."

Annie furrowed her brow. "And go where, exactly?"

"Hana is here with my boat," he replied with a nod over one shoulder. "Surely, we can all figure out how to safely get you and Papa and Stuie safely back to our ship. The sick bay aboard should have what you'll need to—"

"Are you out of your mind, Ritzi?" Annie barked, leaping to her feet. "After Hana has already tried to kill Stuie?" She stabbed her finger Mawro's way, fixing him with a searing glare. "Not a snowball's chance in hell I'd allow that...that woman anywhere near her." Annie covered her face with her hands and shook her head. "Or that I'd leave Stuie behind on this island," she mumbled, her voice cracking. "Right when she needs her mother the most. Right when she needs *me* the most."

Mawro smacked his lips. "Well, how about this, then?" he said after a moment. "I've got a pair of autoinjectors back on the boat filled with carfentanyl. We could administer one each to Hana and Stuie before we embark, which ought to keep them both calm until we reach the ship. Then we'll keep them individually sequestered until I put you all ashore someplace after Papa comes around."

Annie dropped her hands and looked up at him, her shock and disgust clear from the lines crossing her face. "Seriously, Ritzi?" she said, balling her hands into fists. "When me trying to tranq Stuie is what got us into this mess in the first place?" She crossed her arms across her chest and turned away, her nose in the air. "No! I won't do it!"

"Annie, you must listen to me!" Mawro cried as he laid his hands atop of her shoulders.

"No, you need to listen to *me*!" she shot back, squirming within his grasp. "Surely Dory and Top are on their way already to help us. I don't care if I have to administer Niko chest compressions until my arms fall off, none of us are going *anywhere* with you. And that's final!"

Something struck Mawro in the side of his neck, followed by a loud *crack!* from behind the limestone boulder nearest them. He scanned the trees lining the shore back and forth as he plucked the offending object free from his ruff. Holding it in front of his face with his thumb and forefinger, he quickly recognized it as a piece of bark. Glancing down, he met Annie's uneasy gaze. "It that you, Stuie?" he called toward the rock. *"Geugeosi neoya, Hana-ttanim?"*

Hearing no answer, Mawro patted Annie on the shoulder and bounded atop the boulder. His stomach knotted at the sight he beheld there. To one side stood Hana, her mask's faceplate shattered. Mere yards away, to his other side, stood Stuie. Each brandishing fangs and claws, each sizing up the other with wild eyes.

"Jinguem jug! Jinguem jug!" Hana mumbled with feral mirth. Stuie answered her with a snarl before the two werecats scurried sideways like fiddler crabs toward the water's edge. There they jockeyed for position, back and forth, each angling for an opportunity to level a killing strike toward the other's neck. After several feints, Stuie lunged, launching herself at Hana's jugular.

"No!"

Mawro vaulted into the air. Landing behind Hana, he threw his arms around her and clenched her to his chest. She yowled in anger as Stuie's claws sank deep into Mawro's forearm. He bit his lip and gripped Hana tighter, knowing she would tear every member of his family present to shreds if he dared let her go.

Starting with Stuie. Her own daughter.

A loud screech followed by a flash of gray obscured his vision an instant before a wall of water knocked Mawro back on his haunches. He and Hana both coughing and sputtering, Mawro gazed up at the hull of a submersible boat. One larger than his own, driven ashore right between them and Stuie. *What the hell is* he *doing here?*

A trio of crewmen, dressed for combat, burst through the topside hatch. Two of them levelled their high-powered rifles at him over the starboard railing; another dashed over toward the boat's port side, out of sight. Something went fwoosh! an instant later, followed by a pained yelp.

Oh no! Stuie!

The girl stumbled around the bow of the boat, fixing her unseeing gaze upon Mawro and Hana for a moment before her eyelids fluttered closed. She collapsed face first onto the rocky shore, affording Mawro a glimpse of the tranquilizer dart sticking up from her neck. One which would surely be filled with enough carfentanyl to drop a werecat two or three times Stuie's size. "What do you think you are doing?"

"Merely hedging my bets, *Captain*."

Oh shuffled into view. "I didn't want to take the chance of the girl darting off into the woods and delaying us," he went on as he leaned over the railing toward Mawro. "Nor did I want to take the chance of Hana shredding our precious cargo, or you preventing our escape." He pulled some sort of hand-held device from his pocket and held it out in front of him. "So, you had better keep hold of her tightly. With a press of this button, the tiny explosive package we had previously implanted at the base of her spine will detonate. Likely to render her a vegetable for life as much as it is to kill her instantly."

Equal parts fear and anger set the fur on the back of Mawro's neck on end. "You're bluffing!"

A smarmy smile enveloped Oh's face. "Am I? Need I remind you it was my troopers who brought young Lim aboard Blaznikov's ship following your escape from the Chinese?" He snorted, indicating Hana with a nod of his head. "She was Pyongyang's insurance policy that Blaznikov would tow the Party line. 'Harm not the Children of Affliction' and all that." Oh snorted. "Such sentimental rot. But it has proven eminently useful even years after his death. Just look at how fond of Hana you've become, Captain. You could hardly love her more even if she were your own daughter, no?"

Mawro swallowed, his mouth as dry as a cotton ball.

"Oh my God!"

He turned in time to glimpse Annie yank the tranquilizer dart from Stuie's neck. Then she tossed the dart into the woods and jammed her fingers up beneath the girl's jawline. "Sweetie, I'm here...Mommy's here," Annie said between sobs as she stroked at the girl's long black hair. "You're...you're going to be all right."

"She most assuredly will not be if we are not away soon. Neither will your father-in-law," Oh called to her. "But I have plenty of naloxone aboard this boat, along with a portable ventilator and an AED." He turned and winked at Mawro. "And unlike Captain Mawro's ship, *my* ship features a fully equipped trauma suite, staffed by a seasoned doctor and a nurse. Isn't that right, Captain?"

He cast a murderous gaze toward Oh until Hana began to wriggle about. Mawro hugged her tighter, taking care to squeeze the side of her face up against his chest. Both so she wouldn't bite him, and so she wouldn't suffocate.

"Okay. Fine. We'll go with you."

Mawro gaped up at Annie. Tears streamed down the sides of her face. "Don't look at me like that, Ritzi." She indicated Oh with a nod of her head. "Not like this asshole here left us much choice."

With a clap of Oh's hands, the three crewmen sprang into action. "I assure you, *madame*, you will find me the most gracious of hosts. Despite your boorish reception."

A moment later, one of Oh's crewmen made his way up the boat's gangplank cradling Stuie in his arms. Annie followed sullenly behind him, staring at her feet. The crewman quickly disappeared through the canopy hatch. "I'm sorry," she mouthed toward Ritzi before Oh pushed her head down the hatchway and out of sight.

Oh's remaining crewmen approached the boat with Mawro's father laid out on a stretcher. "There's another one lying on the beach over there," the taller of the two men said, nodding over his shoulder. "A woman. Should we go back for her?"

"Leave her," Oh replied. "That one is one of the adult werecats, and we have no need for *their* kind anymore. I've come to realize they're far, far too much trouble."

"What is that supposed to mean?" Mawro asked while the two men plodded up their boat's gangplank carrying his father. After they ducked down the open hatch, the man Mawro had previously seen carry Stuie aboard, popped back up with what looked like an anti-tank rifle over his shoulder.

"It means what usefulness you and Hana had to me is at an end," Oh answered as his man laid down atop the deck of their boat and aimed his weapon at Mawro's chest. "Now that we have the tigrine girl and the elder Doctor Opoworo with us, we have no more use for either of you. And such a bonus, having the girl's mother come also. To ensure the other two do *exactly* as they're told."

Mawro gasped as Oh's crewman racked a shell into the big weapon's chamber. "But don't worry. I'll see that your loved ones are well cared for," Oh said, holding his remote detonator aloft. "And as for Hana, I can assure you she won't feel a thing. You, on the other hand, Captain...well, my apologies. This might sting a whole lot more than a little—"

An angry yowl cut him off. A reddish-brown blur materialized on the deck of the boat beside Oh an instant later.

Tommy?

The younger man thrust his head into Oh's abdomen, knocking them both to the deck. The remote detonator flew from Oh's grasp, landing beside the boat's windscreen. With a *ki-yahp!* Tommy was back on his feet. "Shoot him! Shoot him!" Oh half cried, half gasped as he sat up. Tommy sidestepped the rifleman and kicked the detonator as hard as he could. It skittered across the deck and disappeared over the side of the boat. Giving the rifleman just enough time to draw his sidearm. And to draw a bead on the back of Tommy's head.

A shot rang out. The rifleman let out a pained cry and collapsed into Tommy, knocking them both over the railing and into the water. One of the men from below deck emerged through the hatch, an assault rifle in his hands. A second shot laid the man out flat on his back, a bullet lodged deep between his eyes.

"Kwang! Get us out of here!" Oh cried as he scurried over to the hatch. A third shot ricocheted with a tinny *ping!* off a mooring cleat beside Oh's foot. The boat backed away from the beach, engines roaring. Oh dove through the hatch and yanked it shut behind him. Then the boat came about and sped away toward open water.

"Tommy!"

Hana pulled free from Mawro's relaxed grip. After stumbling away several paces, she turned and hissed at him. Displeasure voiced at Mawro's rough handling of her, she turned again and darted off toward the tree line.

But Mawro didn't notice. He jumped into the water and fished around looking for Tommy, calling his name over and over as he thrashed about. After a moment he stopped and turned, trying to catch a glimpse of Hana. But instead, all he saw was the barrel of a sniper's rifle. With Dory Katczynski peeping at him through the sight at the other end.

"Give me one reason why I shouldn't pull this fucking trigger right now, Mawro."

"Grandpa D! Wait!"

Dory peered past Mawro's shoulder toward where Tommy waded ashore. "Son, this dirtbag trying to bribe you with some sort of waterproof exo or something?"

"These are *my* legs, G-man," Tommy said as he stepped out of the water. "My real legs."

Dory glanced back and forth between Mawro and Tommy, his rifle lost in his hands. "Oh, Niko, you were right..." he said after a moment. "No, wait. This all smells like a setup. Like some kind of trick." Nostrils flaring, he raised his rifle toward Mawro's head once more and took aim. "To distract us all while your accomplices make off with our family!"

"No, no, Grandpa D. That's not it at all," Tommy said as he crouched down and shook the water from his pelt like a dog. "Annie *agreed* to go with Oh."

Dory's mouth fell open. "I...I don't understand," he said at length. "Why...why would she...?"

Tommy hopped to his feet. "G-Nik and I were working in the basement with U-Nat ashore to reduce the chemicals we'd need to rouse Mom from her coma. Stuie went feral and started ransacking the house. Annie tried to tranq her but instead tagged G-Nik with a dart to the neck as he came up the stairs." He sighed and shook his head. "Our equipment broke his fall. Then it all exploded. Whole house went up in flames within seconds."

"So that's what happened," Dory said, his voice barely more than a whisper. "I came across Stuie in the woods earlier. Did...did everyone else get out okay?"

"Yeah, thanks to him," Tommy replied with a jab of his thumb toward Mawro. "Legs working or not—without his help, I'd've never managed to get G-Nik out in time. Then he gave A-squared what naloxone he had on hand from his boat. That's what kept G-Nik's heart beating until Oh showed up."

Dory pursed his lips. "Who offered Annie to get Niko the treatments he needed to survive *if* she and Stuie came too. Is that right?"

Tommy nodded and looked down at his feet.

Dory fixed Mawro with a searing glare. "You could've taken us nearly all out by now twice over, yet you didn't. What the fuck kind of games are you playing, man? Why would you do such a thing?"

"Because he *loves* us, G-man. You and me and everyone else." Tommy smiled a wan smile and glanced up at Mawro. "Isn't that right, Uncle Ritzi?"

With a growl, Dory resumed his firing stance. "So, that's how it is, huh? Well, then tell me, *Ritzi*, just where exactly did you and Hana leave your boat?"

Mawro nodded toward shore. "In the cove by the light tower. Right across the water from Dillinger's Hideout."

Dory gaped at him for a moment, then clicked his rifle's safety. "Which is so named on no map or chart that I know of. Bobby and I were pretty sure Dillinger dodging the cops here on his way to the U. P. to stash his stolen money was just another one of our grandfather's tall tales." He slung his rifle's strap around his shoulder and stepped up beside Tommy. "But it didn't stop my brother from spinning 'em to a new generation of starry-eyed kids who believed whatever we adults told 'em. Including my son Barry and Niko's daughter Alex." Dory rubbed at the corners of his eyes with his thumb and forefinger before turning his gaze toward Mawro. "And her brother. Ritzi."

Mawro winced and sniffled. "Thank you, Dory," he said as he stepped over next to Alex. He knelt down and picked her up, cradling her tenderly to his chest. "I'll run ahead and prep my boat. If we hurry, we likely can still catch up to Oh."

MAWRO WAS HUFFING AND puffing by the time he reached the inlet where their boat lay at anchor. He scanned the area back and forth as he approached and found no trace of Hana. By habit, he tilted his head back and sniffed at the air, regardless of his long-impaired olfactories. After calling out Hana's name, he cocked his head to listen. Hearing no reply, or any sound suggesting she might be nearby, Mawro bounded up to the fallen tree near the water's edge he had indicated earlier that evening as their rendezvous point. There he laid Alex gently down against its trunk and kissed her on the forehead. Then he turned and waded into the water, its frigid temperature invigorating him.

The boat bobbed gently up and down in water deeper than a man's height, though it came up only to the middle of Mawro's chest. He drew in his breath and ducked below the water's surface. Murky water obscuring his vision, he rubbed his hands back and forth across the boat's hull, waterline to keel, searching for any explosive devices Oh's men might have placed. Or any other evidence of sabotage, for that matter. *Merely hedging my bets, Captain* came Oh's words, playing over and over in Mawro's mind.

His inspection revealing nothing untoward, Mawro pulled himself atop the canopy and peered down through the hatch. The first aid kit from which he had taken naloxone vials and plastic syringes earlier in the evening to help Annie save his father still lay open on the seat opposite the helm, right where he had left it. He reached his arm through the hatch and fished around until he felt the carfentanyl autoinjectors. Gingerly, he took each one between two of three fingers and drew his arm back from the hatch. Not daring to breathe lest he drop them, he rolled back on his haunches and blew out his breath when at last he held the autoinjectors safe between his two fur-covered hands.

Mawro stood and clutched the autoinjectors lovingly to his chest. Dory and Tommy would be here soon, and together they would put out after Oh to rescue their loved ones. Hana would be coming with them. Whether she was conscious or not, Mawro would see to it. Oh had tried to kill her before his very eyes earlier, bragging he'd had the ability to do so for *years* already. Mawro couldn't bear the thought of letting her out of his sight again. Not now. Not ever.

"Incoming!"

He gasped and looked up to find Tommy galloping toward the water's edge. With a grunt, the young man sprang and landed atop the boat's canopy beside him. "I saw Oh and his men out there someplace!" he cried, waving his arm back and forth toward the inlet.

An angry roar came from ashore before Mawro could answer. Mawro and Tommy turned as one in time to spot Hana mid-air flying towards them, claws out, fangs bared. The younger man gasped and bunny-hopped away from Mawro before Hana landed atop the boat's canopy. Mawro jammed one of the autoinjectors into the pocket of his canvas shorts, then snapped of the plastic protector covering the needle of the other one with his thumb. Hana, consumed by her feral nature, snarled and gnashed her fangs as she raked her claws back and forth in the air between her and Tommy. "We don't...have time...for this," the younger man stammered as he evaded her attacks. "Oh's boat is launching a rocket attack right at—"

Mawro glimpsed the flash from behind an instant before he heard the *fwoosh*. With a cry, he thrust the autoinjector's needle into Hana's shoulder and bearhugged Tommy and Hana to him. Then he coiled his legs like a spring and launched the three of them together toward shore. He glanced over his shoulder as they flew, just in time to witness a rocket-propelled grenade slamming into the boat's canopy just aft of the helm.

The blast wave slammed into Mawro's back as the three of them bellyflopped atop the rocky shore. He grunted and groaned while a rain of red-hot dust and debris fell atop him, shielding Hana and Tommy from it with his own body. Once the ringing in his ears began to subside, he made out the sound of a boat motoring away from them toward the open lake at wide open throttle.

"Both of you, turn your heads to the side to breathe," he hissed. "And for God's sake, quit squirming around! Don't either of you move until I tell you it's okay." He lay there, panting through gritted teeth, silently counting to one hundred, wondering with each number whether he would pass out before the next one.

Dory called out to him as his count neared fifty. "Oh God, Ritzi, are you okay?" the other man cried as he knelt down at his side.

Mawro winced and turned his head. "Are...are they gone?" he mumbled, meeting his gaze.

"The North Koreans, you mean? Yeah, near as I can tell. I didn't see their boat anywhere, so they must be out to sea already." He glanced back and forth. "Where are the others?"

With a groan, Mawro thrust out his arms and lifted up his torso. Tommy and Hana lie there, their pelts both covered with mud and sand. After Mawro rolled back on his haunches, Tommy sat up. "Hey, gorgeous, no hard feelings about earlier, hm?" he managed in between coughs as he shook Hana by the shoulder.

"I doubt she can hear you," Mawro said before tossing the now empty autoinjector off into the woods. "That should keep her down for a while yet."

Dory nodded and shouldered his rifle. "You okay?" he asked flatly, eyeing Mawro's back.

"Smarts a bit, but I will be." Mawro leaned forward on all fours, then shook himself like a dog so as to rid his pelt of debris. "I'm a whole lot more durable than the rest of you."

"But none of us are indestructible," Dory admonished him. "So, no more heroics. Now, can you stand?"

Mawro nodded and slowly worked himself up to one knee. "C'mon, son," Dory said as he helped Tommy to his feet. "Give me a hand fetching that canoe and dragging it over here so we can get Alex and Hana back to the boathouse."

"But, Dory, I can—"

"Yes, Ritzi, but...but you shouldn't have to. We...we're all family here, right?" Without waiting for Mawro to answer, Dory waved in the direction of their burned-out cabin. "Tommy can get the generator fired up so the boathouse'll at least have lights and a little heat inside. And I can dig out the rations I'd had stowed aboard my boat to pass around." He fixed his gaze upon Hana's unconscious form and narrowed his eyes. "Then I think we all need to sit down and have ourselves a *long* talk."

Chapter Seventeen

Before dawn. **S**omewhere on the **D**oor **P**eninsula.

The trees ahead alongside the road began to glow, illuminated by the headlights of an oncoming car opposite the bend from them. Milda ducked down into the van's passenger compartment, loathe to permit any strangers to see her. Closing time for the local bars had come and gone already. Upon chancing a glimpse of her fur-covered face and pointed ears, a few passing motorists on their way home after last call might well pull over on the side of the road for a nap. More might dismiss the sight as a group of rowdy kids playing some sort of a prank or perhaps someone's derpy dog blissing out during a pre-dawn trip into town for an early breakfast. Nevertheless, neither she nor any of the rest of them wanted to take any chances. They had enough trouble to deal with already.

"Any luck yet?" Top asked without taking his eyes off the road in front of them.

She shook her head. As they began their search, Pawly's scent had been strong and easy to follow. So much so Milda had picked it out almost immediately after morphing in the back of their van. "No. Hardly a whiff since we passed the city limits."

"We'll likely have to suspend our search soon," Nat said as he scanned the landscape back and forth out the passenger seat window. "Farmers will be up before long to begin their morning chores."

Top grunted. "And it'll be light out soon after that."

Milda stuck her head back up through the van's sunroof and sniffed at the air once more. Before losing Pawly's scent, its bitter tang diminishing the further she travelled from town, the path it traced had become straighter. Pawly's rage had surely burned itself out by now. So why had she not returned already?

"She couldn't have gotten far," Milda shouted down toward the two men. "Morphing once in a day takes a lot out of you, never mind twice. She could have collapsed somewhere already for all we know. At least she won't likely move again until dusk at the earliest."

"That would suit me fine," Nat said through a yawn as he rubbed at his eyes with the heels of both palms. "I don't know about you all, but I'm running on empty. What I wouldn't give for a nap and a...right!"

Milda *tsk*ed and ducked her head back down inside the van. "A nap and a what now?"

"A right. As in 'right turn.'" Nat held out his arm, pointing toward the windshield. "Just up ahead there. I *thought* the scenery was starting to look familiar."

She looked up at a large sign alongside the road with RACZKA FARMS emblazoned across it in big white letters. "Glad it does to someone," Top replied as he flicked on his turn signal and began slowing down.

"Where are you taking us, exactly?" Milda asked.

"I remember coming here a time or two with Annie to pick up Pawly on our way back to Chicago from the cabin. That farm is owned by her friend Lana's grandparents."

"Oh, good thinking!" she replied and crouched down behind Top's seat. "Pawly might well be lucid soon if she's not already. She'll likely look for someplace familiar where she can lay low until her shed is complete."

"Like their barn's hayloft," Top added.

Milda tipped back her head and sniffed. "Especially her knowing all this manure around camouflages her scent from someone like me."

"As good a place as any for us to check out," Top said as he completed his turn and began to accelerate again. About a mile down the deserted highway, Top turned off onto a gravel drive beside a clearing.

"The sign we passed on the highway said 'right *two* miles,' Top," Nat said as they rolled up to stone kiosk opposite the drive from a hand pump and a pair of wooden picnic tables. "Why are we stopping here at this wayside?"

Top killed the engine and shut off the lights. "Better to originate our reconnaissance patrol from here. An unfamiliar vehicle pulled off on the side of the road anywhere else around here this time of night is going to garner attention," he said, nodding up the road in the direction of the farm before he exited the vehicle. "Besides, I needed to make a pit stop."

Nat stepped out and pulled open the van's sliding door. An earnest groaning drew Milda's gaze toward the man seated on the floor toward the back of the van. Trying to talk through the gag in his mouth, he wiggled his hands back and forth as far as the handcuffs securing both of his wrists to the van wall allowed. "Tell Top that Lenny here might need one too." He nodded, mumbling what well could have been a "thank you" though Milda could hardly tell for sure.

She hopped out of the van in time to glimpse Top step inside a little brick hut situated at the corner of the clearing opposite them. Milda took a sniff and wrinkled her nose; the thing was an outhouse, just as she had suspected. At least it would cover their scents as they approached the farm.

Seeing no one around outside save for Nat, Milda bounded across the clearing and hopped atop a fencepost. With a grunt, she pushed off and landed on the sturdy limb of a beech tree overhead. With the limb's spring buds only now beginning to form and otherwise devoid of leaves, Milda quickly and silently clawed her way to the top. From her perch high above the parking lot, she surveyed the Raczka family's pasturelands spreading out before her beyond the wooded area surrounding the wayside. Lake Michigan bordered on one side, its waters lapping quietly at the shore now that the storm had blown through. Opposite it lay the highway with the roof of another farmhouse visible in the distance. The Raczka's sleeping cattle huddled together around an enormous knotty old oak tree situated in the center of the pasture. Milda leaned her head back and sniffed at the air once more. She detected no trace of the overpowering stench of manure nor any of Pawly's scent, suggesting the wayside was either upwind or crosswind to the farm. They would need to approach cautiously, taking wind direction and velocity always into account, if they hoped to catch Pawly unawares.

Milda hopscotched from branch to branch until she landed near where Nat sat at a picnic table closest to the outhouse. Just as she opened her mouth to address him the outhouse door creaked open and Top emerged. After easing the door shut so as to prevent it from slamming, he turned to them with his satellite phone to his ear and a horrified look on his face. "Yeah, Nat and Milda are both right here. No one else around, near as I can...what? Lenny? Oh, he's in the van…no, he can't come to the phone. Yeah, still indisposed…right, Milda's helping us track down Pawly and I didn't need *his* fool ass going off on his own trying to find her. Now hold on, let me put you on hands-free…"

"…Nat, can you hear me?" came Dory's voice through the speaker in Top's satellite phone a moment later. "Something urgent you need to know."

"I'm here, Dory," Nat replied. Top sat down at the picnic table and slid his phone over to him. "What's going on? Is anyone hurt?"

"No one is hurt, near as we can tell. But the DPRK strike force ambushed us on the island. They got away, taking Annie and Stuie and Niko with them."

Nat's eyes went wide. He pushed himself away from the phone and stood up, his lower lip trembling. "No…no…" he mumbled as he stepped over the seat of the picnic table and stared off toward the tree line. "It…it can't be…"

"It's a cluster over here," Dory went on. "From what Tommy tells me, Stuie showed up raging and Annie tried to tag her with a tranq dart. She missed and hit Niko in the neck. Then he fell down the stairs and knocked over the equipment reducing the chemicals they need to give to Alex. Cabin went up like paper in fire."

Milda rose and stepped up behind Nat. She began to rub at his shoulders and glanced over toward Top. "But everyone made it out okay, right?" she said in a loud voice in the speakerphone's general direction.

"Yes. Tommy and Mawro saved them."

Nat furrowed his brow. "Why would he do that?"

"Same question I asked Tommy. Right before he told me Mawro is…is *Ritzi*."

With a gasp, Nat pulled away from Milda and dashed over to the picnic table. "What? Ritzi? *Ritzi?* Are you sure? Completely sure?" he said as he slid to a stop on the seat beside the phone. "How is that even possible? And Tommy...how, how can he even—"

"Yes, I'm completely sure. And for the other questions, well, I don't know. Nor do I know how Tommy is managing to walk and jump around without his exo. All I know is he *is*. His exo was lost in the fire."

Nat groaned and rubbed at his face with both hands.

"Yeah, it's a lot for me to take in too, son," Dory went on. "We intend to ask Ritzi many, *many* questions though, just as soon as you get here. Like just where he thinks General Oh might have taken Annie and Stuie and Niko."

Top slammed his fists down atop the table. "No! The island is still a hot zone! We can't risk the civilians any more than we—"

"Oh's strike team has already scored their hat trick, Topper. I don't expect them to return. Especially after ditching their werecat Dynamic Duo."

"Hana's still there too?" Top cocked an eyebrow. "Sounds like a setup to me, boss."

"Yes, Topper, I agree, which is why we've securely restrained them both. Managed to salvage the anchor chain and hauling line from my boat that they wrecked. Mawro was obliging enough to tranq Hana for us so she wouldn't cause a fuss." Dory sighed. "And the cabin is a complete loss, I'm afraid. Fortunately, everyone evac'ed to the point so Annie could try and get a cellular call through after Tommy's satellite phone was lost in the fire. Oh and his people were waiting for them just offshore."

Nat sat upright and crossed his arms over his chest. "How am I supposed to even get to the island, Dory? Hana scuttled both of Bobby's boats and I can't hardly swim there."

"Yes, which is why my old service buddy Irwin MacElroy and his helicopter are standing by on the tarmac in Sturgeon Bay. Mac can be trusted to be discreet, but I don't want him seeing anything 'classified' if we can at all help it."

Top looked up from the speakerphone and met Nat's gaze. "I'll call Washington right after I hang up with you, Dory."

"Good. Get 'em to charter a work boat with an open stern and a container so we can keep everyone out of sight. Have 'em crew it with their own people so we don't have to risk our friends and family being seen by anyone we can't trust."

"Why? The werecats will have changed back by then. Won't an open top runabout do?"

"Hana and Tommy will have, sure, but not Ritzi. Remember that thing eyewitness claimed to see along the river in Szczecin during the university incident?"

"Big as a gorilla, covered in fur, tufted ears?"

"Yeah, that's right. And massive fangs like a saber-toothed cat, don't forget. Suffice to say I no longer have any reason to doubt them now."

"Huh." Top blinked and shook his head. "Alrighty, then. Guess I ought to ask the spooks to get word out. About a crooked shipowner dynamiting two of his own leaky old tubs at their moorings, trying to collect an insurance payout."

"Sounds like as good a cover story as any, Topper. I'll call Mac as soon as I get off the phone with you and get him coming your way. He can do a touch-and-go on the roof of the warehouse to get Nat and then ferry him to the island."

Top *tsk*ed. "We might be a while."

"Why? It's dark out so it's not like you'll be sightseeing. Shouldn't take you more than an hour!"

"Bobby's back in Northport at the RV trying to raise anybody who can come pump out the *Casimir*. The rest of us are together in the service van."

"And I still haven't found Pawly yet, love," Milda added on to Top's reply.

"But you've all been searching for hours now!"

"Her rage likely worked itself out by now, Dory," Nat said, rubbing at his face with both hands. "Given the circumstances, I'm pretty sure she doesn't even *want* to be found."

An uneasy silence fell over them all. "So just where are you, anyway?" Dory asked at length.

"Not far from Egg Harbor," Nat said. "Near the farm Pawly used to sleep over at with her friend back in high school while the rest of us went to the island."

"Right, so let me sign off and get our man here back to town," Top added with a wave of his hand toward Nat. "I'll pick everyone else up after he's away. And hopefully Pawly too."

"Fine. Once you've found her, get yourselves all back to the RV. Hunker down while we all figure out what to do next."

With that Top's phone beeped, indicating Dory had hung up. "Look, I'm pretty shook up about my family being taken and all," Nat said as Top stood, "but getting me to the island can wait."

"Nonsense. We need more details before we can come up with a plan. Details Dory will need your help sussing out of what's-his-face sooner rather than later." He pointed toward the outhouse. "Speak now or forever hold your peace. We need to get going."

Nat glanced over at Milda and narrowed his eyes. "I have no doubt in her skill as a tracker or a fighter. But I don't think it's fair we burden her with bringing Pawly back all by herself."

"She won't have to."

Top pulled a ring of keys out of his pants pocket and strode over to the back of the van. A moment later Lenny stood beside him, swaying from side to side as Top removed his gag.

"Here's your chance to get Pawly back, you lovesick twit. Fuck this up, though, and I'll put your sorry ass on the first bus I can find back to Chesapeake!"

A short time later.

L ENNY WATCHED MILDA AS she pushed off from atop the fencepost, coming to land on the one adjacent to it. Once, twice, three times more, the older woman stole a glance over her shoulder across the pasture toward him. Her tufted ears drew back as she tapped her index finger to her lips, reminding him to keep silent. Lenny nodded in reply before the woman bounded out of sight along the fencerow.

He turned and began tiptoeing along the meadow's perimeter, cradling the air rifle Top had handed him before leaving to deliver Nat to his waiting helicopter. The Raczka herd stood huddled together some distance away around the knotted old oak in the center of the meadow. Milda's words turned in his mind, the older woman having just finished warning him how skittish herd animals like cattle could be at night. One loud noise, one careless move upwind of the herd, one spooked animal alerting the rest could well result in a stampede. Milda herself had told Lenny just moments before she had seen it happen firsthand back in the Białowieża Forest, the stampeding bison snapping tree trunks big around as a person's wrist as though they were toothpicks. But unlike the Forest, Milda had been quick to point out, she and Lenny found themselves here surrounded by pastureland. With no trees anywhere nearby in which she could vault them both to safety so as to avoid being trampled under hoof.

That was hardly the only risk they faced. They might be unlucky enough for someone in the farmhouse to glimpse him and Milda skulking about their meadow like a pair of would-be cattle rustlers. Away from Door County's tourist traps, every pick-up around here likely as not had a gun rack in the back window. Along with a driver inclined to shoot first and ask questions later.

The cows at the edge of the herd stood a silent vigil over their herd mates, turning their heads to follow Lenny's movements along the fence line. Whether the cold or the unblinking gaze of these four-legged butter churns accounted more for his shivering, he didn't know. But he *did* know the sooner Milda finished her sweep, the sooner he could rest easier knowing Pawly was safe. And the sooner all of them could get the hell out of here.

He yelped and stumbled forward after his foot sank into the soft earth up past his ankle. A loud thumping sound rose up opposite the herd from him. Followed by a blood-curdling yowl.

With a gasp, Lenny darted his gaze back and forth across the meadow toward where he had last seen Milda. But where *was* she? The ground beneath him began to rumble an instant before he heard the sound. One that to his ear all too well resembled that of an oncoming freight train.

Lenny cried out as he turned around, staring up at the herd of frenzied cattle bearing down on him. He jumped up and tried to run, but the muddy ground held his foot fast. After planting his face, he rolled onto his back and raised his head. His gaze met the wild, unseeing eyes of dozens of panicked animals. Each the size of a refrigerator, each weighing nearly as much as an automobile.

Each bearing down on him.

A flash of rusty brown streaked by beside him an instant before a pair of hands clenched tight around his shoulders. Whoever it was let out a throaty snarl and gave a yank. After a juicy *schlorp*, his boot pulled free and he flew through the air. Stabbing pain in his shoulders had barely registered before he hit the ground, tumbling end for end until he finally came to rest at the edge of the meadow near the adjoining fencerow.

Lenny rolled up onto his back and groaned, pain rolling across his chest and back as if his shoulders had been dislocated.

"You *stupid* fucker! You could've been killed!"

Pawly?

She knelt down beside him and brought her hand close to his face. Lenny wrinkled his nose by reflex as the strong smell of cow manure wafted over him.

"Yeah, I smell like shit. Not like I had time to bathe, you know." Pawly drew her palms to either side of his head and rubbed along his neck and shoulders. "And, for the record, I never *asked* for your fool ass to show up out here." She *tsk*ed and shook her head. "Playing hopscotch across a pastureland littered with bunny burrows."

After smoothing her hands across the rest of his body, Pawly tugged the hem of the flannel shirt she'd borrowed from him down past the waist of her cutoffs. "Doesn't feel like you've broken anything. Think you can stand?"

With a groan, Lenny nodded and sat up. Pawly rolled back onto her haunches and sprang to her feet, then offered her hand to him. He grasped and pulled, she pulling in return to help him into a more-or-less standing position. "Look, you *know* that I will always—"

She waved one fur-covered finger in front of his nose to shush him. "I was hungry, you know. I've been waiting all night to hunt, knowing rabbits are active at dawn and dusk. Figured you all would give up looking for me by daybreak." Pawly glanced over one shoulder and then the other before continuing. "When Milda showed up, I slathered cowpies all over myself to disguise my scent from her and the cows both. Then I hunkered down in the middle of the herd to wait you out."

With a sigh, Pawly hugged her chest tightly and turned away. "My animal brain sensed the rabbit's warning when you stepped into the burrow across the field. My human brain checked out and I flayed the thing alive in one swipe."

She turned back toward him, the moonlight glinting off the tears welling up in her eyes. "It felt wonderful, Lenny. Because I didn't...I didn't feel *anything*. Didn't have to think about...my dad. How...how I..."

"But it was an accident."

Pawly roared and snagged the collar of his jacket in her claws. "You don't think I *know* that, dumbass? Doesn't make up for the fact that I was the one who went feral, that was the one who lost control. That my dad would still be alive today if...if I hadn't..."

She choked out a sob and let go. Lenny managed to stumble and catch himself as Pawly turned her back to him. "I never want to see myself in a mirror again. Never want to find myself eye to eye with my dad's murderer. Never...never want to risk losing control again, risk hurting someone else I love. Even a stupid fucker like you."

Lenny stared down at the ground and smoothed out the rumpled front of his jacket with both hands. "But where...where would you go?"

"I...I don't know. Stow away on the back of a truck bound for Minneapolis, I guess. Catch out on the first intermodal train I could find heading west." Pawly stared up at the lightening sky and shrugged. "Bail out somewhere inside Glacier National Park. Spend the rest of my life hunting rabbits while I slowly go completely feral."

Lenny shook his head and turned away. "So that's the way it is, huh?" He spread his arms skyward. "I guess this is all *your* world, then. And I just live in it."

"Wait, Lenny, I—"

He turned and met her gaze. "So, I'm just supposed to accept that you're always going to run off and do your own thing? Just like you did after Chah Bahar?" he cried, his nostrils flaring. "What about me? What about *us*? Is there an 'us'? Was there ever an 'us' in the first place?"

Lenny rubbed at his face with both hands. "You know what? This can wait. 'Us' can wait. Right now, your family needs you."

Pawly blinked. "What about my family? Aaah!"

Hearing Pawly's pained cry, Lenny glanced up to find Milda standing behind her. Blood began to trickle down the front of Pawly's flannel shirt from where the elder woman's claws had pierced through skin beneath. "He's right, *Pawlina*."

With a snarl, Milda yanked Pawly to her and muttered into her ear through gritted teeth. Pawly screwed up her face before crying out "Annie? Stuie? *And* Grandpa N? Oh no! Oh God, no!"

"Hey! Who's out there?" came a man's voice from the direction of the farmhouse. The three of them turned as one toward two men, one with gray hair and one with brown, both dressed in T-shirts and sweatpants. The men stood shoulder-to-shoulder on the house's back porch, gazing out across the meadow, each holding one hand to his forehead. And gripping a shotgun in his other.

Milda yanked her claw free from Pawly's shoulder. "There's more to tell, but it will keep," she said as she took hold of Lenny's arm. "Help me get him out of here before the farmer and his son spot us and start shooting."

Pawly clutched at her wounded shoulder for a moment before falling in next to Lenny. After coaxing his arm over her good shoulder, Pawly threw Milda a nod and crouched down. With a grunt the two women bounded off toward the tree line. Lenny peered over his shoulder and glimpsed the sun's rays breaking over the distant horizon, lighting up the sky with hues of pink and orange and scarlet.

Red sky at morning, sailor take warning...

Chapter Eighteen

Dusk, that evening. Chicago's South Side.

Pawly rubbed at her eyes and leaned her back up against the ventilator shaft behind her. Cars and trucks whizzed by on the Chicago Skyway above her perch atop the warehouse roof. Below her, the surface of the Calumet River twinkled in the setting sun. She and her family and their friends had left Door County at first light that morning, even before completing her shed.

They had holed up since in the warehouse beside her great uncle Bobby's boat pier, most of the time tripping over each other in the cramped apartment nestled away in the corner of the mezzanine. Following their escape from Cold War-era Poland with a young Mom and Uncle Ritzi in tow, Grandpa N and *Halmonim* had fashioned it with their own hands from a long-disused production office. What today would barely pass for a studio, the four of them called "home" until shortly after Grandpa N earned tenure at Loyola. Near the same time, Grandpa D had come to possess the apartment building where Grandpa N moved his family, shortly before Uncle Nat had been born. By then, they had all learned how to predict and contain Mom and Uncle Ritzi's feral urges, on account in part of the apartment's secluded location. Which had certainly come in handy for Mom and Dad when she and Tommy had to moved to town, her and her brother both needing to learn likewise in a hurry.

Mom had the single full-size bed in the middle of the room to herself. The rest of them hot-racked on a pair of couches, one pushed up against each adjacent wall, or on one or another air mattresses spread out across the remaining floor. The tiny bathroom had been in use nearly non-stop following their arrival, what with all the werecats shedding and scrubbing and the rest each trying to catch a shower in between. Pawly had done so twice already, believing it might help her nap after being up for nearly thirty-six hours already. But no amount of hot water could purge the horrific images from her Uncle Ritzi's lab of her dad's eviscerated body, his intestines strewn about the floor, flashing through her mind anew every time she closed her eyes. So, she creaked and clanked her way up the spindly spiral staircase to the roof to get some air. Along with a heaping helping of solitude.

A gust of wind on the bare skin of her face and neck made Pawly shiver. She drew the hood of her sweatshirt up over her head and tugged at its drawstrings. It would be another month or so before the wind gave up its bite for the warm caress of summer breezes. At least she had that long to enjoy the evening air before the mosquitoes returned.

She stood, silently thanking her family and friends. They had made good today their collective promise to give her space to sort out her emotions—so long as there was nothing new to report about her mother's condition. Which meant she was still in a coma.

creak creak clank clunk

Pawly snarled, hearing footsteps plodding up the metal staircase below. She crossed her arms and fixed the roof door with her best murder stare as its handle turned and Lenny stepped through. "I *thought* I'd made it clear to you that I—"

"I'm not here of my own volition," he replied with a shake of his head. "Nat sent me to tell you your mom's vitals are steadily improving. She ought to be coming around soon."

She gasped and drew up beside him, her hands clasped together in front of her. "Really? That's...that's great!"

"Yeah. It sure is." Lenny cupped her hands with his and gave them a squeeze. "Apparently, they were able to extract out of Tommy whatever they think gave him back the use of his legs. Then after Jakub and his truck got here with the MGS, they replicated enough of the stuff to treat your mom."

Pawly cocked an eyebrow at him. "Who's 'they'?"

"Nat. Together with that Mawro guy."

She tugged gently on his hands, indicating he ought to follow her. "C'mon. I want to show you something."

They stepped over to the far edge of the roof in time to glimpse the sun ducking behind the massive concrete grain bins opposite Lake Calumet from them. There, Pawly waved her arms toward an empty pier upstream and across the channel. "That's where Uncle Ritzi's lab used to be, right there. The place where our lives all fell apart. Where Top's wife decided to leave him. Where...where my dad died. Where my Uncle Ritzi...that 'Mawro guy'..."

He waved his open palms side to side in front of him. "Hey, I know you're not okay. If you don't want to talk about this right now, I under—"

"No, no," Pawly said, shaking her head. "I want to talk about it. I...I *need* to talk about it." She looked up and met his gaze. "With you. Because, whether I like it or not, this is a part of who I am. A...a part that I'd like for you to finally know. To...to *fully* know."

Lenny took her hand in his and led her over to the edge of a skylight. "Go on," he said, motioning for her to sit.

"We'd all thought Ritzi had died that night, you know. There was an explosion. One I..."

Lenny patted at her back as he took a seat beside her. She took a deep breath and blew it out before continuing. "One I apparently caused during my rage. But Ritzi's body was never found. The Chicago coroner declared him deceased about a year later."

"Guess that means only Blaznikov knew Mawro was really Ritzi, then."

"Yeah, and he wasn't about to tell anyone he didn't absolutely have to. I'm pretty sure he kept Hana in the dark about it, too. Apparently, Grandpa N figured it out though, during the raid on his lab in Szczecin."

Lenny gawked at her. "And he didn't *tell* anybody? That was, what...three months ago now? Almost four?"

She swallowed her lips. "Yeah, that question's been nagging at me all day too."

His stomach gurgled loudly in reply. "Oh, speaking of nagging," Lenny said, drawing his hands together over his abdomen. "One of the men from the security detail Top assigned us said he'd pick us all up some take-out."

Pawly made a face. "And I suppose you won't take 'I'm not hungry' for an answer, will you?"

"Nuh-uh."

"Okay, fine, whatever," she replied with a roll of her eyes. "When's he supposed to head out?"

"As soon as Dory and Nat get back from picking up your grandmother from the airport."

Pawly *tsk*ed. "Pity that we'll miss the pyrotechnics. I'm sure *Halmonim*'ll be cussing them both out in three languages having learned Hana is Stuie's birth mother. Especially after having an entire non-stop flight from Warsaw to grind her axe."

Lenny snorted in reply and drew a folded-up piece of paper from his back pants pocket. "You know this place?" he asked as he held it out to her.

Pawly looked down at the paper, a tri-fold color glossy menu from a hole-in-the-wall Thai place in the neighborhood. "Oh, yeah," she replied, cracking a wan smile. "Their red curry was Sally's favorite. Her stepdad's shop was just downriver from here, so she'd order from this place whenever Tommy and me sortied. Delivery guy would stick the food in the mailbox after taking out the money Sally'd put in there for him. Just to make sure nobody would see us."

"What say you and me order ourselves a whole heap of red curry, then? In Sally's honor?"

"I think that'd be wonderful," she replied, her voice husky.

"Let's go then," he said, taking her hand in his as he stood. "She'd always go looking for you whenever you wandered off by yourself, too."

Pawly sobbed and threw her arms around him. "Don't...don't let me be alone," she whispered as she clutched at him. "Not anymore. I've...I've been alone far too long."

Lenny clasped his hands together across the small of Pawly's back and drew her to him. "Not a chance."

"Thank you. It's what Sally would have wanted, right?" she breathed, drawing her lips to his.

"She's not the only one, love."

ELSEWHERE IN THE WAREHOUSE. A SHORT WHILE LATER.

MAWRO CLUTCHED HIS MOTHER to him as she sobbed into his shoulder, both of them too overwhelmed with emotion to do much else. He patted the back of her head with his fur-covered hand, crying anew spotting more than one streak of silver taking over her formerly pristine jet-black hair. Reminding him of all the time that had passed, time to love and to be loved, without either having happened. Time which none of them would ever get back.

In the space between, Hana and Mawro had come to fill that role for one another. He would see to it that neither he nor his family lost any more such time, see to it that Hana was not losing him but instead gaining *them*. Though the latter, he knew, would prove a daunting task. Mawro had remained by Hana's side the whole trip here to the warehouse, her still languishing in the drugged stupor he himself had induced the night before. Since their arrival, Hana had been sequestered in the armored tool crib. It had once been dedicated to storing explosives for Bobby's marine salvage and demolition efforts, being impervious to stray RF transmissions which might have caused blasting caps to detonate. Because far too many questions remained unanswered. How close *did* Oh or his men have to be to detonate the explosive device he claimed to have had implanted in Hana's neck years before? Could they detonate it by remote control somehow? Could they broadcast such a command via the commercial wireless network? Would Hana be forced to live out her life shielded from cellular signals or other RF transmissions? Or would she be required to isolate herself forever from them, separated by distance or geography or both? These thoughts flooded Mawro's mind, crowding out whatever joy he might have felt being reunited with his adoptive mother at long last.

"We must get to work now, *adeunim*. Yes."

Mawro glanced down to find his mother staring back at him, her eyes puffy and red. She sniffled and nodded toward the tool crib across the shop floor from them. "Take me to the *Chosŏn* woman."

He replied with a grunt and drew himself up to his full height. On one knee, his mother's head came to his shoulder. Standing now, he noticed she was barely as tall as his navel. "Of course, *Eomeonim*. This way."

Dory and Nat fell in beside Mawro and his mother. Together they trundled off across the high bay area, Dory and Nat each lugging one of the two hard plastic instrument cases his mother had brought along. After picking his mother up from the airport, the two men had stopped off at the Brookfield Zoo's examination room to pick up a portable MRI scanner. His mother would use the instruments to search out and mark the precise location of Hana's explosive implant. Then, together, they would assess just what actual threat Hana's implant posed—both to her and to anyone within any proximity.

"She's in there," Dory said, pointing toward the first door to the left of the tool crib. His mother held the door open for Nat and Dory. Mawro bent at his waist and shuffled in after them. His mother closed the door behind herself and gazed about the room for a moment while Dory and Nat lugged the crates over to the gurney Hana lay upon. "You keep her so for *how* long?" she asked, drawing her hands to her hips.

"She's been strapped to that gurney since coming ashore at North-port. Before that we'd kept her secured to one of the litters aboard the *Forty-Four*."

His mother *harrumph*ed and tugged at Hana's bindings. "Need to loosen these from time to time. To maintain circulation. Yes." She turned and met Dory's gaze. "I brought more naloxone. Would like to wake her up once we're finished. For full physical examination."

Dory pursed his lips. "We might have to wait until after we've eaten. Top's men should be here before long with our dinner." He nodded toward Mawro. "Including an entire roasted goose all for you, big guy."

"It is okay. I can administer naloxone when we finish the scans. She likely will not be awake yet following our dinner. But just in case..."

His mother slung her daypack off her shoulder and took a knee on the floor beside Hana's gurney. "Loosen her restraints one at a time while I run scans," she said while she unzipped her daypack and began rummaging around inside. "Massage the tissue underneath and then cinch them back up—oh, good. Here it is."

Mawro's eyes went wide at the sight of the ball gag his mother produced from her pack. "Merely a precaution. To keep her from biting through her tongue should she come around before our return," she said in answer to his questioning stare.

"Is that...is that necessary, *Eomeonim*?"

She shrugged. "You should know. Yes. DPRK agents are trained upon capture to bite through their tongues and bleed out. Lest they betray Party secrets during...torture."

"Which, at the end of the day, Hana *is*, Ritzi," Dory added, reaching up to pat Mawro on the shoulder. "And for all she knows, you and her both have been captured by enemy forces and are being held against your will."

His mother nodded and worked the ball gag into Hana's mouth. "She should respond with favor to seeing you, *adeunim*. And I shall tell her I too grew up in Ryanggang Province. So, she might consent to a full physical exam. But first thing is first," she said, waving toward the crates containing the portable MRI.

Under his mother's direction, Nat and Dory finished uncrating the components and untangling the knot of cables jammed into the bottom of each box. Before long they had the system powered up and running through its self-test sequence.

A projector sitting at the center of a makeshift table constructed from two sawhorses and a sheet of plywood whirred to life once their mother began scanning. Nat knelt in front of a folding chair beside Hana's gurney near her head, tapping at the keys of the laptop connected to the projector. A replica of the laptop's screen then appeared on the heavy canvas hung on the far wall.

Dory took a seat on a wooden bench while Mawro shuffled to the back of the room and plunked down on the floor. Images of Hana's spine and skull flashed back and forth across their improvised big screen as his mother manipulated the instrument across her face and neck and chest and shoulders.

"Wait, *Eomeonim*. Is that it?"

Mawro narrowed his eyes toward a white spot on the screen, about the side of a dime, to which Nat pointed.

"I believe that is our detonator. Yes." Their mother clicked a button on her instrument, increasing the magnification of the screen's grainy image. It indeed appeared to be a small rectangular metal object situated beneath where Hana's head met her neck. "Picture is not great. But I cannot figure what else that thing *could* be."

Dory gasped. "Holy shit. Damn thing's lodged right up against the back of her atlas, if I'm not mistaken."

"You are not," she said, her eyes never leaving the screen. "Detonation pressure. How much?"

Dory sucked in his breath. "I'd heard rumors of DPRK making and marketing such devices, but this is the first time I've ever seen one in actual use myself." He massaged at his forehead with one hand. "C-4 and Semtex each produce detonation pressures in the neighborhood of 250 kilobars, but hard to say what exactly that thing's formulary is."

Mawro gnawed at one knuckle. "Is that enough to kill her if that...that *thing* went off?"

His mother turned to face him. "The force from detonation. Would launch the *Chosŏn* woman's atlas right through her spinal column. Yes."

Shredding Hana's brain stem in the process, as Mawro well knew. The part that controlled body's autonomous functions. Like breathing. He gulped.

His mother blew out her breath and shook her head. "I am sorry, *adeunim*. Truly sorry."

Dory indulged them a moment's respectful silence until asking a question Mawro knew needed asking. "Does the detonator pose an eminent threat to anyone else?"

"I do not believe so," Mawro's mother said, in answer to Dory's question. "It should not be difficult to remove with surgery. That is, if..."

"If what, *Eomeonim*?" Mawro cried, his voice jumping a half-octave.

"We needs must to figure out how to trick the device into not exploding," she replied as she rubbed at her temple. "Somehow. Yes."

Dory's phone chimed just at that moment.

"Which we've got a plan for, big guy. I'll explain over dinner." He fished his phone from his pocket and swiped at the thing's screen with his thumb. "Top's man just arrived with our food. I have to go get it from him because none of 'em except Top himself is allowed back here." He looked up and fixed Mawro's mother in his gaze. "Your call, Sunny," he said, nodding at Hana's still-unconscious form. "If you want to administer the naloxone now, we can check in on her right after dinner."

"It would be best. Then we can finish what we need tonight." She stretched out her arms and yawned. "It has been a long day for all of us. Yes."

Dory snorted. "For you especially. You're the only one here who's crossed seven time zones today."

"I'll help you wrap up, *Eomeonim*," Nat said.

Dory patted at Mawro's shoulder. "Guess you're with me, big guy."

Mawro shimmied himself along the floor with his hands until he reached the door. Then he crouched and bunny-hopped through the open doorway until he was back in the high-bay area. He groaned as he stood, rolling his shoulders and rotating his upper body back and forth at the waist. Growing old was bad enough. Growing old unable to locate a masseuse willing to take on a permanently transformed werecat client would be worse.

L ENNY GAVE PAWLY'S HAND a squeeze as the freight elevator lurched to a stop. She replied in kind before gripping the handles of her mother's wheelchair. "C'mon, Mom, let's go find Uncle Ritzi. I know he's eager to see you. *Halmonim* ought to be around here somewhere, too."

Her mother looked up at Pawly and blinked. Tommy and Pawly and Lenny and Nat had all been there when she had finally come around. The twins' mother appeared grateful for the tea and broth offered her, though she had uttered little beyond an occasional grunt or groan. "She'll likely be out of it yet for another day or so," Nat had assured them before excusing himself to help her grandmother examine Hana. "Her body's been through the wringer a whole lot more than any of the rest of us have."

Pawly and Lenny and Tommy had stayed with her, talking and laughing and carrying on. She responded graciously, with frequent nods and smiles. At least until they had told her that Ritzi was here. Then she seemed to draw into herself, in fact, they had all but had to manhandle her into the wheelchair. Nat had rung them on the house phone indicating their dinner had arrived. And to relay *Halmonim*'s request the twins bring their mother down to try and get some solid food into her.

So Pawly wasn't exactly sure what to expect after Tommy slid the scissor gate open. She pushed her mother's wheelchair into the warehouse and sniffed at the air. Even in her human form, she could tell Uncle Ritzi was around here somewhere. But not nearby.

She knit her brow and glanced over at Tommy. "They're likely over there," he said in answer to her silent question. Raising one arm, he pointed across the shop floor toward the tool crib. "Hana's in the room next door."

Grandpa D stepped through the door as they approached. Uncle Ritzi shuffled along behind, turning away as he stood and stretched. "Oh, hi, kids," Grandpa D said upon recognizing them. He reached up and patted at their uncle's furry side. "And look, Ritzi. Look who's here."

He turned and faced them, his eyes going wide at the sight of the twins' mother, seated in her wheelchair. His panicked stink wafted through the air all around them, strong enough to make Pawly wince. "Alex...Alex, I..."

An angry yowl drew Pawly's attention back toward their mother. Fur already covered her face and forearms as she leapt up out of her chair and launched herself at Ritzi.

"You!"

With a cry, she drew back her fist and landed a punch on the tip of Ritzi's muzzle. He howled and dropped to one knee, cradling his nose between his big furry hands.

Their mother landed and stomped back to face him, panting as if she had just finished one of her marathon training sessions. "How *could* you, Ritzi?" she said, her voice cracking. "Bad enough you abandoned our family, but you had to take that damn tape with you?"

She buried her face in her hands and began to cry. "What were you thinking?" she asked between sobs. "Letting Pawly see it?"

After Tommy exchanged a confused look with Pawly, she patted at Lenny's shoulder. He nodded in silent reply, understanding her message—*let me handle this*. She met eyes with Tommy, then glanced over toward their mother. "Is...is that what you were searching for after the fire, Mom?" Pawly asked as she and Tommy stepped up beside her. She reached out her hand and patted at the back of their mother's gown between her shoulders. A glance toward Tommy revealed a mirror of Pawly's own pained expression. "After Dad..."

Their mother sucked in her breath, holding it for a moment before blowing it out in a rush. "Yes. Yes, it was," she replied at length, her voice barely a whisper. "I searched frantically through the rubble to find that stupid tape. I panicked and went feral, being unable to find it." She gazed up at Ritzi, wiping tears from the fur around her eyes with her thumb and forefinger. "Now...now I know why I couldn't."

Pawly gasped with surprise after her mother grabbed her by the shoulders. "I'm sorry, dear, I...I'm so, so sorry," their mother said in a tremulous voice, shaking Pawly's shoulders with every word. "I was there, I...I *knew*. I've been keeping that secret ever since that horrible night, fearing I'd lose you just as certain as I lost Barry if I told anyone. Ever." Pawly bit her lip as her mother's claws poked through her sleeve and into her skin. "Every waking moment since I've been trying...trying to figure out how to tell you...searching for the right words but they don't come...they never come..."

She fell forward onto her knees and clutched at Pawly's waist, sobbing anew. Pawly reached down and caressed her back, while Tommy crouched beside her and circled her with his arms. Lenny drew up behind Pawly and hugged her to him as she cooed over and over "It's okay, Mom. Mom, it's okay."

They all remained together that way for some time. After giving vent to her grief and anger and pain, her mother's breathing resumed its normal cadence. Pawly patted at her back, knowing her mother's force of will had asserted itself once more.

Their Grandpa D, standing beside the tool crib door, nodded toward their Uncle Ritzi. "After our debriefing, I'm confident Ritzi was unaware Oh even *had* the tape." He took two steps their way and then stopped, as if desiring to keep a respectful distance between them. "Nor had any idea of how Oh planned to use it."

Ritzi shook his head. "He couldn't have asked for a better distraction while he took his captives." He gestured toward the room where Hana lay and *hmph*ed. "Even if he'd asked her and me to give him one."

"All the more reason should get set down around table now," Grandpa D replied as he stepped up beside Pawly and Tommy and their mother. "Everyone's food is getting cold, the others will begin to worry, and I need to lay out the plan me and Monsignor Dryzek came up with to rescue our loved ones. Then we ought to all try and get some rest. We've all got a helluva week ahead of us."

Chapter Nineteen

Forty-eight hours later.

Telltale grunts and yowls echoed throughout the high-bay area as Mawro and his mother exited the freight elevator. A cry from above their heads drew their attention toward where Tommy vaulted from one roofing truss to another, with Hana right behind. After a moment, Tommy dove for the warehouse floor beyond with fangs bared and claws out. He rolled through his landing and stood up, his hands clasped tightly around the middle of an enormous rat, easily the size of a rabbit. Hana drew up beside him with a howl an instant before her jaws snapped shut over top of the rat's head and neck. She wrenched her head to one side, tearing the rat's head clean off of its body. "Hey, get your own!" Tommy protested while Hana shot him a self-satisfied smirk. She mimed a *moi?* gesture as she chewed then dashed across the warehouse floor, apparently scoping out more prey with which to sate her bloodlust. Tommy tore a hunk of the rat's flesh with his teeth before chasing after her.

Mawro crossed his arms and watched them go. "Hana seems pretty taken with Tommy, don't you think, *Eomeonim*?" he said without taking his eyes of the pair.

"He is a handsome young man, yes," his mother replied with a nod. "Eminently attractive to a woman werecat. But she might well be trying to use her feminine wiles so as to distract him."

He snorted. "I'm not at all inclined to think Hana will try to escape. If that is what is concerning you, *Eomeonim*," he said, more to convince himself than to convince her. Upon arriving at the warehouse, Mawro had seen to it Hana was sequestered in the armored tool crib. Dory had been happy to approve such a measure to ensure his family's safety, volunteering to be the recipient of Hana's resulting ire. He had told everyone such precautions were necessary to prevent Hana from seeing outside; to prevent her from knowing the family's exact whereabouts should she consider betraying them to DPRK operatives.

But the real reason was Mawro's fear for *her* safety. For all he knew, Oh had deployed a mop-up crew to cover his escape with Annie and Stuie and his father. Once Oh and his captives were out-of-country and on their way back to Pyongyang, his crew would surely come looking for Mawro and Hana. To tie up Oh's proverbial loose ends, snuffing them out with extreme prejudice. Which, as he had nearly seen himself for Hana, required nothing more than a button press.

He had no idea whether Oh's men could have followed them here. But Dory and that Top fellow both admitted, albeit reluctantly, they couldn't rule out they might well have. After all, the Nohs were clearly still in cahoots with Oh and the other North Koreans. Noh's thugs spotting Hana inside their building could well be just as much a calamity as Oh's men spotting her themselves.

"I am not concerned," his mother replied at length. "I have spoken to the *Chosŏn* woman in private. She believes DPRK cast has her aside like the garbage she and the urchins used to rifle through on the streets of Samjiyŏn to feed themselves. She is no flight risk."

Mawro glanced up toward the catwalk suspended from the high-bay ceiling. A CIA man stood guard, his air rifle held at high port, ready to sight in Hana and drop her with a tranq dart should she make any move to escape the warehouse's confines. His counterpart held station on the other end of the catwalk, out of sight. "That Top fellow's not taking any chances, though."

"Dory would tell you. Washington tasks him thus." She stared up at the two werecats zigzagging back and forth across the high-bay area, four stories above their heads. "It is good that Hana had chance to run now. Will help her recover from whatever atrophy her limbs suffered during confinement. Yes."

Mawro nodded and resumed watching the pair also. After Tommy had gotten the sensor arrays lining the roof and walls of the high-bay area back online, Mawro was well-pleased for Hana to come in here and hunt. Dory had made mention of the sensor network before he and Pawly and Lenny left for Belarus. CIA had installed them years before for testing RF impermeability of his brother Bobby's floating plant, prior to using the boats and barges as mobile covert ops staging platforms. Tommy had reconfigured the network to not only block out any incoming RF signals which might activate Hana's "kill chip," but also to help them determine the thing's exact electromagnetic signature.

A red light began flashing above another tool crib opposite the warehouse floor from them, one they had been using as a combination conference room, command center, and laboratory. "Top told us to expect a call about this time," Mawro's mother said after glancing at her watch. "Let us go so he might call us back. Yes."

Moments later, Mawro sat on his haunches close behind where his mother sat in front of one of several laptop computers. They all lay open on two workbenches, pushed together to form one long one. After several keystrokes, a ringtone began warbling through the speaker situated nearest them atop the workbench. "We are here, Topper."

"Nat and Jakub just arrived in Białowieża with the MGS," came the man's voice through the speaker. "Nat said he'll be setting up shop for when Mawro arrives."

"Good. That he is there and that he will keep busy. Too many worries of Annie and Stuie and Niko otherwise." Mawro's mother glanced over her shoulder at him and then turned back toward the phone. "He can travel anytime. The sooner he arrives, the sooner he and Nat can begin replicating Tommy's DNA. The sooner the Forest Clan members can exorcise their rage. Yes."

"Perfect timing then," Top replied. "Brass has approved our request for a second MAC flight to Europe. Along with a container fitted with Mawro-sized living quarters. It should arrive along with an RF-shielded one for Hana. Both networked together so the two of them can talk and share a movie or three during the flight."

His mother snorted. "They are *so* accommodating, yes? Any more accommodating and Oh's men likely would have never captured our family in the first place."

Top let out a long sigh. "I can't disagree with you there, Sunny."

The tool crib's rear door slid open and Tommy stepped through. "So let me not keep you then," Mawro's mother told Top as Tommy closed the door behind him.

"Fine. I'll get the containers coming to Scott Air Force Base, then get one of my people to truck them up to the warehouse."

"We will be here. Doing what we all need to do. Yes." With that, Mawro's mother poked at her console and terminated the call. "And what I need to do is examine Hana while her heart rate is still above its resting value."

With a curt nod toward Mawro and Tommy, she strode over to the sliding door and disappeared into the corridor beyond.

"*Halmonim* needn't hurry."

Mawro looked over to where Tommy took his seat behind the console and knit his brow. "Just what's that supposed to mean?"

"Wasn't just our hunt getting Hana's motor revvin'," he said without turning around, typing furiously at his keyboard. "She was...oh, how can I put this? She was making certain...*insinuations* towards me. In part why I came in here right away."

Mawro shrugged. "You *are* both werecats, son. 'Instinctual propagation of species' and all that." He drew up behind Tommy and took a long sniff. "It's been years since my olfactories were in tip top shape, but I can't immediately detect anything different about your scent." He reared back on his haunches and tugged at his chin. "I know her better than anyone. I think she's overcompensating for having tried to attack you on the island."

"A simple 'I'm sorry' would suffice." He rolled his chair away from the workbench and met Mawro's gaze. "Don't get me wrong, U-Ritz. Hana's scorchin' hot and all, but it's been only a little more than a year since...since Sally..."

Mawro reached over and patted Tommy on the shoulder. "I'll talk to her if you like. Tell her you still need time to grieve for your fiancé."

Tommy's computer chimed, announcing the data transfer's completion. He shuffled his chair back over to the keyboard and resumed his furious typing, his eyes fixed to his screen. There, before long a profile of Hana's head appeared. "Aha! Found it!" he cried, seemingly eager to change the subject.

Mawro lumbered over to Tommy on all fours and peeked over his shoulder. "Is that a spectrum distribution? From the sensors up in the rafters?"

"Yes. Yes, it is." Tommy pointed toward a flashing arrow beside a small rectangular object situated beneath where Hana's head met her neck. His screen filled with Bode plots, each repainting as the coefficients of their respective Fourier transforms updated. "So, what do you make of this?"

Mawro squinted at the display. "A Nyquist diagram might give us the resolution we need to isolate the changes we're looking for in the transfer function's magnitude."

"Alrighty then." Tommy began tapping away at his keyboard. "Hey, look there," he said a moment later and nodded toward his screen. "Appears this spectrum analysis confirms the chip in Hana's neck has some sort of small transmitter built into it," he announced after scrolling up and down through the spectrum of system responses.

Mawro's brow furrowed. "What would it be transmitting?"

"I'm not sure. Let me...ah, there we go." Tommy adjusted his glasses and stared at the screen. "GPS position, near as I can tell from the structure of some of these data packets. Looks like the thing squawks every two minutes or so. But there are more here than I would expect. Some kind of identifier, maybe? Unique to her?"

"Possibly." To prevent any of his claws from scratching up Tommy's screen, Mawro tapped at the right side of its frame with his knuckle. "What's this other chaff over here?"

"I'm not sure of that either. Looks like this thing squawks more frequently on a different channel, like every fifteen seconds or so. But it appears to change frequency with each interval, so I can't get a bead on—"

"It's a trigger."

Tommy turned to meet Mawro's gaze. "Say what now?"

"A trigger. The thing is a slave. It squawks requesting permission to detonate." Mawro paused and rubbed at his face with both hands before continuing. "If it gets a coded response back from a remote detonating unit, like the one you knocked out of Oh's hands, well...it goes off."

"Oh." Tommy's chin drooped. "Shit."

"Indeed. And we should assume it possesses all manner of active anti-tampering detection capabilities, too. After being calibrated at time of installation, the thing monitors signal diffraction character- istics whenever it squawks. If it senses too great a change, it will know it's been compromised. And detonate immediately." Mawro leaned back against the compartment wall and rubbed at his face with one paw. "DPRK produces and markets similar devices for insurgents and saboteurs worldwide, using just such a frequency-hopping scheme to avoid detection."

"Huh. Is that so?" Tommy's eyes went wide. "Oh! Wait! That gives me an idea..."

Tommy tapped away at his keyboard for a moment, then smacked his palms together in front of him. "Jackpot!"

Mawro cocked an eyebrow at Tommy's screen. "What is that?"

"The spectrum response from Hana's earrings. Stands to reason them and the kill chip would both be channel hoppers, right?"

Mawro combed through his ruff with the claws on one hand. "Well, DPRK's technology development initiative does tend to produce sin- gle devices or systems. Which then end up used in many different applications."

"Right. And these both employ the same frequency pattern." Tommy picked up a pen from the workbench and tapped at the screen with the capped end. "The ones here, here, and here all combine to form one complete sequence. Which then repeats itself..."

"So? How does this help ensure Hana's safety?" Mawro said after a moment.

Tommy shook his head as if to clear it. "Sorry, I was just thinking out loud." He put down his pen and resumed typing. "I wanted to show you what I think ought to happen if we reverse the polarity of the source voltage to her earrings' crystal oscillator."

A new trace appeared on the screen, causing Mawro to gasp. "Her earrings will jam the kill chip's receiver inputs!"

Tommy beamed. "Right! So, it won't *ever* go off, even in the presence of another detonator signal."

"This ought to work, yes. But only as a stopgap measure."

Tommy's face fell. "I...I don't understand."

"DPRK can access commercial cell sites to broadcast activation sequences. I've even heard of them launching drones to sweep areas outside of normal cellular coverage. Oh would gladly send out DPRK operatives across the globe to track her down, if only to spite me." Mawro shook his head and stood up. "Your solution might well be able to shield her kill chip from receiving a remote activation signal via the commercial cellular networks. And it ought to camouflage her from any DPRK sensor networks which might otherwise detect her. Certainly, by now Hana has been removed from Oh's list of friendlies." He waved a hand toward Tommy's screen. "But if someone gets right in close with a handheld detonator, its signal strength might exceed the output of her earrings." He turned toward Tommy and fixed him with a searing glare. "Which is why *no one* is going to say anything to Hana about her kill chip. Not one word. Is that clear?"

"But U-Ritz, I—"

"If Hana finds out about it, she knows good and well Oh might try to use her to intimidate me somehow, someday." Mawro shook his head and rolled back onto his haunches. "She would seek him and his people out herself, then goad them into either detonating the device or shooting her. I...I won't take that chance."

"Fine, have it your way," Tommy replied as he crossed his arms over his chest. "But keeping secrets is what got us all into this mess in the first place, remember?" He turned and glanced up at his screen. "Guess the only sure-fire solution then is figuring out how to cut the damn thing free from her body. Within, like, three seconds."

Chapter Twenty

MEANWHILE, NEAR MINSK, BELARUS...

PAWLY STARED AT THE six cards in her hand and frowned. "Okay, so...I have to call a trump suit now?"

Grandpa D nodded. "Yes. You can also call 'no trump' or *'mizerka.'*" He sighed in response to Pawly's confused look, then glanced back and forth between her and Lenny. "Okay, you two, one more time. Neither option has a trump suit. Calling no trump, your goal will be to win tricks. Calling *mizerka*, your goal will be not to. Clear?"

She fixed a pained smile to her face and muttered "Fine. Clubs." *Whatever.*

"Clubs it is, then," Grandpa D announced before resuming his deal.

Pawly found her grandfather's unflappable calm unnerving. They were seated around a small table inside a windowless room somewhere in the Minsk airport—the place they had been quickly escorted to mere moments after presenting themselves to Belarusian customs officers. Doctored passports in hand, given to them by Top's Washington-based operatives before their flight out of Dulles, she and Lenny and her Grandpa D had tried passing themselves off as a young married couple traveling with her aging grandfather. Headed to a wilderness resort in the southwestern corner of the country, near the Polish border, for a family reunion.

Unlike their fake names, that much *was* true, an apt enough description of their trek to Białowieża for their rendezvous with the Forest Clan and their remaining family. They had undertaken this course of action at Monsignor Dryzek's suggestion. Given Grandpa D was still a wanted man in Poland, the Forest Clan patriarch had thought making their way to Białowieża through Belarus under assumed names would be the best way to fly beneath the radar.

"Hah!" her grandfather cried as he took one final trick, adding to his score and deducting like amounts from each of theirs. Pawly threw her remaining cards down on the table and slid them over toward Lenny. He gathered them up and began to shuffle while Pawly yawned and stretched.

Theories as to why their high-flying plan had seemingly assumed the glide profile of a brick flooded her mind, making it difficult to grasp the rules of this new-to-her card game. Grandpa D had insisted even before they took off from O'Hare two days previous that they play this game in particular if they were ever detained at any point *en route*. Doing so would support their "Polish diaspora family reunion" cover story and help them avoid saying anything which might further compromise their position. For surely the Belarusians were listening to their every word, watching their every move.

Lenny, for his part, followed Grandpa D's lead as best he could. But the furtive glances she stole back and forth at him across the table suggested his asshole was biting at the cheap vinyl cushion covering his chair every bit as much as hers was. Had the Noh family followed them to Uncle Bobby's warehouse? Had they kept them under surveillance until the family's flight out of O'Hare, then tipped off the North Koreans? Had they in turn alerted the Belarusians?

Then again, Grandpa D had warned them Minsk might make a play to capture him, so they might offer him to the Polish authorities in exchange for an outed Belarusian double-agent. Surely her grandfather's former friend Dariusz Luczasik, head of Poland's domestic counter-intelligence agency ABW, would be thrilled having Grandpa D in the Warsaw prison cell instead of its current occupant.

All that aside, the only people she knew familiar with Grandpa D's itinerary included Monsignor Dryzek and a small handful of Forest Clan elders. Had Dryzek sold them out for some inexplicable reason? Had the Belarusian members of the Forest Clan tipped off Minsk themselves, hoping to one-up their Polish counterparts as part of some secret schism?

The working of their room's door handle interrupted Pawly's internal doomsaying. A mustachioed man dressed in a pinstriped charcoal gray suit entered their room and closed the door behind him. He held his hand up to his face and ran a hand through his wavy, graying hair as he squinted down at what looked to be their passports. "Reiner Lutz," he said before handing Lenny his, and "Jadwiga Stupek," before doing likewise with Pawly. "I do not know what laws America has," he addressed her in broken English, waving his forefinger. "But you will need to have your surname changed on your passport before you visit our country again."

"Got it," Pawly said with a polite nod. "Thank you, sir."

The man turned to Grandpa D and handed him his passport. "That would make this last one yours, I suppose, *Pan* Gutowski." Then he slowly stuck his hands in the pockets of his trousers and leaned one shoulder up against the wall beside him. "You are on your way to the Białowieża Forest, yes?"

Grandpa D nodded. "Yes, that's correct."

"Ah, *Belozhevskaya Pushcha* is lovely in the springtime indeed," the man replied in a wistful voice. "I've been to a lovely *dacha* nearby there, just outside of Viskuli. A bit rustic, but I think you'll find it adequately appointed."

"We'll, ah, we'll keep it in mind," Grandpa D replied. "Our family has already made accommodation for us—"

"But Mr. Lukashenko awaits you there, so eager to meet you...Teodor Katczynski."

Lenny's breath caught in his throat. *Oh, shit,* Pawly thought, her lips drawing taut.

The man grinned. "It would be rude for you to deny my boss' boss the pleasure of your company," he said, a lilt in his voice, nodding toward Pawly and Lenny with his chin. "And...decidedly *unpleasant* for these two."

"So, who are you then?" Grandpa D said in even tones. "What do you want with me?" Pawly noticed her grandfather's hand tremble ever so slightly as he waved it toward her and Lenny. "Whatever it is, let me assure you that my granddaughter and her beau here had nothing to do with it."

"Thank you for saying, but we were quite aware of that already." The man drew a leather badge holder from his suitcoat pocket and flipped it open. "To your questions—first, I am Colonel Bortnik. Ministry of Internal Affairs. Second, you have reservations tonight at a bed and breakfast nearby. Compliments of Mr. Lukashenko himself."

Bortnik rapped at the door behind him with one hand. A moment later, two similarly dressed men entered and took up position to his left and right. "These men, together with the rest of my security detail, will watch over you tonight. Tomorrow morning, I will arrive with a fresh crew after breakfast to relieve them. Then they and I will deliver you to Viskuli." He held the door to the room open and motioned toward Pawly and the others with one hand. "We should be going straightaway. The sooner you get your luggage, the sooner you can avail yourselves to our hospitality. You are surely sick of airports now, yes?"

Pawly grimaced. *You don't know the half of it, Borky.*

She and Lenny and Grandpa D stepped through the door single file. Awaiting them in the hallway were three more of Bortnik's gray-suited goons, two men and one woman. They led their procession out into the concourse, with Bortnik walking beside Grandpa D. Lenny and Pawly, hand in hand, drew up behind them. The two other men closed the room door and followed.

As they made their way across the terminal toward the baggage claim, Pawly lost track of the number of what she believed to be "Welcome to Minsk" signs. And found the Cyrillic script on the remaining signboards indecipherable. No one said much of anything else until they arrived at the baggage claim area, where they found their luggage already spinning around on the carousel. One of the goons asked Grandpa D which bags were theirs. After pointing them out, their overseers each picked up a bag or two and slung them over their shoulders. Then they closed ranks around Pawly and Lenny and Grandpa D. "This way," Bortnik said with a wave toward an unmarked gray van parked curbside beyond the window nearest them. In a "no parking" area, natch.

As their procession approached, the van driver got out and popped open the vehicle's rear hatch. "Please, get in, we'll handle this," Bortnik said in English after engaging their driver in a short conversation in what Pawly believed to be Belarusian. "After all," he said with a wink, "you *are* our guests."

One of the men and the woman climbed in first, motioning for Pawly and Lenny to follow them as their compatriots and their driver stowed the luggage in back. Grandpa D sat in the seat in front of them, with Bortnik still at his side. Two more goons took the frontmost bench seat with the last one riding shotgun. As soon as the doors slammed shut, their driver jammed the van into gear and sped off.

Hardly more than ten minutes after leaving the airport, the van pulled into a driveway of a quiet residential street and stopped. Before them sat a large two-story building constructed of white brick. The driver exited the van and walked around to the back while the goon riding shotgun hopped out and slid open the van's side door. One by one, everyone piled out and shuffled off in the direction of the spacious home's front door. Their sullen hosts nodded politely as they all entered. The two huskier men of Bortnik's detail lumbered along behind, burdened with all of their luggage.

Five minutes later, Pawly and her family sat seated around the home's enormous dining room table. After finishing his review of his team's watch rotation, Bortnik turned to the family and spread his arms wide. "I leave you in their care, then. If you need anything, let them know and they shall get it for you. I will return in the morning with a new detail to take you to Viskuli. Now, by your leave, my wife is waiting dinner on me."

"If you would please, lovely, I would show you to your room," their hostess chirped in broken English to Pawly.

Pawly shot Lenny a puzzled look as she stood up. Undeterred, their hostess guided her over to a brightly colored statue of a derpy-looking cat. Bortnik's goons had heaped their bags into a pile beside it, just inside the home's front door. Pawly picked hers out and trudged up the stairs behind their hostess. At the top, to the left, they entered a small room with a queen bed sharing a wall with a petite dresser and a bathroom with a sink, toilet, and shower taking up the wall opposite. She tossed her bag atop the bed and began to unpack.

While stowing her clothes and personal items in the dresser's top drawer, Pawly glimpsed Bortnik through the room's tiny window walking up to the patio of a small house three doors up on the opposite side of the street. A woman with dark hair streaked with gray opened the door as he approached. The two kissed at the threshold, went inside and closed the door behind them. *He'll have a short commute in the morning,* Pawly thought as pangs of jealousy racked her insides. She had been looking forward to spending the night cozying up to Lenny, but their hosts were clearly cut from the same prudish cloth that Grandpa D was.

Their hostess called up a few minutes later, inviting Pawly down for dinner. Or such as it was. A meager meal of stale sandwiches and a soup tasting like it had been strained through a load of dirty laundry. At least she and Lenny and Grandpa D were still together. She and Grandpa D managed a little bit of small talk with their hosts as they ate, making do with the similarities inherent between spoken Polish and Belarusian. Now and again Pawly or Grandpa D would turn to Lenny and give him the play-by-play in English. The remaining time, he just sat there, his expression neutral as he gazed back and forth between speakers. Certainly, he had no idea what any of them were saying. Maybe she and Lenny would linger in the Forest a while after this business was all done. If Pawly was going to keep him around, he would need to pick up the language sooner or later.

At one point in their conversation, their hostess explained she was Bortnik's sister. "So. This really *is* a brother-in-law deal, after all?" Lenny replied with a snort after Pawly translated. Despite sharing a chuckle with Grandpa D at Lenny's snarky comment, Pawly was glad for the arrangement notwithstanding. Bortnik might well have split them up into individual cells in some jail God only knew where, but for whatever monies he was siphoning off to his sister and brother-in-law for hosteling them.

After dinner, Bortnik's goons all adjourned to the derby parlor to watch television. Their hosts joined them after putting their evening tea to draw. At Grandpa D's request, Pawly and Lenny remained with him in the kitchen. They all sat around the dinner table together while the elder man resumed schooling them in *mizerka*. Though Grandpa D trounced them both game after game, his constant wisecracking and table antics made Lenny and Pawly both laugh. For which Pawly found herself grateful.

After a while, their hostess' tea did its work on Grandpa D. After excusing himself to use the bathroom, Pawly leaned up against Lenny's shoulder and sighed contentedly. For that fleeting moment, she envisioned the three of them here enjoying their holiday. Allowing her to shut out their cruel reality—they were being held against their will in a foreign country.

When Grandpa D told Pawly and Lenny upon his return he was going on up to bed, they both agreed to do likewise. Bortnik's people remained glued to their places on the living room furniture, howling as one contestant after another were eliminated on what looked to be Belarus' answer to *Wipeout*. The three of them trudged up the narrow steps one by one leading up to their bedrooms. At the top of the stairs, Pawly turned left and Lenny and her grandfather turned right. She ducked into her bathroom and stripped naked, then pulled on the tank top and pair of gym shorts that she had set out before dinner to sleep in. When she emerged from the bathroom, Lenny was standing there with a blanket in his arms. "Your grandpa thought you might want this. To, you know, keep warm."

She took the blanket from him and tossed it onto the foot of her bed. "I'll just suppose you thought of something *else* that might keep me warm too, hm?"

"Indeed," he replied, taking her into his arms.

They shared a long, passionate kiss until Lenny broke away, having come to know the very limit of Pawly's self-control. "Jakub tells me he's made up one of the buildings at the abandoned sawmill into something of a hunting cottage," he said, wrapping his arms around her shoulders and squeezing her tight. "And that we're welcome to make use of it while were in Białowieża so we can, you know, get away."

"Just like a couple of naughty kids sneaking out of their cabins after lights-out for a secret summer camp rendezvous," she added, the corners of her mouth turning up into a mischievous grin. She drew a finger beneath his nose as she slid past him and stepped over to her bedroom window. There she put her nose up near the screen and breathed deep. Though thick with the strong smell of dogfennel, Pawly managed to make out a trace of a familiar scent.

Milda?

Lenny squinted toward the tree line beyond the house's terraced garden. "What's going on?" he whispered after drawing close to Pawly's ear. "You scent something out there?"

Pawly turned to face him, her brows knit. "Yeah. Milda. I'm sure of it," she responded in kind before turning back toward the window. "In fact," she said as she sniffed at the air, "I can scent her and several more werecats."

"Really? Wow. How did they—?"

"Aht-tut-tut," she replied, placing a finger atop Lenny's lips. "I'm sure they'll answer all our questions in due time. But for right now, just go tell Grandpa D 'the calvary will likely meet us at the pass come morning'." With that, she stepped across the room and stood beside the open door. "Now git. Tomorrow is sure to be a busy day. We should all try to get whatever sleep we can in the meantime."

Chapter Twenty-One

The following morning.

The sensation of someone caressing her cheek startled Pawly awake. "Rise and shine, gorgeous," Lenny said as he sat down on the edge of her bed, dressed in a T-shirt and a pair of basketball shorts.

Pawly rubbed the sand from her eyes and sat up. "Hah. You're funny," she said, running her hands through her hair. "Just as well I look like shit. Too many people around for morning nooky anyway."

"Guess we'll have to settle for morning *coffee*, then." Lenny pecked at Pawly's cheek before handing her a steaming mug.

"Oh, that's good," she said after taking a cautious sip from her cup. "Not as good as morning nooky, perhaps. But I do so love your 'kawfee regulah.'"

"I've had a lifetime of practice," he said, drawing his face close to hers. "Besides, my Bond Girl has saved my ass more than once. I'm eager to repay her any way I can…"

A banging from downstairs caused them both to start. "Outrage! An outrage, I say!" came Bortnik's booming voice from the kitchen downstairs.

"I was merely trying to be helpful, offering for my crew and I to stay on until our relief gets here," Pawly managed to pick out from Belarusian as one of Bortnik's goons spoke. "You need not bite my head off."

"You and yours shall not weasel your way into an extra shift's pay *that* easily, Alexi," Bortnik replied in kind. "Your relief would have been here by now but for someone slashing their van's tires when they stopped to get coffee."

"Sasha and I need to go to town and fetch groceries, Ivan," their hostess chirped, as best as Pawly could make out. "But your van is in our way."

Bortnik snorted. "Alexi, take your crew and go so my sister and my brother-in-law can get their car out of their garage. I can handle things here until your relief arrives."

"What's going on?" Lenny whispered into Pawly's ear.

She leaned over behind him and set her mug down atop the nightstand. Then Pawly bolted out of bed and dashed over to the window, cracking it open before breathing deep through her nose. "She's gone," Pawly muttered before turning to face Lenny.

"Who's gone? Milda?"

"Yes, now go tell Grandpa D," she replied, shooing him toward the door with both hands. "Tell him you and he need to get yourselves cleaned up and packed just as fast as you can. We need to be ready to move. And soon."

NOT TWENTY MINUTES LATER, Pawly emerged from the bedroom and made her way down the stairs. She poured herself another cup of coffee and shuffled over toward where Lenny sat at the kitchen table beside Grandpa D. A flash of color in the front door's sidelight down the hall to her right caught her attention; she turned in time to glimpse a van similar to the one that had brought them here turning up the driveway. She took a sip at her coffee and glanced over toward the living room window, past where Bortnik sat in an easy chair reading a newspaper. "Looks like I'm just in time," she whispered into Lenny's ear.

She waved away his puzzled look and pointed to where several new plainclothesmen and one woman emerged from around the corner of the garage. They proceeded up the walk to the front door and rang the bell. Bortnik folded the paper he had been reading and slapped it down on the end table beside him. "It's about time, Václav," he muttered as he stomped across the living room to the front door. "What the hell took you so...?"

The man's words trailed off as he raised his hands above his head. "We got here just as soon as we could, Colonel," a man replied as Bortnik stumbled backward into the hallway. The speaker appeared around the corner of the portico a moment later, the barrel of his pistol pointed at Bortnik's chest.

"Easy there, Václav," came a woman's voice from behind him. "You know we can't allow any harm to come to him. Or, at least, we can't allow it just yet."

Milda!

The elder woman stepped into view, a bemused grin on her face. She crouched down near where Bortnik sat seated on the floor, trembling. "Though if you don't do *exactly* as we say," she said, taking the man's pallored face in her hand, "I will see to it you beg for Václav to shoot you before we are finished with you."

The one named Václav stepped into the kitchen and waved his arms toward Pawly and the others. "The Monsignor is expecting us," he said in flawless English. "Gather your things, we leave in five minutes."

P AWLY AND LENNY SAT clasping hands as everyone in the van rode along in uneasy silence. Having left Minsk behind them for some while now, she chanced a glance down at her watch. She grimaced, realizing barely forty-five minutes had passed since they left the bed and breakfast. The border—and the Forest—were still hours away.

Václav's people, after revealing themselves to be the Forest Clan members handpicked by Monsignor Dryzek to retrieve them, had backed the van into the house's garage. Václav, they told Pawly and the others, was the Forest Clan's youngest elder and a high-ranking official within Belarus' intelligence apparat. He had brought Bortnik out moments later, hands zip-tied together behind his back, then buckled him securely into one of the van's bench seats, immediately behind the driver.

Pawly turned the mornings events over and over again in her mind as they drove, trying to comprehend just why the Forest Clan had taken him hostage. If it had been up to her, she would have simply sapped the man and let him fall unconscious onto the living room sofa. By the time he came to, they would have been long gone. When the van exited the expressway about twenty minutes later, Pawly figured she would find out what was going on soon enough.

They turned left at the end of the off-ramp. After ducking under the expressway lanes, they turned left again into the parking lot of a run-down warehouse. One of its roll-up doors began to rise as they approached, reversing direction immediately after their van entered. Václav stopped as soon as the door shut all the way and killed the engine. He got out and walked around the van to open the sliding door beside Pawly and Lenny. Everyone else exited the vehicle too, grunting and groaning and working their legs while Václav manhandled Bortnik away from the van.

The staccato, off-tempo tapping of a walking stick against the concrete floor heralded Monsignor Dryzek's approach. "Let's get down to business," he said a moment later before he stepped out into the light streaming down from the warehouse's clerestory.

"My pleasure, Monsignor, as always…" Václav replied a moment before his voice trailed off into a snarl. Claws burst forth from his fingertips, which he used to shred his shirt and suit coat in dramatic fashion. In an instant, auburn fur spotted with brown covered his body. He drew nose to nose with Bortnik and gnashed his fangs at him.

Even in human form, Pawly made out the panicked stink rolling off of Bortnik's body, mixed with the scent of the urine surely trickling down his leg. "Now then, Colonel," Dryzek said after Václav laid his claws alongside their captive's neck. "None of us believe Mr. Lukashenko or his cronies are planning to exchange Teodor Katczynski for whatever Belarusians the Poles have in their custody. Just *why* then did you take him and the others to your safehouse?"

"Because I was under orders to," Bortnik replied through gritted teeth.

"By whom?"

"By the Minister himself—aaah!"

Dryzek *tut-tut*ed. "Now, Colonel, you don't expect us to buy that, do you?" He laid his hand over top of the wound Václav had made from poking a single claw into the side of the man's neck. Bortnik winced as Dryzek patted at it, then whimpered when he showed him a spot of bright red blood on his hand.

"Yes, I do. Because it's the truth—aaaaah!"

"So, will you bleed out before I run out of claws?" Václav clicked his tongue. "Maybe you would like to lay a wager."

Dryzek drew his face close to the end of Bortnik's nose. "Indeed, Colonel. Consider your odds carefully. Václav has come close to your carotid artery already, whether you realize it or not. Oh, and don't forget—he has toe claws, too."

"Why yes, Monsignor!" he said, scraping the very ones Dryzek referred to back and forth across the concrete beside him. "They are more than adequate for this sort of work." With that, he stepped up beside Bortnik and jammed his toe claws into the back of their captive's leg below his knee. Bortnik screamed while Václav raked his toes down the length of his leg, shredding cloth and skin and muscle. "You know, you shall not live long if you keep bleeding like this."

"*Spetsnaz*! It was *Spetsnaz*, dammit!"

The corner of Dryzek's mouth turned upward. "So, you took Katczynski and his family to an undisclosed location like your sister's B&B because the *Russians* are in on this? Now we're getting somewhere." He waved his hands toward Václav to tell him to stand down. "You have my attention, Colonel," he said, grabbing Bortnik's cheeks in one hand and forcing him to make eye contact. "So, just what do their special forces have to do with it?"

"*Spetsnaz* knows...North Koreans are..." the man replied, huffing and puffing, "having a big shindig in Rason...first part of next week. Showing off...their made-to-order mutants...like you." He wrinkled his nose and nodded toward Václav. "And *that* one over there."

The werecat man giggled. "Oh, I don't think so," he replied, his eyes twinkling. "When they made me, they broke the mold!"

"For which we are all grateful." Dryzek turned and motioned toward a heavyset, balding man behind him. "If you would be so kind, Karol. We cannot allow Václav here to have too much fun."

The man nodded and twirled his fanny pack around to his front. After pulling an autoinjector free from its front pocket, he jammed the needle guard into the side of Bortnik's neck and pushed the button. Their captive let out a groan as his eyes rolled up into his head. His lips quivered for a moment before his head slumped forward. Then he went still, his mop of graying hair obscuring his face.

Pawly gaped at Karol. "Is...is he...?"

"No, not at all, young one," Dryzek answered for him. "While your *Halmonim* was with us, she taught Karol here about this particularly strong sedative. Which also has the benefit of subjecting anyone under its influence to vivid hallucinations for hours upon awakening."

A cross between a snort and a cough drew Pawly's attention over to her Grandpa D. His eyes twinkled as he sniggered, then giggled, then began to laugh. He drew his hands to his abdomen and tossed back his head, his laughter echoing throughout the warehouse.

Pawly glanced over at Lenny and shrugged. *Guess the old man's finally gone and lost it.*

At length, Grandpa D raised a trembling finger toward Dryzek. "It...it was *you*! It was all...it was all you!" he said between gasps as he got his breathing back under control.

Pawly knit her brow and glanced over toward the Monsignor. "I don't understand."

After a moment, Grandpa D sighed and stared up at the ceiling. "Kids these days..." he muttered before turning her way. "Don't you see, Pawly?" he said, waving his open palm toward her. "At the airport in Minsk, I was certain though that despite all our precautions, Pyongyang had somehow managed to figure out our itinerary. Then they went and tipped off the Belarusians so they'd be lying in wait. Because this dog-and-pony show of DPRK's surely involves parading around Annie and Stuie and Niko to the Aryan Nations, *Spetsnaz*, Islamic State, and whomever else they invited. They'd do everything they could to make sure none of *us* show up to crash their party."

He glanced over toward Dryzek. "But then this guy here has his man inside the Belarusian security apparat tip off his boss," he said with a nod toward Václav. "Knowing full well how vain the guy is, sure to try and hog all the glory for himself."

Dryzek chuckled. "Suffice to say, me and mine thought Václav was due for a promotion. Which he wasn't going to get until that one finally retired," he said with a snort as he wagged his chin toward Bortnik's prone form. "Though he has served a useful purpose. Because though Václav suspected Spetnaz had Bortnik on the take, the man had been playing his cards close to the vest."

"So, *you* had Václav let slip that I was coming, then dispatched him and the others keep watch over us. But you couldn't risk telling anyone outside the Forest Clan."

"Well, aside from Milda, that is. But I swore her to secrecy to not even tell you, *Pan* Katczynski."

"I understand. Clearly you didn't want to expose Václav nor his position within the Belarusian intelligence apparat. If Pawly or Lenny or I knew all of what was going on, Minsk might try getting one of us to talk by threatening the other two."

Dryzek nodded. "You are quite right."

Grandpa D looked over at Pawly and Lenny and smiled. "So, you see, kids? We were never in any *real* danger. Though I don't know about the two of you, but I was starting to think our goose was well and truly cooked that time."

"And now we have what we need so that you can go rescue your family," Dryzek added, indicating Pawly and the others with the tip of his cane. "Right after you pick up your toys and put them away, Václav."

"Of course, Monsignor," the man replied as he picked up Bortnik's limp form. Another one of the Forest Clan members opened up the back door of the van and began setting all of the family's bags on the floor around them. Václav placed their captive inside the back of the van before the other man jumped in and pulled the van's doors shut behind him.

"Will you need for us and Waldemar to swing by and pick you up?"

Václav shook his head. "No, Monsignor. Elena here left her car at a remote trailhead about eight kilometers or so east of here. We'll ditch this van nearby with our guest inside and have her ferry us all back to the Forest."

"Very well, then. Now go." Dryzek lifted his hand and gestured toward Václav's team, tracing the shape of a cross. "Peace be with you."

"And also with you." Václav jumped into the van's driver's seat as the roll-up door opened once more. The van sped through it a moment later and disappeared down the highway.

Pawly clicked her tongue. "So, what about the rest of us?"

"I've arranged suitable transportation," Dryzek replied before he jammed his fingers into the corners of his mouth and belted out a shrill whistle. A diesel engine fired up from behind a block wall before a box truck rumbled into view. "It may be spartan, but ought certainly to prove roomy enough," he said with a wry grin.

"Let me get that for you, Monsignor," Waldemar called out as the truck rolled up beside Dryzek. He hopped down from the cab, giving everyone a friendly wave as he stepped over to a small lever jutting out from the truck's rear bumper. An electric motor wound up an instant before a deck plate emerged from beneath the truck and extended across the floor behind him. "Going up!"

"Your non-combatants are welcome to remain with us in the Forest until your return," Dryzek said to a moment later, shuffling his way toward one of the bench seats pushed up against the front of the truck.

Grandpa D smiled and patted the other man's shoulder. "Thank you, Monsignor. Just that many fewer things I'll need to worry about."

Chapter Twenty-Two

THAT EVENING. A WILDERNESS RESORT WITHIN THE BIAŁOWIEŻA FOREST.

"MAKE HASTE, DEARIE," MILDA called toward the shower curtain. "We ought to be going soon."

The water stopped running an instant before Hana threw back the curtain and stepped forth from the stall. "I shall be not long," she answered her as she snatched her towel from a nearby hook. Then she took a seat upon the long wooden bench beside her open duffel and began to wring water from the tails of her bob. "We then can go."

Milda glanced up past the shower stalls lining either side of the room toward the wall clock. "Good. Suppose you figured out already it is best one be around Zuza and her fawning minions as little as possible."

"I did. Yes."

After giving her bare skin a quick rub down, Hana bound up her hair in the towel and wrapped it tightly around her head. Then she plucked a bra and panties and a blouse and a pair of trousers from her duffel. "I can finish tending my hair and skin back in my room," she said as she dressed.

Milda snorted. "Nice that they give you a little privacy. At least until Pawly and the rest of her family get here. Those prudes on the council wouldn't dream of allowing her and her lover to even share a room, never mind a bed."

Hana's pale skin flushed. But rather than keep them longer by asking more questions, Milda just shrugged it off. Even before Hana boarded her plane in Chicago, Milda had volunteered to escort her during her stay in Białowieża. Once thought by the Forest's denizens to be the sole surviving member of her seafaring clan, Milda knew firsthand what it felt like to be perceived as an outsider by her fellow werecats. Despite her species, despite who she had previously fought for, Hana was still one of them. Milda was not about to let anyone forget that.

That fundamental point, however, seemed lost on the Forest Clan's elder council. Though Monsignor Dryzek had agreed on their behalf to take Dory and his family and the former DPRK operatives all in, preventing Oh or anyone else from capturing or otherwise harming them, he apparently had seen no need to consult anyone else about it. The council had immediately convened a special meeting here at this resort nestled within the Forest, owned by fellow clansman Stanislaus Kazpierski's family going back generations. Being the annual lull period between when the cross-country skiers departed and the hikers arrived, he and his family had been glad to oblige to fill up their otherwise vacant cottages.

The elders had occupied the Great Hall nearly constantly in the three days since, arguing amongst themselves about the ultimate fate of Dory and his entourage, most of whom they still perceived as interlopers. Though they gave themselves meal breaks and adjourned in the evening to retire to their wives and families for sleep, she could not help but hear them going at it whenever they made their way to the kitchen to pick up Mawro's meals. What, then, had become of the ancient edict "harm not the children of Affliction"?

But today the elders had decided to table the issue and take up debate on their other piece of pressing new business. During breakfast that morning, Milda learned the Monsignor had left quickly in the middle of the night previous, accompanied by several of his lieutenants. She was unsure what sort of undisclosable task they had set out on, but she had said a prayer requesting safe travels for Dory and Pawly and Lenny just the same.

Surely this development had influenced the sudden change in the elders' docket. Before leaving to pick up Hana from the airport in Warsaw, Milda had overheard several of them capitalizing on Dryzek's absence to loudly voice their opposition to his proposal. Leave the Forest and disburse around the globe to ensure their clan's survival? Absurd! Reckless! Suicidal!

Then moments ago, making their way past the Great Hall to the lavatorium's showers, Milda had heard others question the wisdom of Dryzek's decision to permit Mawro and Nat to replicate Tommy's genetic material with the MGS. The machine sat housed in a container on the resort's back lot nearest the tree line. Even if the thing failed to blow up or otherwise manage to set the Forest alight, many nagging questions remained. Could the serum Mawro and Nat hoped to create *really* prevent Forest Clan members from raging ever again? Or would it render them all feral? Reduce anyone who took it to a vegetable? Neither they nor Dory could say for sure. Not like they had the ability to run clinical trials. Or the time.

"I am ready."

Milda glanced up to find Hana standing in front of her, fully dressed, with her duffel slung over one shoulder and her staff balanced atop the other. "Oh. Right then," she replied, waving for Hana to follow her. They emerged from the lavatorium in time for Milda to glimpse Zuza and her entourage headed their way across the parade ground. "Not a moment too soon," she muttered before nudging Hana's shoulder. "Let's go this way instead."

The two women exchanged puzzled glances as they approached the Great Hall. "It is quiet. Odd."

"Huh. Odd, indeed," Milda said, agreeing with Hana. "Maybe if we cut through here, we can get a peek inside at—"

"Such good fortune, eh, Toni? That the remnant of those traitorous seafarers will soon leave our Forest."

"And taking their smelly humans with them. Good riddance."

Milda gasped. Taking Hana by the wrist, she urged her toward a darkened alleyway separating the Great Hall from the keeper's residence. "Don't speak. And don't move," she hissed into Hana's ear an instant before two men rounded the corner.

Forest Clan elders Antonius Bodny and Leokadiusz Brzyski carried on in conversation until they came astride the alcove. "Hey, Leo, do you smell that?" Bodny asked Brzyski as he sniffed at the air.

"Yes, yes I do," the other man replied, his nose twitching. "Smells like women. And...and apricots?"

Uproarious laughter wafted their way from across the parade ground. "Maybe Zuza or one of her friends are using a new shampoo or something," Bodny said as he peered over his glasses toward the lavatorium. "Come, let us go and grab our towels and toilet kits. I want to see if I can locate that loose brick in the wall between the men's and women's showers again."

"Best idea you've had all day!" Bzyski replied before the two men dashed off toward the nearest row of cottages.

Milda made a face as she stepped out from the alcove and onto the sidewalk. "Hardly an impressive specimen, either of those two. Don't you think, Hana? Come on, dearie, let's get you back to your..."

Her voice trailed off as she turned, finding the alleyway empty.

Moments later.

"**I** wasn't expecting you to seek me out again so soon, Hana-*ttanim*. Is everything okay?"

Dim light filtering into the container from the outside allowed Hana to barely make out Mawro's hulking form. Dressed in nothing but his rough-hewn canvas shorts, he sat on the edge of a mattress made from what looked like cotton waste stuffed into a covering of hastily stitched together pieces of burlap.

"You tell me, Papa. What is this I hear about all of us leaving the Forest? Was it not Agent Katczynski's idea we come here in the first place?"

The oversized bed fashioned together from salvaged structural steel creaked and groaned as he stumbled upright to face her. "I figured you would hear about it sooner or later. Though I had hoped it would be later and not sooner."

Hana crossed her arms across her chest. "So?"

Mawro rubbed at his temples with both hands. "Okay, I'll tell you what I know, but don't tell anyone else these things. Dryzek himself sternly warned Nat and Tomasz and me not to say anything. At least not until the elders make their announcement to the Forest Clan members.”

“Right then. Not a word,” Hana replied with a nod.

“With Dryzek’s help, Dory believes they have figured out where his loved ones are being held captive.”

Hana’s eyes went wide. “Where? Where are they?”

“Back in North Korea. Oh is taking them to Rason for some sort of dog-and-pony show. Foreign bidders have been invited to try and buy rights to whatever ailuranthropic transformation serum they will develop in the future.”

Mawro waved his hand toward the door. “So, most of the family and their allies will deploy to a ship currently underway in the Sea of Japan between Vladivostok and Chŏngjin. Including me.”

She snorted. “I will be glad, then, when we are away from these other—”

“*I* will be deploying to Korea, Hana-*ttanim*. That Top fellow and the others will need me to prevent the child from going feral during our operation.” He shook his head from side to side. “But you are *not* coming. Now, when we are finished there, rest assured I will be back here as soon as I can. Then we will figure out together where to go next.”

“I cannot simply languish here, Papa!” Hana cried, clenching her fists at her sides. “Not while you return to DPRK. You and I both know well and good Oh would shoot you on sight. It is suicide to trust anyone with your back other than me.”

Mawro let out a long sigh. “I don’t see us as having much of a choice. Your oxygen mask was destroyed back on the island. I don’t have any way to sample Stuie’s DNA, so I can’t possibly build you another one. Especially not on such short notice.” He raised both hands to his shoulders, his palms open. “And we both know what would happen if you come into contact with the child without it." Mawro lowered his hands and shook his head. "Neither Dory nor I are willing to take such a risk. I'm sorry, Hana. You're just going to have to trust us."

Hana snarled and spun on her heel, then stomped her way to the door. After slamming the door behind her, she made a beeline for her cabin. She rubbed at the corners of her eyes with her thumb and forefinger to stave off the hot tears welling up there.

"There you are!"

Hana gasped and looked up to find Milda trotting up alongside her. "Is something wrong, dearie?" she asked after placing a hand on Hana's shoulder.

She stopped and turned to look eye to eye with the elder woman. "It is...is nothing."

Milda cocked an eyebrow at her. "Are you sure? If there's something I can do to help, you need but only ask."

A flash of inspiration gave Hana a start. "On my second thought, there *is* a favor which you can do. Yes."

LATE THAT SAME NIGHT...

"RIGHT! CUT RIGHT!" MILDA cried as she bounded from branch to branch, high above the forest floor. Down below, Hana complied, bringing her to within striking distance of the panicked spikehorn. Though Hana had dutifully followed her instructions to the letter for the duration of their hunt, Milda knew their success was solely in the other woman's hands now.

Hana quickly demonstrated herself a proficient closer. She sprinted alongside the deer and lunged, sinking the claws on both hands deep into the thing's flank as her momentum carried her over the deer's back. Knocking the deer's front legs out from under it with her own body, Hana clung tight to the deer as the two of them tumbled to a stop. Accompanied by the deer's mournful bleating, Hana reared back on her haunches, bore her fangs, and plunged them deep into the deer's neck. After a quick shake of her head, Hana spat out a softball-sized chunk of flesh onto the ground beside her. Blood gushed forth from the savage wound while the spikehorn's final breath gurgled forth from its ruined throat. Then its head slumped to the ground and it laid still.

By the time Milda touched down beside the deer's carcass, Hana had already torn open the thing's abdomen. She knelt fishing around inside the steaming cavity with both hands until she cried "Aha!" With a swift tug, Hana pulled the deer's liver free and jammed one end of it into her mouth. After ripping off a hunk, she turned to Milda and nodded. "I needed that. Oh, so much," Hana mumbled as she chewed. "I am obliged." She swallowed and held up the remainder to Milda. "Have rest. I insist. Yes."

Milda took the dripping liver from Hana and raised it to her mouth. "Thank you," she replied before taking a big bite. "Now, when we're finished here, dearie," she went on around a mouthful, "we really should be getting back to—ow!"

Hana looked up at Milda with wide eyes. "What is wrong?"

Milda worked her tongue back and forth over the jagged edge of whatever she had bitten through. After waving one hand toward Hana, she drew it to her face and pointed at her mouth. Then held her palm open and spat out everything she had been chewing. She squinted down at the fleshy mass at something glinting in the dim light shining down through the canopy from the night sky above. With one finger on her other hand, she poked at translucent surface. Sharp and hard and broken.

Hana stood and stepped over to Milda. "What did you find?"

"It looks like glass," Milda said, her brow furrowing.

"I wonder. From where could that have come?"

"I don't know, dearie. Here in the Forest, we've come to expect coming across a stray piece of buckshot from time to time in a kill. But I don't ever...ever recall seeing..."

Milda stumbled forward, managing to catch herself by sinking her claws into the bark of the tree closest to her. She looked up at the tree's trunk and gasped. It and everything within her field of vision circled round and round. As her stomach began doing flip-flops, Hana laughed from somewhere off to Milda's right. She glanced up to find the other woman standing there, watching her, a smarmy smile spread across her face.

"First time for everything. Yes," Hana purred before Milda lost consciousness.

Chapter Twenty-Three

A church in the town of Białowieża. Wee hours, the following morning.

Pawly stared at the spot on the floor between her knees until the curtain beyond the pew to her right swooshed open. She lifted her forehead from her folded arms and glimpsed an older man walking briskly down the aisle toward the church's vestibule. She glanced around to confirm she was the last person remaining in the sanctuary and sighed.

After sitting up in the pew, Pawly pushed the kneeler up with the toe of her sneaker. She stood and glanced at her watch before stepping over toward the confessional. Now or never. Parishioners—almost entirely Forest Clan members, Monsignor Dryzek had told Pawly and her family—were already beginning to arrive in advance of Easter Vigil Mass. The clan elders and their families were likely already aboard their shuttle too, on their way here from the resort.

They all had much to seek after prayer for. Pawly and the others would be leaving on their rescue mission to Korea early Easter morning. And they had several occasions for which to give thanks. Nat and Ritzi's success in replicating Tommy's regenerated genetic material with the MGS, had brought the twins' mother back from the brink. Just that afternoon, after much debate, Forest Clan elders had approved Dryzek's recommendation. In the coming days, they would commence rolling out treatments for their kinsmen, to quell the effects of their Affliction's rage once and for all.

Soon the church would be full, possibly for the last time. Once their species' enduring survival no longer bound them to this land, Dryzek had urged his fellow clan members and their families to leave the Forest behind them. To start new lives, the world over.

Pawly stepped into the tiny booth and drew the curtain closed behind her. Her mouth was dry, her palms sweaty. Grainy images of her father's dying moments from the surveillance tape flashed through her mind on a continuous loop as she crossed herself and knelt down once more. Just how long *had* it been since her last confession, any-way? High school? Basic training at Great Lakes? She could hardly remember. Hopefully Dryzek wouldn't ask.

After clasping her hands together, the door behind the metal grille fixed to the wall in front of her slid open. "Welcome, child," came the priest's soft voice from behind the rice paper covering the opening.

"B-bless me, F-father, for I...I have sinned," Pawly mumbled in reply with her head bowed. "It's been..." She clicked her tongue. Why did she have to go and say *that*? "Well, it's been a long time since my last confession. I...I accuse myself of the following sins..." A lump filled her throat, feeling all the world as if she had swallowed a bowling ball. "K-killing my father...and—"

The rice paper panel slammed open. "No, daughter, you misun-derstand," Dryzek said as he met Pawly's gaze. "Allow yourself to feel the guilt so it might pass, sure," he went on in a harsh whisper as he fixed her with a hard stare. "But know, in it, that you have *not* sinned. You and I and the rest of our kind were created by almighty God with

His purposes in mind, killing instincts and all, just like every other living thing. None of us can change that. Nor should we be idolatrous enough to think we ought to try."

Images of the humans among Pawly's family and friends flashed before her eyes. *Halmonim*. Grandpa D. Grandpa N. Uncle Nat.

Lenny.

"But...but what about those I care for?" she whispered in reply. "Those outside our kind? Those that...that I *love*?"

Dryzek sighed and rubbed at his face with his hands. "Centuries ago now, we collectively chose to cloister ourselves off from humans as best we could for that very reason. Those of us near them learned to live double lives, one among our own kind and another, very different one we were required to present to everyone else." He leaned back in his chair to rest his head against the wall behind him. "But your mother, your uncle—none among their clan could have predicted the evil those Soviet submariners would inflict upon them that terrible night afloat on the Baltic. Nor do anything about it when it happened."

She blinked. "What...what does this have to do with them?"

"Their parents had taught them our ways. As your great-grandfather Andrzej would have right up until he and the others were murdered. But after that, Nikodemus and Seon-Yeong and Teodor would come to care for your uncle and your mother. They...they did not know what they did not know."

The man leaned forward in his chair. "And at the time, Milda was in no position to teach them. She was alone and Jakub was a mere babe in arms. She must have believed we wouldn't have been able to either, us being opposite the Iron Curtain from your mother and uncle after the Opoworos left with them for America." He turned his head to stare blankly at the back of the confessional door. "And she was right," Dryzek went on after a moment's pause, during which Pawly realized he had been referring to her mother's adoptive parents and her father's father by their given names. "So, we never pressed Milda for details or followed up further."

Pawly met Dryzek's gaze after he turned back her way. "Ilya and I had just been seated as our Council of Elders' youngest members. And we're the only ones from that time yet alive today, though Ilya has been declining fast. We should have sought out your mother and uncle after the Soviet Union collapsed. Kept tabs on them, kept tabs on you and your brother. Been there for you when you came into your own." Then he hung his head and stared at the floor. "But we did not. You and Tomasz and your family had to go about figuring out how to werecat all on your own. Which is why your father's blood covers *our* hands, not yours. Our penance obligates us to prevent that from ever happening to your family again."

She could hardly believe her ears. Who was confessing to whom here? "Monsignor, I—"

The rice paper slid closed, obscuring Dryzek from Pawly's view but for his silhouette. "Now about that beau of yours. Tell me, child, have you and he been...intimate?"

Pawly bit her lip. "Uhm, well...yes. Yes, we have."

"Americans," Dryzek mumbled. "Once, child?" he said, his voice returning to its previous volume but still soft. "Twice? Three times?"

"A...a few more times than that."

"I see."

Silence passed between them. Just as Pawly wondered whether the man had fallen asleep, he cleared his throat.

"Oh, yes, Monsignor. That's all. I ask for absolution."

"Very well. When you see Milda at Mass, ask to borrow her rosary if you don't have one with you. Retire with your beau afterward to a quiet place and pray through it together. Then go straight to bed—in your separate rooms. I shall pray he takes the hint."

"You don't know him like I do," Pawly replied with a chuckle. "He can be a bit thick sometimes."

"'Knock and it shall be opened unto you,' my child. Now, do you recall the Act of Contrition?"

"Not well, no…but I am sorry for these sins. And for all my others."

"Close enough. *Dominus noster Jesus Christus, te absolvat*," he began to chant quietly, "*et ego auctoritate ipsius te absolvo ab omni vinculo excommunicationis…*"

Dryzek's rapping on the grille opposite her returned Pawly's awareness to the present. "I *said* 'Give thanks to the Lord, for He is good.'"

"Oh. Yes. Yes, He is. And…oh, yeah—'His mercy endures forever.'"

"It does indeed, my child. Now, go in peace."

She crossed herself and stood. "I shall, Monsignor. Thanks be to God. And thank you…thank you, too."

Pawly emerged from the confessional into the empty sanctuary and made her way to the vestibule. Lenny awaited her there, idly scraping with his fingernail at the camework joining two panes of an antique stained-glass window together. "I was beginning to wonder if you were okay," he said, offering her his elbow, "but I didn't want to crowd you."

She flashed him a shy smile and looped her arm around his. "God and the Monsignor and I had a lot to talk about," she said, nodding over her shoulder toward where Dryzek shuffled along behind. "About my dad. And about…us."

"Figure he said we need to keep things platonic between us for a while, huh?"

Pawly bit her lip and nodded.

"Well, that sucks," Lenny replied with a snort. "Here I was hoping to take you on a blanket laid out beneath one of the Forest's thousand-year oaks—"

"Not in *church*, you ass," she hissed into his ear. "Honestly, Lenny. Is that *all* men ever think about?"

"There you are!" came the sound of Grandpa D's voice before Lenny could answer. Pawly looked up in time to find him bolting up the vestibule steps, Jakub right behind.

Pawly cocked an eyebrow. "Where's Milda?"

"That's...that's what we came here," he replied, leaning against the railing at the top of the steps, "to...to talk to you about."

She shook her head. "I don't understand. What's wrong, then?"

"We don't know, Pawly," replied Jakub as their grandfather caught his breath. "The crew at the refectory kitchen asked me to take your Uncle Ritzi his dinner, because they hadn't seen that Hana woman since mid-day. When I did, he told me that she had left with my mother early this afternoon to go hunting in the Forest."

Dryzek emerged from the sanctuary and stared up at the clock hanging on the vestibule wall. "Milda ought to have at least a half a dozen *sernik* whipped up by this time of night, for us all to enjoy once Mass was over."

"Which is why both me and Dory here are worried, Monsignor. Apparently, no one has seen her since then either."

"Yes, that is indeed worrying, young man. And not just on account of my sweet tooth." Dryzek tugged at his chin with his thumb and forefinger. "Your mother hasn't missed an Easter Vigil since your last bout with the croup."

"That's farther back than I remember. Ma told me later I wasn't even that long out of diapers at the time."

Dryzek waved an arm toward Pawly. "You and your mother were with Milda on a hunt your last time here, yes?"

Pawly averted her eyes. "Well, yeah, but I don't think I remember just where we—"

"Don't worry about getting there," Jakub said. "I'll take care of that. But I could really use your help looking for Ma once we arrive."

"No, that's not it." She looked up toward Dryzek. "I seem to recall the Forest Clan members are rather...uhm, territorial about their hunting grounds."

The priest held out his open palm and waved it side to side. "You needn't worry about them, child. All of them will soon gather here in the sanctuary to light candles. I'll see to it this Mass runs long." He looked up at Pawly and winked. "I have an extra special homily in mind, one that ought to buy you ample time to conduct your search."

"Take Tommy with you," Grandpa D said. "Annie said it will do him good to stretch his legs a bit." He sighed and shook his head. "Just be careful, all of you. Because we don't know if Hana might be up to something," he went on as he gripped the stair rail tightly with a trembling hand.

Pawly worked her arm free from Lenny's and stepped over beside her grandfather. "Are...are you all right?" she said, resting her hand atop his shoulder.

"I...I will be." He reached up with his free hand and patted the back of hers.

Jakub levelled his finger toward Lenny's chest. "We could use your help. Someone ought to stay behind in the van while we're in the woods to make sure no one interferes with it."

Lenny glanced over at Pawly and then back to Jakub. He nodded. "Okay."

"So, everything is decided," Grandpa D said, looking around at each of them in turn. "You should all go, then."

"Not until after I beseech St. Joseph for your protection," Dryzek said, crossing himself. Pawly and the others followed suit as the priest lifted his hands and closed his eyes. *"Ad te beate Ioseph, in tribulatione nostra confugimus, atque, implorato Sponsae tuae sanctissimae auxilio, patrocinium quoque tuum fidenter exposcimus..."*

Chapter Twenty-Four

A truck stop near Glinojeck, Poland. Just before dawn.

HANA FLICKED ON HER turn signal and guided the van up the expressway exit. At the top of the ramp, she completed her turn and motored up to the truck stop's main entrance. She ignored the sign directing cars to the parking lot out front beside the petrol pumps. Instead, she followed the truck route, past the diesel fueling stations, past row upon row of parked tractor-trailers and straight trucks. When she reached the rear of the parking area, she glanced around at the tops of the light poles looking for camera housings. Locating a spot where the van would best hide her from any given camera's view, she pulled up as close as she could to the fence at the edge of the asphalt and killed the ignition.

Sleeping geese lined the banks of the retention pond situated opposite the chain link from her, all the way to the tree line beyond. This would do nicely. Anyone spotting an Environment Ministry van parked here might well conclude someone was simply busy gathering data on migration patterns. The dim light of pre-dawn, after all, would enable one to get an accurate count of the geese before they rose and resumed their flight.

She sat there for a moment, watching tendrils of steam rise from the surface of the retention pond. Letting out a long sigh, Hana worked one finger beneath the pink knit neoprene mask covering her face and neck and scratched at her cheek. More pressing matters demanded her attention. The sooner she sloughed off her shed fur and resumed her human guise, the sooner she could attend to them.

Hiking her stocking cap up so as to camouflage her tiger-like ears, Hana stepped out of the van and slid open its side door. She grabbed her duffel, slung it over her shoulder, then pulled the door shut. Rubbing at her coiled-up tail through the fanny pack covering the slit in her jeans, she glanced quickly back and forth between the van's driver and passenger seats. Satisfied she had everything she would need, Hana yanked Milda's keyring from the van's ignition and let it drop to the floor. Then she poked the driver's door lock button and slammed the door shut behind her.

Lights from the truck stop cast a glow in the sky above the rows of trucks spreading out across the landscape in front of her. Hana hiked her duffel's strap atop her shoulder and set off toward them, not once looking back at the abandoned van.

Hana entered the truck stop and squinted up toward the overhead signs. She managed to decipher enough of their text to make her way over toward the shower area. "Perfect," she mumbled, approaching the yellow-and-black striped barrier blocking off the hallway in front of her. "Hello? Anyone here?" she called out in Polish.

Footsteps echoed from around the corner past the hallway barrier. "I'm sorry. We're closed for cleaning until..."

The voice trailed off as a young man, dressed in an attendant's uniform, rounded the corner. Hana stifled a chuckle as he stood there, gaping at her, his eyes wide. Maybe he had never met a burn victim face-to-face before. Good.

Hana averted her eyes. "I...I want to find a place here I might..." she said in a small voice "...you know, change."

"Oh...oh, I see," the young man managed at length. He nervously glanced back and forth between Hana and the first shower room behind him. "I just finished cleaning this one," he said, pulling the barrier aside and waving her through. "The soap dispenser is full and the towels are fresh. Take whatever time you need."

Hana blinked. "Don't I need to pay for a key or something?"

"I haven't opened my till yet," the young man replied, shaking his head. "But I don't want to keep you waiting. My father was burned in an industrial accident some while back now, and my mother changed his dressings like clockwork."

She smiled behind her mask, taking care to squint so as to convey her gratitude with her eyes. "Thank you. I really appreciate this."

The young man nodded toward the empty booth behind her. "Though I would appreciate your coming to find me when you're done. Once I get the rest of these rooms swabbed out, I'll be right back there behind the desk until my shift is over."

Hana nodded and ducked past him into the shower room, closing and locking the door behind her. Then she sat her duffel down on the bench beside the shower stall and reached around behind the nape of her neck for the mask's zipper. She groaned and grunted as she pulled it free, her damp fur clinging to the mask's insides. Gazing at her disheveled face in the mirror above the sink, she began scratching at her cheeks. Her fur came off in clumps, suggesting the mask might have actually helped hasten her shed. That would be helpful, she realized as she glanced down at her watch. The bus to Gdańsk was due in twenty minutes, so she had no time to lose.

By the time she finished a quick shower and brief brush-out, her tail had completely receded back into her body. Recalling the young man's kindness, she scooped as much of her shed fur as she could with her hands into the waste bin beside the sink. Then she wiped up the rest with a towel and wadded it up into a ball beside the bin.

Hana scrutinized her naked form in the mirror. Satisfied her human guise had fully returned, she rummaged around in her duffel for a suitable change of clothes. Finding them, she quickly dressed and repacked her duffel. After zipping it closed, she dug her last pair of twenty *złoty* bank notes from the bag's side pocket and laid them on the shower bench. Then she emerged into the hall, turning opposite the direction the young man said led to his desk. The corridor led past several more shower rooms and back out into the hallway. Hana peeked around the corner and spotted the young man talking to two men standing in front of his booth, both wearing truck driver's uniforms. She darted around the corner and down the hall until she came to an open doorway. Drawing up beside it, she realized from the sound of clanking plates it must be a service entrance into to the truck stop's restaurant.

After stepping through, Hana spotted a man in a dingy white uniform beside a large sink, his arms immersed in soap suds past his elbows. "Excuse me, I think I'm lost," she called out to him.

The man glanced over his shoulder for only a moment before turning back to his work. "Tourists," he muttered low enough that surely no human would have heard him. "Dining room is through that door over there," he said in a louder voice, nodding his head in that particular direction. "One of the waitresses can show you out. Or seat you, if you prefer."

She glanced back and forth at the stacks of plates and cups, many of them dingier than the dishwasher's uniform. "No thank you," she replied. "I'm...I'm not hungry." *Not anymore, anyway.*

Hana exited the dish room and strode across the restaurant's serving area to the entrance. Once outside, she scanned back and forth along the front of the building. An inter-city bus sat parked beside the curb nearest to the truck stop's main doors, a line of passengers awaiting their turn to board following their meal stop. She set off towards it, picking up her pace upon spotting *GDAŃSK GŁÓWNY* scrolling across its destination indicator.

Meanwhile, back in the Białowieża Forest...

L ENNY GROANED AND BLINKED, quickly throwing an arm over his eyes to shield them from the blinding light. He smacked his lips and sat up in the driver's seat of the van. The sun's rays streamed from over top of the trees, lighting up the icy remnants from the winter's snow covering the ground beyond the edge of the gravel parking lot. He gazed back and forth at the tree line in front of him out the van's windshield and frowned. It was morning already. Neither Pawly nor Tommy nor Jakub had returned from their search for Milda and Hana. And, given the tingling sensation within his bladder, it had been quite some while since he had last emptied out, before leaving the church back in Białowieża.

Shivering from the cold, Lenny keyed the van's ignition. Its engine rumbled to life, affording Lenny occasion to breathe a relieved sigh.

He had had the presence of mind before nodding off to crack open the windows so as to allow in fresh air. Instead of the van's engine having stalled, apparently the vehicle had some sort of automatic engine shutoff to conserve fuel or something. Dryzek had arranged on the fly for them to borrow this jalopy, so no one had seen fit to ask a lot of questions before speeding off.

After pulling at his door handle, Lenny carefully stepped out into the snow. Shuffling back and forth to make sure his feet would not slide out from under him on the hidden ice, he high-stepped to the end of the van and strode off toward the outhouse opposite the parking lot from him. He glanced back and forth across the patches of dirty snow, their white parts gleaming in the dawn's light. His gaze followed the set of tracks from their vehicle to where they disappeared around the bend in the potholed gravel road leading out to the highway. Accompanying the two other sets of tracks they had all seen upon their arrival the night before, which he and the others quickly concluded belonged to Milda's Environment Ministry service van. Carefully examining the tracks in the snow had suggested to Lenny a driver and passenger exited the vehicle, though only a driver got back in.

Tommy had suggested that Hana might have been hurt somehow and Milda had gone to get help. But Pawly, having faced Hana before, cautioned of her trickery. In the unlikely event Hana had somehow overpowered Milda, she could well have carried her back to the van as a hostage.

Jakub had cast the tie-breaking vote. His mother knew every square meter of these woods. Hana, a newcomer, did not. If anyone would have been carried out of here, it would have been her. But he believed they ought to search the area anyway. Because if there had been some sort of tussle, and if his mother had emerged the victor, she would have certainly gone straight to the Bodny family home near the main road to use their telephone. With that, Jakub and Tommy and Pawly sprouted fur right before Lenny's eyes before bounding off into the woods together to look for her.

Hours had passed since then, as Lenny's bladder reminded him with each step. Upon reaching the outhouse, he reached out for the handle and gave it a pull. The door opened but a mere crack before a padlocked hasp prevented him from opening the door further. He looked up at a small red placard on the outhouse door in front of him. Its white letters surely spelled out some variant of "closed for the season"—he did not need to know a word of Polish to figure that out.

Lenny swore and stomped around behind the outhouse. The nearby underbrush would afford him at least a little bit of privacy, good. He undid his fly and relieved himself, *ahh*ing loudly and longly while his bladder emptied out.

As he finished, he thought how aggravated Dory would surely be at this divergence from his carefully choreographed itinerary. Surely the elder man would be worried sick about his lover Milda, about her son and his grandchildren; he would be desperate to know they were all okay. Yet Lenny was certain Dory and Top had already shipped out for Redzikowo regardless, taking the container concealing Mawro with them. Because both of them knew better than to keep a MAC flight waiting, especially one tasked with ferrying them all the way to the Korean Peninsula.

A *thump* from inside the outhouse gave Lenny a start, nearly causing him to snag his pubic hair as he zipped up his pants. A groan followed. From what sounded like...a *woman*?

He quickly put himself back together and leaned his ear against the side of the outhouse. "Hey in there!" he cried before pounding on its wall with the heel of his palm. "Can you hear me? Are you all right?"

The woman inside grumbled what sounded to Lenny like an urgent reply, despite its being unintelligible. As if the woman were trying to talk around some kind of gag. "Hana, if that's you in there, slap or bump the wall once. If it's you, Milda, twice."

Thump. Thump.

Lenny gasped and darted around to the front of the outhouse. He grabbed at the door handle and pulled, but the padlocked hasp held firm. "I'll call for the others, Milda," he shouted at the door, drawing forth from his pants pocket the dog whistle which Jakub had given him earlier. "We'll figure out how we can get you out of there." Then he crunched his way through the snow to the tree line and blew the dog whistle as hard as he could.

A mumbled cross between a curse and a snarl rose up from the outhouse behind him. "Oh, I'm sorry. I should have told you to cover your ears. But, then again, I suppose your hands are bound together, aren't they?"

Thump. Thump.

"Fair enough. I'll be right back."

Lenny dashed through the snow and into the trees. There he drew the dog whistle to his lips and blew one more time.

"Keep your shirt on, dumbass! We heard you the first time."

Lenny smiled and turned toward the sound of Pawly's voice. She bounded into view a moment later, Tommy right behind her.

"I'm glad to see you two," Lenny said. "Where's Jakub?"

"He should be here soon," Tommy answered him. "He was sweeping an area where the underbrush is thicker, making for slow going."

"Well, you can help me free Milda then and surprise him when he comes."

Pawly's eyes went wide. "You know where she is?"

"I'm in no mood for horsing around, Lemony Rinse," Tommy said, crossing his arms. "The three of us have been running ourselves ragged all night trying to find her."

Lenny shrugged. "I wouldn't have believed it myself if I hadn't...well, maybe you should just come see for yourselves."

The three of them shuffled off through the snow. "Milda! I'm here with Pawly and Tommy," Lenny cried as the three of them approached the outhouse. "Let them know you're in there."

Thump. Thump.

Pawly swore loudly and hopped atop the small building's roof. She leaned over the eave and drew her nose up beside a metal grate in one wall near the roofline. "She's in there all right," she cried as she hopped down. "Been right under our damn noses this whole time!"

"Her scent camouflaged by the contents of the cesspool beneath, Sis." Tommy walked around to the front of the outhouse and eyed the padlock and hasp below the door handle. "Which I'm certain Hana knew full well it would."

"Here, allow me," Pawly said as she stepped up beside Tommy and took hold of the hasp. "Gotta practice for when I manage to get my hands around that Bengal bimbo's neck."

With a *ki-hahp*, Pawly began to tug at the hasp and padlock. Though she wrenched it this way and that, it held firm, no matter how much she shouted and screamed and swore. "Don't just stand there with your mouths hanging open, dickheads," Pawly cried, casting her searing glare back and forth between Tommy and Lenny. "Each of you grab a shoulder and help me pull!"

The two of them did as they were asked. "Okay," she said, steeling herself, "all together now on three. One...two...three!"

They pulled. Hard enough for the padlock to slip through Pawly's hands, sending the three of them all flying backward into a snowdrift.

They thrashed about until someone hauled Lenny upright by the collar of his pea coat. After regaining his footing, he turned to find Tommy beside him. Past him stood Jakub. "You three. No time for goofing off," he bellowed in English as he hauled Pawly to her feet. "We are looking for Hana and my mother, yes?"

Thump. Thump.

"We are, but it was Lenny who finally found her," Pawly replied, pointing toward the outhouse door. "She's in there."

"Mamo? Jestes tam?" Jakub shouted toward the outhouse, eliciting another urgent-sounding yet unintelligible reply from within.

Whiskers twitching, Jakub stomped over to the outhouse door. The hasp and padlock denied him entry, clanking as if to mock him whenever he yanked on the handle. A low growl rumbling forth from somewhere deep in his throat, he seized the padlock in one hand and flicked his wrist. The entire hasp pulled free from the door and jamb with a tinny *pop*. Jakub tossed the crumpled hasp aside, its padlock still attached, and flung the outhouse door open. *"Mamo!"*

Jakub scooped Milda up into his arms and carried her over to a nearby picnic table. Lenny ran on ahead and brushed snow of off the end of one bench with his pea coat's sleeve. Tommy drew up close as Jakub set her down, taking her shoulders into his hands to help keep her upright. Pawly bared her claws and slipped one behind the gag in Milda's mouth. After ripping the gag in half, she knelt in front of Milda's feet and began working and the bindings around her wrists. "Where's my van?"

"We don't know," Pawly answered for them. "It was gone when we got here."

The woman worked her jaw open and closed several times before she went on. "Hana asked if I could unlock the outhouse for her to use it before our hunt, so I did. After we took our kill, she slipped me some sort of drug and I passed out. Then she must have made off with my keys."

"And locked you up in the outhouse before driving off with your van," Jakub said, punching his hand with his fist. He met Lenny's gaze, then wagged his chin toward their vehicle. "Bring our van around. I want to get Ma home to rest. Then you and me and the twins here have a plane to catch."

Lenny nodded and ran off across the parking lot. Waldemar and his box truck would certainly be awaiting them in Białowieża, ready to ferry them all to Redzikowo. Having the werecats ride in the truck's cargo area while they morphed back and completed their shed would save some time. Whether it would be enough to reach Dory and Mawro before Hana showed up in their theater of operations was anyone's guess.

CHAPTER TWENTY-FIVE

HANA BLINKED IN THE sun shining down upon the street outside the bus terminal. She stretched and yawned, having been unable to get much sleep on the ride here. One of the few seats left open on the bus had been located in the rear of the vehicle adjacent to the lavatory; every time she managed to nod off, the toilet flushing or the lavatory door slamming shut would wake her. Soon, very soon, she would have an opportunity to take her rest.

But for now, she strode off down the street, focused on the task at hand. The street outside the bus terminal was all but deserted this Easter morning. Once the church bells started pealing in celebration, that would surely change, as hungry churchgoers flocked to whatever place they agreed to gather with friends and family for brunch. Her thinking again about food set her stomach grumbling. The little bit of the deer's liver she gulped down the previous night had not stuck with her long at all. Maybe she would pick up something quick so she might sate her hunger. For that she would need funds—funds which could never be traced either to her or to this city. Of just the sort she intended to get her hands on here, in fact.

A block and a half away from the bus station she came to an ancient warehouse, repurposed into a self-storage center several years ago during a downtown renovation initiative. Surely because the space-constrained new residents of the lofts constructed in the old factory across the street would want some place close by to keep their things.

Hana entered the lobby and poked her access code into the electronic lock beside the inner door. Its display flashed green as it buzzed her in. Once inside, she followed the familiar route to a row of storage units, each little more than a meter wide. She let her duffel slide to the floor and reached up for the combination lock attached to a hasp on the side of the narrow metal roll-up door. After twirling it right, then left, then right again, the lock popped open. Hana pulled it back through the hasp and jammed the lock into her pants pocket. Then she rolled up the door, revealing an empty unit save for another duffel, similar to her own, sitting on a shelf about chest height.

After unzipping the duffel, Hana set aside a bag of toiletries and a couple changes of clothes. She snorted as she picked up a box of tampons, its plastic wrapping still intact, and shook it back and forth. An exhausting night spent cold and hungry and soiled on a park bench, awaiting a long-delayed rendezvous with one of ChongPol's vessels, had prompted Hana months before to squirrel away a shoreside "comfort kit" like this one in each of the ships' ports-of-call. Such irony, having no further need for them since. Or, more accurately, such irony at having no further need for them until *after* DPRK decided they had no further need for her.

Hana set the box down atop the pile of clothing and rummaged around in the bottom of the duffel. After plucking out a black leather wallet, she backed up into the middle of the corridor. Bathed in gray-blue light courtesy of the sodium vapor lamp buzzing high above her head, she rifled through the wallet taking a quick inventory. Several hundred *złoty* worth of bank notes, several hundred more in American dollars, and a pair of prepaid credit cards. Each card bore a different alias, matching the two passports Hana had brought with her in the other bag. Pyongyang knew about one of the aliases, but Hana had taken pains to see no one would ever know about the other.

She stuffed the wallet into the back pocket of her pants and picked up the bag lying on the corridor floor opposite the storage unit. After pulling out her passports, she jammed them into the bag on the shelf and zipped it shut. Then she hefted the bag from the shelf and slung its strap over her shoulder. Leaving the door of the now-empty unit open, she strode quickly to the lobby, then out into the street.

After retracing her steps to the bus station, she continued up the block until she reached Gdańsk's main train station. Passing through the main entrance, she quickly made her way to the first women's restroom. Once inside, Hana glanced down beneath the stall doors. Certain she was indeed alone, Hana marched over to the trash receptacle near the row of sinks and stuffed the bag she had brought with her from Białowieża into it. Then she briskly strode out of the restroom and down the concourse until she reached the ticketing booths. "Please, one ticket. To Warsaw. Very next train due out," she stammered in Polish to the gray-haired PKP clerk standing behind the first open window she came to.

"Why certainly, miss," the man replied, pulling at one rim of his glasses as he peered back at her through the bars. "Are you needing an express train? Or would you find a local making all stops acceptable?"

Hana shook her head. "It does not matter. Either will be fine. Yes."

Sŏnbong-guyŏk, North Korea. Hours later.

OH BURST THROUGH THE door into the control room, his security contingent fanning out as they entered behind him. "Director Yin! What the hell is...?"

His voice trailed off as his gaze fell upon where Yin lay flat on his back on the control room floor. The scientist's legs leaning up against the side of the elder Opoworo's wheelchair; his feet and ankles rested in the man's lap. Oh glanced down at Opoworo, seated in his chair with a smug look on his face.

Oh snorted and stomped over to the control room's console. There he poked a big red button beside a red flashing light there, silencing the klaxon blaring above their heads. "Somebody tell me what the fuck is going on here!"

Yin groaned and raised his head. "These...these *two* insisted upon interfering with our intervention!" he cried, nodding toward Opoworo.

"As I have since coming to in your ship's sick bay, as you'll recall. That you all let Annie and me handle Stuie," the man in the wheelchair shot back, narrowing his eyes. "But this time, I was just sitting here, minding my own business, when you tripped over me."

"Only because *she* shoved me into you!"

Oh covered his eyes with one hand and began to rub at his forehead. "And just where is the girl's mother now?"

As Yin shakily got to his feet, he waved toward the aluminum door frame separating the control room from the adjacent isolation chamber. Shards of glass from the door littered the dusty floor of the chamber opposite them. "She's in there."

With a snarl, Oh darted his gaze back and forth across the control room. "Where is your guard?"

"Over here, sir!"

Oh whirled around to find two men from his contingent hauling the uniformed guard to his feet. The man cradled his nose with both hands, blood dripping from between his fingers. "Guy says the mother snatched his rifle from his hands and then smashed his face with its butt end."

"Then she did likewise to the isolation chamber's door and pushed me," Yin added. "I dropped the controller for the girl's shock collar as I fell. She picked it up and dashed inside."

Opoworo rolled his eyes. "Only because you wouldn't listen to her!"

"Her fears we might damage the girl's central nervous system if we delivered a pulse out of synch with her heartbeat are completely unfounded," Yin replied, his hands on his hips. "I told you both we are sure it is a safe and effective technique to quell the girl's rage."

"And *we* both told *you* not to coax Stuie into raging in the first place. You should have left well enough alone!"

"Enough!" Oh cried before whirling around to face the troopers holding the injured guard upright. "Get this fool out of my face. You two there," he said with a nod toward the pair nearest the isolation chamber doorway, "make sure no one or no *thing* comes through that door without my say so." Then he turned and met eyes with his remaining men in the control room. "The rest of you, get up to the catwalk above the isolation chamber and stand by with your tasers for my signal. Now move!"

After his troops scurried off, Oh turned and stepped through the doorway into the isolation chamber, glass crunching under his feet. "Where did you last see the girl, Director?"

The other man waved a hand over toward a pile of construction rubble heaped up into one corner of the isolation chamber. "Over there. Her mother is surely close by."

Oh nodded and entered the chamber. Soon he spotted Annie Opoworo, frozen in place, her gaze fixed on something obscured from Oh's view by a boulder-sized chunk of broken concrete. He tiptoed toward her, managing to move silently until the toe of his boot connected with a jagged piece of metal hidden in the dirt and dust. It skittered across the floor, clinking and clanking, until it bounced off the concrete chunk and disappeared from view. Annie gasped.

Something *roared*.

A flash of orange and black streaked through Oh's line of vision before something threw him bodily up against the broken concrete. When his world stopped spinning, he stared up into a pair of wild, feral eyes, framed by locks of long, black hair. The girl hissed at him with primal fury, baring her sharp fangs. Then she started, yanking at the shock collar around her neck as her hiss morphed into a pained yowl. Her eyes rolled up into her head before her arms went limp and she fell forward. Landing spread eagle on the dusty floor, the girl whimpered once and then lay still.

"I *could* have let her eat your face, you know."

Oh looked up and met Annie's smoldering gaze.

"I think that makes as good a case as any why you ought to trust Niko and me," she went on, nodding toward the control room. "Besides, we know we need you just as much as you need us right now."

Oh glanced over at the girl's prone form. "Fine. Have it your way." He raised his head toward the catwalk encircling the isolation chamber and cupped his hands to his mouth. "Stand down, all of you," he shouted before stomping off.

The elder Opoworo sat seated in his wheelchair beside the control room's broken door frame. As Oh approached, a surprised cry drew his attention back over his shoulder toward where the girl's mother knelt beside her daughter. Sitting upright on the isolation chamber floor, the dazed girl gazed about the room, blinking rapidly. Her fur-covered ears twitched back and forth, as if she were struggling to process who and where she was. The girl's mother mumbled something into her ear before throwing both arms around her and crushing the girl to her chest.

"I suppose you'll be wanted in here," Oh said after he opened the door and waved him through.

Opoworo flashed Oh a sly smile as he wheeled his chair past him. He rolled over toward where the girl's mother knelt clenching her daughter to her chest, her body heaving.

"A word, General."

Oh looked up and frowned, seeing Min Soo enter the control room. "Yes, yes, I had seen you had called me." He stepped through the door and pulled it closed behind him out of habit. "I've been a little busy," he added, waving an arm toward the broken door. "We have less than forty-eight hours between now and when our guests begin arriving."

"Make sure your people know to check the guest list carefully, General. We might have an unexpected 'plus one.'"

Oh growled and rubbed at his temples. "Dammit, man! Speak plainly for a change, wouldn't you?"

"Hana's credit card has been used to purchase a bus ticket at a truck stop in Poland along the E77 motorway, far from the Białowieża

Forest. Then it was maxed out at the Warsaw airport, purchasing a few million airline miles from a Lufthansa ticketing kiosk."

Oh cocked an eyebrow at him. "Have you confirmed it was indeed her?"

"I cannot," he replied with a shake of his head. "All I can figure is that either she's removed her earrings or that someone has tinkered with them."

"I doubt she would go anywhere near an airport if the former, for fear she might rage herself in a crowded terminal. Or even in mid-flight."

Min Soo shrugged. "Then the latter, perhaps. From what you've told me about that Tomasz Katczynski fellow, such a feat might be well within his capability. Especially with Mawro helping him."

"It matters little either way," Oh replied. "Because I do not believe she is heading to Rason. She would have no reason to, not even knowing we're here. Besides, even if she did, I'm certain Mawro made sure she knows every soldier in the People's Army would have orders to shoot her on sight." He patted at his suitcoat, above his inside pocket beneath. "And if she does come, does somehow manage to elude them, I will not hesitate to detonate her kill chip should she dare to intervene," Oh said with a snort. "But we will have plenty of time to deal with her later." He glanced through the control room window toward where the Opoworo family sat holding one another. "Come, Min Soo. Right now, we must begin preparing our star attraction for her big debut."

Chapter Twenty-Six

Sea of Japan, off the Russian coast. Thirty-six hours later.

Tommy peered past Jakub's shoulder out the window of the helicopter's cabin. The looming shadow lumbering through the fog was quickly replaced by a view of the *Kamchatsky Trader*'s deck after their pilot began their descent. He glimpsed the big white "H" surrounded by a green circle painted atop the hatch cover nearest the ship's superstructure, until the nose of their craft came about and made a beeline for it. The crewman sitting opposite the cabin from them knelt down on the deck and slid the cabin door open. "Everyone. This is your stop," he shouted in halting English over the din as he leaned out toward the skid. "Be ready. Alight on my signal. Yes."

He glanced up toward where Lenny and Pawly sat opposite the cabin from them. Tommy was sure Lenny would have rather fast roped down to the deck, eager to recapture the thrill of the numerous VBSS insertions during their tour together aboard the *San Jacinto*. Truth be told, Tommy would have been happy to follow him down. Grandpa D had likely figured as much and taken steps to minimize any risk to Tommy's still-fragile musculoskeletal system. Express orders to their pilot received via coded message from the *Trader* after putting out from Vladivostok were to drop his passengers on the ship's deck, period. Lenny had not pushed the point either, knowing Top was keeping him on a short leash too.

Their pilot brought them gingerly down atop the helipad. After a barely noticeable bump, the crewman straightened up and waved them out. Lenny hopped out first and extended his hand to Pawly. After Tommy and Jakub scrambled out behind them, the crewman handed them their duffels one at a time. The four of them crouched down and shuffled their way over to the steel staircase at the edge of the helipad. After the helicopter's cabin door slammed shut behind them, Tommy glanced back over his shoulder. Their crewman tossed him a casual salute through the cabin window as the bird lifted off. The helicopter traced a wide arc past the ship's stern and plunged into a fog bank, making all possible speed so as to return to its oil platform home base before burning up all its fuel.

A whistle caught Tommy's attention an instant before Top stepped into view around the corner of the cargo hatch. "Dory asked me to bring you all to them as soon as you came aboard," he said, nodding toward the ship's stern. "This way."

Top strode off along the deck and the four of them followed. A moment later they ducked into a passageway leading below deck, then descended a staircase situated against one of the aft hold's bulkheads. The beam from Top's flashlight flashed back and forth across dimensional lumber, steel rebar, and bulk bags silkscreened with large red Cyrillic characters. Likely containing some sort of powdery material—lime or fly ash or Portland cement or whatever.

"Watch your step," Top said as he pulled open a bulkhead door and motioned them inside. After high-stepping over the threshold, Tommy spied Ritzi in the far corner of the hold compartment, naked but for what appeared to be a pair of cargo shorts fashioned from scraps of tent canvas. His uncle reclined upon some sort of oversized bed, fashioned together from pieces of rusted metal.

"You all had a reasonably pleasant trip here from Białowieża, I trust."

Tommy turned toward where Grandpa D sat, finger steepled, seated behind a long folding table with an unreadable look on his face. Here in theater, about to commence operations, Tommy knew his grandfather would already have his game face on.

"Yes. Yes, we did," Pawly replied for all of them as she followed Lenny into the compartment.

"We had to scramble to find charter flights on short notice," Top added as he pulled the cabin door closed behind him. "So, whatever was coming in this general direction, we booked for you."

Uncle Ritzi sat up and swung his legs over the edge of his bed. "I'll bet you they at least got to get out and stretch their legs a bit whenever they landed." He met Tommy's gaze and leaned his way, the bed frame groaning under his weight. Cotton waste protruded from one corner of the mattress cover, haphazardly stitched together from mismatched swatches of burlap. "I was cooped up aboard that MAC flight all the way from Redzikowo to Osan Air Base in South Korea. Bastards wouldn't even let us leave the plane when we took on fuel after landing in Dubai."

"Hardly a pleasant sixteen hours for Dory and me either, Ritzi," Top spat back as he took a seat beside Grandpa D. Tommy and Jakub and Pawly and Lenny each sat down across the folding table from them. "And that was before we rubber-tired over to Sokcho all stuffed into your container with you to be put aboard this leaky old tub."

Grandpa D rubbed at his forehead. "Give it a rest, both of you. You can both give our MAC crew a one-star review later." He blew out his breath and turned toward Tommy and the others. "Forgive us if we're all a bit cranky. We've been cooped up below deck like bilge rats since, waiting for the rest of you to get here."

Top crossed his arms. "Sokcho to Vladivostok, then Vladivostok to Rason and back again. Since we had to wait for the rest of you to catch up, we were forced to make another turn to avoid breaking our cover." He turned and made a face at Ritzi. "More than enough time for us all to get on each other's nerves, suffice to say."

Grandpa D leaned forward and planted his elbows on the table. "But what's on my nerves even more than *you* two, Topper, is just how far behind these delays have put us. As it is, we'll barely arrive back in Rason ahead of Oh's dog and pony show."

Tommy gulped. Bortnik had told them about the event after they had captured him back in Belarus. Their loved ones were Oh's star attractions, especially Stuie. If he and the others arrived too late to affect their rescue, then God only knew for sure when they would have another opportunity. If ever.

"And on top of all of that, we've got this wildcard now to deal with," Grandpa D went on as he looked up at Tommy. "When was the last time you managed to get a fix on Hana's location, son?"

"When we changed planes in Kazakhstan. We knew already she'd flown out of Warsaw, and picked her up again in Frankfort."

Grandpa D stroked his chin. "That's Lufthansa's main hub, isn't it?"

"It is, Agent Katczynski," Lenny said before Tommy could answer. "My parents and I used to fly to Frankfort every couple years or so as I was growing up to visit my dad's aunts and uncles and cousins. Lufthansa flies practically everywhere around the globe out of there," Lenny added.

Pawly smacked her lips together. "If Hana was flying with them, she could be just about anywhere by now."

"Thank you, Lenny. And quite right, Pawly." Grandpa D turned his attention back to Tommy. "So was Frankfort the last location you'd confirmed her at?"

Tommy pulled his knapsack up into his lap and unzipped it. "Yes. I didn't dare try nailing up an encrypted connection via satellite uplink while we were on layover at Beijing."

"That was wise," Grandpa D said with a nod. "Sitting in front of an airport window beside an open briefcase with a parabolic antenna sprouting out of it might attract the kinds of attention from the Chinese none of us could afford. Doing so then would have only set us back further. But now, we need to know where Hana is."

"Is that key server aboard and online?" Tommy asked as he drew out his laptop and set it on the table in front of him. "And has the antenna been fully deployed?"

"Yes, I set them both up myself," Top answered him as Tommy powered up his laptop. "At least it got me above deck for a while on the way back from Rason."

"Okay, thank you." Tommy drummed his fingers on the table top in front of him while his laptop's boot sequence completed. Then he launched his encryption app and glanced down at the alphanumeric sequence displayed on the digital readout of a key fob-like device attached to one of his knapsack's zipper pulls. After entering in the proper characters, a tinny *bing* from the laptop's speakers informed Tommy the app had finished executing its secure connection routines. "Okay, I'm in," he said as he tapped furiously at his keyboard. "Now let me get the map up here... import the updated dataset from the geolocation algorithms...and then we see what we can...oh. *Oh.*"

Grandpa turned his way. "What, son? What is it?"

"Apparently, Hana landed several hours ago at an airport in mainland China."

"Which one?"

"Shenyang." Tommy adjusted his glasses and hunched over in front of his screen. "There's a trail leading north out of there, so she must be relying on ground travel now."

"Let me see!" Grandpa D cried before bolting up out of his chair.

"Right here," Tommy replied after Grandpa D rushed up behind him. He traced the route on his screen with his finger. "Looks like she's headed toward Changchun."

"Then she's headed right for us."

"How can you be so sure, Dory?"

Grandpa D stood and met eyes with Uncle Ritzi. "Because the twice-daily train to Changchun continues all the way to Yanji in the Yanbian Prefecture."

Uncle Ritzi gasped. "Which borders North Korea!"

"And not hardly more than thirty miles overland to Rason from there, if I'm not mistaken," Top added. "In her tigrine form, I'm sure she could make up that distance in no time."

"This is your show," Grandpa D said to Top, holding both his open palms out to him. "Figure you'd've hatched a plan already, so let's hear it."

"All right, then." Top stepped over to his laptop and started poking at its keyboard. The projector on the table in front of it whirred to life, reproducing the image of the map on his laptop's screen on the bulkhead opposite them. "This, right here," he said, twiddling his cursor over an array of gray circular objects surrounded on three sides by thick green forest, "is the Seungri Chemical refinery complex." He moved his cursor toward the ocean, then followed the coastline up an inlet to a harbor lined on all three sides with gray concrete wharves.

"This is Unggi Bay; the harbor and the town around it are known as Songbong." His cursor kept on along the shore until it stopped beside a jetty connecting the mainland to a long and skinny island offshore. "And right here, in the middle of all this open land, is the Emperor Hotel and Casino. Built in part to attract foreign businessmen to the region."

"Let me guess," Lenny piped up from where he sat beside Pawly. "To allow Pyongyang to showcase the region's burgeoning industry. And that deep water port I saw you whisk by in nearby Rason."

"Pretty smart for a puddle pirate, isn't he, folks?" Top replied with a wink. "Correct on all counts." He stepped up to the bulkhead and pointed toward a semi-circular structure situated just inland from the Emperor Hotel. "This is an amphitheater built to entertain DPRK's guests with concerts and circus acts and other live shows. It was constructed over top of a small cogeneration plant, cut into the hillside here, just opposite this ridge from the refinery. Massive pipes bored beneath the ridge deliver waste steam from the refinery to supplement on-site boilers providing power and heat to the hotel and casino. Steam ejectors provide air conditioning during the summer months."

Pawly whistled. "Warm in the winter and cool in the summer? I suppose applicants from all the country are climbing over top of each another to get a job there."

"If Sunny were here, she would surely remind us such perks are reserved only for the Party's upper echelon. And members of their most trusted military units," Grandpa D added.

"Yes, which is why the spooks back at Langley believe staffers here are all part of some sort of DPRK covert operations group," Top said with a nod. "Likely every room is bugged. Housekeepers surely rifle through every guest's luggage and personal items every time they make the rooms up, too."

After Top tapped at his keyboard, a series of mug shots replaced the aerial images from the North Korean coastline.

Lenny *hmph*ed. "I recognize some of those guys from my Coast Guard human trafficking briefings. Those two on the left operate one of the biggest drug smuggling rings out of El Salvador." He pointed at the right side of the screen. "That wild-eyed guy there is from Cambodia. No illicit goods move in or out of Phnom Phen without his say so."

"Everyone in the stevedore's union received similar training," Jakub added, "to keep alert for signs of human trafficking while unloading ships from foreign ports." He nodded toward the screen. "Those two fellows next to the Cambodian are both former Spetsnaz guys. Do not be taken in by their smiling faces. They're known to deliver anyone who crosses them piece by piece back home to his family. Or *hers*."

"And those three in the center?" Top curled his lip. "They're Americans. Leaders of the Aryan Nations from Idaho," he said in low tones, his voice almost a growl.

Pawly yawned and stretched as the mug shots disappeared. "Fine, upstanding citizens on Oh's VIP list for his little shindig, huh?" she asked as their screen repainted with the terrain map they previously been viewing.

"Yeah, and most of 'em hate each other." Top crossed his arms and leaned his back up against the bulkhead nearest him. "Which is why I doubt DPRK's people will go pawing through their stuff while they're here. Any of this crowd would likely as not accuse another guest of trying to get a leg up on them in the bidding or something. And then stab them in the temple with a piece of room service flatware as soon as their DPRK handlers' backs were turned."

Grandpa D buried his face in his hands. "All the more reason we need to get Niko and Annie and Stuie out of there as soon as possible," he said through his fingers.

Top stepped to the head of their table and leaned forward, resting his open palms on the table top. "Now that we're all here, that's exactly what I plan for us to do."

Uncle Ritzi's ears drew back against either side of his head. "But what about Hana?"

"Yes, she's the one variable we can hardly account for. Which is why we need your help to find her for us. Tommy?"

Tommy reached down into his bag and pulled out a hand-held transceiver. "On the way here, I reprogrammed this unit to monitor the new squawk frequency we configured Hana's earrings to use." He stepped over toward Uncle Ritzi and held the thing out to him. "When Hana's in range, you can tell what direction and how close she is by monitoring signal strength and bearing."

Uncle Ritzi leaned over, squinting at the device. "I don't see any extendable antenna. The thing's effective range would be markedly limited even with one."

"You're right, big guy," Top said before Tommy could answer. "Which is why you and Tommy will need to hold the high ground." He stepped over to the terrain map and waved his hand back and forth near the center of the image. "This ridge surrounds the Emperor Hotel on three sides. We expect her to approach from the west, likely skirting the Seungri Chemical refinery to help camouflage her scent from us." He pointed to a spot on the ridge near where a straight line drawn between the refinery and the hotel might intersect. "If we deploy you right here, Tommy assures me that instrument will pick up Hana's earrings if she's anywhere in the valley below."

Uncle Ritzi drew back onto his haunches and frowned. "That won't help if she makes it to the amphitheater before we do."

"True." Top motioned toward where the ridge met the seashore down the coast from the Emperor Hotel. "Lenny will pilot the semi-submersible we have aboard and drop you here. Then you can make your way toward the middle of the ridge." He followed the ridgeline with his finger until it intersected the shoreline near the harbor. "It should be dark by the time our ship is on approach to Songbong Harbor," he went on, turning to Pawly and Tommy. "As the ship makes way to its berth, you two and Jakub will bail out here beside this breakwater. It should give you adequate cover until you make your way ashore and into the tree line. Follow the ridge until you meet up with Ritzi. You'll have an instrument like Ritzi will have, so between all of you we should know whether or not Hana's already at the amphitheater." He sighed and shook his head. "If she is, then we'll be forced to scotch the mission. Try again some other time."

"But Topper, we can't just—"

"Can't be helped." Top met Uncle Ritzi's gaze and crossed his arms. "Oh will surely evacuate his prisoners to a safe location as soon as the carnage starts. We'll just have to make sure we get into position before Hana arrives in-theatre."

He resumed his place in front of the terrain map and pointed once again at the ridge. "Assuming that we do, the three of you will split up. Tommy will remain atop the ridge to help Mawro. Pawly, you and Jakub will proceed through the woods and on to the amphitheater. Find a place to hide until Oh is ready to show off Stuie to his bidders."

Pawly and Jakub exchanged looks. "How will we know when that happens?

"Remember how you rage whenever someone threatens a loved one in your presence?" Grandpa D said before Top could answer. "We think they'll do likewise with Stuie and the others."

Pawly clenched her eyes shut and shook her head. She did not want to imagine what the North Koreans might do to Annie and Grandpa N in hopes they might goad Stuie into raging.

"Right you are, Dory. We believe he plans to demonstrate to his potential buyers how DNA from a juvenile like Stuie can help them continually change up their ailuranthropic formulary." Top stepped over to Pawly's seat and rapped on the tabletop in front of her with his fingers. "And when they do, we need you to use the dart gun you'll have to administer the same stuff your uncle gave your mom to pull her back from the brink."

Pawly cocked an eyebrow at him. "And that's going to do what exactly?"

"It should immediately change Stuie back, that's what. But only if our timing is spot on." Uncle Ritzi paused, waiting for Pawly to face him. "The formulary of the anti-serum used on your mother is that of an adult dose," he went on, rubbing at his forehead with one hand. "We cannot administer it to a child such as Stuie without compensating for her still-developing physiology. Give her too little, she may be over the wall and out of sight of Oh's guests before her human form returns. Give her too much...well, it could stop her heart."

She gulped. "How...how will I know how much serum to use, then?"

"You won't," Uncle Ritzi replied with a shake of his head. "But I will. Right after you establish connection to the telemetry unit in the pendant she wears around her neck."

Pawly looked over at Tommy. "And how am I supposed to go about doing *that* exactly?"

"Just drive that transmitter stake I told you about on the trip here into the ground somewhere near the main stage," Tommy answered her. "Then press the button on top of the thing to activate it. It'll receive the RF signal from Stuie's pendant and then broadcast a ULF one through the earth. We'll receive it with the stake at our location. Then U-Ritz here can analyze Stuie's vitals and tell me to tell you the exact amount of anti-serum you'll need in the dart to shoot her with."

She groaned and rubbed at her forehead. "Enough with the technoporn already! Wouldn't it just be easier for Jakub and me to just snag 'em all and then make a run for it?"

"No. But you're not completely wrong either," Top replied, wagging his finger at her. "We want every one of Oh's guests to see us render his whole ailuranthropic human enhancement program worthless in real time and with their own eyes. When they revolt—which we're sure they will—that's when you two will swoop in and carry off Niko and Annie and Stuie. We're banking on your either outrunning or outmaneuvering DPRK's security forces as you make your escape, and we want to give you every advantage possible."

Pawly sighed and looked up at him. "Alright, fine. Once Jakub and I have everyone, will we fall back following the same route?"

"No, because you'll both be encumbered. Follow the ridgeline back to where I showed you Ritzi would come ashore," he said, tapping at the bulkhead wall beneath the image with one finger to emphasize his point. "Lenny will be cruising back and forth off-shore, waiting for you. Hop aboard as he skirts the shallows. When we finish unloading and put back out again, he'll return you back to the ship."

Top turned back toward Tommy. "Should you sight Hana during the operation, see to it she stays away from the amphitheater. Shoot her full of carfentanyl if you have to. After Pawly and Jakub exit the theatre, you and Ritzi will bring her with you to the place you disembarked. Follow the coast south to this little spit of land here at Kwak-tan," he said, tapping at the map. "After discharging his passengers, Lenny will head that way to pick you both up. Once everyone's aboard, our captain will lay course for Sochko." He nodded. "And that will be that."

Grandpa D stood up and stepped over to the bulkhead door. "Now, if you'll excuse us," he said as he pushed a button beside the door frame, "Top and I have a whole lot of details we need to work out yet. Our ship's steward will be here momentarily to show you to your berths."

After Top stepped over beside Grandpa D, he folded his arms across his chest. "We're several hours out from Rason yet, which is why I'm ordering all of you to quarters until further notice. See to it you all get some rest. Because you're gonna need it."

CHAPTER TWENTY-SEVEN

RASON, NORTH KOREA. THE FOLLOWING EVENING.

A ROUND OF APPLAUSE rose up from the audience gathered within the amphitheater. Mawro glanced up from his instrument and carefully drew aside a branch with one claw. He peered through the evergreen boughs concealing the position he and Tommy had taken up atop the ridge toward the sparse crowd below. For the last twenty minutes or so, ushers dressed in tuxedoes dashed back and forth the length of the amphitheater escorting one small group of well-dressed guests after another to their seats.

Though the amphitheater appeared spacious enough to seat a couple hundred people, tonight's crowd consisted of barely more than few dozen. Oh and his staff had surely drawn up a seating chart ahead of time, ensuring each rival group would be separated from the others by several empty aisles. So as to minimize the likelihood of an aggrieved bidder starting a brawl following a failed bid.

Representatives from rogue states and criminal enterprises the world over had come to witness the fruits of Pyongyang's revamped human enhancement program. Each of their organizational sponsors sought to create a werecat army of their own, tasked with carrying out whatever means they believed justified in accomplishing their ends. DPRK would gladly share their successes with whomever among those gathered was willing to open up their wallet the widest. After wining and dining his potential patrons at Rason's luxurious Emperor Hotel for the last two days, Oh's dog and pony show was now getting underway to encourage them to do just that.

As their applause died down, a man dressed in a white tuxedo approached the grand piano in the center of the stage. He sat down, shook out his hands, and got to work banging out one of Haydn's concertos. A video montage began to scroll across a large screen set up at the rear of the stage as he played. Mawro squinted toward an image he recognized as Hana, sporting the battle dress uniform she had worn during the operation at Chah Bahar. Blaznikov bounded along beside her until she broke off and engaged Pawly, the pair of them battling tooth and claw as a violent firefight erupted all around them.

Talking points in Korean, Russian, and English began scrolling across the bottom of the screen as the video continued. Mawro guessed Oh's event organizers would be speaking into their lapel mics from somewhere near the stage, beaming their words to ear buds worn by the gathered patrons via an encrypted radio transmission.

Stories Papa used to tell him and his sister Alex from his clandestine activities during the protests leading up to Poland's Solidarity Movement flashed through his mind. Meetings taking place across the country in seedy bars and nightclubs chartered for an evening's invitation-only event. With house bands playing as loudly and raucously as they could, their organizers made sure passers-by on the streets outside the venue—including agents from the MSW secret police—heard only what the event's organizers inside *wanted* them to hear and nothing they did not. Just as Oh now employed the virtuoso so as to distract anyone milling around outside the adjacent casino from the event's true purpose.

The video cut away just prior to the explosion that would cost Blaznikov his life, ending in time with the pianist's performance. The man stood and took a bow in response to the audience's polite clapping. Oh appeared, also dressed in a tuxedo, stepping up beside the pianist before announcing the man's next selection—by *Chopin*.

Mawro bit his lip, his mind swimming. Ought he chalk up Oh's choice to include selections by a *Polish* composer as mere coincidence? He sat watching the performance, transfixed, until the pianist played *Minute Waltz*'s last note. Then Oh waved a hand toward the wings of the stage to his left. "Honorable guests. You all will certainly enjoy this next piece. Yes."

Mawro swore under his breath as he spotted Stuie and Annie and Papa being led from the wings, each wearing a set of casual clothing. The audience resumed clapping as a half dozen men, likely packing heat beneath their cummerbunds, led his loved ones to a row of empty chairs on stage set up to face the piano. The applause died down as the pianist launched into a stirring rendition of *Revolutionary Etude*. The video resumed playing on the big screen a moment later. The crowd *ooohed* and *aaaahed* at the sight of Hana and Stuie locked in mortal combat on the pier in Gdańsk Harbor from last Christmas Eve before Pawly had intervened.

He darted his gaze back and forth across the amphitheater grounds but could find no trace of either Pawly or Jakub. Where the hell *were* they? Glimpsing a gray streak disappear around the corner of one of the roof's support beams made him feel better. A moment later Pawly and Jakub emerged over the crest of the amphitheater's roof, both of them shimmying along on their bellies. At the roof's edge they logrolled over, one after the other, and disappeared.

"They're in, Tomasz. I expect they will try to hail us momentarily. Are we ready?"

"I'm sweeping the band now," Tommy replied, the tufts at the top of his ears twitching as he twirled at one of his radio receiver's tuning knobs. A copper-clad steel stake protruded from the receiver and into the ground, driven into place after the two of them first took up their position. "Just shave off a little more of the sideband and I ought to be able to...ah, there they are." He started tapping at the keyboard of his laptop, a USB cable connecting it to the receiver unit. "Link's up, initiating decryption algorithm, Pawly's transmission should be coming through right...now."

Mawro lumbered over next to Tommy and leaned over his shoulder, trying to get a look at his screen. But the bezel Tommy had affixed to it earlier obscured his view from the side. "What's she saying, then?" he asked with a sigh as he rolled back on to his haunches.

"That she and Jakub have taken out the snipers already."

"And have they been able to establish a connection to Stuie's pendant?"

"Yeah, the stream just now finished buffering...oh. Oh, wow. Hey, U-Ritz, I think you'd better see this." Tommy turned the laptop sitting across his legs toward Mawro and tapped at the top of the screen. "Her vitals are through the roof already."

He leaned down and peered at the screen, able to see what was on it now that he was facing it straight on. "We'll have to work fast. First, I'll need you to plot her heart rate on a logarithmic scale..."

Mawro and Tommy spent the next several minutes manipulating the data streaming in from Stuie's telemetry pendant via their below ground connection. Together they filtered out corrupted data from her vital signs, eliminated outlier values, and normalized the coefficients of the remaining residuals. Then came several passes of the scrubbed data sets through their polynomial regression algorithm. "There. That's how much she'll need," Mawro said, tapping at the screen of Tommy's laptop with one furry finger near to the nexus of the resultant curves. "Tell Pawly that Stuie will need 285 milliliters of serum."

Tommy shook his head. "The tranq darts she has were all made up ahead of time, each pair containing an exact quantity. She won't know whether to round up or round down, though."

"They're in fifty milliliter increments, aren't they?"

He nodded.

"Tell Pawly to use the 300-milliliter darts first. If she manages to miss Stuie with both of them, instruct her to use the two-fifties." Mawro bowed his head and crossed himself. "But Stuie was cut from Hana's genetic stock. That might not be enough to make a tigrine completely change back to—"

"Oh, shit!" Tommy cried, his ears standing erect. "I completely spaced out about Hana!" With a snarl, he turned and began banging away at his keyboard.

"What? What about her? Your rig there is sweeping the bands looking for a blip from her Pearls, right?"

"It *was*," Tommy replied without looking up from his screen. "Those regression algos we needed to run really bog down the processor, so I shut down the tracking process until we finished our number crunching. Relaunching it...now."

Several seconds of silence passed between them. "Well?"

Tommy turned away from his screen and pointed off toward the southwest. "Got a bead on her. She's approaching from that direction."

"Range?"

"About half a klick and closing fast," Tommy replied as he stood up. "We'd better get going, then."

Mawro laid one enormous paw atop Tommy's shoulder. "Sit down, son. You're not going anywhere."

"But U-Ritz, Top told us that—"

"—that escaping with Stuie and Annie and Papa was our highest priority, yes he did. Which is why I need you to relay those dosage instructions to Pawly and confirm they have the intended effect on Stuie. If Pawly is forced to use the lower dosage darts, she and Jakub might well need your help corralling Stuie so the buyers see her change back." He raised his other paw to where he knew Tommy could see it and wiggled his fur-covered fingers. "Besides, I can't type very well on such a tiny keyboard as you have."

"But how will you find Hana, U-Ritz? Didn't you say your sniffer's been on the blink since the night...the night that Dad..."

"Yes, I did, and it has." Mawro reached down with one paw and patted at Tommy's cheek. "But if Hana is moving as fast as you suggest, she's likely not paying any attention to how much noise she's making. I'll surely *hear* her, even if I'm not able to immediately scent her." Then he turned and bounded off. Tommy called after him about forgetting the carfentanyl dart, but Mawro paid him no mind.

Leaping tree to tree, rock face to rock face, Mawro made his way along in the direction Tommy had indicated, pausing every so often to listen. Before long he picked up sounds of rustling leaves and snapping branches, punctuated now and again with grunts and growls. He dropped down to the ground and approached their source, which he surmised to be Hana, near the mouth of a small ravine.

Mawro tacked back and forth, hoping to avoid getting anywhere near upwind of Hana. But then the wind shifted suddenly, surely carrying his scent in her direction. A gasp followed by the sound of bark dropping to the forest floor after being ripped from a tree limb left no doubt.

He swore loudly and gave chase. Though her smaller size made Hana far nimbler, Mawro knew from his past hunts his brute strength would allow him to jump farther. She would require two bounds to cross from one side of the ravine to the other to his one.

After several volleys, Mawro worked Hana into the narrow end of the ravine. With a sheer rock wall blocking her escape in either direction, Hana turned and faced him. "You must let me take Oh out!" she cried in her native language, her balled fists trembling at her sides. "The Katczynskis told me he had already tried to have you killed once, Papa. He will surely not stop until he succeeds."

Mawro drew himself to his full height, trying to look as stern and imposing as he could. "He already tried to have you killed once too, Hana-*ttanim*," he replied in kind.

Hana's brows knit. "He did, did he? I do not recall when. He must have caught me unawares somehow. All the more reason why I needs must catch him unawares now—"

He belted out a roar, cutting her off. "You're not to go anywhere near that amphitheater, do you hear me?"

"But you...you are..." she stammered in reply, her eyes wide. "And I...I am..."

"Am that girl's mother, Hana-*ttanim*. The product of the pregnancy which you yourself tried to abort."

She gaped at him with her mouth open, apparently too stunned to speak. "Which I did not know myself until just before Oh captured her back on Pilot Island," he went on, if only to fill the crushing silence between them. "Nat and I believe the trauma you suffered that night years before is why you rage whenever you get near to her."

Mawro stepped up and gently squeezed Hana's shoulders with his paws. "Stuie is *his* prize now, one he will stop at nothing to protect. He will not hesitate to detonate the explosive device he had secretly implanted at the base of your neck as you and I fled the Chinese." He leaned forward and gingerly took her into his arms. "I cannot permit that happen, Hana-*ttanim*. I love you. As if you were my own daughter."

After a moment's embrace, he stepped back and knelt down to meet her gaze. "Sit this one out. Let me and the Katczynskis effect the girl's rescue. I'll administer you a sedative afterward so you and me and them can all leave together safely. How does that sound?"

Her expression remained vacant for a moment before hardening into a mask of fury. "I will kill him. I will kill him with my bare claws!" she replied, beginning to hyperventilate. "He shall not see me coming. And you shall not see me going!"

Hana drew something from a pouch on her bandolier then launched herself into the air. Once eye-to-eye with him, she clapped her hands together and thrust them both toward Mawro's face. A cloud of dust surrounded him an instant later. He gasped as blinding pain exploded across his face, like a thousand needles assaulting his eyes. The realization he had inhaled the remainder of the red pepper released from Hana's *metsubushi* egg came an instant too late; his mouth and throat were already aflame.

Mawro dropped to his knees and fell forward, curling up into a ball with his arms crossed over his face. He remained that way, coughing and hacking, willing himself not to rub at his eyes. After moments that felt like hours, the pain began to subside. The burning in his throat lessened, along with his coughing, allowing him to breathe more normally.

At length he sat up and looked around, tears obscuring his vision. He gazed all around the narrow end of the ravine as he blinked them away. Not a trace of Hana to be found. Anywhere.

Mawro silently cursed Hana for her stubbornness. Then he began cursing himself—for allowing Hana to get the drop on him with such a predictable move, for allowing her to endanger herself, for allowing Oh to endanger them both. Heart racing, he leapt to his feet, knowing Hana was surely making her way to the amphitheater this very moment.

"Ow!"

Pain shot up his left leg. Mawro stumbled backward onto his buttocks and pulled his injured foot toward him, expecting to see a wound of some kind inflicted by a snake or a spider or a scorpion. But instead, he found a silver ball dangling by a short length of chain, connected to a metal stud impaled into the folds of skin between his two middle toes.

With a gasp, he plucked the thing from between his toes and held it up to his face. It was one of Hana's Pearls, all right. The very earrings that not only helped keep her rage in check, but also afforded Hana her only defense against Oh remotely detonating the kill chip implanted in her neck. His stomach sank as he looked over beside him, spotting the earring's mate among the twigs and acorns littering the forest floor.

Mawro gingerly picked up the other earring off the ground so as not to crush it, then jammed the pair of them into the pocket of his canvas shorts. With a mournful yowl, he bounded off toward the amphitheater. Tears began streaming down his face again, but this time not from any pepper.

Chapter Twenty-Eight

Moments later...

THE AMPHITHEATER'S SCREEN WENT dark a moment before raucous applause and cheers rose up from the audience. Pawly twiddled at the end of her whiskers as the pianist stood and took his bows. She knew full well their accolades were for her and Tommy and Hana and Stuie and all the other werecats featured on Oh's highlight reel, not for him.

Even if the men and handful of women seated in the stands below her rooftop perch were inclined to appreciate the man's mad phat talent, high class scumbags were scumbags still. But for Stuie and the others, none of them would be here now. And Pawly and her team were themselves here now to remedy that.

As the applause died down, she reached over to where her air rifle lay at her side and drew it around to her front. After plucking one of the two serum darts Tommy had directed her to use from her bandolier, Pawly racked open the rifle's chamber and slid the dart inside. The pianist began playing again, another piece she could not recall the name of. But, like several of the others, its melody brought to mind another silly ditty from the countless *Animaniacs* episodes she and Tommy used to watch every afternoon after school.

Pawly turned her attention toward her loved ones, seated in a row off to the pianist's right. After laying the rifle's barrel atop her forearm, she hunched her shoulders forward and peered through the rifle's scope. Selecting a point slightly above and upwind of Stuie's neck, she centered her scope's crosshairs over it.

Then she glanced up, scanning the roofline over the amphitheater stage. Seeing no trace of Jakub she bit her lip, knowing he ought to have been in position by now. She could manage carrying Annie and Grandpa N out of here by herself if Stuie remained conscious and could be counted on to keep up. But the girl raging during their escape presented a far greater risk than waiting on Jakub. Since he would help get them all out of here once Stuie was down, he was needed.

A collective gasp from the audience drew Pawly's attention toward the amphitheater's main screen. On it played the surveillance footage from her Uncle Ritzi's lab that horrible night years before, just as her teenaged self had raked her razor-sharp claws across her father's midsection. "Oh no, not now! Dad, I...I can't..." she squeaked, red haze obscuring her vision.

Then she saw stars. After logrolling across the pavilion's concrete roof from the force of the impact, she sucked in her breath and let out a pained yowl. Then a hand clamped down over her muzzle, forcing her mouth shut. "Knock it off already. Need I remind you that you used to thump me every bit as hard sparring at the *dojang*?"

Next thing Pawly knew she was being hauled upright by her shoulders. Once on her feet, she shook her head and blinked until Tommy's face came into focus. "Dust out them cobwebs, sis. We need to go. Hana's here."

Pawly gasped and glanced around, her eyes wide. "She *is*? Where?"

"Right now, I don't know. Jakub went to go look for her. I spotted her heading this way after Uncle Ritzi tried to—"

A roar cut him off. Pawly and Tommy both turned toward the stage to glimpse Stuie in mid-air, vaulting toward them. The girl landed in a crouch atop the roof nearby, then bounded off. "Why is she...?" Pawly muttered before Hana's feral scent registered.

She gasped and glanced over at Tommy. The panicked look on his face told her he could tell Hana was raging, too. "Shit! She must've given Jakub the slip somehow," he said, craning his neck to try and spot her. "Then managed to get close enough to Stuie to set them both off."

Pawly darted her gaze back and forth across the rooftop nearby them until she spotted her air rifle. "Stuie ought to stop raging if I tag her and she changes back, right?" she called over her shoulder to Tommy as she bounded over to it.

"She ought to, yeah."

"Good. Maybe it'll calm Hana down too," Pawly replied as she picked up her rifle and took aim. "Then Uncle Ritzi can..."

Pawly's voice trailed off as she drew her face close to her scope's eyepiece. Compressed gas hissed from a fissure between the back of the rifle's barrel and its stock. She grabbed the bolt and yanked it toward her, attempting to extract the dart. But the mechanism wouldn't budge.

She growled and hurled the useless weapon to her feet. "Dammit!" After taking a knee, Pawly reached into the pouch strapped to her thigh and began rummaging around. "Rifle's toast. Doubt I can even get the fucking dart out without breaking it open," she said as Tommy trotted up beside her. "I'll have to poke Stuie with our backup dart myself."

"You two will need to herd her back into view of the patrons first."

Pawly and Tommy both turned as one to find Jakub approaching. "But what about Hana?" Tommy asked him.

"Leave her to me," Jakub replied as he cracked his knuckles. "I'll run interference while you two lead Stuie toward the stage. Come now, let us do this. So that we can all get the hell out of here."

Then he bounded off, not bothering to wait for acknowledgement from either of them. Pawly growled and rapped Tommy on the chest with the back of her hand. "C'mon!"

She sprang and followed after Jakub, with Tommy right behind her. The three of them soon came upon Hana and Stuie, the pair's raging scents strong and musky. They paced around in a circle opposite each other on the far corner of the pavilion's roof, snarling. Jakub landed between them and faced Hana, knocking Stuie roughly to the floor as he backed away from the elder woman. Then he crouched down and sprang, narrowly missing Hana with the claws on both hands as she leapt to one side. "You want some of me, whelp?" he called to Hana as she hopped back up. "Come and take it, then!"

Jakub hopped over the edge of the roof and disappeared, with Hana right behind him. Stuie got to her feet, casting furtive glances back and forth between Pawly and Tommy, as if unsure of just what to make of them.

Tommy took a step toward the girl, his palms wide open out in front of him. "Hey, squirt, remember me? Your favorite cousin? Think you could just maybe—?"

Stuie reared back, hissing. "Guess not," he replied with a defeated sigh. "Worth a try, I guess. You'll take the right, sis?"

"And you cover the left, bro. Just like tailing deer on St. Martin's Island." *Except Stuie is smaller. And bitey-er.*

He nodded and lunged for Stuie. She dodged him and broke right. Pawly held short and let the girl dash past, allowing Tommy to catch up. "Corner her in the rafters above the stage so we can keep out of sight before I stick her. Then when she falls, everyone in the stands ought to be able to see her change."

Tommy hollered in agreement before the pair of them set off after Stuie. But cornering the girl proved far more difficult than Pawly had anticipated. She yowled in frustration after Stuie evaded her needle for the seventh...no, the eighth time? The girl was crazy fast, what with her small size and tigrine form. And fast was what Pawly knew she and Tommy needed to be to complete their task. The more energy they expended chasing Stuie, the slower they would be able to make their escape with her and Annie and Grandpa N. And though she and Jakub had taken out Oh's rooftop snipers before commencing operations, there would certainly be no small amount of small arms fire coming their way once they were spotted. Taking any fire while trying to extricate their loved ones put them all at grave risk, but it could hardly be helped.

And if Oh spotted Hana before Jakub managed to subdue her...

Pawly shuddered at the thought. No werecat deserved that. Nor Uncle Ritzi watching the woman he loved like his own daughter end up a vegetable. Or worse. She had to get this deal done.

Taking the dart between her teeth with its needle jutting out of the left side of her muzzle, Pawly sprang, slashing at Stuie with the claws on both hands. The girl managed to parry her attack, then went on the offensive. Pawly ducked an instant too late, allowing the tip of one of Stuie's claws to catch the end of the dart. It pulled free from between her teeth and tumbled toward the stage below.

"No!" she cried. Tommy peeled off and plummeted toward the stage like a gull diving for a fish. An instant later he vaulted up and over their heads, coming to land beside Pawly. "Take it!" he yelled, waving the dart in her direction. After she snatched it from his hand, Tommy puffed out his chest, making himself look as big as he could. Claws on both hands fully extended, he roared and began to swipe at the air near to Stuie's head and middle.

Appearing as though her feral instincts had concluded she was outgunned, the girl belted out a panicked yowl and leapt up toward a pair of stage lighting uprights. Pawly's heart pounded in her ears while the two of them closed in. Before slamming into the wall beyond the uprights, Stuie cut a sharp corner and began to double back—just as Pawly had wanted her to. *We've got 'er now!*

Pawly and Tommy flanked Stuie as they sprang their trap. The girl attempted to change course an instant too late, her arm catching on the crossbracing of one of the amphitheater's roofing trusses. Her momentum slammed her bodily into the steel latticework. But she was stunned only for an instant. Tommy grunted as Stuie sank the claws on both her hands deep into his chest near each shoulder. "Now!" he cried through gritted teeth, clamping his hands atop hers.

Pawly stuck the dart back into her mouth and pushed off the col-umn in front of her with both feet. High above the stage floor she flew toward where Stuie dangled from the truss. After throwing her arms around her, Pawly thrust her head sideways and jammed the needle deep into the girl's neck. Stuie cried out, struggling to break free from her grasp. Pawly pushed the plunger home with her cheekbone before thrusting Stuie clear. The girl tumbled to the stage, managing to stick a wobbly landing. She turned and glanced up at Pawly before her eyes rolled up into the back of her head and she passed out.

Annie cried out and bolted from her seat. An instant later, she was at Stuie's side. Annie drew her ear to Stuie's mouth, as if assuring herself that her daughter was indeed still breathing. Clumps of or-ange-and-white fur pulled free from the girl's head and neck as Annie checked her vitals. By the time Grandpa N drew up alongside, Stuie was well into her shed. Together he and Annie propped the girl up and guided her over to their seats. Her face a disheveled mess of shed fur, Stuie's human form quickly returned. For *everyone* to see.

Which, Pawly noticed, everyone surely did. A man from the audience, standing closest to the edge of the stage, glanced back and forth between Oh and Stuie. After a moment, he fixed Oh with a disgusted stare and began yelling in a language Pawly did not recognize. He tapped another man standing nearby on the shoulder, gesticulating wildly toward Oh and Stuie. Each of them did likewise with another. And then, another.

"We gotta get them out of here," Tommy said after scaling the rafters between them. "Preferably *before* the riot starts."

Pawly snarled. "Now or never, I guess. Let's go."

By the time they leapt down from the rafters, the crowd had worked itself up into an angry mob. Pawly picked out variations of "you've cheated us!" in English and Korean from among their shouts.

"Please, gentlemen," came Oh's voice, shouting over the din in Korean, "if you would return to your seats, I'm sure we can all work out an amenable resolution."

"Save it! Pyongyang's treachery has been laid bare for all to see," one of them spat, jabbing his finger at him. "Courting us and our money when you've got some sort of werecat anti-serum waiting in the wings? That you could be so brazen!"

Oh opened his mouth to say something, but an angry roar cut him off. Hana landed behind Oh's accusers and bounded over their heads to the stage. She stepped toward Stuie and the others, gnashing her fangs and brandishing her claws, until a cry from above drew her attention upward. An instant before Jakub tackled her.

"Get a net around the girl!" Oh screamed to his security detail, his panicked voice rising above the din. "And kill the others. All of them!"

"No!"

The stage rumbled beneath Pawly's feet, absorbing the impact from Uncle Ritzi's bulk as he touched down. Then he bounded up and grabbed hold of the truss holding the stage lights aloft. With a grunt and a heave, he tore the thing free from its mounts and sent it hurtling toward the stage in a shower of sparks. It crashed down atop the piano, narrowly missing Oh and pinning several of his security troopers beneath it.

Hana, having managed to wriggle free from Jakub's grasp, leapt to her feet. Mawro barred her across her chest and shoved her bodily up against the ruined rigging behind them. After drawing nose to nose with her, he belted out the most menacing roar Pawly had ever heard.

The other woman blinked once, twice, then looked up into Uncle Ritzi's eyes. Shock, anger, and resentment played across her face, followed by a calm look, one of tranquil acceptance. Pawly recalled Grandpa N and Uncle Nat going on about just such an intervention during their voyage across the Atlantic after Christmas. Something about reestablishing equilibrium to the brain's neural circuitry, much like a defibrillator firing does for a quivering heart.

And it had *worked*. Just like when Uncle Ritzi had done likewise to Pawly aboard Uncle Bobby's tugboat after Sally was swept overboard. But Hana still appeared to be mostly out of it, her gaze darting to and fro around the ruined stage as if trying to piece together just where she was and what exactly she was doing here.

"Here, Pawly!" Uncle Ritzi cried as he frantically waved her over. "Reach into the right front pocket of my shorts. Take out Hana's earrings and stow them somewhere," he said after Pawly bounded up next to him. "Pin them back on her the very first chance you get, but for now just get ready to run."

After doing as asked, Pawly glanced around at the twisted jumble of metal surrounding them all on three sides. "Run *where*, exactly?"

Uncle Ritzi bounded over the wall behind them and shook out his hands. He clasped his fists together and whirled them around in a circle. A *boom* louder than a thunderclap echoed through the amphitheater after his balled fists slammed into the wall. Brick and mortar flew inward with explosive force, creating a hole large enough for them all to pass through. "Get Hana into the tunnel," he said, nodding toward the corridor beyond. Then he turned and waved to their remaining loved ones. "The rest of you, follow me!"

CHAPTER TWENTY-NINE

M AWRO SKIDDED TO A stop at the intersection of two corridors and stared up at the ceiling. Jakub bounded up alongside, panting, cradling Annie in his arms with Papa draped across his shoulders, fireman-style.

"Which…which way now?" he asked as Pawly, a woozy Hana slung over one shoulder, and Tommy, clutching an unconscious Stuie to his chest, joined them.

"That big pipe there with the green banding and white arrows ought to point us toward the boiler room," Mawro replied, pointing out the line bearing a "condensate return" label in *Chosŏngul* from among the tangle of plumbing above their heads. "There should be a service entrance adjacent to it. We would park our trucks there, then wheel in the cages containing our 'star attractions' so we could show them off whenever VIPs came calling from Pyongyang."

"Sure to be some trucks there now," Pawly added as she finished pinning Hana's earrings back into place. "I'm sure we can convince one of the drivers that we need his rig more than he does."

Tommy clicked his tongue. "Only if we hurry. Oh's troops might be stumbling all over each other at the moment, but it won't take long for him and his officers to reassert discipline. Right, U-Ritz?"

"Couldn't agree more, my lad," Mawro said before nodding his head in the direction indicated by the arrowhead on the pipe label. "This way, everyone."

Before long, the corridor led them to a high bay area. In the center sat a large steel pressure vessel. Two small pipes, one each connected to the vessel's top and bottom, ran along the ceiling and into a narrow tunnel where they disappeared from sight. Mawro recalled being briefed years before on the hazards posed by the superheated steam they contained, delivered here from the nearby chemical plant to supplement this secondary boiler to furnish heat and light for the amphitheater and hotel. He and his crew had made sure to check and double-check the locks on every one of the cages housing their ailuranthropic test subjects each time they wheeled one through here. A superhuman berserker running amok near a high-pressure steam boiler salvaged from a Cold War-era Soviet warship would have been *bad*.

"So far so good," Mawro announced as he waved everyone into the room. "Jakub might have a hard time fitting through there, burdened as he is," he said, pointing at the man door on the wall opposite them. "And I am certainly too big. But there should be a control button for that roll-up door there beside it, just on the other side of the wall from—"

"Halt!" boomed a male voice from a loudspeaker high above their heads. "None of *you* are going anywhere."

The lights came up an instant later, flooding the entire room with their blindingly bright beams. Mawro squinted up at the mezzanine to find what looked to be an entire platoon's worth of men dressed in riot gear, each of them drawing a bead on him and the others with their assault rifles.

"Why Captain Mawro! This is indeed an unexpected surprise."

Mawro grimaced and looked up to find Oh standing at the mezzanine rail, speaking into the mouthpiece of a handset tethered to a service panel mounted in the wall behind him. "And yet, a decidedly unwelcome one. Though I appreciate your delivering us more fine specimens," he said, waving his arm Mawro's his loved ones. "But that hardly makes up for the damage you've done. All our work to date is *useless* now!"

Oh cradled the handset between his head and shoulder while reached into his suit coat pocket. "I shall enjoy seeing you shot," Oh said through clenched teeth as he produced a small box and pointed it toward them. "But not nearly as much as watching you watch *her* die first."

Tommy gasped and glanced over at Hana, still slung over Pawly's shoulder. "He's too close, U-Ritz!"

Mawro reached over toward Pawly and yanked Hana to him. Then he clutched her to his chest and sank his fangs deep into the base of her neck. She let out a pained cry, then fell silent and still in his arms. Mawro ripped away a chunk of flesh and worked his jaw until he felt the kill chip's metal housing between his teeth. He spat the thing out, sending it skittering across the floor until it exploded with a loud *bang* an instant later.

Snarling, Oh threw his now-useless remote up against the wall behind him. "All right, you son of a bitch," he hollered, returning his attention to Mawro as he clenched his handset with both hands, "have it your way!" He glanced up at his fire team's commander and shouted in Korean, "Spare the youngling. Kill all the rest!"

Mawro turned to Pawly, holding Hana's limp form out in front of him. "Quickly, take her!" he cried, having hardly handed her off before he lunged toward the steam line directly above him. Taking it between his hands, he placed both feet on the pipe and pushed off as hard as he could. The thick steel pipe groaned and gave way, sending an enormous plume of superheated steam upward toward the mezzanine. Oh's commander hurled him to the deck an instant before the remaining soldiers were swallowed up by the scalding-hot cloud. They shrieked and dropped their weapons, several of them hurling themselves over the mezzanine railing in their panic. Billowing steam quickly obscured Mawro's view of the doomed men. But even above the steam's loud hissing, his preternatural hearing picked out the sickening *splut* each of them made upon impact with the boiler room's concrete floor. Three stories below.

When Mawro turned around, he found Hana lying on the floor face down. Pawly knelt beside her, jamming her wadded-up jacket into the gaping hole in the other woman's neck to staunch the blood squirting forth with every heartbeat. Tommy, having laid the still-unconscious Stuie beside him, unbuckled his belt and tugged it free. Then he crouched opposite his sister and looped his belt around Hana's shoulders, fixing her makeshift compress into place.

"I'm fresh out of ideas," she cried as Annie came trotting up beside them. "Anything else we can do?"

"Not much with a wound *that* deep, in such a critical place," Annie replied after bending down to examine the twins' handiwork. "I'm...I'm sorry, Ritzi," she went on, glancing up to meet Mawro's gaze. "Without an OR nearby, I doubt even *I* can do anything that would save—"

"The serum!" Mawro cried. "We only used a few of the darts to inject Stuie. Where are the others?"

"They're all right here," Pawly replied, patting at her bandolier. "Except for those three hundred milliliter units we used already."

"What is this 'serum' you're talking about, Ritzi?" Papa asked as he shuffled up beside Stuie. "Didn't you merely administer her a sedative to quell her rage?"

"I'll explain later. Hana will bleed out if we don't hurry. Annie, I'll need you to administer a pair of two fifties as near to Hana's transversa colli artery as you can. Then shoot a five hundred straight into her jugular. And hurry!"

"On it!" she replied, holding out her hand. "Just as soon as I can get—"

"Right here, Annie," Pawly said, plucking the three darts from her bandolier and handing them to her.

Annie rubbed her hand back and forth over the blood-stained fur covering Hana's neck and shoulders. Seconds ticked by with agonizing slowness as she sought out suitable injection sites nearest to the other woman's gaping wound, then delivered the serum per Mawro's instructions.

He sighed and rubbed at his face with one hand. "That's all we can do for now. Should stop the bleeding and keep her breathing, at least. But it might be *days* before she wakes up." He turned toward Tommy. "Longer before we'll know if she'll ever walk again."

Tommy nodded and gazed up toward the plume of steam billowing forth from the ruined pipe. "Sounds like the troops on the mezzanine are mustering on the ground floor," he said after cocking his head to one side. "I doubt that will keep them much longer."

"The lad is quite right." Mawro waved his hand toward the tunnel leading to the chemical plant. "Everyone, get inside."

"You heard the man," Jakub said as he drew up behind Niko and Annie. "Alley oop!" he said as he bent down and hefted them up, one sitting atop each shoulder. Tommy gathered Stuie into his arms while Pawly gingerly worked her arms beneath Hana. She stood and faced

Mawro, one arm beneath the compress around Hana's neck, the other situated in the small of her back. "Her bleeding seems to have stopped, Uncle Ritzi. Just like you'd said it would."

"Very good. You all go ahead of me." Mawro gazed all around, flexing his fingers. "I'm going to find something big and heavy I can drag behind me into the tunnel so Oh's people can't…"

A *screeeeeee* came from above Mawro's head an instant before Papa's panicked cry: "Ritzi! Look out!"

Mawro glanced up and gasped, registering an enormous section of the mezzanine as it plummeted toward him. He sprang to one side, but not far enough. The mass of steel and concrete landed with a deafening *crash*, pinning his left leg just below the knee. With a pained yowl, he collapsed to the floor. Pawly and Tommy and Jakub raced to his side, laden with their charges. Annie leapt from Jakub's shoulder and crouched down beside Mawro. She poked and prodded while he struggled to get his breathing under control, inhaling deep and then blowing it out forcefully. "It…it's bad, isn't it?" he asked at length.

Annie met his gaze and swallowed her lips. "Yeah, Ritzi, it is. Your tibia is snapped clean through and your fibula is likely fractured also. Not to mention the rest of your leg, it…it's…"

"It's okay, Annie," he replied, wincing. "You and Stuie and the rest of you will all be okay. I shall see to it."

Papa knelt beside him, his eyes wide with terror. "But son, we can't just—"

"I'd only slow you all down, even if you could carry me!" Mawro propped himself up on his elbows, groaning from the exquisite pain. "And besides, my life was forfeit the night Barry died," he said in a small voice as he reached up and stroked Hana's forehead with the back of his massive paw. "So, I must depend on *you* now to save hers."

Tears began to stream down the sides of Papa's face. "Ritzi, I…"

"Do this, Papa. Please. For me," Mawro said, his voice cracking. "And tell *Eomeonim* and Alex and Nat and Dory that I love them. As much as I love you...all of you."

Papa threw his arms around Mawro's head. "I will, son. I love you, too," he mumbled before choking back a sob. "We all do."

A loud popping drew everyone's attention to the tunnel entrance in time to glimpse the jet of steam sputter out. Oh's officers barked out orders as the plume began to dissipate, surely preparing to renew their offensive. "Papa," croaked Mawro, "it's time."

After one final squeeze, he stood. With Annie already having re-sumed her perch atop one shoulder, Jakub knelt down beside Papa and offered him his other. "I'm proud of you, son," Papa said as Jakub raised them both up. "Never been more so."

Mawro smiled a wan smile as Jakub bounded off. "Goodbye, U-Ritz," Tommy said as he followed, clutching little Stuie to him.

Pawly drew close, nodding toward Hana's still form in her arms. "We'll care for her. I promise."

"Thank you, dear. Barry would be proud of his 'lil' fighter.'"

She nodded and blinked, tears streaming anew down the damp trails between her eyes and jawline. Then she turned and dashed away down the tunnel to catch up with Tommy and Jakub.

Mawro watched them go, indulging himself with a small, sad smile. After they disappeared around the bend, he turned to find Oh ap-proaching, his remaining soldiers right behind. "Sergeant Pak, you and your men go on ahead and take up position behind the escapees. The rest of us will circle around to the chemical plant and intercept them."

The soldiers acknowledged Oh's order and broke ranks. Oh stepped up beside Mawro's head and crossed his arms. "But before we do," he said, fixing Mawro with a searing glare, "we need to take out the trash."

"Indubitably!" Mawro spat back as he reached up and took hold of the wreckage pinning his leg. He screamed, venting his pain and rage, and hurled the mass of steel and concrete into the mouth of the tunnel. It bounced back and forth, up and down, like a ball travelling down the length of a musket barrel after firing. Spearing, crushing, shredding every soldier in its path until it slammed into the wall at the first blind corner and stopped.

"Shoot him!" Oh cried, his hands shaking at his sides. "All of you, shoot him!"

Mawro rolled upright and managed to stand shakily on his right leg while fire rained down on him. His flesh ripped, his bones snapped, his mangled left leg dangled uselessly below his knee. By the time he spotted the relief valve jutting from the side of the boiler closest to him, he was blind in his left eye and deaf in his left ear. Blood dripped from his face and jaw in a dozen places. His chest felt like it was on fire. How many bullets had he taken already? How many of his internal organs had been damaged beyond repair?

Did it really matter?

No. No, it did not.

"We shall *end* this," he cried out in a loud voice, his heartbeat thundering in his ears. "Here. Now!"

Mawro leapt up and grabbed the boiler's relief valve, grunting as the hot metal seared his paw pads.

Grant me strength, Barry!

With a roar, he gripped the valve with both hands and set his feet atop the boiler's scorching surface. "No! Stop him!" Oh cried out from behind. "Kill him before he can—"

The valve ripped free from the boiler's outer shell. Permitting the boiler's entire contents to escape in an instant. Explosively.

The shock wave slammed into him, hurling him backward across the boiler room. Blinding him. Deafening him. Taking his breath away.

And then, Ritzi felt nothing.

Nothing at all.

CHAPTER THIRTY

**AFLOAT ON THE NORTH ATLANTIC. THE FOLLOW-
ING WEEK.**

STUIE STEPPED FORWARD BEHIND Ewa as Karolin took her place in the middle of the batter's square. It lay on the deck in front of her, fashioned from pieces of white plastic pipe wrapped with red electrical tape, making it appear as though it were made from giant peppermint sticks. The boys hooted and hollered from the other side of a line marked out with duct tape across the deck about a dozen or so yards away. They were doing their best to distract Karolin, much like they had for the other girls. If the batter whiffed the ball, it could very well land on the side of the tape nearest her, in "hell", where she would be out and have to go sit down. Even if it landed in the "heaven" side nearest the boys, they might well have an easy time tossing it back into hell before the batter could run to the first flag. And she would be out then, too.

But Karolin was not about to go easy on the boys. Shooting them all the stink-eye, she gritted her teeth and tossed the ball up into the air. She powered through her one-armed swing, sending the ball soaring over the line—and the heads of the boys standing closest to it. The boys in the back row cried out in alarm as the ball hurtled towards them. One face-planted onto the deck before the ball bounced over top of him. His teammate managed to tip it with his finger, sending it careening over the railing. The boys groaned as one as the ball plummeted toward the water and disappeared.

"Nice going, Piotr," their team captain Jerezy cried as he stomped over to the where the other boy sat shaking his head. "The girls are tied with us now."

Karolin blew the boys a kiss as she rounded the third flag, herding Jadwiga and Weronika back to the nest ahead of her. She ran up to the nest's flag and smacked it with her arm, sending it fluttering back and forth. "And we're gonna beat you, too!"

Jerezy glanced down at his watch and then back up at Ewa and Stuie. "I doubt it. Time is almost up and your weakest hitter is at bat. Followed by that new girl."

"Ewa and Nastusia have been practicing together," Karolin shot back. "Which I might suggest you have Piotr and Pawel do more often to improve their catching." She picked up the open tennis ball can beside her, turned it upside-down, and shook it up and down for him to see. "We might be forced to call it a draw, though. Seems you're not the only thing around here with no balls left."

Jerezy snarled and poked at his watch. "Hey, Artsyom!" he called out to a boy from behind him. "Go below and ask your folks if they've got any more we can use."

With a nod, the other kid darted over to the edge of the deck and disappeared down the stairwell. Karolin plunked down atop the deck and crisscrossed her legs. "Okay, everyone, take five. Hey Wiktoria, send that water jug around, will ya?"

The girls all followed Karolin's lead and sat down. The others all around Stuie began yammering on among themselves, switching back and forth between Polish and what she had been told was old Belarusian. Stuie nodded and giggled at what she thought were the right times. It was a challenge for her to follow them whenever they spoke fast, but she understood enough to get the gist of it. Which boys each girl thought was hot, which boy each girl thought was a clod. Often times being, in fact, the same person.

But no matter what they said or how they said it, they were all werecats. Kids just like her. Stuie stretched out her legs in front of her and sighed, satisfied just to sit amongst them.

Their ship had been steaming westward across the Atlantic for several days now, bound for New Brunswick, part of the plan Grunkle D and Monsignor Dryzek had presented to the Forest Clan elders to rehome its members across the globe. She had been unsure just what Grunkle D had meant about an "arms race," though. But whatever it was, he and the Monsignor made a really big deal since how every werecat would need to do their part in preventing one.

The parents of the kids all around her, along with a number of adults who lacked children, were eager to leave the Forest and start new lives for themselves elsewhere. A number of them had left already after the ship made a midnight call to Oslo, their first port-of-call. More would surely leave when they reached St. John. Though they would likely make port sometime tomorrow afternoon if the weather held out, Grunkle D and the Monsignor had told everyone to wait until darkness fell before going ashore. It would be the same for her and her family when they and whoever else remained arrived in Boston. She and her parents would immediately head back to Chicago, where she would resume her homeschooling. But following a bit of shore leave, the others would return to Poland for another load of "cargo." This one bound for Korea, Japan, and eastern Russia.

Stuie bit back a twinge of sadness. This comfortable feeling, surrounded by her own kind, would not last, and would likely never come her way again. She shook off the awful thought, reminding herself instead of all of the online pals she would soon have from the world over. Planning future meet-ups with them and their families for herself and her own family, whenever and wherever their future travels took them. Stuie would see to it that for the rest of her life, wherever she might go, she would never be far from those like her.

"Got one!"

She turned toward the stairwell from where Artsyom's voice had come. He trotted over toward Karolin, waving the ball he held in his hand back and forth above his head. Jerezy frowned as he drew up beside them. "But it's all black. What's it made out of, solid rubber?"

"Near as I can tell," Artsyom replied, giving the ball a squeeze. "My mom told me we've used up the last of the tennis balls they had on hand, and we won't be able to get more until after we make port again. But then Dad rooted around in his things and found this, which the hospital had given to him after the last time he'd had surgery on his hand." He bounced the ball up and down a couple of times. "He says it's more like the sort of ball you're supposed to play *palant* with, anyway."

"Might sting a bit trying to catch it," Jerezy said, sneering toward Karolin. "Think you girls can deal with that?"

Karolin answered him with a snort. "Also means it'll go farther when me or my girls hit it. You and the other boys are the ones catching, not us. So, the only stinging going on here will be you and the other boys from your loss." She turned toward the crowd of kids and waved her arms. "All right, everyone. Let's play ball!"

The kids all cheered as Artsyom stepped over and handed the ball to Ewa. "Better make it count. Got enough time left in the game for only one more rotation," Jerezy said, poking at his watch once again. "One more out for you girls, then me and the boys will have our last turn at bat."

Karolin wrapped her arm around Ewa's trembling shoulder while Jerezy hustled back over the line. "Just do your best, lil' sis, okay? That's all your team mates and I could ask for. And whatever happens, happens."

"O-okay, I...I'll try."

Stuie patted her on the back. "And I'm sure you'll do it, Ewa," she added, flexing the muscles in both arms as the other girl took her place in the batter's box. "Small but mighty. You and me both."

Ewa flashed Stuie a small smile. "Thank you, Nastusia."

Then she tossed the ball into the air, her eyes fixing upon it as it fell. After taking pause for an instant, Ewa gripped her *palant* with both hands and swung as hard as she could. It connected, sending the ball straight and true toward the heaven zone. "All right, Ewa! Way to go!" Karolin cried as Stuie and the other girls whooped in approval.

Then the ball struck the spar jutting up from the middle of the afterdeck with a loud *smack*. Instead of rolling lazily back their way like a tennis ball would have, it hurtled back directly toward them. "Look out!" Karolin cried as she shoved her sister to the deck.

Stuie dropped down into a crouch. "I got it!"

"Nastusia, no! Let it go!"

But she jumped anyway, determined to snag the ball out of the air as it whizzed by. Arms to one side as if cradling a baby, Stuie caught the ball. It struck her palms with force enough to whirl her around in mid-air, upsetting her balance. She landed on the edge of one foot and tumbled into the railing, her momentum carrying her right up and over.

Stuie screamed, seeing only ocean beneath, until a rusty streak flashed past her eyes. Then came darkness as something squeezed her tight around her head and neck and back. Her stomach fell as if she were once again aboard Great America's *Goliath* before she crashed on to something solid and tumbled to a stop.

With a groan, Stuie slowly rolled herself to a sitting position. "Holy shit, kiddo! Are you all right?"

Stuie blinked up into Tommy's face. His tufted ears drew back alongside his head as he narrowed his eyes at her. "You nearly gave me a heart attack."

"But, Tommy, I didn't mean to—"

"Shhh, kitten, I know," he said, laying one of his furry fingers over her lips. "I came out of the stairwell and saw you stumble into the railing after catching that fly ball."

"Nastusia? Tomasz?" came Karolin's voice from somewhere above their heads. "You both okay?"

"Yes, thank you," Tommy called back after cupping his hands to his mouth. "Came topside to tell you kids the adults have the rabbits all ready below for your hunt. Could you please tell the others and start taking them down?"

"Oh, okay. Our game was over here anyway."

Tommy turned toward Stuie and chuckled, his whiskers twitching. "I wouldn't be so sure about that."

He drew his closed fist near to Stuie's face and then slowly opened his fingers. "You caught it!" she squealed, seeing their ball in his hand.

"Wanted to see your team finish strong, small but mighty," he said, holding it out to her.

Stuie gasped as she reached for the ball, seeing the orange and white fur sprouting from her hand and forearm. "Well would you look at that," Tommy replied with a smirk. "Looks like you get dibs on some bunnies. So now, let's get you—"

"Stuie, it's dangerous here!" came her mother's voice an instant before she dashed through the screen door located opposite the platform deck from them.

Tommy blinked. "A-Squared, what are you—?"

A raspy squeak cut him off. He and Stuie whirled around to find a sickly pale woman sitting up behind a mooring winch. She clutched a white bedsheet to her chest, darting her gaze from side to side. Her black, disheveled hair flapped back and forth across her high cheekbones until she fixed her narrow eyes upon Stuie.

She felt the hair on the back of her neck stand on end. Was this woman scared? Angry? Possessed? Stuie could hardly tell. But the red haze burbling into the edges of her vision made clear she ought not stay here to find out.

"Annie, I've got 50 ccs of carfentanyl on me," Dad said as she stepped through the screen door. "But if we need more, we can..."

"No, I've got some already," Mom replied, patting at the pocket of her lab coat. "Go find Alex and Pawly and bring them back here. Right away."

With a nod, he disappeared back through the screen door. "Now Stuie, I need you to keep still," Mom said as the sound of his footsteps thundered down the passageway. "I took all of Hana's bindings off when we rolled her out here to get some sun. Don't move a muscle until your father comes back with... Tommy, what are you *doing*?"

The red haze advanced, narrowing Stuie's vision as Tommy drew up to the woman's bedside. She closed her eyes, imagining roots growing out of her feet and into the deck below her. To keep herself from bolting.

Tommy gently caressed the back of Hana's hand. He mumbled something in Korean which sounded to Stuie like "Can you hear me?"

The woman blinked up at him. "Where am I? What is this place?" she answered in halting English.

Tommy turned and met Mom's gaze, then motioned her to join him at the woman's side. "On deck outside the sick bay of a ship in the middle of the North Atlantic. You were injured badly during our escape from Rason. And unconscious since, until, well...just now."

Hana began hyperventilating. No one moved except for Stuie's mother placing her thumb atop the syringe in her hand. After several tense seconds, Hana's breathing slowed. "Where is...where is he?" she asked, her voice barely louder than a whisper. "Where is Mawro?"

"His leg was crushed beneath a section of the amphitheater's boiler room mezzanine after it collapsed. He...he insisted we leave him there...insisted he cover our escape...insisted we get you to safety. Then, halfway through the tunnel back to the chemical plant, the boiler exploded." Tommy shook his head and sighed. "I'm...I'm sorry, Hana. There's no way he could have made it."

Hana's hands dropped to her lap, and she began to cry. Stuie glanced up at her mother and bit her lip, unsure just what Hana might do next. After a long moment, she rubbed her eyes with the back of her wrist and sniffed. "Where are my Kindred others, then?" Hana asked before fixing her gaze on Stuie. "And this one." She sniffed at the air and knit her brow. "I...I know you." She looked up at Mom, a puzzled look on her face. "I understand not. Raged I met you time and again. But...but not now."

"For which the rest of us are all grateful, rest assured."

Everyone turned to where Auntie Alex had entered the room, Dad and Pawly right behind her. Her aunt and cousin were both in human form, though from their scent Stuie knew they were ready to morph on a moment's notice. The elder woman stepped up to the foot of the bed and crossed her arms over her chest. "Maybe someone else can help us all understand *why*. Nat?"

Dad stuck his hands into the pockets of his lab coat and nodded toward Hana. "Mawro tore out the explosive device implanted in your neck with his teeth. Then Annie injected you with a serum we created from samples Tommy allowed us to take after he began walking again." His chin dipped toward the floor. "Mawro believed it would heal whatever spinal damage you'd sustained, just like what they'd taken from Tommy did for him. Given time, that is."

Hana reached up and patted at the bandages covering her neck and upper back. "But yet. I do not rage now. Why?"

"The Monsignor assures us each of your kind almost always rages when they first morph. And that individuals may rage later in life upon experiencing strongly painful or fearful emotions." Dad smacked his lips. "Papa thinks the serum Ritzi insisted we give you somehow stifled your response. But none of us can say for sure, Hana."

"Lim."

"Excuse me?"

"I am Lim. Lim Young-Hee," Hana said, her gaze fixed upon when her hands lay folded together in her lap. "Blaznikov named me 'Hana.' It means 'One.'" She looked across the room at Stuie and knit her brow. "Clearly now, I am no longer. To you all further I shall be 'Lim.' Yes."

"Which is what Ritzi called you when he and I brought you to the Chinese refugee camp, in shock and bleeding out." Auntie Alex looked up at Stuie's mother and father with a pained expression on her face. "Isn't that right, Annie?

Mom stared at the floor, balling both hands into fists.

"My husband, father to my children, and now my brother. Both dead," Auntie Alex went on, her voice cracking. "Simply because everyone in this family kept far too many secrets for far too long. I know this is a big ask of the two of you, but please, Annie, Nat…make it *stop*."

Dad pursed his lips. "She's right, Annie."

Mom said nothing as tears began to run down either side of her face. "Come stand over here, dear," she said in a small voice and reached out for Stuie's hand. Mom led her over to stand between Pawly and Auntie Alex. She knelt and took Stuie's hands in hers while the two women each placed a hand on one of Stuie's shoulders. "Lim here…carried you in *her* womb. She's…she's your real mother."

Stuie stared at Lim, her mouth hanging open. Grandpa N's words from their meeting back on Pilot Island flooding back, confirming what she couldn't bear to hear then. What she could not bear to hear now. Red haze ebbed and flowed from the edges of Stuie's vision as wave after wave of emotions crashed over her. Who was she? *What* was she? And what was she to *whom*, exactly?

Burying her face in her hands, Stuie began to sob. She cried and cried and cried, saying nothing. Because crying made sense. Nothing else did.

Then she felt a hand tousling her hair. She looked up into Lim's face, seeing damp trails beneath her eyes too. "She is right, little one," she said in a soft voice. "And yet, she is wrong."

Stuie sniffed and wiped at her eyes with her forearm. "I…I don't understand."

"Since Rason, this fellow here had sat with me," Lim said, glancing over at Tommy. "For hours I lay, unable to move more than my eyelids. Listening to him talk about you, little one. And the rest of your family. Your father. Your mother. Yes."

She reached out her arms and embraced Stuie around her shoulders. "I...intended you harm, child. Then and now. And for that...I am sorry. So sorry."

Then Lim placed her hands aside of Stuie's cheeks and gently turned her head away from her, right towards...

"Annie is your mother, dearest. She loves you. She has loved you from the moment she rescued you from my savaged womb. Which I...I myself had..."

Lim let go of Stuie, pulling her knees to her chest as she began to cry anew. Mom stood up and rubbed at her back. "Life had been unkind to you, girl. You were scared. Alone. Had been taken advantage of. All while caring for other children, barely more than a child yourself." She looked down at the floor and shook her head. "I...I can't say with certainty that I...that I might not have done likewise."

An uneasy silence passed between them. "Papa and I have a theory, Lim," Dad said, at length. "I don't think you ever really *wanted* to hurt Stuie. But her very presence inside and outside of your womb triggered some sort of fight or flight reflex within your feral mind. Which the serum we administered to you appears to have quelled."

Lim blinked, her face blank. "So...so I need not worry about raging anymore? Even without my Pearls?"

"No," he replied, reaching over to pat her hand. "And no werecat, nor their loved ones, ought ever to again."

Auntie Alex stepped over and grabbed Pawly and Tommy by their shoulders. "C'mon, kids. Let's leave them be. Besides, we should let the rest of the family know what's going on."

"Make sure to tell Monsignor Dryzek, too."

She turned and looked at Dad. "Tell him what, exactly?"

"That Hana...I mean, Lim, that Lim has come to. He wanted us to wait until then before saying a private Mass for our family to celebrate

Ritzi's life." Dad met Lim's gaze and patted at her hand. "Would that be okay with you?"

Lim nodded. "I…I think Papa would like that," she replied, smiling a small sad smile. "Yes."

Chapter Thirty-One

ASHORE IN THE FLORIDA KEYS. DAYS LATER.

L ENNY AWOKE TO THE sound of waves gently lapping at the sailboat's hull opposite the cabin wall. He patted at the space beside him, finding it empty except for Pawly's beach towel. She and Lenny had both wrapped towels around themselves before lying down together for a nap, not wanting their wet bathing suits to leave their tiny bed damp.

He rolled onto his back and stared up at the overhead mere inches from his face. Sunlight streamed into the cabin through the narrow window situated to the left of the companionway above the head. Was it evening already? They had plenty of food and fresh water aboard and could easily remain at anchor here on the lee side of Big Torch Key until morning if they wanted to. Pawly could even indulge her urges by wading ashore to take down a key deer or something, both of them confident no other person would be around to hear. His parents had told him the native torchwood would burn even when green. Maybe he would build them a small fire to roast himself any leftovers from Pawly's kill while waiting for her shed to complete.

Neither he nor Pawly were in a particular hurry, and that was by design. Top announced to his weary and worn-out crew as they finished their work in Boston that they were overdue for an entire month's shore leave. Nat and Annie had agreed for Lim to spend time together with Stuie upon their return to Chicago. Their plans included a day out at Great America during opening weekend, with Stuie eager to introduce Lim personally to *Goliath* and *Wild Bull* and all the other coasters there. After her parents had requested Tommy accompany them, he did not complain—not the least little bit. He assured Nat and Annie he would keep an eye on them both. Though Lenny figured his old shipmate would certainly be keeping his eye more on Lim than on Stuie.

Lenny and Pawly had disembarked for the Keys the morning following Top's announcement. They had pledged to each other they would remain incommunicado with everyone until their arrival back in Massachusetts to visit the rest of Lenny's family. By the time he caught up with his uncles and aunts and cousins, he and Pawly would be due back aboard ship. Then they would commence the next phase of the Forest Clan's dispersion, this time bound for the Far East.

Dad would not need his sailboat back in Marathon until the end of the week, after which he would begin fitting it out for this year's Buccaneer Blast Regatta. Which was why Lenny's stomach knotted up upon hearing Pawly's voice topside. She jabbered on in what he had come to recognize as Polish, pausing now and again. Lenny realized she was talking with one or another of her family members on the satellite phone his parents had insisted remain aboard in case of an emergency. He had known Pawly to be stubborn and determined when she took notion to, so whatever had prompted her to break their joint vow of silence had to most certainly be of dire importance. *For fuck's sake, what now?*

He wiggled out of their cubby and crouched down in the companionway. After pulling on his T-shirt, he stood up and spied Pawly beside the helm. She gazed out at the shoreline fifty or so yards beyond their stern, twiddling absentmindedly at the hem of her beach shirt with one hand while holding the phone to her ear with the other. A moment later, she turned and met his gaze before waving him over. Pawly plunked down heavily atop a seat board and he slid up beside her. As Lenny reached over to put his arm around her shoulder she launched into a tirade, lambasting whoever the poor slob was on the other end of the line. Though he could only make out the occasional word or phrase, her tone told him more than plenty.

Pawly stood up and stepped over to the cooler pushed up against the transom. She picked up a clear plastic cup from a hole molded into the cooler's top filled with some sort of bright maroon liquid and handed it to him. The familiar smell of vodka and cranberry juice brought a smile to his face. A chunk of freshly squeezed lime floated atop a right proper Cape Codder, served just the way he liked them. He looked up at her and mouthed the words "thank you" before taking a long, slow sip. She nodded and rolled her eyes, flapping her thumb and fingers together on her free hand while holding the phone at arm's length out to him.

He leaned forward so as to better hear Agent Katczynski and Monsignor Dryzek's voices booming through the phone's earpiece. Was the brain trust having second thoughts about their dispersal plans? Forest Clan members were no longer solely dependent upon killing to sate their primal urges, that much was true. Yet Katczynski and Dryzek were insistent that any group or government foolish enough to attempt exploiting werecats for their own ends found their perceived advantage negated—quickly, discreetly.

Permanently.

Lenny gulped down the last of his drink as Pawly ended her call. "I woke up and saw you were still sleeping, so I came out here to spread out and read my book so I wouldn't bother you," she said while she returned the satellite phone to its charging enclosure beneath the helm. "This thing was blinking when I sat down. I scrolled through the missed call list and recognized Grandpa D's number. So, I called him back and, well...you know the rest."

He made a face. "I know you and he and Dryzek were talking. Though about the only Polish I know is *proszę* and *dziękuję*. Aside from the swear words Tommy taught me while we were at sea together aboard the *San Jacinto*. And I picked out more than a few of those."

Pawly shrugged and sat down beside him while avoiding eye contact. "Clearly they're questioning whether they covered all the angles with their dispersal plans for the Forest Clan."

"They're a little late, don't you think?" Lenny leaned back on his seat board and stretched out his arms along the gunwale. "I mean, proverbial cat's out of the bag already."

She pulled her knees to her chest and swung around to face him. "Yeah, I told them much the same thing. But they're concerned bad actors somewhere in the world might yet make a play to coerce our kind into doing their bidding. Even going so far as to pit werecat against werecat."

"Can't hardly blame them. What with you and Hana...er, Lim, I mean," Lenny said, waving a hand toward Pawly. "There *is* precedent for that."

"I know. Which is why they asked me to head up a force protection unit for them. To include Lim, in fact."

Lenny blinked. "They want you to do *what*? With *her*?"

"Well, the term is mine, but it sums up what they were looking for. Officials representing the nations to which we've been delivering the

Forest Clan refugees all agreed to grant them asylum. So, Grandpa D and the Monsignor want us to conduct periodic welfare checks on them. To make sure no one *does* exploit them, governments or otherwise." She snapped her wrist and flexed her fingers, staring at the claws poking through the bare skin atop her fingertips. "And if we find that they are, well..."

He clasped his hands together over his abdomen. "I suppose you and Lim are *eminently* qualified for such a task."

Pawly turned and flashed Lenny a big grin. "I went for the hard sell. Scored us a stateroom to share aboard the *Archer* and all the food and drink we want. Getting paid to travel the world, just so long as we only ever go ashore under an alias." She narrowed her eyes and smiled a sly smile at him. "And I forced a major concession out of Top, too. He's arranged for the brig at Chesapeake to sign over sole custody of you to me. Though abandon all hope I'll soon let you forget it."

Thoughts flashed through Lenny's mind of Pawly dressing him up in a maid outfit. She burst out laughing, seeing his pained expression. He laughed nervously along with her, trying to be a good sport. But before long her laughter trailed off, her smile fled, her gaze fell upon the deck around her feet.

"But..."

Pawly gripped the edge of her seat and sighed. "That's where you and Tommy come in. The pair of you will work undercover to investigate all the werecats we check in with, making sure they're not offering their Talents to anyone for their own undue gain." She narrowed her eyes at her receding claws. "Because if they *are*, well..."

Lenny rubbed at his chin for a long moment. "So. You going to do it?"

"'Harm not the Children of Affliction,' right?" she answered him in a small voice. "My kind has been exploited for centuries because we were unable or unwilling to police ourselves. We have to take responsibility. Now. Figure that if I do, then Dad and Uncle Ritzi won't...won't have..."

He took her in his arms and squeezed. Pawly let him hold her close while they swayed back and forth in time with their boat's gentle rocking. Before long, Lenny grew uneasy with the silence. He peered over her shoulder toward where the setting sun filled the evening sky with brilliant hues of crimson and scarlet and vermilion. "Red sky at night, sailor's delight," he said, desperate to change the subject.

Pawly took his face in her hands. "How about you delight *me*, sailor?" she asked with a sultry grin before clamping her lips over his. Lenny returned her passionate, greedy kiss, all too eager to oblige.

THE END

AFTERWORD

This book and the rest of the FOREST EXILES SAGA, each featuring the modern-day remnant of an ancient clan of werecats, are the books I wanted to read but couldn't *find*. The paranormal sci-fi thrillers which I had in my heart to write. Thank you, dear reader, for letting this one into yours.

Share your thoughts, please—and help others who might enjoy the book to discover it—with a review on Amazon:

Link:

https://www.amazon.com/review/create-review?&asin=B0CNHJJQ23

QR code:

Or please post one at the site of whichever vendor you purchased this book from. Reviews on Goodreads also are both greatly helpful and greatly appreciated. Thank you.

Acknowledgements

This novel was over twenty years in the making. Neither it nor my other books would have been possible but for my previously having written fanfiction for anime, manga and anthro fandoms. Several of the friends I made along the way number among my longest and staunchest supporters. Thank you to Ken Wolfe, Mike Morrey, Daniel Snyder, and Laura Lee for their providing a sounding board as I detailed my series outline. They also, along with Angela Carina Spears and Deanna Vaughn, encouraged me throughout the drafting process. Thank you all.

A number of people also helped during the book's editing phase. Deserving special mention are the members of Allied Authors of Wisconsin, most notably David Michael Williams and Christopher Whitmore. Thank you. Others I'm grateful to include beta readers Jodi Herlick, Frances Pauli, and "Filigree". Thank you, and again to Ken, Mike, and Dan for their help here, too.

I also want to recognize those who have helped me develop and execute plans to get this book and the others in the FOREST EXILES SAGA series in front of the very people most likely to enjoy them. People like *you*, dear reader. Jess Owen, R. A. Meenan, Matt Doyle, Chris Brucker, Stephen "Scuba" Coghlan, "Wolfie," and "APC" along with Ken, David, Christopher, Carina, and Filigree once again—thank you, one and all, for helping me see my vision through.

And a shout out to my "super fans," chief among them Breana Sprinkle and Bryan Potratz. Your kind words and ardent support as I complete this leg of my creative journey help affirm all the effort and sacrifice has indeed been worthwhile.

Lastly, and most importantly, I want to thank the One who makes all things possible:

> *For God so loved the world,*
> *that he gave his only Son,*
> *that whoever believes in*
> *him should not perish but*
> *have eternal life.*

(John 3:16 ESV)

About the Author

Boyhood interests in trains and electronics fostered Mark's career as an electrical engineer, designing and commissioning signal and communications systems for railroads and rail transit agencies across the United States. Authoring industry trade magazine articles, coupled with long-time participation in anime, manga and anthropomorphic fandoms, led him to write paranormal sci-fi thrillers featuring the modern-day remnant of an ancient clan of werecats. Growing up in Michigan, never far from one of the Great Lakes, Mark and his wife today make their home in Wisconsin with their son and a dog who naps beside him as he writes.

Mark is a member of Allied Authors of Wisconsin, one of the state's oldest writing collectives, and the Furry Writers' Guild, dedicated to promoting quality anthropomorphic fiction and its creators.

Visit Mark's web site...

Author Mark J. Engels (mark-engels.com)

...and subscribe to his mailing list to receive details on release dates, special promotions, and in-person appearances.

You may also connect with him via these platforms:

amazon.com/stores/Mark-J.-Engels/author/B074Q51T9R

https://twitter.com/mj_engels

facebook.com/mark.engels.39

linkedin.com/in/mjengels/

goodreads.com/author/show/17095069.Mark_J_Engels

Also By the Author

Check out the entire FOREST EXILES SAGA
using the link below or the QR code at right:

https://www.amazon.com/dp/B0C572FW6N